A Death *at the* Palace

M.H. Baylis

First published in Great Britain in 2013 by Old Street Publishing Ltd
Trebinshun House, Brecon LD3 7PX
www.oldstreetpublishing.co.uk

ISBN 978-1-908699-16-9

10 9 8 7 6 5 4 3 2

A CIP catalogue record for this title is available from the British Library.

Typeset by Old Street Publishing Ltd.

Printed and bound in Great Britain by CPI Group (UK) Ltd, Croydon, CR0 4YY

To my beautiful wife, Emma

Chapter One

The crossing paths of a pair of jets formed a perfect X above, as Rex Tracey lit an incense stick at the shrine in his front garden. It wasn't aeroplanes he could hear, but their after-effect: the hollow plastic roaring of wheeled luggage being dragged across paving. The sound was there, too, as he left for work, as he waved to the Colombian lady who had recently moved in two doors down, and as he nodded, with more reserve, at the old rabbi who'd lived in the house on the corner since there had been a house on the corner.

The luggage-sound would be the soundtrack to his lunchtime sandwich, his lullaby and, one day, his requiem. It was the theme of Wood Green, as unique to it as certain clicks and whistles to the hill-tribes of the New Guinea Highlands. All along the road towards the tube station he could see them, the arrivers: wispy Polish girls with feather-cut, plum-dyed hair, the boys uniformly shaven bald in short leather coats. Two dozen, identical, red-brick-terraced and satellite-dished streets away to the east, there was Tottenham Hale; from there a fast rail link to Stansted airport and the nine-quid flights to Krakow, Wroclaw and beyond. At any point in the day, but especially the mornings, some were coming, some going. The Kurds around the minicab office eyed them morosely, because these newcomers never took cabs, perhaps, or just because they were the newcomers.

But young people with luggage always have a certain optimism, and this seeped into Rex as he limped down past the bus station and the toilets that were always locked. The sign – This Toilet Is Shut Indefinitely Because Of The Mess A Person Did

– made him smile, although he'd seen it a hundred times before. His foot ached badly. A team of faerie washerwomen seemed to have shrunk his clothes in the night. He would be forty before his Oystercard needed its next top-up. But it was a sunny morning. He loved being able to walk to his work, through this ugly, lovely, teeming part of town. And he was seeing his GP tonight. Things were on the up.

For some, only spring and summer can be seasons of rebirth, but Rex Tracey's soul drew strength from the smoke of bonfires and the watery light of an October sun. The warmer months had been less fun: he'd gorged, without much joy, on fatty sausage and Polish beer in the evenings in his yard, pained by floating snatches of Slavonic in the lane outside. His time had been measured out by weekly visits to a once close relative who only sometimes recognised him – and far less frequent contact with a Lithuanian girl who didn't love him anymore. At points in that low country of the spirit, he'd even thought of leaving his beloved Tottenham.

Rex was a broad man of average height, with thick dark hair, and he limped because of an accident he'd had nearly a decade ago. People often looked at him twice, partly because of the way he moved, partly because he always wore a suit, but mostly because his face seemed to remind people of someone, or something. Friends and colleagues sometimes observed that he looked sad and you would, perhaps, need to have known him quite well to determine that this morning, Rex Tracey was happy.

He hadn't, contrary to the advice of his workmates, joined a dating site, taken up Tae Kwon Doh or given up wheat products. His brain had simply had enough of circling around the same old topic. He found, imperceptibly at first, that he could again follow the thread of a newspaper article, even one in the *Guardian*. He could bear to look at her sketches on the office wall. He could pass by the photocopier without remembering that filmic moment when he'd snagged the buttons of her jacket in the mesh of his hunting bag, and so commenced their affair. He couldn't quite see one of those high cheekboned, Tartar-eyed girls without recalling her lips and the way she spoke, and perhaps he never would. But there was no doubt he was over the worst, and as more leaves fell, so his fortunes seemed to rise.

'You don't look so good, Rex.'

It was a typical Eastern European pleasantry. He hadn't recognised the girl delivering it until she was standing right next to him. She had a sharp little nose, green, slightly slanted eyes, and she wore a pale blue suit, studded with rhinestones.

'Aguta. *Labas.*' He kissed her on both cheeks, an awkward manoeuvre as all around them there were people pouring off buses into the Tube Station. 'Are you going to work?'

'Yes, but then I saw you from the bus and –' She took a breath. 'Rex, I wanted actually to ask you something. Have you seen Milda?'

There it was. The first of the day's mentions. He was over Milda. But he wished people would stop going on about her, all the same.

'Well, Aguta, we split up quite a while back, so...'

'She hasn't been doing some more work for the newspaper?'

Milda had never really done much work for the newspaper. Susan, the boss, had hired her as a temp to do some general office admin, and found her wanting. She'd also, in common with the rest of the staff, liked her too much to give her the sack. The last concrete task Milda had performed for the *Wood Green Gazette* was doing a sketch of everyone who worked there.

'She stopped all that when we... you know. She's at that café down on Green Lanes now.'

'So you've seen her?' Aguta asked.

3

'Not for some time. Why?'

'Because,' Aguta said. 'I am bladdy worried, actually, about Milda.'

How many times had he played this conversation in his head? Aguta would intercept him in the aisles of the Lidl, or knock on his door in the middle of a storm to say just this: *I am bladdy worried, actually, about Milda.*

Aguta, her best friend from Primary School 'Young October', Co-operative Street, Klaipeda, Lithuania, would then add that Milda had never been the same since they split up. That she still loved him. That Vadim was not such a good man, after all. Please, Rex, please, call her on the telephone. She is sorry about everything.

'It was Dovila's birthday yesterday. She didn't come. Didn't call even. I tried her on her phone. Psh. Nothing.'

Rex had to admit this sounded odd. Months ago, before they split up, she'd told him she was saving for Dovila's birthday. He'd asked her how old the kid was going to be. 'Ten,' she'd said, in that way of hers, as if somehow it was quite amusing to be ten. Milda adored Aguta's daughter. Which was why, he guessed, Aguta was worried.

'So she's only been missing a day. Why don't you go to the house?'

Aguta pulled at one of her vast, hooped earrings. 'Vadimas disgusts me,' she said, giving his name the Lithuanian ending. 'I am reluctant to visit him.'

A mean little part of him couldn't help being cheered by this. He'd tortured himself with the idea of Vadim as a regular, stand-up guy, beloved by all of Milda's friends. He was no longer torturing himself with this idea, of course. But still...

'Let's try her now,' he said, reaching into his pocket for his new phone, forced upon him by his boss. It was black and card-thin, and bristled with functions he had no intention of using. He was intending to go back to his old phone after a decent interval.

'She said they were having problems,' Aguta said. She paused, as Rex waited in vain for an answer, then jabbed awkwardly at the touch-screen in an attempt to end the call. 'See? Just always answerphone.'

There was no point leaving a message. For girls like Milda, topping up a few pounds at a time, dialling voicemail was too expensive. 'Maybe she's just gone somewhere for a while,' he suggested.

Aguta shook her head. 'She wouldn't disappoint Dovila, whatever else she had going on.' She spoke precisely, her accent sometimes the only sign of her origins. A single mother who toiled at the back of Wood Green's Shopping City doing beauty treatments, she spoke far better English than Milda, the university graduate.

A shaven-headed man in a white tracksuit top passed by and thrust a leaflet at them. Rex took it without looking at it. 'I don't know, Aguta...' He gazed out on the High Street as a wide, flapping-floral-trousered trio of Kurdish ladies rolled by with bags. The shops were opening up. He was running late for the paper's Monday morning conference. Should he be worrying about an ex-girlfriend who'd been incommunicado for a day? 'I don't know what I can do.'

'I wouldn't come to you if I wasn't worried.' Aguta fingered the cross around her neck. 'I got a bad feeling about this.'

Rex sighed. Morbid superstition seemed to be an integral part of Lithuanian identity. He missed Milda. Missed the way she would do anything with him, from a night in a nasty pub to a séance at the Spiritualist Church, because it was all new to her, all interesting, all worth trying. He missed her manners. Her way of being a woman so old-fashioned it was almost tribal. And the careful, intense way she performed every action, from stirring a cup of tea to making love. But he'd been uneasy with that part of her – her habit of saying that certain people carried 'the look of death', or her refusal to wash her hair when the moon was waxing.

Even so, as Aguta spoke, Rex felt a darkness as he stood on that busy little corner, a faint chill upon his skin. He knew what she meant. Somehow, it didn't feel right.

'I'll see what I can find out,' he said. 'I'm sure it's nothing, though.' He was about to reach for his wallet and give Aguta something for her daughter, but then he had another idea. 'Would Dovila like this phone? For her birthday?'

Aguta rolled her eyes. 'Rex. Where we live, they would stab her for a phone like this.' She patted his arm. 'But you're right. For Dovila, getting a mobile would be like marrying a prince. And I wouldn't mind her having one, to be honest, if I could find one that the other kids didn't steal... No... Rex...'

She stood objecting, as Rex rummaged in his bag, and proffered the beloved, battered, six-year-old handset he'd been hanging onto. Then, as soon as it was in Aguta's hand, she just nodded curtly and stowed it in her handbag.

'You're a kind man. Milda was stupid to end it with you.'

Rex shrugged, embarrassed.

'She knew it, too.'

Aguta departed, in her creaking blue suit, leaving Rex with the new phone he loathed, a faint but definite sense of unease, and a crumpled leaflet in his hand. He glanced down at it.

RUNNING OUT OF ROOM

Beneath this heading, the leaflet declared that the area was too crowded. Controls needed to be put in place. Recent immigrants needed to go home. The authors called themselves the British Workers' Action Party. They had a phone number. Squinting across the road, towards the rude newsagents that Rex never went in anymore, he could see the man in the white tracksuit, dishing out his leaflets with limited success. Rex wondered if he should nip across and talk to him. He decided to ring the number on the leaflet instead.

No one answered, and the ringing was soon replaced by the expectant bleeping of a fax machine. He folded up the leaflet, crossed by the traffic lights and made his way to the office.

Of course, the area was, in a sense, running out of room. Walking up Wood Green High Street to the shops on a Saturday lunchtime, for instance, was like participating in some Fritz Lang vision of the future: a conveyor belt, every race packed nose to neck, marching in slow formation. Some of that was down to the ridiculously narrow pavements, the thoughtless siting of the bus-stops and the constant digging by the water and gas and cable companies. Even so, it was true: more people were coming, all the time. You could tell that from various indices. The names on the satellite dishes, for a start: DigiTurk and Hellas1 now giving way to PolSat and RusTel.

The entrance to the newspaper was behind the high street, fronting onto a car park shared by council offices and a supermarket. You needed sharp instincts to cross it on foot, not just because of the erratic parking techniques and the delivery lorries, but also because many of the two-wheeled local road-users had adopted the car-park as a cut-through. Rex kept one eye on the vehicles, another on the ground, where all the cigarette packets were.

The fag packets provided the most accurate gauge of who was coming and going. When Rex had moved in to the area, the health warnings were still in English. Then it became Polish, then to Bulgarian and Rumanian as the citizens of those countries were granted the right to seek work here. Today, the language he saw most often on the car park floor was Hungarian. So were the other smokers going home, or was everyone just budging up to make room? Did the British Workers Action Party know, or care? Whatever the answer, there was, Rex sensed, a story in it.

A loud buzz caught his attention. He glanced up to see a kid on a moped, heading straight towards him. Startled by the speed, he moved to one side, only for the moped's grey-clad rider to swerve in the same direction. The kid was aiming his bike at him.

He had just enough time to see, inside the mysterious folds of the hood, a pair of eyes staring coolly ahead, more through him than at him. He could smell the diesel and the hot metal before his instincts told him to dart out of the way, between an pair of parked cars.

The kid sped past without a glance. Rex gazed after him, heart banging. What had that been about? The sensible part of him said: nothing. Just kids. And Tottenham. And mopeds. But that made things worse, rather than better.

* * *

He was halfway up the office stairs, ringing the number on the leaflet again, before he remembered that he hadn't bought a coffee. Two weeks ago, this would have presented no problem, but the machine in the kitchenette had broken, and Brenda Bond, the paper's receptionist and layout editor, had refused to replace it, on the grounds that everyone drank far too much. The caffeine made them irritable and careless, she said, and she bore the brunt of it. No one ever argued with Brenda. They just bought their lattes from the shop on the corner. Rex, with his aching foot, decided to do without.

'KP Kill Pests,' said an Eastern European voice as the call was answered. Rex hovered on the landing, thrown off guard.

'What?'

There came a sigh. 'KP Kill Pests. Is it existing job, new order or just query?' *Chast kviri* was how she said it, reminding him instantly, painfully, of Milda.

'I thought this was the British Workers' Action Party.'

'Oh.' A pause, protracted rustling. 'That is a small mistake. The boss sometimes diverts his private phone to the business line. Can I take a message?'

Rex smiled. What would potential recruits and donors make of it, dialling the number of the new racist party only to find themselves talking to a Polish receptionist?

'So the person who runs – what is it – KP Kill Pests – also has something to do with the British Workers' Party?' Pest control and racism: unwanted guests, pollution. Appropriate to the point of poetic.

'The proprietor is Keith Powell,' was the tart reply. She was all briskness now. 'Do you wish to leave a message for him?'

'I'm from the *Gazette*,' Rex said, giving her his contact details. 'I'd like to speak to Mr Powell about his party, and the leaflets he's been handing out on the High Street.'

'He's in a meeting.'

What kind, Rex wondered. A sales rep with a new kind of rat-trap? Or shaven-headed minders and moth-eaten flags in the back room of a pub?

'If you'd just tell him I called.' Then he added, 'And also tell him there's already a group called the BWAP. Bangladeshi Women Against Prostitution.'

He went into the office, grinning, although he doubted that Powell's receptionist got the joke, or was bothered if she had. Not being bothered by jokes seemed to be a big part of the Slavic identity. They presented a stern, critical front to the world, as if only they understood how serious it all was. 'You really think you've got a right to be happy, don't you?' Milda had once said to him. Inaccurately, as it happened.

He passed by her sketches of the office staff on the walls: bold, fat charcoal lines that were part calligraphy, part theatre. There'd been moments when he'd wanted to take them all down, but he knew no one would let him. A daft impulse always made him breathe in when he went by them, as if he might catch a trace of her from the paper. He no longer did this because he needed to; now he just did it because he always did. And in doing so this morning, he registered how stale the office smelt, of old sandwiches and the bottom of coffee cups.

'Wazzup!'

Ellie Mehta, twenty-four, all treacle hair and rosy cheeks, clicked off her Facebook page and span round in her chair. She was wearing a tight-fitting, military looking trouser suit. She smelt, as she did every morning, of lemon shampoo and mints.

'Have we stopped having this place cleaned?' Rex asked, sweeping a sandwich carton and a crisp packet from the sticky desk into the already-overflowing bin. The place was a tip.

Ellie just shrugged. 'The cleaner's gone AWOL. Anyway, it's been, like, way busy?' Rex tried not to wince – at the terminology, and the way it was phrased as a question, when it wasn't a question. 'Some bloke going postal in a GPs.'

'What GPs?'

'Bryant Villas,' Ellie said. 'Isn't that the one where Diana works?'

'What happened?'

'I've only got a few details. That Mauritian Special Constable rang me, the one who keeps trying to get me to go bowling with him? I'm no way going to though because I saw this tweet he'd...'

'Details?' Rex said, gritting his teeth. His junior had the face of an English rose, the body of an apsara dancer and a temperament that would have tested the Buddha.

'Er…' Ellie checked the Post-It on the front of her computer. 'Male. 30-40. Dark hair and eyes. Says he wants to see a doctor. Receptionist says he needs an appointment. He gets threatening. Doctor comes out. Talks him down a bit. He vanishes before the Feds get there.'

Rex was already dialling Diana's number.

'It was Dr Shah,' Ellie added, with a faint smirk. 'Not Dr Berne.' Rex put the phone down. 'But I'm sure she'd appreciate a call anyway. Show her you care.'

There were many things Rex wanted to say to Ellie in that instant, but he was prevented by a shocked cry coming from the office of his boss. He looked up to see Susan Auerglass, dark-haired and pale in the doorway, replacing the phone.

'The cleaner's not coming in,' she said.

'We'd guessed that,' Rex said.

'Magda isn't coming in,' Susan repeated blandly, 'because someone attacked her on her way to work.'

* * *

These days, he kept it in a Throat Pastilles tin at the back of a drawer in the kitchen, a drawer where his wife had once stored excess tea towels and the little labels she stuck on jam jars. In there, also, was a handful of silver milk bottle tops. These they'd collected, he remembered, for the neighbour-child in the Seventies – a 'Blue Peter' appeal, never fully explained, but which somehow converted milk bottle top foil into dams for Africa.

A different child was upstairs now. A woman, really, but so slight, so funny in her ways, she could have been a little one. He could hear her using the water closet, as she called it in her quaint, old-fashioned way. How had she picked that up, he wondered, growing up where she did? When she came down, she would want to work with him, and there would be no time, so he had to put the tin away now. But he needed to see inside it first.

The tin smelt of nothing except metal. Nor could you smell anything upon the lock of hair inside, not any more. He knew that, but there remained a power in it, same as a crucifix. Time was in that little box, and just by fingering the brittle, blonde fibres, he was back there, in that border town in the winter of 1952, with the breaths of the sleeping like a gas leak and the muted tramp of the dancers' feet on the wooden boards, and the girl. The memory of the girl was still strong even now, but he found it impossible to savour without the bitterness of what went before, like a photograph of something lovely, which had to be dipped in acrid chemicals before its beauty could be brought within his grasp. At each re-playing, he had to steel himself to face the prologue, found his thumbs gripping the seams of his trousers as if he was truly back there, barely seventeen but about to be born.

The London he saw today often reminded him of that sprawling camp on the Austro-Czech border. As he queued with his groceries in the headache light of the Morrison's, an overheard string of Slavic words would spawn memories of defeated, sagging figures stamping their feet in the mud, eyes beseeching for the stub of a cigarette. The lot of them crossed by lines of wire, as if drawn in the pages of a school exercise book. Displaced persons. That was what you had to call them, then. When they were in the hospital – they were often in the hospital – they became patients. Not inmates or internees. And never prisoners. It was odd to be so polite, when they were confined in draughty huts behind wire-fences, and when everyone running the camp, soldiers and orderlies alike, assumed they were all Nazis or Soviet spies, even when they had numbers from Dachau and Sobibor tattooed on their arms. Fucking nest of Krauts and Bolshies, was how Philips described the place.

In his mid twenties, Philips was the chief of the orderlies. Perhaps it was his lustrous moustache, or the way the Bootle slums had prematurely ravaged him, but everyone who met Philips found themselves behaving as if they were in the presence of someone older. It was a mistake he actively encouraged. The formidable Sister Hornby called him Mister Philips, the nurses called him Johnny and made sure he was never disturbed when he took to the latrines with a mug of char and a newspaper. Philips had rights over the little walk-in cupboard next to the pharmacy – this was where he could be found with Parry and Unsworth, playing pontoon for Passing Clouds, or discussing things in whispers. Once he'd walked past and seen the three of them fingering a peach-coloured camisole in there. Looted from one of the half-burned houses in the town? Ripped from one of the refugees? Either was possible. Philips had cruel good looks, black hair and blue eyes, and he was involved in the sale of petrol. Parry and Unsworth were his acolytes: the one slight and shifty, the other huge and unfinished-looking. There was a joyfulness about the way these three hated him, an enthusiasm that could have almost been mistaken for fondness.

But he knew no one was fond of him. He knew it had nothing to do with his weak voice or his failure to understand jokes. Or even the way he always seemed to be there, unnoticed until it was too late, when a Nurse was adjusting her stockings in some private corner, or an orderly was being treated to the Major's sarcasm – when anyone was engaged in something to which they wanted no witness. These traits of his, they added to it. But they weren't it.

Philips, actually, he found he could bear. He'd come across

his kind before at the village school. The toughest boys left him alone, settling instead for a casual contempt, with perhaps just the odd shove when they had a girl to impress and no other ready means of doing so. It was the weaker ones he had to fear. For instance, when the rosters were drawn up, the sly Parry ensured that his was the shift begun in the savage chill of dawn. When a body had to be removed from the bunk-houses, or crawling sheets were incinerated, the task inevitably fell to him. So, too, when a sudden bountiful blip in the supply lines allowed a brief season of razor blades or American chocolate bars, he came to understand it would dwindle just before his turn. These he accepted as simple facts of his existence, no different from the manner of his birth or his upbringing. It was the fun he could not stand.

The fun was Unsworth's speciality. Fittingly for a man like a fleshy, overgrown boy, Unsworth had commenced with practical gags of Beano standards: vinegar in his tea, cold beer in his boots. He'd withstood them all in silence, even though that only made his tormentor more determined, just as his unblinking stare had once goaded his foster-mother to an ecstasy of slaps and threats. Less bearable were the girly mag and single sodden sock in his locker on inspection day, but even then there'd been compensation, because Nurse Morrisson had taken his side and said, in her beautiful Hebridean song-speak, that the older men should be ashamed.

But the nurses, who'd been happy to treat him as a sort of pet in those early months, seemed to change as the tricks became crueller. Unsworth had spotted him lingering over an advertisement about thinning hair although, in reality, his hair wasn't thinning: it was simply thin. So he'd gathered a handful of pale, blonde hair from the barber's shop in the camp, and placed it on his pillow to give him a scare. And then the hair, because it had come from the refugees, had been full of lice, so his mattress had had to be burned and he'd been forced to undergo the ignominy of a scalping and a painting with the purple dye. And when he trod the wards with a bald, plucked head, he'd seen how the Nurses had glanced away, heard during tea-break the contempt in Nurse Reece's voice as she giggled 'just like a turkey!' For the first time, he wondered – idly, as if day-dreaming – if it had to be this way.

He didn't blame anyone for his treatment. His mother had sought to abort him. Failing in that endeavour, she had abandoned him at the house of some nuns. He had not been meant to survive. Pale, weak-sighted and prone to illness, he'd been sent from the city to a foster-home in the Suffolk countryside. There he'd watched the life of the fields and seen within in it the explanation for his own position. God, in addition to Seeing Everything A Little Boy Did And Thought, was like his foster-mother and her three daughters. Powerful, unfathomable, capricious: creating life only to pluck it away, juxtaposing the glories of a fern with the ugliness of a slug. He had been scheduled for destruction by the Almighty, but somehow slipped the noose. So he carried the mark of something that should not have been, and mankind could not help but feel revulsion when he crossed its path. This explained his fine, white-blond hair and his tiny eyes, and the fact that his skin was just one shade paler than normal. It was why even the motherly dinner ladies at the school shrank back from him. It explained everything.

Until, in that winter of 1952, in his 18th year, he glimpsed something else. There was a festive air, even throughout the series of draughty huts that formed the camp hospital, as the nights grew to their darkest and the air so cold it hurt your teeth. It was only just December, but permission had been granted for decorations to be hung, and these the Nurses had cut cleverly into continuous skeins from a shipment of glossy magazines. His hair was growing back, and aside from the nicknames and the quips about his pale skin, he seemed to have slipped for a while beneath the radar of the normal folk.

Charged with tacking the paper-chains to the walls of the men's ward, he'd had to borrow a stepladder from Philips' store, and mysteriously been offered a tot of schnapps by the man himself. Philips was sodden with drink, as if some great central bone had been removed, and his sharp features were dissolving further with each sip. With liquid eyes, Philips had shown him a photograph of a plate-faced, defiant-looking little girl and said that if anyone hurt his daughter, he'd swing for him. As he watched the older man blinking owlishly at this snapshot, he'd run his hand lightly over the NAAFI ashtray on the desk. And, as if the inspiration came from the cold clay itself, he'd suddenly thought of swinging it into the side of Philips' skull. It was the first time he'd had such a thought since his childhood. He saw no connection between it and the way he was treated. It was just an idea, like the snatch of a song that might pop into your head when you were mopping floors. Then Philips had glanced up from the photograph. 'What are you doing?' he'd asked, quietly, as if he'd forgotten that he'd invited him in. 'Creeping round like a fucking ghost.'

Later, while he was at his task, perched several feet from the ground, there'd been a terrific crashing from the women's ward. In itself this wasn't remarkable: the camp held many who'd been in the East, witnessed the ovens and the cattle-trucks, and it was a rare night when no hoarse, half-conscious bellowing split the blue-black dark between the bunkhouses. But the warmth and the smell of alcohol and the abject screams of a young voice combined to remind him of the foster home and its routine miseries, so that he wasn't truly alert when the girl came charging into the room. She was blonde and naked, and her voice was raw with shouting. In her hand she had something that flashed, like a scalpel. Nurses froze, while the men in their beds – mostly gaunt internees with hacking coughs – shifted upwards, hopelessness temporarily cured by a flash of pink nipples and pubic hair. She ran around the ward, cursing and then pausing, almost comically, to brush some books off the desk of the nurse's station. Then she stood still, the knife in front of her, as if modelling for a sculptor. A Nurse from the women's ward – he'd heard her referred to as Kathleen – came running in, with Philips behind her. The girl tensed, as if about to spring at them.

'Now then, girl, what's all this about?' Philips asked, softly. 'What's the matter, hmm?' The drunken orderly crooned at her, as if to a frightened horse. Observing from the stepladder, quivering with alarm, he was amazed that Philips could make his voice so gentle. 'No need for all this, is there? No one's going to hurt you.'

This, he thought, was how men behaved, and why he would never be one. They knew what to do. They were undaunted. His foster-mother again: 'Boys don't tell tales. But perhaps you're not really a boy at all…'

Philips began to inch towards the girl, talking all the while in that soft, soothing voice. Alcohol fumes from his breath filled the room until it seemed a spark from the stove would ignite them. The girl trembled, at one point almost letting her knife-hand fall. Philips saw his moment to make a leap, but as he did so, she spat in his face and slashed him. Philips sprang back, cursing her, and the girl darted away. Stumbling over the books, she crashed into the step-ladder and he fell on top of her, clutching at the air.

He was aware of a numbing pain on one side of his face, the smell of her saliva and the feel of her soft skin. He wanted only to get away, but she was thrashing at him, and some instinct made him thrash back, flailing arms and legs and occasionally connecting with hard surfaces that may have been skin and bone. Something tore at his ear. Then the flailing stopped and he heard laughter. Blurred shapes pulled into focus and he saw the entire ward, shaking with mirth.

'Don't ye know where to put it, lar?' Philips knelt down to him as two Nurses pulled the naked girl away from him. He glanced away in confusion, pulling himself upright on the nearest bed. In the bed was an old man, his face dappled with sickness and filmy eyes. With damp lips, the man made a circle of his thumb and forefinger. Then he inserted the index finger of his other hand into the circle, wheezing as he did so, his crackling phlegm like the percussion for some wider orchestra whose sole purpose was the mockery of him. They were all laughing: the sick and the strong, the free and the confined. 'What a fucking treat that was,' Philips sighed gratefully, wiping a bead of blood from his cheek.

'For pity's sake!' Nurse Morrisson snapped. At first he thought her anger was directed at them but then he saw the stone in her eyes and knew that it wasn't. 'Clean yourself up before Major Adams sees you!' And he passed, under a gauntlet of pointing fingers and jokes he couldn't understand, to have his bitten ear seen to by a plump Nurse who shook so much with laughter that it took an hour to finish the job. So he was late for the afternoon rounds, and Nurse Morrisson said something to Sister Hornby, who had a word to Major Adams and they put him on the Nights after that.

They had tucked him away, an embarrassment, but he was grateful for it. The fact of Philips being drunk in the afternoon had reached the Major's ears and he'd been placed on a charge. Red-eyed and shivery without drink, Philips began regularly to lose his temper and had struck Unsworth with the heel of his boot. He was pleased to be out of the way. Most of all, he was pleased that he had to work the night of the Christmas party – a Thursday so cold that everything went still, as if it was held in ice.

The refugees and the camp staff had been brought together in Hut E, for a night of dancing. There was a gypsy violinist and a Polish accordionist who were meant to be playing duets, but as they got drunker, their melodies clashed. Listening to it all, thirty feet away in the heat of the hospital, he started to feel queasy.

At half-past eleven, seeking relief, he stole into the isolation ward, where the TB cases were housed. He'd had TB as a child, and fancied that gave him immunity. In any case, he didn't care. Major Adams was very strict about the TB patients being kept cooler than the others and that, on nights like this, made their ward the most bearable place in the camp. In the darkness, drugged and weak, they slept, and it had become his habit to creep into their room and watch them. The smell in there was of ether and diseased breath and unwashed hair. It gave him an odd, trembling feeling: a kind of power to have entered somewhere forbidden unseen, to be watching people at their most vulnerable. In the moonlight their faces shone like angels. But they could be sealed in the snapshots of his memory, doing the most embarrassing things. He'd watched the gypsy-looking woman asleep, rocking back and forth with the meagre hospital pillow between her legs. The old man who claimed to have been a rabbi, sucking his thumb. The two Latvians who looked like SS soldiers, curled up in the one bed. He pored over these images, sometimes transplanting them with the heads and faces of Philips, Parry, Unsworth and the Nurses. He came to feel that it wasn't a curse he had, for seeing people as they chose not to be seen. As witness of mankind in its weakest, secret moments, he was close to God.

Laughter outside the windows made him freeze against the wooden wall. A woman's voice played a melody he remembered from his foster sisters with the village boys: I'm telling you to stop, because I want you to keep doing it. He dared to glance through the glass, feeling the cold pane jab against the tip of his nose. He saw Nurse Morrison playfully batting a man on the arm as they tottered towards the nurses' quarters, her free hand adjusting her dress. The man spoke and he knew it was Philips. His heart began to beat harder, and he was not sure why. Was it the sight of Philips with Nurse Morrison? Or was it that, in the bed to the side of him was the girl who had run into the men's ward with the scalpel two weeks ago? On the evening of that day, Nurse Morrisson, regretting her harsh words, had told him not to worry. The girl, she explained, had been 'got by some soldiers' and was 'a little, you know, in the head.' None of which he had understood, except the fact that Nurse Morrison was being kind to him again, and that it was no longer quite enough.

Now she was beneath him, the girl, lying in a twisted shape like a swastika. The lung-types – this was what Philips called them – experienced violent swerves of temperature in the night, and in one of those she must have flung all the covers from her bed. He made to pull the sheets and the itchy, linseed-scented blankets over her, but paused at the sight of a naked thigh and tentacles of dark hair. It wasn't these, but the contrast between bare flesh and the printed hem of her thin nightdress that seized his attention. Took him to that day he'd had to walk through the village in a short cotton frock of his foster sister's, all the while pulling it desperately to cover his bare-legged shame. The taunts of the children, the sniggers of the labourers outside the Market Arms. His hair, finer and blonder than the girl's in the bed, teased into tiny pig-tails by his foster-mother. *Now let's see if you lie to me again.* It was June's dress she'd made him wear, the oldest sister. June who chased him down the street with her friends, chanting Who's a pretty girl. June he'd surprised at the allotments with the copper-haired boy.

And June's piebald rabbit which, freed from his humiliation into shirt and trousers again, he'd taken and gently squeezed until it stiffened and thrashed and then fell limp. Hid it where nobody but he knew, deep in the woods beyond the brook. He remembered how warm the rabbit had felt, for so long after he'd killed it. And wondered, in a move so bold it took his breath away, if the girl would feel so warm after she died, and placed his hand upon her mottled cheek. Was she one of those Nature had pencilled in for dispatch, or would she survive to become stout and weary like Sister Hornby? She stirred a little, fleeing the clamminess of his fingers, and shifted in the bed, so that the full extent of her pubic apron revealed itself to him, like the cities of life he'd uncovered under stones.

The pillow lay to one side of her, and he took it up and smelt it. Sharp thoughts and equations replaced ancient feelings. If God saw everything, and he saw everything, then his was a power equal to God's. God could try to wipe him out for his mother's sin, but he too, had the power to decide who stayed and who went. He had already killed one of God's Creatures, after all – and nothing had happened to him. And now the girl squirmed as he climbed on top, and sealed the pillow over her face and clung to the sides of it, feeling her flailing knees knock against the rough serge covering his back. The horsehair in the pillow crackled, as her head twisted about. He could still smell her last stale breath as he pulled the nightdress down and covered her neatly with the bedclothes. Scared that he might one day forget it all, he took out his pocket knife, and cut a tiny swatch from the girl's hair, storing it in the breast pocket of his tunic.

Sixty years later, in his small house in the far north of London, he rubbed those locks between his fingers, hoping the power they still held might float up into the air of his living room and away. He wanted it to go now. He was no longer strong enough to resist it. A pact, kept for decades, had almost been broken up like pie-crust. And he'd sworn to himself, of course, that this had been different, a different type of life-taking, not a return to his old longings at all. But it had felt the same.

He heard her feet on the stairs, two steps, then a pause, two and a pause, like always. He saw what she was doing, without the need to see, because she always came downstairs that way, as though not wanting to miss some detail of the journey. And as much as he liked that, he longed for her to go away. With her little habits and her funny expressions, always leaving that strange, sad perfume in the air, so pale, so intense, he wondered what he might end up doing.

Chapter Two

'I'm still not getting the peg,' Susan said, back to her usual, bullish self an hour later, as she argued with her staff over the contents of the next edition. Rex ground his teeth. He knew, as they all knew, that theirs was just a local paper in a district of North London that would never acquire a gastro-pub. With the exception of Ellie, who was young, and Susan, who owned the paper, everyone on the staff was there because they had nowhere else to go. But Susan, being from somewhere along the East Coast of America, conducted all her business as if she and her band of disciples were responsible for bringing out the *New York Times*. It was daft, if you thought about it; but if you didn't think about it, in a way it made work much more enjoyable. Often more frustrating, too.

'A bloke just gave me this leaflet,' Rex said, brandishing the offending article for all to see. '"Fascists hand out leaflets on High Street on Monday morning." What more of a peg do we need?'

'And what better publicity could they hope for?' Susan said, toying with one of her dark ringlets. She had, Rex often thought, remarkably kittenish ways for a woman in her late fifties.

'What I don't get, right, is, right —' Terry, the photographer, shifted awkwardly in his chair. His six colleagues all turned to him. 'You've got that Polish bird attacked up at Ally Pally last week. Now it's happened to Maggs the cleaner. That should be your lead story, shouldn't it? Two Polish birds in the same place in two weeks? I mean, young women,' he added, with a nervous look towards Ellie.

In spite of his terminology, there were a few murmurs of approval. Terry sat back in his chair, folding his arms.

'The first girl was called Ilona Balint,' Susan replied. 'She was Hungarian. What happened to her, actually happened seventeen days ago. And we covered what little information there was in the relevant edition of the paper. But still, I take your point. Is this something we should be leading on?' She spread her palms out towards the staff, as if inviting their views, although the staff knew it was never that simple.

'In other words,' Rex said, 'at the same time as two Eastern European women have been brutally attacked in the same way, in the same place we've also got a new political party handing out leaflets saying all the Eastern Europeans need to go home. '

'Rex, we don't know that the person who attacked Magda is the person who attacked the Hungarian girl. And we certainly don't know that the motive for either or both of them was...'

'He pulled out her hair,' Rex said. 'Isn't that what we reported? Someone pulled a great chunk of hair out of the Balint girl's head? And now someone's done it to Magda.'

There was a pause, as everyone thought about the office cleaner. She wasn't exactly a chatty soul, but she cheered the place up. Always came in wearing parakeet colours, shocking pinks with queasy greens, and sang little snatches of Elvis as she cleaned.

She'd been found by a van driver taking a cargo of pastirma sausage and salty cheese on the high, mountain-pass circuit around Alexandra Palace to avoid the permanent log-jams of Wood Green High Street. He'd almost knocked her down as she stumbled out from the trees.

'Both young, attractive blondes, walking across Ally Pally,' Rex finally said. 'Both grabbed by the throat. Both given a brutal new hairdo. Pure coincidence? No. Same attacker, same targets. And this BWP group is targeting them, too...'

'You're lumping them together because they're young blonde women,' Ellie said. 'But Ilona Balint is a Hungarian lettings negotiator, and Maggs Wysocka is a Polish music student working part-time as an office cleaner. And people are always getting attacked around Alexandra Palace,' she added. 'It's a big space, surrounded by park and woodland, with lots of hidden bits. And this is a violent area.'

'I thought we were supposed to call it vibrant,' Rex said.

Susan ignored him. 'I agree it needs covering,' she said. 'In brief. And if and when Maggs is ready, we'll see if she wants to talk to us. But in the meantime, come on. I say this every week.' Susan rapped her desk with a biro. 'Biggest disparity between rich and poor in any London borough. Biggest growth in disparity in any borough in Western Europe. School meals cut. Libraries closed. Care budgets slashed for the elderly. That's our story. Not panicking people with a story about some whack-job in the park.'

'And every week I point out that the word 'budget' on the front page sends people into a coma!'

'We're not leading on budgets. We're leading on the business at the Surgery,' Susan said.

'What?' Rex sat up in his chair. He heard his phone ringing outside, at his desk, but ignored it. 'No way, Susan. I am not writing that as our lead story.'

'You are under no obligation to,' said Susan in her chilliest mid-Atlantic accent. 'Ellie – I want interviews with the Receptionist, with Dr Shah... and see if anyone who was in the Waiting Room can give you a line or two. You just need a link...'

'Mental health budget cuts?' Ellie suggested, scribbling furiously.

'Perfect.'

Rex groaned. Susan pointed at him with her biro. 'The oldest resident in Haringey is 101 today. I want an interview and snaps. Something uplifting, Rex,' she added pointedly. 'And some ideas for the competition, too. It's six months since we ran the last one.'

'Wasn't it like this in Berlin in the Thirties?' Rex said. 'Nazis marching to power, and all the local papers doing stories about cats up sodding trees?'

He was annoyed now, not only because Susan wouldn't see his point, but because she'd handed the lead story to his junior. It was Susan's management style: part Zen, part prankster. They were all supposed to rise to the challenge and surprise themselves.

'Rex,' Susan said, looking up with a sigh. 'Interview this little fascist rat-catcher if you must. I can't imagine he'll have anything new to say. I can imagine even less why I should give him any publicity. But I'll read it. That's the best you're going to get.'

Rex sat back, glum in victory as the weekly meeting went into its final phase. Brenda, who sub-edited the paper as well as manned the phones, announced some new protocols for the spelling of Albanian names. One of the Whittaker Twins – Rex could never tell one whey-faced, bulbous headed member of the advertising sales team from the other – asked for sponsorship for a Fun Run. Rex wasn't listening. He sensed his piece about the British Workers' Action Party was doomed to sit around the page 21 mark, somewhere between the local sports and the Laureate of the Ladders column. If it got in at all.

The end came and the staff drifted out to their desks. The light was flashing on Rex's desk phone, but whoever had called had left no message. Rex sighed, impatient to go, but having to wait for Terry as he scrabbled around the office getting his stuff together. The Geordie photographer possessed a vast quantity of equipment, all of it stored in locked metal suitcases scattered about the office. Keys for these had to be located, items had to be decanted into satchels and shoulder bags and bomber-jacket pockets. Terry had a passion for war photography, stored volumes of it in his Tottenham flat, but Rex often wondered how his colleague would actually fare in a war. They'd have drawn up a peace treaty by the time he'd made it beyond the hotel lobby.

As he watched his colleague, Rex was reminded, somewhat incongruously, of the delightful spectacle of Milda's morning preparations. Like the Japanese tea ceremony: formal, balletic, involving dozens of embroidered silk bags. That she never put any clothes on until the last moment gave it an additional power.

He'd kept just one photograph of her. Not a naked one: she was underneath a tree in Highgate Woods, in her sternest Communist librarian's outfit. Trim woollen suit, horn-rimmed glasses, hair in a bun, but smiling in her mysterious way, as if she might just be on the verge of shaking the hair loose, tearing off the blouse and making howling love on the nearest surface.

You could also see the watch. Rex had won her a watch at the funfair, on a day-trip to Clacton. A gaudy, see-through plastic thing, digital, and pale blue. If ever anyone wanted to know the meaning of the word gewgaw, you only had to show them this watch. Milda had loved the word, and claimed to love the watch, sporting it as her one concession to the modern age.

And that photograph, the only one he had left, was on the old phone. The phone he'd given to Aguta to give to her daughter. Ellie had transferred all the important phone numbers to his new device, but he hadn't asked her about the picture of Milda because he didn't want anyone to know he still had it. So that was that. Probably a good thing.

Ellie was nowhere to be seen, and Terry was still faffing, so Rex made use of the interval to call Diana. She was with a patient, but he left a message on her voicemail. 'See you around eight-ish,' he said, his spirits restoring as he thought how refreshing it was to have a new girlfriend who could understand every slack nuance of the language, someone you could leave voicemail messages for. Diana wasn't officially his girlfriend, of course, it had only been one round of drinks, two sit-down kebabs and a kiss, but he had hopes. 'You're going to get a visit from my young assistant,' he added. 'Don't let her wind you up.'

No sooner had he replaced the receiver when the phone rang again. Number Unavailable.

'Hello... Hello...?'

A distant roar greeted him, like heavy traffic. Then a clatter – a receiver dropped from a height rather than replaced.

Rex shrugged and hung up as Terry finally came across, garlanded with bags and photographic baubles. 'Ready, boss?'

'It's off. That was the old folks' home on the line. The borough's oldest resident just carked it.'

'Fuck off,' Terry said, agreeably.

As they went past Reception, Lawrence Berne was leaning over the desk in a manner that he no doubt thought was waggish, telling Brenda and Ellie about the opening night of the Hornsey Players' production of 'The Boyfriend'.

'And speaking of boyfriends,' Berne said, in an unnecessary *basso profundo*, waggling his shaggy eyebrows. 'When is my niece going to make an honest woman out of you?'

This was a reference to Diana, and was met by the female part of the audience with a peal of laughter. It troubled Rex that all the women in the office appeared to adore Lawrence Berne, the genius behind the 'Laureate of the Ladders' column, local historian and theatre critic to boot. Especially Brenda: vast, sixty year-old, no-nonsense Brenda, *Gazette* gate-keeper, fundamentalist sub-editor, mother of five, policeman's wife. How could Brenda be impressed by a bloke with a year-round suntan and a bow-tie? He didn't wish he wasn't dating Lawrence's niece. He just wished she wasn't his niece.

'She's married to her job,' he said, getting out of the doors before Lawrence could respond.

'What a twat,' Terry said, gently but with feeling, as they crossed to the car park. And then, 'Your car or mine?' Terry always forgot about Rex and cars. Rex didn't mind. In fact, he liked the fact that Terry never remembered he didn't drive. It was better than the awkward dance everyone else did, that polite yet painful way they managed to drag the issue of his not-driving up by so very pointedly not dragging it up.

'Let's get something to eat first,' Rex suggested. 'You never know, maybe he really will croak before we get there.'

'I could go another Egg McMuffin,' Terry said, having noisily eaten two of these items throughout the conference. 'Have you lost something?'

Rex was gazing back at the building, and the route between the cars. The route the kid on the moped had taken. Had that really happened?

He turned back to Terry. 'I'm not going to McDonalds.'

They got into Terry's lovingly preserved 1980 Chevette, stowing the photography kit on the back seat. A quirk of the car's design meant that if you sat down heavily in the passenger seat, the glove compartment sprang open. It did so this morning, depositing a gaudy scarf onto Rex's knees. It was a pastiche of the Burberry print: Pepto-Bismol pink in place of the red horizontals, canary yellow where the black vertical stripes ran.

Rex stuffed the scarf back into the glove compartment, wondering idly who would wear such a garment. Then he remembered that he'd seen it dozens of times, around the neck of the only person on earth who could possibly wear it and not look silly.

It belonged to Magda Wysocka, the cleaner.

They drove along Green Lanes, through the heart of North

London's Turkish community. There were jewellers first, all in a line, with that bright yellow gold so popular east of Athens, then they passed a row of grocers with identical displays of fruit and veg. 'Saw that in Istanbul once,' Rex said, more or less to himself. 'With Sib. You get one street – all they sell is typewriters. Next street – hooks. Just hook shops. How do they all stay in business?'

'Aye. Well,' Terry responded. 'Funny lot, your Turks.' He glimpsed a quartet of head-scarfed girls in tight jeans passing down the pavement, arms linked. 'Mind you, I wouldn't say no to a shish kebab,' he added meaningfully.

They drove on, slowly, because there were roadworks, as always, and half a dozen vans with long, agglutinated Turkish words on the sides were blocking the way. *Hizmetinizdeyiniz. Mahdumlari.* Roads of neat, Edwardian terraces sprouted off left and right, and a metal sign announced that this was the Haringey Ladder. As with the Southfields Grid and the Wimbledon Toast-rack, Rex wondered why these names stuck, why people seemed to like the idea of a community laid out like a piece of metalwork.

They parked in one of the ladder-roads, walked back to the Lanes, and there, next to a dim hall where old Greeks gambled, found the 'Good Taste' café, a lone beacon of British builder's breakfasts amid the variegated stews and flatbreads of the Levant. The clientele wore high visibility vests. The staff came from Eastern Europe and included Rex's ex-girlfriend, Milda. Or generally did. Today there was no sign of her. Instead, the tall, cheese-complexioned girl from the Czech Republic was by the till. She didn't like Milda and so, out of some perverse logic, was always very pleasant to Rex.

'Milda finished now here,' she told Rex, hardly able to disguise her pleasure. 'Fight wiz boss, maybe one month ago, she walks out. Dat's it… You want Heart Attack?'

He declined the café's famous 'Heart Attack' breakfast in favour of a toasted cheese sandwich. Terry tried and failed to make the girl blush with some witticism, then meekly ordered a burger with egg. 'Can I have a word with the boss?' Rex added, as she left. 'When he's got a moment?'

'Why d'you want the boss?' Terry asked, folding a paper napkin into a swan. 'You after a new job?'

'If Susan keeps chucking out my ideas I might think about it.'

'Bosses.' Terry gave a philosophical shrug. Rex sometimes wished he could be more like Terry, resplendently unconcerned about so many things. But that attitude also frustrated him. Susan was wrong to think he wasn't concerned with issues. It was just that Rex's issues weren't the same as hers.

'Come on,' he leant forward across the blue Formica table top. 'You live right in the middle of Tottenham. You've got every nationality under the sun in your building: South Americans, Somalis, Kurds. You want running battles between them and the skinheads? Fire-bombs? Smashed windows? Think what that'll do to your equity.'

Terry's flat round the back of Bruce Castle, the intricacies of its mortgaging, and the dimensions of its ever-fluctuating equity, were among the few things Terry was concerned about. But today, he wouldn't be drawn. 'I couldn't give a shite,' he said, rubbing his buzz-cut, copper-tinged skull. 'I've got two Polish lads in there paying three hundred a week. Actually, it's probably thirty of them paying a tenner, but like I said, if it's in my bank on the first of the month, I couldn't give a flying one.'

'Why not?'

'Moved in with me bird, haven't I?' Terry beamed. 'Gated mews in Leytonstone.'

'Does she mind you giving lifts to beautiful, blonde Polish girls? I assume you were giving her a lift, rather than anything else?'

'I'm not with you.'

'Magda. The cleaner. That's her scarf isn't it, in your car?'

'Ah. Right.' Terry nodded. 'Yeah. I gave her a lift in. On Friday, I think it was. When it was raining.'

'Pity no one gave her a lift today,' Rex said, lost for a moment in gruesome thoughts of what had happened up at the Palace. 'What makes one person want to do that to another person?'

He was speaking to himself. Terry had gone to fetch a newspaper from one of the other tables. The café-owner came across with their food. He was a tiny, dolorous-looking Greek, with the sort of profile you might find on an ancient vase. He'd always seemed fond of Rex, but when Milda's name was mentioned, anger flashed in his eyes.

'To be honest, she was on final warning with me before she started all this.'

'All this what?'

'Look. Right. Mate. I'm not being funny with you,' the man said, in his melodic London-Greek brogue. 'But actually. She was nicking stuff, actually. Stuff from the fridge.'

'She was nicking food?' The idea was impossible, comical even. Milda had found a twenty-pound note once and handed it in – much to the mirth of the desk-staff – at the police station. She had berated Rex for getting on the 29 bus without a valid Oystercard. She was so honest, if you asked her some innocent question, like, 'How are you?' she'd really tell you: cystitis, lost bank cards and all. There was only one explanation.

'It must have been a mistake.'

The Greek shook his head sadly. 'I don't think so. Carrots, cabbages, cauliflower – big box of stuff.' He waved his hands in a hopeless gesture and started to turn towards the counter. 'It's stupid. They can have anything they want to eat. They don't need to nick it.'

'But what did she say? When you caught her?'

The proprietor held his hands up, shook his head again. 'If you see her, tell her to talk to me. The job's still here, to be honest… What can I say?'

He walked away. Rex didn't want to leave it like that, though.

'Have you got a bit of paper?' he asked.

Terry tore off a miniscule fragment of the newspaper.

'A proper bit. One I can write on.'

The photographer pulled a card out of his wallet. It was from a business calling itself Eazylets. Rex scribbled a name and an address on the back of the card, then passed it across the table to Terry, who wiped his fingers on his jeans and held up the card. 'Who's Afaz Demirkol?'

Rex didn't answer. He was staring at the name of the Lettings Agent printed on the other side of the card. It seemed familiar.

'I said – who's Afaz Demirkol?'

'The Borough's oldest resident. Wish him a Happy 101st Birthday from me,' Rex replied, as he stood up, and walked out of the café.

* * *

He didn't understand how, because he'd been doing it for decades without any problem – but somehow, today, he'd got on the wrong bus. Instead of taking him down to the allotments in Palmers Green, it took him east and then south, so quickly it felt like an act of violence. And by the time he realised it had happened, he was going down Blackboy Lane.

The experience frightened him because he'd heard about it. Heard about it happening to old people. That they could be bewildered in the present, yet remember everything that happened fifty years ago. And he remembered everything that had happened here, down the lane the Council were always trying to rename.

The tall corner house was still there. A shop on the bottom floor sold car alarms and car stereos now, but he could remember every detail of the old interior. None of the people he passed on the bus had been around then. They hadn't even been in this country, he guessed, and nor, in most cases, had their parents. It was a different area then – instead of the Turks and the Jamaicans and the Ghanaians, there were Irish and Jews and other people with a distinct, prominent set of features that only belonged to North London. He saw those features sometimes, still, though separated and married to new ones: a fleshy mouth here, a pair of heavy-lidded eyes there, and he remembered the Carringtons, who'd given him his first job after the army.

Mr Carrington was a chiropodist: big business, he used to joke, after a war when everyone had had to squeeze their feet into army boots. It was true enough, though – he converted three rooms at the top of his house for corn-planing and bunion-easing, and a whole decade after the war, they had people in them until long into the evenings. Carrington had been with the RAMC, and this was where he'd picked up the trade. Not much different to a bit of pruning, that was what he used to say. He had sandy hair and jolly eyes, in contrast to his wife, who was, in the words of the man who delivered the coal each Monday, a great long streak of misery.

He'd spent the first six months sweeping up the cheesy-yellow shards of skin from the floors, stocking up the instrument trays with new blades, making sure the waiting room had newspapers, air in the warm weather and some semblance of warmth in the cold. Then, for reasons unclear, Mr Carrington had declared that he had spotted something in him: a real flair for the business. From that point on, two days a week, he went to learn the muscles and the bones of the feet in a stuffy hall in Holborn; the next two days he swept as usual; and on the last one and a half, he was permitted to cut the callouses from selected pairs of feet, under the close supervision of Mr Carrington himself.

Eighteen months in, even though he still didn't have the certificate he needed, they let him cut unsupervised. There was a poplar tree outside his window, and he found he could cut away without looking at his work much, just staring at the branches outside, and remembering how the winds had made the wheat-fields sway like the sea when he'd watched them as a boy. He found the customers' sore spots without looking, without talking, just with his fingers. That which had made his hands, and indeed the whole of him, so unnaturally soft and yielding, gave him strength in this job, because he could feel the contours of peoples' feet, and know just where it was right to cut away, to smooth with the plane, or salve with the balm or sometimes just rub the pain away making circles with his fingertips. They made little sighs, sometimes, the people on the couch, when he did that – the big burly men in tweed suits, and the haughty, hard-looking women, and he found he enjoyed having the power to make that sound come out of them. People asked for him again, and it amused Mr Carrington to book them in. He found he enjoyed seeing people with their shoes and socks off. They always looked so pale and vulnerable that way, on the couch, with the soft velvety soles facing towards him, the odours they could not mask.

It was a November day in 1955. In bad weather, more people came – the cold made them notice their feet more, the damp made their shoes fit less well. He'd had customers from seven in the morning, solid, right the way through lunch – only had to time to wolf down an apple whilst old Mrs Lally took an age over her ancient, Edwardian button-up boots. The coal in his scuttle was quite used up, and when he went down to the cupboard in Mr Carrington's room for more blades, his employer had laughed at his nose, the tip of which seemed to have gone red in the cold. 'Get yourself a handful from our living room,' he'd said, something he'd have considered unthinkable, except that Mr Carrington had come halfway down the stairs with him, and he knew Mrs Carrington had gone into Hornsey for a dress fitting.

In the living room, kneeling by the grate, he breathed in the strange smells of the Carringtons' house. They boiled up coley for their cats, and this mingled with the vanilla of Mr Carrington's pipe tobacco and the fruity scent of the furniture polish to make a heady cocktail. He didn't want to carry a handful of the coal all the way up the stairs as he'd only need to go two flights back down again to wash his hands, so he took a sheet of the *Gazette* that they left by the fire for lighting, and wrapped up a few of the smaller lumps in that.

He was just twisting the paper around the coal when Mrs Carrington came in. She had a leaf stuck to the side of her shoe.

'What are you doing in here?' she asked. She had a way of smiling so only the muscles of her mouth moved whilst her eyes remained like the fish in the fishmonger's window. He mumbled that Mr Carrington had said for him to come and take the coal.

'Did he?' she said, as if it might not be true. She wore too much make-up around her eyes, so that when she looked at things, it was as if she was pointing at them. Now she pointed with her eyes at his parcel of coal and the torn newspaper left in the grate. 'I hadn't read the *Gazette* yet,' she added. And she stayed where she was in the doorway, towering over him, as he squeezed past her and went to the stairs. There was a rustle as he passed by the bulge of her belly, and the fabric of her woollen skirt moved against the stiff petticoat underneath. It made him shudder.

He shuddered again when he arrived back in his room. A red-headed girl was sitting on a chair, taking off her stockings. He saw her pale flesh under a smart, dogstooth patterned skirt.

'Mr Carrington showed me in,' she said. 'I thought I'd just get on with it 'cause it takes an age to undo these laces when my hands are cold.'

Her fingers were red, like meat. He nodded, going over to the fire and putting the coals in to hide his face. She had a North-country accent, a bit like one of the Nurses he'd worked with in Austria. He got a good blaze going, happy to face the fire instead of the girl.

'Shall I just get on the table?' she asked, brightly. And before he could answer, she'd lain on it. He sorted out his tray of sharp instruments, hating her now. Why ask his permission, he thought, if she was going to do something anyway? Why talk in that happy, sing-song voice, when it was obvious that she, like everyone, despised him?

She gave a big yawn and said she worked nights on the buses. He calmed down a little as he began to shave away the callous on the edge of her right big toe. You could look like her, he remembered, in your tight sweater and your smart skirt, you could have milky-white thighs and French scent, but your feet would give you away. Your callouses, and your misshapen nails and the dark hairs on the bridge. You could be as fish-eyed as Mrs Carrington, as cruel as any foster-mother, and still, at the end of the day, there'd be a pile of hard, yellow shards on the floor to remind everyone what you really were. In this job, he saw people: looked down into them, up them, saw everything, like he'd been told Jesus did.

'I'm just going to rub some salve into your heel,' he said, reaching for the bottle of peppermint-scented lotion on the wooden stand. She gave a faint murmur and shifted her legs slightly. A tiny part of her slip showed against her knee – rose-colour against the paler bloom of her flesh. From the rhythms of her breath, he knew that she'd fallen into a doze. He glanced back at her knee – at the hem of the slip and the soft skin. God did that sort of thing often, he thought – set two things against each other to show you His wonder. A dewdrop on a leaf. A curl on a collar – two things, unremarkable alone, arresting when put together.

He felt a thickening between his legs and a dryness in his throat, as he moved from her right foot to touch the criss-crossed padding of her left sole. Sometimes, from songs and snatches of what he overheard on buses and in shops, he got a sense that other people felt these things, too, but they felt them in a different way, a way they invited and welcomed. His heart fluttered and he felt the corn-plane slip a little in his dampening fingers. For him, these feelings only meant anger; inside his head, a magic lantern show went by, composed of his foster-mother's thin lips, the tauntings of her daughters, bare legs, stinging slaps, yanked hair and nakedness, burning shame and punishing, probing, exposing hands.

'Did he?' he heard Mrs Carrington saying again. 'I hadn't read the *Gazette*.'

He thought how easy it would have been, as she'd made him squeeze past her rustling, padded belly, to reach out to the folds of her powdered neck and to pinch and squeeze. The shock he would see in her eyes. The way she'd thrash. The sense of injustice in her dying gestures, as if, for once, the whole order of the universe had been reversed, and the weak become the strong.

This girl's neck was nicer: long and pale, with a little floral scarf around it. When he'd squeezed the life out of the rabbit, there'd been softness, then something fibrous and grainy, and finally, something like the moment you crunched down on a gobstopper, a great, muted, satisfying crack from deep within the beast. The body of the girl in the camp hospital had made a sound like that as well – not her neck, he thought, but just the ligaments and cartilage of her bed-bound limbs stretching as she bucked and struggled under the pillow. He wondered if this girl lying here, with her red curls and her swelling sweater, would make a cracking sound as well. He found himself wanting to hear it again.

And then, as if Jesus had been real, and had heard his secret thoughts, as he stood over the sleeping girl on the table, there was sudden, sharp crack. Not from her neck, though – it came from the fire behind, making him jump and making the girl wake up, too. The first thing she did as she awoke was to give him a friendly smile, her nose wrinkling up and the corners of her eyes lifting outwards.

'Blimey. I think I was out cold,' she said. And she smiled again. A real smile.

To see such a thing, to be the recipient of such a thing, instead of fear, indifference, disgust, made his legs shake. Her name was Caroline, he discovered later, and she came from Belper, in Derbyshire. He never went there, not in the whole of their time together, but the name of Belper, in Derybshire, assumed the importance of Canaan and Gethsemane in his own legends. A girl from Belper smiled at him, treated him as if he was meant to exist alongside her, and he was forever changed by it. They married in her Church in Stoke Newington, about six months after their first meeting and when he stood at the altar, he made his own vows with his own God. He would never do it again, he said, never squeeze and smother, never wait for the crack, not as long as Caroline was with him.

* * *

Rex took the 141 up to Palmers Green. It was on that bus route that he'd last seen her. After an evening working late at the paper, he'd walked down to the Pamukkale Restaurant for a lahmacun. They only served them after 8 pm, for some reason, and it had been well after that on a wet Thursday, a little way into Setember, the street almost deserted. As he left, with the teardrop of lamb-studded bread warming his pocket, a city-bound 141 had sailed past, like some ghostly galleon, Milda its only cargo, sitting where she always did, on the right-front seat of the top deck. That snapshot of her, pale and alone, with her Soviet administrator spectacles and her little Fifties coat, was an eerie image, one that had troubled his subconscious for weeks before Aguta had appeared with her speculations. He'd sent her a text after seeing her, but she'd never replied. He decided she might have been freaked out by him saying he'd seen her, per-haps thought he'd been stalking her. He almost texted again, to say that wasn't the case, but luckily his dignity kicked in.

Now, upstairs on the bus, sitting where she sat, he caught a glimpse of the tv transmitters on the top of the Palace, the biscuit-brown brick towers below. Milda had been confused about Alexandra Palace, thought some real royalty lived up there on the hill. It had saddened her to learn that the Victorian hulk was just used for bric-a-brac fairs and the odd bit of ice-skating.

One hot Thursday night in the office, Lawrence Berne had given them all a long lecture about the old Princess of Wales, who'd opened it and given it to the people for entertainment and education, complete with its music halls and libraries, and how apt it was that the first tv broadcasts had issued from its tower.

*So actually it's tv station and place for jumble sale*s – Milda had concluded drily – *but in England, that is Palace. Ha!*

Rex found himself smiling at the memory. He wondered what she'd say now, if she were to suddenly sit down next to him. She always felt so light and fragile beside him, like a bird that might suddenly fly away *Ai! Such a silly bag, Rex*. He still remembered, with diamond clarity, the first words she'd said to him, as she tried to extricate her buttons from the net on the front of his satchel. He'd felt so awkward, he hadn't even noticed that the beautiful new office temp knew his name.

And what would he say, when he found her? He was over her. It was over. He was seeing Diana now. But how could he explain that he'd been worried about her, without seeming as if he still had feelings? It occurred to him that he wouldn't be mentioning this visit to Diana. She wouldn't get it. He wasn't even sure he did.

Green Lanes was one of those roads people called arteries, a painful term that made you think of skinned beasts and blood clots. It was appropriate. This improbably long and straight passage was an old cattle-drovers' route, from Hertfordshire pastures to Smithfield slaughter. From country to city, life to death. Similar contrasts were to be found today. At the southern end, two miles and cultural light-years away from Rex's manor, was Newington Green: a young and artsy place, full of people who worked from home and called their children Milo and Edie. That zone ended abruptly by the old water-tower, giving way to velvet-clad Hasidim, then several hulking, half-empty blocks. After that came the teeming bazaar of the Turkish quarter, then the bland, consumer-conveyor-belt of Wood Green, the whole ribbon of civilisation finally flickering out on a high flat plateau above the city, a windy place jagged with pylons and giant, creaking storage units. Nobody, not even local history bores like Lawrence Berne, could explain why it was Green Lanes in the plural, instead of just a Lane.

At the very top of it, where the mighty 141 concluded its passage up from Waterloo, Milda lived, in a squat by the North Circular. It wasn't hard to find the house: a chunky, between-the-wars affair that could have looked respectable without the metal shutters and the main road running by. Many of the properties around were squatted: brown steel sheets over the doors, flags in the upper window denoting the nationalities of the new residents.

He didn't remember the number – houses on the North Circular ran well into the nine hundreds – but he knew it was by a crossroads, and that the place to its left was derelict. Or rather, it had more or less burnt down, but was, incredibly, still occupied by the people who had set light to it. *Chankiss*, Milda always called them, contemptuously. Junkies. She was a very proper girl, the squat her one nod to rebellion. She never swore, never took drugs, never broke a promise, and certainly never lied or stole. All of which made her, in her own way, and to Rex's heart, the most attractive sort of rebel of all. But the Milda he'd heard about today didn't sound like the girl he knew.

Rex banged on the metal door of the squat, creating thunder within. From inside, he could hear quick footsteps, the ever-present dance music being turned down. Unexpected visitors caused anxiety. An Albanian who had once lived there was under threat of bailiffs, and the bailiffs weren't the sort who'd care that he wasn't there any more. Then, as Milda had often explained, there were the electricity, gas and water people, keen to investigate the continual theft of utilities. And the police, raiding the makeshift brothels. And the bored Turkish youths who sometimes knocked on the door – almost politely, she said – in search of a fight.

A head poked from one of the upper windows: a middle-aged, weathered-looking man. Rex gazed up at him, squinting in the sun. 'I'm looking for Milda,' he said. The head disappeared. There were more footsteps and after a silence in which Rex felt sure he was being watched, the sliding of bolts. The man appeared again. He had so many freckles, his face was almost khaki, but his eyes were the colour of the sea in holiday brochures.

'Ah,' he said. 'The journalist.'

From this courteous, slightly mocking introduction, Rex knew this was Vadim. Much older than he'd expected. He had wavy, sandy-blond hair and a bandaged hand. He led Rex through the dark, fungal hallway into the kitchen, where a group of hefty boys in workboots and overalls was smoking grass. They were young, with cropped hair and pale skin; some still had acne. Rex recognised a couple of faces: fellow Lithuanians he'd been introduced to in the street when he was with Milda. At a word from Vadim, they all trooped out, acknowledging the interloper with grave, yet not unfriendly nods. Somewhere else in the house, the music was turned up again.

'Maybe you don't want to sit on our sofa in your handsome coat,' Vadim said, seating himself at a table covered in computer parts. He said it smiling, so that Rex couldn't decide whether it was an insult or not. He decided it was, and sat on the sofa, which offered all the comfort of a sock stretched over a coat-hanger. The floor was bare boards, but other than that, the kitchen looked quite bearable – no worse than the places Rex had lived in at university. Vadim picked up a soldering iron and squinted at some obscure piece of circuitry before him.

'I am sorry, I must finish this because... I must finish it by tomorrow.'

'Where is Milda?'

Vadim shrugged. He was sinewy and powerful-looking – Milda had said something about him being in the army for a while. In fact, Vadim seemed to have done everything for a while: worked in a bar in Frankfurt, something indistinct in Finland. Now he mended computers – when he wasn't fitting kitchens, or importing smoked fish.

'She said maybe she might go to see Birgita,' Vadim offered. 'Do you know that girl?'

'The artist.'

'We are all artists perhaps,' Vadim grinned, showing small, crooked teeth. 'Even you.'

It was one of those annoying, cool, European-squatter-type comments that meant nothing. Rex dismissed it. 'When did she go?'

'I don't know,' Vadim replied, glancing up. 'Three weeks ago, maybe.' He looked away again.

'And you haven't heard from her since then?'

'No.'

Rex stared distractedly at the bright blue holdall by the side of the sofa. This didn't sound like Milda, either – a girl who couldn't pass ten minutes without informing someone where she was and what she was doing by text and telephone. Rex's refusal to do the same, his need to go off the radar for an hour or two, had troubled her greatly, and contributed, he suspected, to the death of whatever they'd had together.

'Excuse me, Mister Rex. But is this any of your business when I speak to my girl?'

'Maybe not,' Rex said. 'But Aguta was worried about her, because she didn't come to Dovila's birthday yesterday, so I promised I'd find out if she was okay.'

'Aguta,' the man said, simply, lifting a savage-looking hunting knife from the jumble on the table, and twisting it next to his temple. 'Crazy bitch.'

'You don't think it's odd for her to have missed the kid's birthday?'

'Many things Milda does is… odd. You know that. You tried calling to her?'

'Voicemail.'

'I will be, er, straight with you, okay?' Vadim put his tools down and rubbed the bridge of his nose. How old was he? Fifty? 'We had an argue, actually. Quite big argue. She quits her job at cafe, she's got no money, she wants to borrow from me… So – I tell to her, after time, no, sweet-cheeks, get another job. So she slams the door, and she goes to see that friend Birgita. So – she wants me to call up her. Darling darling, I am so sorry, come home, without you I can't live. So – I won't. Understand? Even she doesn't go to the kid's birthday it's same thing – she wants Aguta to blame me. Nasty Vadim! Games, games all the time. She cannot help it. It's communism.'

'Communism?'

'Under communism everybody learnt tricks. Steal, cheat, manipulate. Now, all those people are coming here to your country, Mister Rex, and they only know to live as they lived before. Anyway. On you she doesn't need to play tricks anymore.'

Rex sighed. What Vadim said wasn't entirely untrue. And the older man's attitude was probably more healthy than his own. Even now, even after she'd left him for this sour old soldier, he was still running around London worrying about her. He stood up. Vadim showed him to the door. By the radiator he saw a pile of final demand letters addressed to Adem Dushku – the debt-ridden Albanian, he assumed.

'I was a journalist also,' Vadim said. 'For a while. In Kazakhstan.'

What a city. Only here, in a mildewed squat, could you meet a man who'd been a journalist in Alma-Ata, and now fitted kitchens in Arnos Grove.

As he came out of the door, he almost bumped into a tubby Turkish man in a leather coat. 'You Vadim?' he asked. Rex gestured behind him. Vadim looked suddenly pained, as if Rex, or at least someone, had committed a social gaffe.

'Taxi for Stansted yeah? Any luggage?'

'In a minute,' Vadim said tightly. The driver walked back to the road.

'Going for a trip?' Rex asked.

'Vilnius,' Vadim replied, sharply. 'I better go. Actually.'

* * *

Later, Rex was waiting for a southbound bus amid a raucous throng of boys from the nearby school. Exuberant and smelling of bubble-gum, no doubt the only danger they posed was to someone's eardrums. All the same, a stout woman carrying a lap-top case crossed the street to avoid them. That made Rex remember what Vadim had said about the computer he'd been repairing. Why had he said he had to finish it by tomorrow, when he was plainly on the verge of leaving the country today? Why had he looked so awkward when the taxi driver appeared? He didn't understand, but it bothered him.

The feeling did not ease as his bus travelled south down the Lanes, past the boxes of fruit and vegetables outside the grocers. He could believe she'd disappear in a sulk to make a point with Vadim; even, at a pinch, if the argument had been harsh enough, avoid Dovila's birthday. But lose her job, over a bunch of carrots?

His phone rang. It was Ellie, in the office. She spoke in the bland, affectless fashion of someone very angry. He couldn't be bothered to find out why. Keith Powell, she said, could meet him this afternoon, at his house. Rex took down the address, noting the postcode with surprise.

'Thanks,' he said. 'How did you get on at the surgery?' There was no reply. Ellie had hung up.

He shrugged, resting his head against the cool glass of the window, letting the street go past in a blur. Among the medley of colours, one item drew his attention, and forced him to focus. A pale blue sign for the Eazylets lettings agency. The signs were everywhere along the street. Rex remembered he'd been looking at the same logo a few hours back, on the card in Terry's wallet. He also remembered why the name on the card had been familiar to him. Ilona Balint. The first girl to be attacked.

* * *

Rex thought he had a good idea of the sort of man Keith Powell would be. One of the dwindling tribe of blue collar Tottenham whites. Bull-necked and defiant, they drank in the few taverns where the Cross of St George flew. They consumed Carling by the bucketload. And they prided themselves on their good relations with their Asian newsagents and their Turkish kebab vendors. But it only took the tiniest spark – a bent wing mirror, a case of miscounted change – for some of them to turn into roaring, racist psychopaths. Their sons and daughters spoke perfect patois – they had half-Caribbean babies, sometimes, too – but that didn't make them any more accommodating when the matter of housing, or school places, or women in burkahs cropped up.

Powell's address didn't fit this profile. His street lay in the protective shadow of Alexandra Palace, at the intersection of the three, defiantly middle-class hamlets of Crouch End, Hornsey and Muswell Hill. At one end of it, a little shop sold organic bread. As Rex shuffled along through the fine drizzle, fashionable mums gazed up from brand-new buggies and pushchairs. He began to wonder if Ellie had given him the right address, but there it was: the silver Luton, shining rudely amongst his neighbours' Audis and lovingly-restored camper vans, like a tradesman refusing to use the back door. On each side, painted in stout black letters, was 'Keith Powell – Kill Pests'.

Rex rang the bell and waited. Silence and birdsong were broken by the rasp of a scooter engine. Rex swivelled round. The sound had made him anxious. He was relieved to see a chunky, grizzled-looking black man drive slowly past, the clipboard on the handlebars announcing him to be a trainee cab-driver, learning The Knowledge.

The door opened, and man in his mid-thirties stood before him. He was dressed in smart jeans and a striped jumper, with his dark hair drawn into a little fin: the uniform of the North London media-type.

'You're wet,' Powell said. 'Did you have to park a way off?'

Rex said nothing, wanting to avoid the car conversation. Powell's accent was flat and featureless. South-eastern and possibly working class, he thought, but subject to some deliberate bleaching process. Like Powell himself, judging from his appearance.

'Are you really called Rex Tracey?' Powell asked, as he took off his coat in the hallway. 'You should have been a private detective with that name.'

'Well. I do find things out,' Rex replied, for perhaps the eight-thousandth time in his life.

They sat in a bright front room decorated with black-and-white photographs and Ikea nick-nacks. It was a thoughtfully laid-out space, very male, with its leather cushions and silver orbs. Powell didn't wear a wedding ring, Rex noticed, as he poured out Darjeeling tea. They could also have had Earl Grey, Lapsang, or half a dozen fruit and herbal blends. A neo-Nazi van driver who offers you a choice of teas. The world was changing.

Keith Powell seemed to think so too. 'We're well aware this country has been built upon waves of immigrants,' he said earnestly, his hands mimicking the open, 'trust me' gestures of a certain recent Prime Minister. 'We're not challenging that. And we're not trying to pretend there's any such thing as a pure white Englishman. All that rubbish was deconstructed decades ago.'

Deconstructed? Rex had rolled his eyes before he'd had a chance to restrain himself.

'I didn't always drive a van, you known,' Powell said. 'I was a teacher. Up in Corby. History and PE.'

Rex had already noticed the bookshelf on the far wall, stuffed with popular history: the Reformation to the Rolling Stones. 'So what happened?'

'Too much form-filling and liberal fascism.'

'Liberal fascism?'

'As in, I can't tell a black lad to take off his Bob Marley cap because that's infringing his human rights. As in, I'm not supposed to be in a room on my own with a female pupil. As in –'

Rex stopped him. This all felt engineered, fake. The variety of teas, the big words. The fact that Powell's front room smelt of cigarettes, but he wouldn't smoke, and there were no ashtrays or lighters to be seen. He wanted to disguise certain things, yet he couldn't hide the angry glee with which he warmed to his theme. The sense of injustice, the use of home-made terms like 'liberal fascism'. And how quick had he been to mention blacks?

'You're called the British Workers' Action Party. What kind of action are you talking about?'

'Not the kind of action you're thinking of,' Powell retorted. 'This whole thing started out just me and some local lads, working blokes, meeting up in a room on the Lanes, to talk about things. We never wanted to be a party, as such, just a sort of informal pressure group.'

'So what changed?'

'The fact that every third shop around here sells Polish sausage.'

Rex laughed derisively, but Powell joined in, as if they were sharing a joke. 'Don't quote me on that. But we're being swamped, aren't we? Every school round here is stuffed with kids from Eastern Europe, who can't speak English and won't learn because they'll probably only be here six months. We haven't got room for every single person who wants to come here.'

'But you're not really talking about all the other immigrants, are you? Your leaflets target people from the eastern bloc and the former Soviet Union. And you've just said yourself that these are mostly short-term visitors. So why not let them do what they want, and go?'

'Because they'll be replaced by others. We're not a transit camp. Some controls have to be placed on it all, and if the government is reluctant to do it, then people have to fight.'

'Fight?'

'Through public debate.' Powell was interrupted by a bleeping sound from upstairs. He stood up. 'Sorry, someone's sending me a fax. Must have run out of paper.'

'I didn't know people still used them.'

'We buy supplies from Rumania.' He shrugged, and turned round at the door. 'Mention in your article that my company does business with Eastern Europe. We even have a Polish girl on reception. This isn't about xenophobia.'

'Spell that for me?' Rex said. Powell responded with a smile, and a good-natured V-sign, as he ran upstairs. Rex was surprised. How many people flashed the V's nowadays?

He drifted over to the walls. The photos were self-made, executed with a real feeling for light and shade. All lonely seaside scenes, with a complete absence of humans. Powell's artistic world seemed to be a coastline, ravaged by wind and sea, under threat from barnacles and other pitiless invaders. Maybe that extended to his politics, too.

He moved over to the bookshelves, and thought it would be funny if there was a copy of *Mein Kampf* in there. Then he saw that there was, which he didn't find so funny. There was a piece of paper sticking from the top of it. He pulled the book out. It belonged to Corby Central Library. The slip of paper was a letter from the Probation Service, dated a month ago, its language so bloated with jargon that it was all but impossible to understand. The gist, though, was that Keith Powell was a 'probation service user', attending monthly meetings with his 'probation service provider' at an address just off the Archway Road. So Powell had form. And he had a copy of Mein Kampf. Not that possession indicated belief, of course. But still...

Rex went into the bright, spare bathroom – the bathroom of a single man, he decided, from the position of the loo seat to the peppering of stubble in the basin. But then, on the way out, he saw in the waste basket a tube of aloe vera foot gel, and a couple of cotton wool pads. The sight of them gave him a quick stab of nostalgia for Milda and the strange, fragrant detritus she left behind whenever she spent the night. Did Keith Powell have someone like that? Or was he just a Nazi who looked after his feet? It was important, perhaps, if you were going on marches all the time.

'You a bit of a scooter boy?' Rex asked Powell. He was in the little hallway, looking at the green fishtail parka on the coathooks as his host came back down the stairs.

'I restore vintage Lambrettas, actually.'

'Just restore them?'

'The best ones are like vintage wine. You don't ride them. You just have them. You into scooters?'

A scooter, of some sort, had very nearly been into Rex that morning, but he didn't say so. In any case, he had no idea what a Lambretta looked like.

'I've kept thinking I've seen you before somewhere,' Powell went on, as he opened the front door. 'Now I remember where. You drink in the Victoria Stakes, don't you?'

Rex inclined his head slightly. He was there sometimes. He was in most pubs sometimes.

'I'll buy you a pint if I like the piece,' Powell said as he saw Rex out.

'Erm. Yes,' was the best Rex could manage. He wondered whether Powell was profoundly stupid or dangerously clever. Did he imagine they were friends now?

'Just one thing,' Rex said, turning round just as Powell was about to shut the door. It was a trick he'd seen on *Columbo*. 'Where did you say your group had its meetings?'

'I don't think I did,' Powell replied smartly. 'But by all means mention it. Everyone's welcome to our meetings. Tuesday evenings. Eight till ten. In the Good Taste Cafe.'

* * *

When I went to the surgery, I found it eerily quiet, as if some trace of the horrifying events still lingered in the air.

'Ellie!'

Rex's voice rippled the stillness of the early evening office. The Whittaker Twins continued murmuring into their headsets. Ellie looked up briefly, then went back to typing, smiling and talking softly into a mobile cradled between her chin and her neck. Rex saw the logo of her favourite social networking site on her monitor. He felt a trembling in his jaw.

'I'm sorry, yeah?' Rex almost shouted into the mobile he'd just snatched from his colleague. 'But Ellie's got this, like, thing to do? Called a, like, job?' He slammed the phone down on the desk. Ellie's perfect, almond-shaped eyes were wide. He knew he'd gone too far.

'*That* was assault,' she said hoarsely. She glanced around for support, but no one was looking.

Rex ignored her. He tried to calm down. 'I need to talk to you about this piece, Ellie, it's just…' The word wouldn't come. 'You're not writing a ghost story.'

Ellie looked sullen and said nothing.

'And you never write a news report in the first person. You know that.'

'Dr Shah?'

'What do you mean, Dr Shah?'

'He's the first person in the article.'

Rex stared at the tiled ceiling. She wasn't thick, he knew that. The very opposite. But how did you get four 'A' levels, get through three years of a degree at Bristol, followed by a year of NCTJ training here in London and still not understand the difference between florid Victorian-Gothic prose and a few paragraphs for the local rag? How could she not know what the first person was? He knew what he'd sound like if he opened his mouth, so he didn't. Interpreting his silence as some sort of scheduled break, Ellie picked up her phone again and started texting. Rex glared in teeth-grinding silence. After a while she looked up.

'What are you getting in such a state about?' she said, letting her hair fall over her face in a sulky curtain. 'You expected me to mess it up. That's why you called the Surgery before I even got there. And guess what? I did. I messed it up. So now you can write the piece yourself, can't you?'

Ellie's voice had started to wobble before the end and her eyes filmed over. Before Rex could answer, she had fled from her desk into the toilets. She'd started a drama degree before switching to journalism. Perhaps it had been the wrong decision.

'A word.'

Susan summoned him from across the office. Loud sobbing emerged from the Ladies.

'Ellie is an extremely bright young woman, Rex.' Susan closed the door and topped up her mug with green tea, all silently. She sometimes appeared in Rex's dreams as a ghost – slender and dark and exotic, like a long-dead Byzantine princess. 'Yes, she is,' she added, seeing his face. 'And the only reason she isn't flourishing under your tuition is because you undermine her. Whenever she speaks, you get this pissy, bored look on your face.'

Rex sat up in his chair, aware from the way the accent had shifted from Boston Old Money to New Jersey Dockyards that this wasn't one of Susan's chats. It was one of Susan's bollockings.

'If I didn't know you better, you know what I'd say? I'd say, "Ellie's a kid who's going to go places. Rex – he's been places. And that's why he has such a problem with her."'

Rex started to speak, but she interrupted. 'But I give you more credit than that, Rex, as a professional and a human being. You know what I think? I think Ellie is a young, intelligent and attractive woman, and for reasons that have been obvious to everyone in this office since the start of the summer, that's the kind of woman you're angry with right now.'

'That's psycho-twaddle, Susan.'

'You're not over Milda, Rex,' his boss said. 'You're still very hurt. And I think you should go back for some counselling.'

They'd worked together a long, long time, here and elsewhere, but sometimes he didn't like this intimacy, this reminder that Susan knew so much about his past. 'I'm planning to sleep with my GP,' he said savagely. 'Does that count?'

'Cheap. Have you seen Milda lately?'

'No one seems to have seen her lately. She's not at the café anymore.'

'How do you feel about that?'

'I don't care! She was the office temp. We had a fling. All right, more than a fling. A relationship. But she left. We split up.'

'What about Syb? Have you seen her?'

'Syb kind of picks up on my mood. And I don't like to upset her.'

Susan smiled. 'So you admit you're in the sort of mood that upsets people.'

'Sod off,' he said, but more gently.

'Play nicely, Rex. Ellie's an okay kid.'

'She sends bloody text messages while I'm speaking to her!'

'None of which bothered you at all when Milda was around.'

Rex opened his mouth and closed it again. She had him there, and it annoyed him.

'Tell yourself it was just a fling if you like, Rex. But you looked happy. Happier than I'd seen you in ten years. You made Milda happy, too.'

'Well – thanks for reminding me what I lost.'

'I'm reminding you because I want you to give yourself time to get over it. Admit it mattered. Admit you're hurt. Grieve!'

'Susan. Jesus.'

'Your Keith Powell interview's good,' she said, suddenly swerving onto a new topic. It was typical Susan style. Rex imagined the scene in her head to be a continuous, hurtling ticker-tape. 'Very funny. I'll put it in if there's room, but just so you're clear, I'm not making any spurious link to the two attacks up at the Palace.'

Before Rex could answer, the door had opened and Ellie had come in, her face blotchy and streaked.

'Rex?' She spoke in a theatrical whisper as she handed him his phone. 'I thought it might be urgent.'

'Rex Tracey.' He stood up and took the phone out of the office and into the stairway, which smelled as ever of toast and radiators. 'Hello?' At first there was no reply, then a voice crackled on the loudspeaker, startling him.

'Rex, it's Mike Bond.'

Mike Bond was Brenda's husband, a Detective Sergeant for as long as anyone could remember at St Anne's nick, and a font of valuable information for the paper. The staff lived in fear of the day Mike retired.

'What have you got for me, Mike?'

'Another girl's been attacked at Ally Pally. She's in the North Middlesex.'

'Does she have a name?'

Bond ignored the question. 'Poor kid. Same as the last one. Well – not the same, actually. Worse. A lot worse…' He cleared his throat. 'Lithuanian, we reckon she is, this time.'

Rex's heart squirmed. 'A name, Mike?'

He was out of the door before Bond had finished struggling with the name.

Chapter Three

The North Middlesex was a place under permanent siege. Burly Congolese security guards paced the corridors, and a complex one-way system was in place, so that no one could get from the A&E entrance into any of the consulting rooms or the wards without being escorted or entering a PIN code. This might have had something to do with infection, but it had more to do with people.

Rex knew the system well. He loathed the place, but the job took him here at least once a month, more when the weather was fine and the gangs spent more time on the streets, disrespecting each other. In spite of all the precautions, he was able to wander unaccosted into the Intensive Care Unit. There were no nurses: machines did all the looking-after here, machines in three, large-windowed rooms, arranged in a horseshoe around a tiny lobby. He didn't need the posters – in English, French, Turkish, Somali, Kurdish, Bengali, Urdu and Albanian – to tell him to wash his hands and put on a gown.

Each of the three rooms housed a body, but Rex knew instantly which one to look at. Through the observation window he recognised the cello-like curves of the shoulders, the narrow waist, a wisp of her almost brass-coloured hair. Seeing this hair on the hospital pillow, as he'd seen it so many times on his own pillows, he knew that Susan was right. He still cared. He hadn't come here on the trail of a story; he had come because Milda had carved out a space inside him, because he still cared about her, even if they weren't and never would be together.

He took a step inside the room. She'd never been big, but

now, surrounded by all the tubes and the hissing, bleeping machinery, she looked tiny, like a premature baby. She must have been badly hurt to have ended up here, and he could see a heavy white dressing covering one side of her head. But she faced the other way. And he knew that he had to look. He moved round the bed.

'What are you doing? Who are you?'

A stout, furious nurse filled the doorway, a plastic hat covering her afro like a cloud.

'Hey! I'm calling Security. Who is this man?' She voiced her thoughts, an African trait, he had noticed. 'Where is that policeman?' She bustled out of view, all crackling apron and outrage.

'You don't need a policeman. I'm – ' Rex's voice faded away as he saw the face on the pillow. The bone white skin. The orange stain of the iodine. The rust-brown of the dried blood. So many colours. Like the fruit and veg outside the grocers. He heard muttering in the corridor. Was the nurse talking to someone, or just herself?

'Rex. You're not supposed to be in here. What are you doing?'

At the sound of his name, he glanced away from her, to the voice in the doorway. Even in the cap and gown, Mike Bond looked like an old policeman.

'I thought…' Rex was shaking. 'I thought it was her, Mike.'

* * *

The tea tasted somehow like the women who served it: of face-powder, lavender and lilies. There was no currently no cafeteria at the hospital – Lawrence Berne had, in fact, offered a ditty on the subject to the *Gazette*, beginning with the couplet: 'I fancied a bun or a teacake/After they'd checked out my prostate.' In place of the normal facilities, some ladies from a church in Barnet served hot beverages and flapjack from trestle-tables in the waiting area. Rex sipped his drink gingerly, then put it under his chair as Bond appeared, carrying a blue, plastic sack. He was a big man, with a heavy, jowly face and white hair whipped into tight waves, like something from an ice-cream machine.

'This was the book,' the policeman said, easing his bulk into a chair and pulling from the sack a pale, green, cloth-bound book with a Lithuanian title. This was sealed inside another bag for evidence purposes, but Bond let Rex handle it. The bag was big enough to allow him to open the book and see Milda's name inside, in her handwriting. She'd written, typically, in fountain-pen. Somehow this book of hers had ended up in the hands of that forlorn creature in Intensive Care.

'That's the only thing we've got with a name on,' Bond went on, pulling another, plastic-shrouded item out from his sack. The next item was a dirty, fabric handbag with a flower-print. There followed various of its contents: a paintbrush, lip-salve, a railway ticket from Leyton High Road, and a torn envelope. Rex read the words on the envelope out loud. 'Hodja Nasreddin.'

'Someone you know?'

'He's a sort of Islamic folk character,' Rex said, absently, staring at the fragment of envelope. 'But look – that's an 'N' underneath it. It's part of a postcode.'

'An Islamic folk character who lives in North London.'

'There used to be a restaurant with that name, just off Newington Green. It's a squat now.' Rex sensed rather than saw Bond's raised eyebrows. 'I went there once with Milda.'

'Brenda said you were seeing one of those girls,' Bond said, gathering back the bagged items. 'But I didn't know her name. I'm sorry. That must have been a fright for you.'

Rex shrugged. 'We split up, actually. Back in July…'

'Never exactly the sort to stick around, are they?'

Rex looked at him. 'Who aren't?'

Bond lowered his voice. 'An awful lot of these Eastern bloc girls

59

are just here for trouble.' He jerked his crenellated hairdo back in the direction of the wards. 'That one certainly was. You only had to look at the clothes she was in. You know what I mean.'

'What was she wearing, Mike? A t-shirt that said Please Throttle Me and Pull Out A Chunk Of My Hair?'

Bond sighed, as if Rex were being deliberately obtuse.

'He did worse than that this time. He cut out a chunk of her scalp the size of a sardine tin.'

'He scalped her?'

Bond nodded. They were both silent for a while, until the policeman tapped the cover of the book. 'You're certain this is your girlfriend's book?'

'I'm certain my ex-girlfriend wrote her name in it,' said Rex slowly. 'It's her name. It's her handwriting. And she always writes in fountain pen.' She does everything carefully, he wanted to add. Wants everything to look beautiful, even if it takes hours to do it. Bugger all use as an office temp, of course.

'So there's a good chance she knows that kid in there,' Bond said, jabbing a thick thumb in the direction of the wards behind him. 'How can we get in touch with her?'

'I've been wondering the same thing myself.' Rex gazed morosely around, at the peeling walls and the curling lino. At the posters, executed in vivid, third-world graphics, proclaiming the wisdom of hand-washing and the dangers of an infant's cough. Why did he have to spend so much time in this place?

Later, outside, in a breezy car park surrounded by garment factories and lock-ups, Rex rang the office.

'It's not Milda,' he told Susan.

'Thank God.' He heard Susan relaying the news to other people behind her, then murmurs of relief. 'We'll talk later. Do you want a drink?'

'I'll call you.'

'Ok. And Rex?'

'Yes.'

'Do you know where Milda is?'

'No. She's not at the café. No one seems to know where she is.'

'I'm going to contact the agency she came through. Someone should be warning all these girls not to walk through the Palace.'

As they got in the car, Bond went through all the things that had happened to the girl now in the ICU. She'd been found unconscious in the grounds of Alexandra Palace, with strangulation marks to the neck like both of the other girls who'd been attacked up there. The scalping, though, was a ghastly new departure – neat, almost workman-like, it had exposed the skull beneath. She'd had a small brain haemorrhage, and now they were worried about sepsis in the wound. The girl was seriously unwell.

'You reckon it's the same person behind all three attacks?'

Bond sighed, shifting a box of rubber gloves off the dashboard and stowing it on the back seat. 'Don't know. Seems likely, though. Maybe pulling their hair out wasn't giving him enough of a thrill. Maybe he can cut them quicker.'

'Or slower,' Rex added. 'Sick bastard.'

'Still no nasties, you know, down below,' Bond mused, with a policeman's mix of callousness and delicacy. But he went on to add that the buttons had been undone on the third girl's jeans, as if perhaps the attacker had been on the verge of something, but been surprised.

Bond gave him a lift to the crossroads, where Green Lanes hit the North Circular. It was right next to the squat where Milda lived. Rex pointed it out before he left the car, but Bond merely took a note of it and drove on.

He wanted a drink. There was a pub over the road, which over the years had undergone countless changes of management and design, without ever becoming any more attractive. Now it was calling itself a 'Polish Sports Bar'. Rex just wanted a dark corner, out of sight, where he could drink steadily, from relief and sadness, but mainly from memories.

Ten years ago he'd stood next to another bed like that, seen another broken girl, possessed and violated by all the equipment that kept her alive. Bond's final words on the subject, before they'd switched to holidays and roadworks, swung in and out of his mind, like an ancient church bell. 'If she gets through the next 48 hours, they think she'll be all right,' he'd said. 'In one way, at least.' The girl he'd watched a decade ago had turned out all right, in one way. Desperately, heart-breakingly not in so many others. He wouldn't be able to cope if that happened to someone else close to him.

A bus went by, carrying another bright-blue sign for the Eazy-lets agency. The sight brought a thought to the surface: the third girl – because she was, without doubt, the third girl, now, part of a definite sequence of events – had had a railway ticket from Leytonstone in her bag.

And that gave her one thing, one unsettling, unthinkable thing in common with the other two girls. He didn't want to address it. He also knew he had to.

A quick call ascertained that the agency was open until 7 pm, and that Ilona Balint was still working there. He caught a bus back to Wood Green.

The North London office of EazyLets was in between a Caribbean takeaway and shop that unlocked mobile phones, but didn't sell them. At that hour, Ilona Balint was the only person in there. She was a tired-looking, metallic blonde, whose make-up almost, but not entirely obscured the natural beauty beneath. She came to the locked door, looked him up and down and asked him his business before undoing the catch to admit him. A coloured scarf did not quite hide the red marks around her neck, and a pale blue woollen hat announced, rather than disguised, the hank of hair Rex knew had been removed in the attack. He tried not to stare.

'You want to register with us?' she said stiffly, sitting down at the desk.

'A friend of mine recommended you,' Rex said. 'Terry Younger.'

Ilona Balint shrugged the shoulders of her pale grey business suit and flipped through a drawer. She was young, Rex saw, looking at her hands, but something had withered her. Was it the job? Hungary? Or what had happened at Alexandra Palace? She'd got off lightly compared to the last girl, but of course she wouldn't see it that way.

'He was very pleased with the place you found him in Leytonstone,' Rex prompted. 'The gated mews.'

Ilona Balint narrowed her eyes suspiciously. 'I let a place out last week but…' She turned her attention to a bulging notebook. 'Yes. There's a Mr Younger on the tenancy agreement but I never met him. Only his partner.'

'You've never met Terry Younger? Skinny bloke? Bald? Funny accent?'

'I know the accent because he rang me to ask about parking space,' she said. 'But that's it. I never met…' She paused as Rex pulled a copy of last week's *Gazette* from the nearby coffee table. Thanks to a recent edict of Susan's, mugshots of all the team were now featured on the back page. 'No,' she said, shaking her head. 'Never seen him.'

'Oh. Well. He speaks very highly of the agency.'

She stared at Rex coldly for a moment or two, then asked him to fill out a form. Rex was so embarrassed by the encounter that he did so, painstakingly, and then spent several minutes looking at pictures of one-bedroom garden flats in the Wood Green area. Had this been a stupid idea?

He had answered that question in the affirmative as he reached the front gate of his house, with a newly-purchased bottle of raki in his hand. Someone had left something outside the gate, and the light down the lane was so poor that he almost walked into it.

His stomach lurched when he saw what it was: a hospital wheelchair, cheap and battered, with a pole on one side so that a drip could be affixed. He pushed it aside and went in.

With a glass in his hand, and the news on the tv, he reminded himself that people were dumping things and playing pranks around this area all the time. It was chock full of students, and a good proportion of them were training at the North Middlesex. Nevertheless, the sight of the hook-like tip of the drip attachment over the fence out of his window troubled him. He had another drink, then went out and pushed the contraption over into the next road. Someone else might be spooked by it in the morning. But not someone with all the reasons he had.

* * *

'Promise me you'll do something about that foot?' Brenda Bond said as he limped into the office. His tight smile in response only intensified Rex's headache, but it was all he could manage. If he actually made a verbal promise, he knew she'd hold him to it. Every day Brenda brought a family-sized ice-cream tub of freshly-made rolls to the office with her. Most of these she ate herself, but the rest were forced upon those *Gazette* staff-members she thought were looking 'peaky'. She now advanced the opinion that Rex was looking peaky, and invited him to approach the desk. Vast yet carefully dressed, bejewelled and coiffed, the paper's receptionist and sub-editor reminded Rex somehow of a ship, or an island. She wore rings she hadn't removed in ten years.

'I didn't know you could still get fish paste,' Rex said, through a mouthful of roll.

'You can't,' Brenda said, adjusting her towering hair-do. 'That's my rhubarb jam.'

He went upstairs quickly. It was Wednesday. Deadline day. The paper came out tomorrow morning. Ellie was at her desk in a short, grey dress over an ivory-coloured blouse. The outfit, and her tied-back hair gave her a chastened, penitent look, as if she were making a new start. She also looked very young, and Rex resolved to make a new start with her, too.

Susan stood in the doorway to her office, her back towards the staff. Some sort of new cyber-hub was being installed, an item which promised to simplify her life, but which everyone except Susan knew would only complicate it further. As if in prophecy of the chaos to come, polystyrene nuggets and cable ties had spilled out across the doorway, the rumpled shirts and waistbands of two baffled IT types could be glimpsed further within and even on the other side of the office, Rex caught the whiff of new plastic and sweat.

Rex went through his morning routine: reading emails, listening to messages, checking his diary. A thin jiffy bag had come for him in the post, and he found that the anonymous unexpectedness of it made him nervous. He'd spent a restless night, reflecting on the way the day's puzzles all seemed to relate to him. He knew that Milda's disappearing act wasn't his fault. Nor was he involved in the attacks up at the Palace, or Keith Powell's gang of apparently reasonable racists. Yet somehow, because all of those things had been book-ended by a kid trying to run him over in a car-park and the wheelchair outside his house, they seemed to point back to him. He knew where this line of reasoning came from. He knew where it led, too, and he was afraid if it.

He took a deep breath and slit open the envelope. It was a

CD. From the makers of his new telephone. Featuring a new, upgraded Tutorial with bonus features. He shoved the thing in the bin. What kind of phone required you to have lessons in it?

Luckily one of the Whittaker Twins wanted copy for an advertorial, the subject being SoTo, alias, South Tottenham, alias, the bit between Turnpike Lane and Seven Sisters, and why it was such an up-and-coming place for young professionals to invest right now in a two-bed flat with balcony and de Bouverie bath fittings. He rather enjoyed these assignments, the hyperbole of the local estate agents having reached such levels during the recent recession that nothing he could say would look out of place.

'Hewn by artisans from the finest synthetic materials, this luminous new-build sits astride the mighty Philip Lane, basking in the reflected glory of a dozen kebab shops…'

It wasn't the copy he would give them in the end, but after a draining Monday and a rough night he was finding relief in a bit of silliness. Then he was interrupted by Ellie: she'd rewritten the Surgery piece and wanted him to take a look. This he interpreted, as a good sign.

'Hunt For Surgery Attacker' ran her suggested headline. Aside from the fact that the man hadn't attacked anyone, and no one was actively hunting him, it was a decent, open-ended, story-still-to-be-told sort of headline. She'd laid out the facts clearly enough in her piece. An agitated, dark-haired man, unshaven, in jeans and leather jacket, had asked for an appointment at the GP surgery on West Green Road where Diana worked. On being told that he needed to be registered with the practice, he'd become violent. His accent was described as 'foreign-sounding', and his violence had frightened the Receptionist into pressing a panic button. But before the police had arrived, Dr Shah had come out of his consulting room and spoken to the man, who had then run away. Ellie's piece included a quote from a terrified

Turkish mother, who'd been in the waiting room with her asthmatic three-year-old son at the time. It also made a link to the overstretched mental health services in the borough. 'Overstretched' was a well-chosen word. To the sort of readers who sympathised with Keith Powell, it meant there were too many immigrants. To those of another mindset, it evoked images of exhausted professionals, accorded neither the respect nor the resources they deserved.

It was a good piece. He wondered vaguely whether Ellie had been taking the piss with the last version. He glanced at her.

'What?'

'Nothing. It's a good piece. Spot-on, actually. Well done.'

'Seriously?'

Her face broke into the most artless, shy and touching smile. He almost felt like reaching out giving her a hug. Before this could happen, Susan was upon them both, phone in hand.

'You're here,' she said, by which she meant that he had not been at some earlier, more desirable point. 'Two hair-yanks and a scalping. It's more than coincidence. I want to go big on it. Timeline, interviews with police, local women's groups, maybe a psychologist...'

Rex and Ellie both scribbled notes. 'See if Ilona Balint and Magda will give you some interviews for page 2. Ellie – that could be for you. Well. You know. Divide it up amongst yourselves. And do we know if Victim Three has given any descriptions yet? What's the kid's name, anyway? Who was she?'

'I've got a lead on that,' Rex said. 'But she won't be giving anyone any descriptions for a while.'

'What about the Surgery piece?' Ellie interjected. 'Rex said it was – '

'That's off,' Susan replied bluntly. 'A non-story. Okay? Let's talk again after lunch. Oh, and Rex. I called that temp agency.

No dice on Milda. Try and find the kid, will you? I'm only going to worry.'

With that, she was gone. Susan's flurries of energy could be annoying, but they were the reason everyone had a job. A former news editor on the *Times*, she'd combined some ancestral stock-options with two divorces and a redundancy pay-off to purchase this ailing local title before the owners closed it for good. National quality, local news was what it now said on the *Gazette's* masthead, and that was the idea behind the whole venture. A local paper, properly done: all the usual ads and splashes but with real stories in between, a real attempt to get the readers involved in the issues that affected their lives. And nothing could affect their lives more directly than some freak going round attacking women.

'I think she's right about the victim interviews,' Rex said to Ellie with a smile. 'You'd be perfect for that. And you get on well with Maggs, don't you?'

Ellie stared at her screen, sullenly joggling the mouse.

'Ellie?'

She turned to look at him. 'I worked all night on that piece. And she just spiked it like that. No discussion. Didn't even look at it.'

'That's just how it is sometimes,' Rex said gently. 'My first boss always used to bang on about it.' He mimicked the man's lugubrious Midlands accent. 'The news dussn't stay still, Rix, and nor can we.'

Ellie's plump, oxbow mouth turned ever so slightly upwards. 'He really used to say that?'

'He had a cliché for every occasion. But he was right. It's something you'll have to get used to if you want to stay in this game.'

Rex sensed that he'd blown whatever goodwill he'd managed to gain, but before he could retract his last words, his chair was swung violently round. His first thought was that Susan had been listening and was about to rebuke him for being patronising. But it wasn't her.

'Good morning, Rex.'

Angry, dressed in her khaki suit, Dr Diana Berne looked like an Israeli commando. Rex suspected he was about to get the Gaza treatment. And he knew why. A fat book landed in his lap. It was something he'd lent her, about the temples of Angkor Wat. She had been going to give it back to him. Last night.

'Oh God, Diana,' he began. 'Sorry…'

'It doesn't matter. I was on my way to a house-call, and I thought you'd want your book back.' As her hand brushed chestnut curls away from her eyes, the bracelet on her wrist jingled with agitation. She turned to leave, but then said, 'If you'd changed your mind, you could have called, or sent me a text, you know.'

'I didn't change my mind. I just… I had to chase a story and I… Well, I forgot.' Rex felt himself going red. His mouth was doing him no favours this morning. Was he really a journalist, someone paid to put things neatly into words?

Patches of red also bloomed on Diana's cheekbones, but not from embarrassment. 'Well, thanks,' she said. 'Thanks a lot.'

She walked out, then turned back in the doorway.

'I don't mind you forgetting. It's what you did after that.'

'What do you mean?'

'You don't recall the six silent calls between the hours of two and five this morning? You must have been off your head.'

She left.

'I never made any calls to you,' Rex said lamely, to thin air. He glanced around. There was a look of blissful fascination upon Ellie's face, like a spectator in the electrifying final moments of a tennis match.

'Before you do anything on the lead story,' Rex said, lashing down any nuances of vocal or facial expressions that might reveal his feelings about the foregoing incident, 'I want you to come up with an idea for the competition, write the copy, and talk to the Whittakers about getting one of the advertisers to give the prize.' Ellie opened her mouth to speak, but Rex held up a hand. 'Do it. Mention nothing about what just happened. And I'll let you do half the front page as well.'

He left. From Ellie's silence, he assumed they had a deal.

He'd just stepped into the car park when someone grabbed him and hissed in his ear.

'Cunt!'

He felt himself pulled with savage force into the dank service alley at the side of the office building and slammed against one of the huge metal bins. His head connected with iron.

'D-don't!' was the only feeble thing that could come out of his mouth, as his attacker lunged.

'Don't what?' Terry spat. 'Don't fuck you up like you've fucked me up?'

He pushed Rex away and now, for the first time, he was able to register what had happened. Terry had attacked him. He felt warm blood trickling down his neck from his head.

'What have I done?'

'My Missus thinks I've got debt collectors after me, or I'm living under an assumed i-fucking-dentity because I'm a kiddy-fiddler or something!'

Rex snorted. It was the wrong thing to do. Terry grabbed him by the collar.

'You think it's funny?' He pushed Rex away, white with rage. 'That girl in the Lettings Agency. She's been texting my Missus. Tells her you've been in the office, asking funny questions about me.'

'I didn't ask any funny questions,' Rex said, shakily restoring his collar to its usual position. 'I just said I knew you, and you'd recommended her agency, and I was looking for a flat.'

'She didn't believe a word of it! And why the fuck should she?' A red flush crept upwards from Terry's collarless stonewash shirt. 'Because I never did fucking recommend it, did I? So what were you playing at? She thought I was being investigated or something.'

Rex sighed. He had a choice. Lie, and probably come up with something even less believable. Tell the truth and get beaten up.

'I thought it was odd that you had Maggs' scarf in your car,' he said, staring straight ahead at the side of the building. 'And then you had a card from Ilona Balint in your wallet. The two women who were attacked, both had a link to you. So did the third one. She had a rail ticket from Leyton in her bag.'

Terry's eyes widened and then narrowed. 'So you think I'm –'

'Thought. In fact, never thought. Wondered. Worried. Looked into. It's what I do, Terry. It's my job.'

There was a dreadful pause. Rex readied himself for the proper kicking. The longer the pause went on for, the more he wanted it over, and the kicking to start.

'I always thought we were mates,' Terry said, quietly. 'Silly fucking me, eh?' Then he walked out of the alley.

* * *

There was no longer anything green about Green Lanes, but the area at its southern end, Newington Green, still possessed a circle of land roughly that colour, with benches and railings. Attempts had been made to smarten this up over the years, with modern, brightly-painted play equipment, a little café for the parents, and a modern, automated toilet which people had dubbed the Cosmic Loo because of the way its fluorescent, junkie-deterrent lighting glowed at night. No attempt had been made to smarten up the local Brew Crew, however, who teetered glassily on a pair of benches by the western entrance, and gave Rex filthy looks because he was a man, in a suit, with a mobile phone in his hand.

He wasn't actually making a call. So far he had managed to get Diana's number up on the little screen, but he was still weighing up what to do with it. A younger version of himself might have been pleased to have had this furious, curvaceous Jewish girl, with all her dark ringlets, turning up at his office and bawling him out. The present version had to admit he'd found it quite exciting. The difference was that now he knew there were real feelings at stake, in along with the drama. You didn't get to being single and childless at their age – Diana's birthday was a month after his own – without having had a fair deal of romantic trampling. She was slow to trust, he knew that, and his not turning up must have hurt. At the same time, you didn't pull a scene like that one in the office if you didn't want a response. It had been more of a challenge, he felt, than a straightforward rebuke.

'Wanker!'

He didn't look back. For a start his neck was aching too much from Terry's assault by the bins. And if he didn't look round, he could at least try to convince himself that the Brew Crew were shouting at someone else. Probably not, though, and maybe they had a point. Plenty of people seemed to think he was a wanker today.

But Diana... Did he want her challenge? Why had he pushed her out of his mind so completely last night? Maybe it proved what Susan had said, that even if he no longer loved Milda, he wasn't over the loss of her. In that case, was it fair to be getting involved with someone else? The task of getting to know Diana – more accurately, getting her to know him, with all his dark corners and conversation-stoppers – seemed long and hard. Too hard. But was that just nerves? Or nerves and laziness? He knew what came from doing nothing. Nothing.

'Diana?' – he was through to her voicemail – 'Look, I'm genuinely sorry. Please let me make it up to you. Give me a call. And, you know, if you don't, I'll give you one. I mean – I'll try you again.' He took a breath. 'And, just for the record, I was very drunk at four this morning but I never rang you. Honestly.'

He'd meant to say more, but he was walking, and as he neared the squatted restaurant formerly known as Hodja Nasreddin, he heard shouts and bangs. Glancing up, he saw four or five Turkish boys, clad in the obligatory uniform of the North London street-villain, milling around the doorway. A girl with a nose ring and dreadlocks piled up on her head like a haystack was shouting, while one of the boys bashed the spray-painted metal shutters with a piece of wood. Rex stood watching a little way off, by the bins.

'It's my uncle's restaurant,' another boy was saying. 'All you Russians got to pay me if you want to stay here.' His sideburns, Rex noted, had been shaved into rococo swirls. As, in fact, had the sideburns and necklines of all his compatriots.

'Your uncle must got a lot of nephews,' shouted the girl. Rex recognised her as Birgita, a friend of Milda's, whom he'd met once before. She'd been dressed as a sort of 1920s tweedy lesbian back then. Now she wore a grey t-shirt with KAOS written on it. 'Every week, one of you coming by and says this is your uncle restaurant.'

Rex gave the tiniest of laughs – more of a snort – forgetting how sensitive the average skunk-smoking street hood was to subtle vibrations. The peaks of five, carefully-skewed baseball caps turned to look at him.

'Whatchu want, old man?' The spokesman pimp-rolled over to him, in perfect imitation of a gang-banger from South

Central L.A.. These guys spent a lot of time on their look, Rex reflected, as he was slammed up against the wall. Three assaults in one day. Not quite a record, but close.

'Rex Tracey,' he said, smiling over the pain. 'From the *Gazette*.'

Ten, narrowed eyes appraised him. Teeth were sucked, one set after the next.

'Your name's really Rex Tracey?' the spokesman asked. Rex showed him his press card. 'Sounds like a movie star, man.' His friends laughed.

'I was,' Rex said. 'But you know what Hollywood's like when you hit forty.'

He went flying against the wall again, this time injuring a different part of his head on the brick.

'Don't chat shit to me!' the gangster hissed, so close Rex could not only feel the carefully-clipped stubble but also see how young he was. Nineteen? Maybe not even that. 'Report something in your paper about these rats, bruv!' he said, gesturing towards Birgita. 'Breaking into our houses, nicking the gas, dealing drugs. Maybe all that gas gonna blow up in their faces, man.'

A siren sounded nearby. Rex's attacker pulled away.

'You gonna write something like I tell you?'

'Mehmet, man, come out, man.' His friends were getting antsy as the siren came nearer. 'Come out, man.' Mehmet pointed two fingers, held together, gun-fashion, first at Rex, then at Birgita, and ran away with his crew.

Birgita tutted. 'Welcome to the rat-house.' She stared curiously at Rex. 'I know you from somewhere, don't I?'

* * *

Just before Hodja Nasreddin closed, Rex had eaten an indifferent dinner in there: the bulgur wheat in the Akçabat köfte had been undercooked, like grains of cat litter, and he'd had to get up and pretend to leave in order to get anyone to take his money. There was a certain, deliberate sadness called *huzun*; some people considered it to be a national trait of the Turks, almost a point of pride. But it wasn't *huzun* at Hodja Nasreddin that night – half the dishes had been off, the fridge had made a loud hum over which bickering could be heard from the kitchen. When Rex had passed by a week later, the restaurant was shuttered up, never to re-emerge.

A couple of the original, red velvet banquettes were still in one corner, along with a faded photograph of Izmir and a *nazar boncuğu* – the ubiquitous eye-shaped amulet – over the door to the former kitchen. But far from merely squatting the building, Birgita and her cohorts had transformed it. Striking canvases hung on every wall, sharing space with a cracked leather sofa, a toy train set and a huge, stuffed pelican. The wooden floor, and what tiny bit of the wall-panels remained visible were spattered with coloured oils. The smell of these mingled with the fumes of a calor-gas heater, freshly-peeled tangerines and Birgita's rolling tobacco.

She had a wide, flat face with a snub nose. She sat, open-legged like a tribal fishwife, on a low stool, allowing Rex a seat on the vintage sofa. He'd have been glad of it, except that there was a mattress directly behind the sofa, and on it, a thin man wearing only a pair of grey, pain-spattered jeans, asleep. Rex sipped sorrel tea and tried to ignore him.

'Police was here already,' Birgita said, flatly, as she peeled another tangerine and popped segments of it in her mouth. 'Asking about the girl that got attack. Her name was Marina Krelkina.'

'And she lived here?' Rex put the tea down. It tasted truly unpleasant.

'Sometimes here, sometimes squat in Dalston, Leyonstone…' Birgita waved a hand on the air, symbolising the girl's wanderings.

'She lived in a squat in Leytonstone?' Rex clarified, remembering the railway ticket in the girl's bag. He felt a fresh wave of shame about Terry.

'Squats all over. But not here.'

'You just said she stayed here.'

'And here is not squat,' Birgita replied, testily. 'This place costs five hundred fifty pounds a month. The owner allows to us cheap so it doesn't become crack house. It is not a squat.'

Rex held up a hand in surrender. 'But this girl – Marina – she knew Milda? I mean – she had one of Milda's books.'

'Yes, and she had Mark's laptop, as well,' Birgita said, archly. 'She didn't deserve that… that scolping thing. But she is *vagis*. Thief.' The man behind the sofa yawned and stretched – a blast of unbrushed teeth floated up towards Rex. 'Actually, when police come I am just glad they don't say nothing happened to Milda. This is my thought. Imagine it. Rex.' She shivered. 'Somebody going round, doing that to women.' She tapped her head. 'Ugh.'

'So you're worried about Milda?' First Aguta, he thought. Now Birgita. And Susan. Not to mention himself.

'I had bad dream about her,' Birgita said, distractedly picking a piece of lint off one of her hanging canvases. 'Last time I saw her, maybe three weeks ago she wasn't happy.'

'Because of the row with Vadim?'

Birgita snorted. 'Vadimas is just a man. She had lost her job at café, and she was sick.'

'Sick?'

'Headaches all the time. She felt…' Birgita span a finger in the air. 'What do you say?'

'Dizzy?'

'Dizzy and sick.'

Before Rex could ask more about this, the man behind the sofa stood up and left the room, making a brief grunt towards

Birgita. 'Mark,' she said, with a wry look in her eye. Whoever Mark was, it was clear he didn't always sleep behind the sofa.

'I said it was a spirit sickness,' Birgita went on. 'Go back to home country, walk in forests, visit the trees, don't visit doctors. She was thinking to go on bus. You know, some boys of ours got a bus? One of your old Routemeisters. East Ham to Vilnius, once a week, full of money.'

Rex had heard about the bus, about all the buses, in fact, leaving various parts of East London for cities behind the former Iron Curtain. 'You think she might have gone back home? No one's seen her for a while.'

Birgita shrugged, revealing a freckled shoulder and a purple bra-strap. 'It costs quite a lot, that bus. But if you can't fly…'

Rex nodded. Milda hated aeroplanes.

'… I hope she has. It's the only place she'll find what she needs.'

'What do you mean?' Rex liked Birgita: the paintings, her coolness with the thugs outside. But still, throughout all this talk of spirit sickness and prophetic dreams and finding what you needed, he'd wanted to shake her and shout, 'Yes, but what do you bloody mean?' in her ears, just as he'd ended up wanting to do with Milda. And he remembered, in that instant, why they'd split up.

'She is too good,' Birgita answered, after rolling another cigarette. She rummaged in an archive box on the floor and pulled from it a heavy piece of paper. She passed it to Rex.

It was a portrait of Keith Powell, facing slightly to the right, eyes aloft, like a parody of a Soviet propaganda image. Closer up, he could see it had been made of fine strips of news print. He saw a string of numbers. The fragment-words 'resourc' and 'immi'. She'd made it from British Workers' Action Party posters. The man, quite literally, in his own words.

'Do you know him?' Rex asked, turning it towards Birgita. 'Local fascist leader,' she said, as if it was quite normal to have local fascist leaders in Newington Green. 'You see this now? She can draw, then she can paint. Last time I see her, now she starts to work with a camera. I told her: you know Milda for some artists this is a curse. Really. Too many languages. She doesn't know which is the… the mum-tongue.'

'Mother tongue,' Rex corrected, absently. He remembered, when she'd once complained about being artistically stuck, getting one of his old cameras out of the cupboard under the stairs and giving it to her. Two days later, it had been back in there, unused, not a word said. So how had she arrived at photography now? Who'd given her a camera and managed to inspire her? He looked down at the image of Powell and remembered all those artistic shots of fairgrounds and fishing boats on his walls. Had it been him?

Birgita coughed hard, then wiped her mouth with the back of her hand. 'I have to go to hospital,' she said.

'They'll just tell you to stop smoking those things.'

She shook her head. 'No, I mean – I got to go the hospital now. For a…' She waved a hand over the lower half of her body. 'Appointment.' She stood up, and held out a hand. As he shook it, she laughed huskily and said, 'I just wanted Milda's picture.'

He handed it back, feeling that this moment probably symbolised his leave-taking with Milda, and her whole world. They'd had fun, a sweet, funny time together, but ultimately, very little in common. She'd almost certainly hopped on a bus and gone home without telling anyone. He had a headache, a neck ache, a back ache. And a big story to write.

The old restaurant stood on the end of a row of shops, some thriving, others in a perpetual cycle of new beginnings and bailiffs' notices. There was an alleyway between the off-licence and the café, and as he walked past it on his way back towards the green, he sensed a flurry of movement. The man who'd been asleep behind the sofa, Mark, now stood in the alleyway, zipping up a little pocket in the arm of his bomber jacket. Behind him was a boy on a mountain bike. Grass? A loan? Rex walked on quickly. Not his business. None of it was any of his business.

But then, sitting on the top deck of another 141 as it sailed past the low, flat buildings of the health centre, he found himself wondering if Milda had visited a doctor with her complaints. Perhaps she had, and her worries had been settled. Or she'd had bad news. Or possibly she'd believed Birgita's anarchist-art-collective-hippy-squatter bullshit and stayed away from medicine and carried on and just collapsed somewhere. Somewhere dark where no one would come to help her.

* * *

At first he was only going to get rid of the pill packets and the bottles, but the urge to sweep the whole thing away became too great. He started with the bottle the girl had been holding. MS-Contin, morphine tablets, his wife's name printed on the label. As he dropped it into the bin-bag, he felt again a prickle of the anger he'd felt when he'd come upstairs and seen her there, in their bathroom.

There were other medicines, too: anti-nausea drugs to go with the chemotherapy, dihydrocodeine from the early days when the pain still went away, some herbal rub from the time when the doctors couldn't give her pains a name, and kept sending her away, telling her it was only stress, nothing to worry about. It was, in reverse, a catalogue of her death.

Outside, past the rabbit hutches, he'd made a fire-pit from bricks he'd found in a skip. There was dry garden waste waiting in there already, along with some old newspapers and all the rubbish the schoolkids shoved over his wall during the course of a term. He enjoyed lighting the first match, and when he'd put it in and the fire, tentatively, began to catch, he struck another and another, and found, eventually, that he had used up a whole box of matches.

Caroline hadn't understood what she was asking. Couldn't have known of the pact he'd kept all these years, or how intimately connected that was to her. Other people, he knew – he'd read about it in the papers – were happy to do it. Not him. It hadn't mattered what things she had claimed when torn apart by the pain. And if the girl hadn't interfered, he would have explained.

At first he'd seen her as a sort of saviour. It was only later, much later, in the bathroom, that he'd recognised what she'd really been.

He threw the contents of the bin bag in, item by item, watching them twist and yawn and shatter in the heat. Standing there, so close to the ashes and the smoke and the flames, he remembered his fury with the girl again, how out of control it had made him feel in his stomach and his legs. How his rage had burned so strong that it seemed to erase things from his memory – he couldn't, for example, remember anything about the rest of that day, where he'd been, what he'd done with himself. Or the girl.

* * *

As Rex walked from the bus stop to the office, a smoky drizzle had started to fall, and he remembered a little snippet Milda had told him about her school days, just at the end of communism. They hadn't been allowed out when it was wet, like in English schools, in fact, but instead of making a racket in the classroom as the English kids did, these junior revolutionaries had to walk, in silence, in a circle, around the gym. Just doing that, in silence, for an hour. That was why she hated rain. And that, he thought, was why he'd found her so fascinating. Her memories. So different from anyone else's.

Something caught his eye on a strip of wall between an estate agent's and a halal butcher. Maybe it was to do with the way he spent his days, but the typeface drew his attention before the words. 'Wrong Time Wrong Race' said a small, A6-size hand-bill on the wall, in the cheap, chunky lettering of the BWAP. It made Rex think of neckless men in bomber jackets, shouting things on the terraces. But someone more intelligent was behind this poster. Below the headline were a few lines pasted from the free paper they gave out on the tube – these referred to the three girls who'd been attacked recently in the area. But, in a few well-chosen phrases, this little square of paper put a whole new spin on the link between immigration and crime. These girls had been attacked because they were newcomers, the poster said. They weren't responsible for the violence, but they were, nonetheless, the reason it was happening. It was a work of marketing genius, as if Keith Powell's gang of fascists had hired an ad agency to give them the edge. Then again, maybe Powell had done it himself. He was clearly a bit of an artist. So was that what had pulled him into Milda's orbit? Or her into his?

Rex succeeded in taking a picture of the poster on his mobile phone, and quickened his steps back to the office. With a group like this operating in the area, so keen to make capital from violence, Susan couldn't possibly refuse a big piece. It proved everything he'd been saying.

The office was cleaner, thanks to the efforts of a tiny, skull-faced Spanish lady who'd been brought in by an agency to cover Magda's absence, but it was too warm, and it smelled of peoples' lunches. Rex took a deep breath and headed straight over to Terry, whose knobbly, Norseman's skull was bent over the desk as he rummaged through the drawers.

'Now I can't find me bastard hundred-mil macro…' he muttered, before seeing that it was Rex who'd approached the desk. He fixed him with a baleful gaze.

'Terry. Look. Sorry. Can you blow this picture up for me?' Rex said, handing over his mobile. 'You know what Susan's like – she won't even look at it if it's not headline size.'

Terry continued to stare.

'Can we just forget about the other business?'

The stare went on.

'I'm sorry, Terry. We *are* mates. I mean, I hope we still are. And perhaps if I'd remembered that we are, then I might not have… I mean I would have just asked you outright, and not…' He was jabbering. 'Can we just chalk it up to inexperience? Or my immense stupidity?'

'We can chalk it up to you being a fucking knob-head, yes.' Terry inclined his head towards Susan's office, through whose slatted blinds could be seen the seated forms of the editor and Ellie. 'But I'd leave your Nazis for a bit if I were you. You're wanted in there.'

It soon became clear why. 'I'm not paying Ellie a Grade One salary for charitable reasons,' Susan said, as he went in. 'I expect her to be learning as she works. And I expect you to be taking charge of that process.'

Ellie stared at her feet.

'You've been out most of the day,' Susan continued. 'You've had your mobile switched off, and you've left your assistant with nothing to do.'

'I didn't mean to switch it off, and it's only actually just after lunch,' Rex said feebly. 'And she did have work to do. I asked her to take charge of the competition.'

'I've done it,' Ellie interjected. 'The changing face of Haringey. Kahn's are giving a free tripod to the winner and camera bags to the runners-up.'

'She achieved that in the first half hour of your absence,' Susan went on, stuffing various bits of cutting-edge technology into her handbag. 'And since then, I've had her on the lead story.'

'So we're exactly where we would have expected to be if I'd been in the office – except that I might have checked her copy earlier, and instead I'm going to be doing it now.'

Standing up, Susan gave Rex a long, cool look. It suggested that his logic might not be at fault, but many other things still were.

'I want everything on my desk by close of play this evening. And then tomorrow, Ellie and I are going to The Old Dairy for a nice, long, leisurely lunch, to which you are not invited, and while we're there, she's going to talk me through every line of the lead story, explaining all the changes you and she made and why.'

'Fine. But can I just show you this?'

Susan waved his hand away as he produced his mobile phone poster picture. 'I'm late for the accountants.'

With that, she took a powerful-looking coat off the hooks and swept out. Rex and Ellie looked at one another, for once equals in sheepishness.

'I wasn't trying to make trouble for you,' Ellie said, her cheeks reddening. 'I got hold of the first girl, Ilona, and she said she'd do an interview if we paid her expenses, and I wasn't sure if we could do that, so I asked Susan and…'

'My fault. I should have given you more of a steer,' Rex said, glancing at Susan's original Fifties school clock. 'We'd better get cracking. And Ellie?'

'Yeah?'

'If you've got any questions about editorial policy, never ask the editor. That's what Brenda's for.'

* * *

Ninety minutes later, Rex was polishing the main article, while Ellie finished an interview on the phone. She'd already been onto one of the ICU nurses at the Middlesex, and discovered that Victim Three, alias Marina Krelkina, the book thief, was showing signs of improvement. Now, she was talking to Dr Nicky Pryce, consultant psychiatrist at Pentonville Prison, and from the sounds of things she wasn't letting him go.

'So he's collecting trophies, that's what you think, and there's a strong possibility that he's rehearsing for something bigger...'

Rex smiled. She was good: keeping Pryce on the phone, letting him enjoy the conversation, at the same time as wringing him for all the droplets of printable information she could extract. It was almost ruthless, and all the more impressive for being something she did naturally, without training. Or perhaps it wasn't without training. Maybe drama school had done her some good.

Another paragraph slotted onto the page, and Rex allowed himself another check of his phone, another glance at his inbox. It contained a curt missive from Diana.

Explain yourself. Salisbury. 8.30.

No sign-off. No kisses. But a chance, all the same.

His smile vanished as Terry returned from downstairs and tossed him another jiffy bag. Brown this time. No stamp or postmarks. Just REX written in marker pen. 'Gonna open it?'

Rex didn't reply. He knew he was being stupid. But a mysterious envelope, at that moment, promised no joy. It was a creaking door, a summons. He couldn't help but see it that way.

He tore it open and examined the contents. Inside, packaged in gaudy cellophane was a pair of black, rubber handcuffs. Not the kind the authorities used. Sexy Handcuffs, said the lettering on the packet. Part Of The Tie 'n' Tease Range. There was no note.

Terry chuckled. Rex felt oddly relieved. The doubting was over.

He wasn't imagining things. Someone was trying to spook him.

'I reckon your bird's forgiven you,' Terry said.

Rex shook his head. This wasn't Diana. Not her style. But someone's way of sending a message. Or part of one, to be studied and decoded in conjunction with mopeds and wheelchairs. And whatever nastiness might come next.

'I'm beginning to think someone's got it in for me,' he said blankly.

'Well, that's because you're a twat,' Terry said, returning to his desk. 'And it's your turn to do a tea-run.'

As he went down the stairs, it occurred to Rex that he should take care when he crossed the car-park. Then it occurred to him that it wouldn't matter. The next thing would be different, predictable only in that he could predict nothing about it. The thought frightened him, as undoubtedly the sender of these signs intended.

But why? Who wanted him scared? As a journalist he crushed toes and accrued grudges all the time, of course. The recent difficulties with Ellie and with Terry were just tiny fragments of a stream of wreckage, boxwood splinters in the ongoing tsunami of his life.

This was the work of someone creative. Someone who communicated in metaphors and symbols. The only person he knew like that was Milda.

Brenda wasn't at her desk when he went by, but the book she'd been reading was open on the counter. It was called Living With A Violent Man, and it clearly wasn't a work of fiction. The sight of it briefly distracted him from his other worries. Brenda normally read novels about badly-used girls in 1920's pit villages. This wasn't her thing at all.

He was about to pick up the book when the outer doors swung open, making him jump. Aguta came in, cat-eyes flashing, smelling of hairspray.

'Ok listen, I've gone to Milda's house, right, and one of those boys there said she isn't there, and Vadim's not there, but he said he thought Milda gone home to see her mum.'

'Hang on. Who said that?' Aguta's English seemed to be suffering alongside her heart-rate. In the meantime, Brenda had returned from the toilet and installed herself behind the desk, stowing the book out of view.

'That boy in squat!' Aguta replied irritably. 'But then, listen, so okay, I went to internet café, on a Skype, I talked to sister. Milda's sister, called Niela,' she added stonily, in case he was thinking about stopping her flow again. 'She told me Milda hasn't come home, nobody expecting her, they don't know anything from her.' She came to a halt, breathing hard.

'So why would the boy in the squat tell you she'd gone home?'

'The boy in the squat said to me Vadim told him that,' Aguta replied, firmly and precisely. 'And now Vadim has gone as well.'

Gone somewhere on an aeroplane from Stansted, Rex thought. And he didn't want me to know. Before he could say anything, the doors went again and Susan walked in. She didn't even glance at Aguta.

'Is the piece ready?'

'Not quite, I'm –'

'You've got twenty-seven minutes,' she said, glancing at her watch.

'Susan. Jesus. Why are you treating me like some office junior with an attitude problem?'

She clipped up the stairs without answering. Rex looked at Aguta. 'I can't help right now. I'm sorry.'

'Tonight?'

'Tonight it's…' He was about to make an excuse, but changed his mind. 'Aguta, look. Milda and I aren't even talking to each other these days, and I've got a lot on my plate.' He thought about the handcuffs, upstairs in his desk. If they were from her, what could they mean? Stay away? Free me?

He was about to suggest that she call Milda's sister again and find out the last time they'd heard from her. Or she could go back to the squat and find out when Vadim was expected back. There were a lot of things she could do, but before he could mention them, Aguta had left.

* * *

Powell was right. The area was changing. Being invaded, even. But, Rex reflected as he sat wedged into a tiny corner of The Salisbury, it wasn't incomers from Eastern Europe packing out the bar and drowning out his thoughts. It was people who couldn't afford to live in Islington. Already, the pub had started doing Scrabble Nights and slightly serious quizzes; at the table next to him, a trio of achingly pretty young women was discussing where to film an episode of 'Law and Order'.

He remembered trying to explain to Milda why he loved this area. Why even its bleaker sights – the listless, smoking men outside the snooker halls, the African shops with no stock beyond ten yams and a case of condensed milk – were as vital to his soul as trees and birdsong to a country-dweller. Why he no longer wanted to live in a place where everyone looked and dressed and spoke like him, even though that might have been safer and quieter. He was never sure Milda had understood why the people around him mattered so much. She was interested in the world, but less in its people, more in its patterns and arrangements of colours. And so, so many times, a thought would cross his mind, and she'd see it on his face, and ask him to explain, but he'd end up saying, 'Nothing', because the effort of explaining it, and having it then not understood by her, seemed too much. Their relationship hadn't ended, but fallen into silence, like a pair of travellers approaching their destination.

He realised he was sitting in the very seat where he'd first kissed her. That wasn't ideal. Here he was, moving on, supposedly. Telling her best friend she was none of his business any more. Telling himself it had just been a fling, a spring and summer – inappropriate, but fun. But still Milda was everywhere. In every corner.

His worries disappeared as he felt a gentle tap on his shoulder. He turned with a smile.

'Oh.'

'Not the girl you were expecting?' Susan said, with a dry smile. She'd changed into a new outfit, he noticed. 'I wondered if you'd got time for a quick one with Bilal and myself?'

She indicated a handsome young man at the bar. Bilal was the Assistant Press Officer for Haringey Council, and a rising star of the local Lib Dems. A serious man, with seriously good suits, because his uncles imported cloth from Ankara. And an orange-juice drinker. Rex shook his head.

'I'm sorry to read you the Riot Act today,' she went on. 'The copy was great.'

Rex shrugged. 'I haven't really been switched on lately, you know, but...' He held out a hand, as if reaching for the brighter future. Susan nodded.

'Share some of that talent with Ellie. She deserves it.'

She wandered off, leaving Rex to wonder if Susan, and indeed all women of her type, had a designated day and a night perfume. Then she came back. 'If you're thinking of staying and soaking, I wouldn't,' she said. 'They're doing Scrabble in about ten minutes.'

The Scrabble came and went, in fact, as did another pair of pints, without any sign of Diana. She was either paying him back, or unavoidably detained. The solution, of course, was to ring or text. But something held him back: a sense that he deserved her to be late, or not show up, and didn't have the right to ask about it. He was also certain that, whether she came or not, he wanted more to drink – a desire which necessitated a swift trip across Green Lanes to the Nationwide cash point.

Football was afoot that night – to be precise, a match between Trabzonspor and Fenerbahce – and the jubilant fans of one or other team were tooting their way down the Lanes, waving flags from the windows. It looked like a revolution might have done, seen from street level: happy and hopeful and altogether rather fun. And, Rex thought as he picked his way across the busy road, markedly less boorish than the English way of celebrating sporting triumphs.

As he crossed back with fifty quid in his wallet, he was beeped at by a big silver people-carrier. He assumed it was carrying more Turkish football fans, so he gave it an awkward wave, passed in front of it and carried along his way.

But it slowed down. A window wound down.

Rex speeded up, but the people carrier kept pace with him. Somebody wanted something. Another bit of intimidation? Jesus. Not today, he thought. Not after everything else.

'Were you going to stand me up again?'

Diana was in the front of a big taxi, it emerged, seated next to a grinning Somali driver, with a huge pouch of qat bulging in his left cheek. The back of the vehicle was filled with Ikea bags.

'I thought if you were showing up this late you'd need a very big drink, so I went to get more money.'

'Good. I'll have a very big vodka tonic,' Diana said. 'Sorry I'm late.'

Rex made a sort of Gallic *de rien* gesture and went back into the pub, spirits renewed. He jostled his way to the bar counter, but it didn't really matter where he stood. The Salisbury, as Diana's Uncle Lawrence had so often pointed out in his columns, was a classic Victorian corner house, and boasted the longest bar in North London. Out of some inverse logic, the management only ever employed one, angry girl to cover said bar. By the time he'd managed to attract the girl's attention, Diana had come to stand with him.

'That nice driver's going to take all my Ikea stuff to my house and leave it down the side. Can you believe that?'

'I didn't know you were going shopping.'

'To be honest, I hadn't planned to, but I had a shit day, and I needed cheering up before I...'

Her voice trailed off, and he caught a look in her eyes that told him she'd said too much, and knew it. Why would she need cheering up? Because meeting him would probably make her feel worse? Or because she wanted to be on good form when she met him? Rex decided not to ask. 'You went to Ikea to cheer yourself up?'

'It's lovely in there!' she said, rather loudly, touching his arm. 'There's never anyone around at tea-time. You get yourself a plate of meatballs and a glass of red for a fiver, and you come out with new glasses and duvet covers and chopping boards for the cost of a couple of cinema tickets.'

Rex said he'd never thought of it quite like that.

'Then you get a Somali-Cab back home, and those guys are all super-bright, they've got the World Service or Radio Four on all day and they're high as kites on that stuff they chew, so you have a lovely conversation with them. Trust me, Rex, it's a treat, Ikea.'

'Perhaps we should have met there.'

Diana spotted a couple leaving a table and she swooped over to bag it. She seemed breathless, nervous, even anxious. And why had she gone all the way up to Edmonton if she knew she was going to meet him? He began to wonder if this drink was a good idea.

As the barmaid brought the drinks over, he suddenly had a clear line of sight across the bar. In the crush on the other side, he saw a familiar face. By the time he had worked out who it belonged to Keith Powell was disappearing into the Gents. Not alone, but in the company of two bull-necked, shaven-headed men in casual sporting gear.

Rex left the drinks at the bar and followed the men into the toilets. Powell was cropping up too much today – in the picture Milda had made, in the new, inflammatory posters. And the camera. Could Powell really be the one who'd given Milda a camera? He had to know.

You are hitting middle age when you start to notice the quality of public lavatories. Rex had long thought that The Salisbury's were a shining example of the genre. Original door handles, oak panelling, ribbed glass and big, vitreous wash basins. To piss in there was to take part in local history. Maybe Lawrence Berne should put that in his column.

The trio didn't spring apart as Rex walked in, but they looked as if they had. To confirm the general impression of wrong things afoot in that chilly, fishy place, Keith Powell gave him a wide, eager grin.

'Who are these?' Rex asked, noticing that one goon had a horizontal groove across his nose, whilst the other sported a vertical one down his chin. 'Your Media Team?'

The Media Team glared, whilst Powell did his best to look hurt behind his chunky media spectacles. The hurt look lasted all of a millisecond before he gestured to his two companions and they headed straight back out through the door. As they did so, both hand-dryers switched on, whistling like jet engines.

'They didn't stay long,' Rex observed.

'Are you running that interview tomorrow?' Powell asked casually.

'We felt your organisation was good enough at getting its own publicity,' Rex replied, leaning up against the noisy hand-dryer. 'And making publicity out of tragic events.'

Powell shrugged. 'Like you, we have to respond to the news.'

'Or make the news.'

Powell snorted. 'You think we're the ones attacking the girls? Why don't you think about about the lorry-loads of Rumanian sex offenders showing up here every day?'

A boy in ripped jeans, a lumberjack shirt and an exquisite set of Edwardian facial whiskers came in at that moment, and made his way across to the urinals. Rex suppressed the urge to smile, and then saw that Powell was doing exactly the same thing. This was the man's trick. Making you think he was just the same as you. It was sinister.

'Seen Milda lately?'

If Powell was surprised, he didn't show it. 'No, actually. How do you know her?'

'How do you?'

'I met her at the café.'

'Swapped photography tips, did you?'

'Erm…' Powell looked genuinely confused now. 'I don't think so. We were just, you know… she worked in there… I ate in there. We have our meetings there, so… We talked sometimes. Why?'

'So you had your meetings in there, where you and your pals discussed chucking out all the Eastern Europeans, but somehow, in spite of that, you struck up a little friendship with one of the Eastern Europeans serving you your bacon sarnies?'

'It wasn't like that. We're not talking about chucking anyone out.'

'You're fond of Lithuanians, then?'

'Individually,' Powell replied coldly. 'Yes. Can I go now?'

Rex wasn't in Powell's way, but he stood aside just the same.

Powell stalked out, letting the door slam.

By the time Rex had retrieved the drinks and found Diana, she had her arms folded and had torn a beer-mat into a dozen very small pieces.

'What took you so long?' she asked, ignoring the drink.

'I'm just very bad at getting noticed by barmaids.'

She didn't smile. This wasn't looking good.

'I'm just going to say what I've got to say and get it done with, okay?'

'Okay.' This really wasn't looking good.

'I know it wasn't you who made those phone calls. I mean, I don't know who it was, but I believe you when you say it wasn't you. Sorry.'

'It's okay. I'm sorry I stood you up.'

'I don't want you to be sorry. I just want you to be straight with me...' She took a deep swig. 'I get the feeling you're not really into this. I mean – there's always something going on. You make an arrangement, but you don't show up. Or you show up late. Or you show up on time, but you're thinking about something else.'

She had listed three types of failure. And they'd only been out four times. This relationship – if it could ever have been called that – was slipping away in front of his eyes.

She took another drink. 'I can't work out if you've got some terrible secret, or you're just not that bothered. And you know, I'm not sixteen any more. I don't want you in my handbag. I don't want worshipping. I just want to know, that when you're with me, you do actually want to be with me.'

Rex took a long pull of his drink and stood up. 'Come on.'

She frowned – her eyes flashing – in that moment, no longer a Jewish GP from East Finchley but a tribeswoman of the Negev. 'Come where?'

'I do want to be with you,' he said. 'Really. But I need to show you something.'

Chapter Four

There had been holy women on Muswell Hill since pagan times. There was an underground stream that fed a well, and its water, so legend told, had once cured a travelling chieftain of the scrofula. Around the place there had arisen a shrine, its original caretakers transforming into nuns as the new faith spread around the land, and the mossy well became known as Muswell Hill. The Sisters of Saint Veronica of Jumièges now counted this spot, high up above the Tottenham marshes, as their own. Encircled by trees, invisible except from the top deck of the 144 bus, the religious house was a mystery to many a long-standing resident of the area, and those who caught a glimpse of its lichen-covered tiles from the terrace bar at Alexandra Palace usually thought it had something to do with the park groundsmen.

She was sitting in a high-backed chair in the tv room when Rex and Diana came in, her slender fingers softly brushing the green felt fabric as if they were searching for something. The nuns loved tv detective shows, and tonight's viewing was an old episode of 'Taggart'. She might have been following it – Rex couldn't tell. Nor could any of the experts her family occasionally sent her to.

As they drew up chairs in the warm, musty little room, she hiccupped and asked them if they had any biscuits. At least, that seemed to be what she had said. The various pins keeping her jaw together had eroded the gums, and those teeth that had been saved were now falling out. Her voice sounded rough, as if she might not have used it all day, but she was as slim and elegantly turned out as ever, her red hair tied back neatly, her favourite green cashmere cardigan done up to the neck. Rex could smell Mitsuko, a dab of which went on each wrist, every morning, as it always had. She didn't need eyes to put that on.

'There are two of you,' she said, as if she'd caught him out in a deception.

'I've brought a friend,' he said, smiling at Diana. 'Syb – meet Diana. Diana. This is my wife.'

Every time he said those words, he remembered standing on a pavement in Marylebone, on a Friday night in December 2003, the smells of brake fluid and vomit in his nostrils. He was standing, but he couldn't feel the pavement beneath him. A policewoman with grey hair and a double chin asked him who the passenger was, and he heard his own voice as though from a great distance, saying, 'That's my wife.'

He'd said 'that' – not 'she' – and it was odd, because in the moments just before he'd crashed the car, Sybille had been berating him for not introducing her by her name and referring to her as 'my wife' all evening. They'd been on his newspaper's table at a press awards bash, and Sybille had been sandwiched between a small, angry mother of twin autistic boys, whose production manager husband cheated on her, and the production manager husband. She had not enjoyed herself.

That, and the business of Rex not calling her Sybille, and his drinking too much, had only been irritations. The real issue was the deputy editor bowling along, full of Scotch and soda, and asking her if she was excited about New York. Rex hadn't told Sybille about New York. He'd told her that he was up for an award because of his big series of articles about ethnic London. He'd told her that the editor had made encouraging noises. He hadn't told her he'd been offered a job in New York, though, because he'd known exactly what her first reaction would be.

He had intended to tell her. He had intended to convince her, gently and with patience. He had planned to find apartments to show her on the internet, to book a crossing on a freighter because she had always wanted to make a long sea journey some-where. But he couldn't do any of it until they'd got Christmas with her parents and her sister out of the way.

It was raining lightly, and they couldn't get a cab after the awards, and Rex found he had left the umbrella in the back of the car outside the office, and by the time he'd gone there and unlocked the boot, the rain was coming down more strongly, and it seemed a reasonable idea to drive home the short way to Camden. Sybille had been too angry to challenge him about it, she just wanted to get home and slam the door and ignore him for a few days. Nothing goaded Rex as much as his wife's silences, though, and he hadn't yet made the long acquaintance with quietness that would characterise the next eight years of his life. So, as he drove, he forced her to argue with him, mak-ing what was said, on both sides, angrier and less forgivable all round.

It hadn't been a make-or-break kind of row, though, just the standard complaints between men and women when they spend their lives together. She over-reacted. He didn't listen. He'd clearly decided they were going to New York, whether she wanted to or not. She'd clearly decided, in a split second, that she couldn't leave the sweaty embrace of her family to go and live in one of the world's most exciting cities. He didn't think her job in London was important. She just wanted a dreary, suburban existence like her sister. And so the charges passed back and forth as rain pin-pricked the windscreen and the car's inefficient heater burned their knees.

In time, by the Sunday afternoon at the latest, they would have worked things out, because they loved each other, and they'd both forgiven far, far worse – and in any case, neither was wholly in the wrong. But by the Sunday afternoon, as it turned out, Sybille was in a coma and Rex was losing his mind. That came about, partly because his wife – convent school educated, the daughter of two Parisian lawyers – had this uncanny habit of saying things that were quite funny in the midst of very serious discussions.

'There's only so many times I can go for a walk in Central Park and eat a Cuban fucking sandwich.'

She spat that out as they sped over some traffic lights in Beaumont Street. And she meant, quite reasonably, that she wouldn't have a job in New York, and that the usual tourist diversions would not be enough to sustain a life there, but her way of saying it made Rex snort with laughter, and he glanced across at her as he accelerated, in that moment failing to see the motorcycle courier cutting right across in front of him through the drizzle. Memory turned into splinters of sensation after that point, like a tapestry scene pulled into its separate threads. Sybille screamed, everything lifted up in the air.

Later, he would understand that the car had mounted the kerb, and hit some scaffolding, and an unattached pole had passed through the windscreen on the passenger's side. At the time, though, there was only a crunch, a bang, a shaft of fluorescent orange light and a feeling passing up his left foot and leg so cold, so strong it was almost serene. So the last words Rex's wife spoke to him, spoke to him, as her, as Sybille, the red-headed girl he'd loved since university, were 'Cuban fucking sandwich'. Neither of them had ever eaten a Cuban sandwich. Rex wasn't even sure what it was.

An ad break took over from the Glaswegian detectives. Deftly, Sybille switched off the sound with one remote control, turned soft music on with another. She turned her head towards Diana and asked if she was comfortable sitting next to the radiator.

'You can't sit on the other side,' she added. 'Rex always has to sit on the broken side.'

She'd said this before, and it was true. Rex did always sit on the side of his wife that was smooth and shiny and mostly not there. There was little hair on that side of Sybille's face, nothing you could reasonably describe as a brow or an eyesocket – nothing but barren grafted skin. He'd started to sit there, he supposed, so that he'd become used to the way she looked. Or to show other people that he could do it. Or so that she knew he didn't mind.

But she knew, of course, that he did mind. Even though the old Sybille had been sieved through metal and glass, parts of her had retained their old form. The parts that were sharp, and clever. And angry. And that was why he sat there. Because he deserved to look at her, and deserved her anger.

The music sounded ultra-modern: all bleeps and synths and sampled voices. A breathy French newscaster, a shouty American commercial, a fruity English poet with hectic drumbeats in the background. Rex had never heard it before. He wondered where on earth Sybille had got it from. Presumably not from the nuns.

Having shown a corner of herself, Sybille retreated into the gnarled woodlands of her mind, and pretended that Diana was a small child. She asked her what school she went to, and what her favourite subject was. Diana, who was asked dozens of impossible and unreasonable questions every day, merely smiled and said it was P.E. Sybille said she hated running about, but the nuns didn't make her do much. Everyone laughed at that – too long, too loud.

Then Sybille turned her clear, sightless eye to Rex, and fixed him with a gaze he wanted to flinch from. 'He's been walking in the park for days and his mind is disturbed,' she said.

'Whose mind?' Rex asked, knowing there'd be no answer, but unnerved by the comment all the same.

The swing doors opened then and Sister Florence rustled in. Perhaps that was who Sybille had meant – the person who would be found soon. A tiny, brisk and efficient Belgian, Sister Florence spoke French to Sybille, and for this reason alone, Sybille's family trusted Sister Florence above all the other nuns. Tonight, though, because Rex was there, she spoke in English.

'Tchah!' Sister Florence cast a disappointed look at the tv screen as the programme began again. 'Police again. Sybille, you are missing the Andrien film on the fourth BBC canal.' She gave Rex a conspiratorial wink. 'A Belgian director. Vairry good!'

The arrival of this busy, friendly soap-smelling creature changed the atmosphere, and after a few pleasantries, Rex and Diana left, heading up a steep path through trees to the bus-stop at the top of the hill. They sat on the narrow red seat, close, but silent, with the marsh-plains of East London flickering below them like a console.

'What a place,' Diana said, twisting back to look into the trees. 'What is it – a nunnery?'

'Religious orders often look after people,' said Rex. 'Nuns were the first nurses, you know.' He thought he'd better explain that – Diana being Jewish – but she replied sharply that she knew all about the first nurses.

'I suppose they're too busy praying to do anything about the cobwebs.'

Rex smiled. It was a warm, damp, cave-like place, forever prone to visitations of silverfish and spiders.

'They sweep them out,' he said. "But they always come back."

'Not if you open the odd window.'

He couldn't work out if she was being critical of the place because it had unsettled her, or if she was trying to be helpful. At any rate, a young Polish couple came along and sat, busily entwined at the other end of the seat, and Rex and Diana fell into an embarrassed silence. Rex had hoped at various points during the day that he and Diana would be ending their evening like this couple. He knew now that they wouldn't.

'I'm guessing you were both in an accident,' Diana said finally, as the bus arrived.

'I had the accident,' said Rex. 'But it happened to her.'

Actually, it had happened to a lot of people. Sybille's father had had a stroke eight months later. Her big sister Aurelie had divorced within a year, checked into a drying-out clinic within two. Her nephews, twin boys called Sylvain and Olivier, had moved from the Lycee on the end of their street into a series of boarding schools. And as the bus sank back down towards Turnpike Lane, to the kebab shops and the Thai sauna and the swaggering packs of boys, Rex told Diana all about it.

The Sisters of Saint Veronica of Jumièges didn't seem to believe in miracles. They just said their prayers, and they tried to make Sybille and the handful of other broken humans in that house as comfortable as they could. Rex didn't believe in miracles either, but he knew the supernatural had intervened in his life that one, wet December night.

They had breathalysed him at the scene, and the breathalyser said his blood alcohol level was very low. He'd tried arguing the point, but in the wreckage of the car, Sybille died – the first of three deaths – and amid the drama of bringing her back to life, he was forgotten. He'd tried to stand up from where they'd settled him on the kerbside, but his leg wouldn't work, so he'd looked down and seen the bone coming out of his suit trousers and fainted then.

Later, it emerged that the motorcyclist was full of amphetamines, and had had a near-miss with another car ten minutes earlier, and so everyone – policemen, nurses, mental health workers, Sybille's parents – said it wasn't Rex's fault that his wife was blind and brain-damaged, and would never walk again. Sybille's sister, eventually, came round to the same point of view, or at least, said she had when she was sober. Sybille never said anything on the subject, even when she was able to.

Even at half-nine, the traffic was crawling around the junction with Green Lanes, so Rex and Diana joined the general exodus from the bus at the stop by the Wetherspoon's instead of waiting to reach the modern, steel and glass terminus over Turnpike Lane tube station. An assortment of rheumy, battered-looking men and women was supping at the tables outside the pub, taking in the diesel fumes and the damp. A few nodded at Diana.

'Patients?' asked Rex.

She ignored him. 'You could have been in New York, and you're here. And once a week, you go up that hill and... crucify yourself in a nunnery. You hardly got off scot-free, did you?'

'I didn't get what I deserved.'

'That's what that creepy little... temple thing in your front garden's all about, isn't it?'

'It's a shrine. You said you found it interesting.'

'That was before I knew what it was there for. It's all crap, Rex!' she said, causing a pair of brightly-robed, bible-clutching Africans to look up as they flapped by towards the church on Duckett's Common. 'It's all just random. A lot of people are happy with that. I am. The ones that aren't... they have to find some way of making sense of it all. Go to church. Visit little old ladies. Give all your sodding money away.'

'Do you want it? You could get some new lino for the Surgery.'

Rex moved towards her, but she stepped back, into the aura of a lamp-post, and was suddenly illuminated.

'I need time to take it all in.'

'So it's all just a random part of life, I should stop making such a big deal out of it... but you need time to take it in?'

His tone had been bitter, and he regretted the words as soon as they were out. Diana's eyes flashed. Exactly as his wife had been, he suddenly thought. Beautiful when angry; least touchable when most desirable. 'What are you doing?' she asked.

'Going home on my own, I'm guessing.'

'That's not what I meant, Rex. You knew I was going to react. You wanted me to react, or you wouldn't have made that big song-and-dance about taking me up there…' She glanced round and saw the 41 bus to Archway turning the corner into Turnpike Lane. Its arrival seemed to make up her mind. 'Look – I've got an early start – I'll see you around, okay?'

She ran across the road to the bus-stop by the Tube entrance. Rex wondered if she would turn around, but he knew he wasn't going to wait and see.

* * *

When his phone woke him at 5.30 am, his first, forlornly hopeful thought was that Diana was ringing him. Unable to sleep. On her way round.

His second thought was that it might be his persecutor.

His third thought was that Diana had received strange calls. The same as him. Had she received any unwelcome gifts? Surely she would have mentioned it.

He fumbled for the phone, summoning a live image of his sitting-room onto the screen before answering the call. He swore.

'Language. I'll be outside yours in ten minutes,' said Terry's hoarse voice.

Rex rubbed his face, and averted his eyes from the raki bottle on the coffee table. He'd passed out on the sofa, and now he didn't feel good.

'Ready for what, Terry?'

'One of them squatter houses on the North Circular's burnt down.'

He clicked off and Rex hauled himself up, glad, in a way, to have something else to fill his thoughts.

Ten minutes later, he was outside, trembling in the orange half-light under the lamp-post with two steaming mugs of coffee, watching Terry reverse down the lane. They covered a lot of fires in the paper, partly because the area was rammed with old, overcrowded, barely-managed properties, but mainly because Terry was in a football team with several members of the fire brigade. Whenever something was burning down, they rang him up, and the paper went along to snap it.

Terry was talkative, chewing and sniffing constantly as they drove up to Palmer's Green along the deserted Lanes. As the morning light bled into the sky above North London, it looked angrier and angrier, combining with the dull, shuttered buildings to give the place a lonely, forbidding look, like a mountain pass just before a storm. Rex let his forehead rest against the cold glass of the passenger window.

'Seen the paper?' Terry grunted. He motioned with his head to the back seat where a brand new edition of the *Gazette* lay next to all his camera equipment. The headline read: Three Attacks In Three Weeks.

Ellie had done well: a timeline, and a map of the attacks, with the names of the victims and what scant descriptions they had been able to give. Susan had kept true to her word and included his interview with Keith Powell – right next to the column Lawrence Berne was now calling a 'blog' – and edited to around a third of its rightful length.

'He smokes and he's a short-arse. All they need to do is arrest every Turk in Haringey,' Terry opined.

Rex groaned. 'Ilona Balint said she thought he smelled of fags. Maggs said he seemed small, and the Krelkina girl hasn't said anything.'

'He strangles them and he yanks their hair out,' Terry argued. 'Or scalps it out. Any way you look at it, that's someone who hates women.'

'I'd agree with that. But why does that mean it's a Turk? Most Turkish guys I've met worship their mums and their sisters.'

Terry pondered this for a while. 'Suppose it's got to be a Red Indian then.'

'I'm booking you on Haringey Council's next Diversity Workshop, Terry.'

It was that hour when London's traffic is a rumble instead of a roar, and the vehicles on the North Circular were mainly lorries. They sped on past the fire engine and the police cars and the blackened house.

As he stepped out of the car and shook his foot back to life, Rex recognised a number of Terry's fireman mates, along with D.S. Bond and a blond, broad-faced, somehow Dutch-looking D.C. whose name escaped him. The other, instantly recognisable thing about the scene was the smell of gas.

'Waiting for the Gas Board,' Mike Bond said, by way of greeting, as he moved his weight slowly from the ball of one foot to the other. The Dutch D.C. – whose name was Orchard – nodded coldly. He was taking a statement from a red-eyed girl in a Breton shirt and black dungarees. One of the squatters, Rex guessed.

'Was the fire still going when you got here?' Rex asked, glancing at the house. One of its metal shutters was dangling off, and all around it, stretching up to the open windows of the first floor, and across to the front door, the wall was blackened. A near-perfect map of Japan.

'More of an explosion by the sounds of things,' Bond said, blowing on his fingers. 'Happens all the time – they're always tampering with the meters.'

Rex remembered the gang-banger with the decorative facial hair. His visceral hatred of the squatters. *Nicking the gas* – he'd said. *Maybe some of that gas gonna blow up in their faces.*

'I just told to you, there were three men outside, banging upon the door!' the girl shouted. She had fine features, and spoke with a faint accent. 'I looked out, one of them told me piss off back to Russia and then they pushed something through the letter box.'

'What like? A North Sea gas grenade?' queried D.C. Orchard, clearly rather proud of his joke.

The girl scowled.

'Did he really say that?' Rex queried. 'Piss off?'

'He shouted piss off back to Russia, and he made that… Winston Churchill sign to me and he walked off. And one of the others was doing something down there, and I couldn't see it, but then he pushed something through the door.'

'What's the Winston Churchill sign?' asked Bond, in a kindly voice. The girl made a 'V for victory' sign with her fingers. Everyone frowned.

'You mean like that?' Rex suggested, flashing the same sign in reverse. She shrugged.

'Sir?'

A young, Chinese-looking WPC emerged from the front door.

'There are spent matches all around the front step. Like someone was trying to light something.'

The squatter-girl nodded, vindicated, until one of the firemen said, 'There's no way a few matches could have set that off unless the hall was drenched in petrol, or it was full of gas.' D.C. Orchard smiled, thinly.

The Leak Response Team from the gas company called, to say they were a few minutes away. Terry snapped the damage from all sorts of interesting angles, and tried to do the same with the squatter, who wasn't having any of it. In the meantime, Rex looked at the spent matches with Mike Bond.

'Lucky she was the only one in, and right at the top,' said Bond.

'I didn't know anyone still used matches,' Rex said, looking down at the step. There were some in the weeds at the side, six or seven right by the door, and a few more on the path itself. More than anyone needed to light a cigarette.

'I didn't know anyone still said "piss off",' Bond observed.

"Or flicked the V's," Rex added. Except that, as he said that, he remembered someone doing it to him, not long ago. The same person who'd been in a conspiratorial huddle with a pair of thugs in the pub toilet. And put up posters, telling Eastern Europeans to go home.

"You know much about Keith Powell?" he asked Bond, as casually as he could.

'The Nazi bloke?' Bond frowned 'What – you think he did this?'

'Maybe,' Rex said. 'Maybe some of the people he knows. And he's got a criminal record.'

Bond looked at him. 'How do you know?'

'He's on probation for something. I saw a letter in his house.'

Bond's unruly eyebrows rose. 'Probation for what?'

'I don't know. But if we did – I mean – if you did, then it might...'

'We'll look him up.'

Rex decided not to share his thoughts about Powell's fondness for flicking the V's, or his chumminess with the thugs in the Salisbury toilets. They'd sound silly. Or too obvious. But most crimes, in his experience, were obvious. That was why the police managed to solve them.

The Gas Board van finally arrived, and Bond ambled off to

greet its occupant. Rex looked back at the house for a while, then eastwards along the row. Next door was a modest, legitimately-occupied home whose residents were up and moving about. A bird cage in the ground floor window and some stone ornaments on the lawn outside gave some clues. They'd be near, or just past retirement age, Rex guessed. Greek Cypriot, or Irish, here a long time, and hard, hard-working. They'd have pictures of gap-toothed grandchildren on the mantlepiece. Flintstones-style fireplace, tablemats with pictures of dray horses on them. What did they make of the squat next door? Night-long parties, thrown by kids who stole the electricity for their sound systems and never went to work?

Maybe Powell's mob had nothing to do with it. Maybe people like this old couple had sons. Maybe they were gangsters like the boys he'd run into at Newington Green. Or maybe they were mostly law-abiding, tax-paying, strapping great big sons, who didn't want that going on next door to their old mum and dad, next door to the house they planned to inherit. He found himself suddenly thinking about Olivier and Sylvain, Sybille's Parisian nephews. He'd last seen them six years ago, when they were twelve. They were all pleases and thank-yous and damp handshakes, yet murderously protective of their increasingly chaotic and alcoholic mother. When kids were asked to protect their parents, they took it seriously.

He noticed to his surprise that the house on the other side of the smart one was also blackened with soot. It looked in an even worse state, as if it had been bombed in the Blitz and never repaired. So these people – Rex saw a stout woman with steel hair adjusting the curtains and peering out – these people were marooned here, on a road that had turned into a motorway, surrounded by houses that kept bursting into flames. What a way to live out your days.

There was a moment of eye contact between Rex and the woman in the window, and he thought about going across and asking her some questions. Two things stopped him. The first was his realisation that the bombed-out house was the same house he'd seen from the other side on his last trip up here. It was, itself, next door to the house Milda lived in. Or, it seemed, no longer lived in.

The second thing was an argument, between the girl in the dungarees, and a tall boy in a green tracksuit top, who had just shown up on a mountain bike with no saddle. The argument was in German, but none of the onlookers needed any knowledge of the tongue to understand that the girl was very angry with the boy, and the boy didn't have a leg to stand on. She kept pointing at the pavement a few feet away, or more accurately, at the gas main situated there, which was being closely inspected by the man from the gas company.

As Rex wandered over, the gasman held up a few links of a thin metal chain.

'This is it,' he said. 'See – when we switch the supply off, we put a chain on, to stop anyone unauthorised switching it back. But they' – he glanced meaningfully at the squatters – 'can break them with a pair of bolt cutters.'

'So they left the gas on?'

'We *didn't*,' said the girl. 'We switched it off when we moved in here last week, and we rang you' – she pointed at the gasman – 'to put the supply on the meter.'

'You got a record of that call?' asked D.C. Orchard. His tone made it clear that he suspected, and hoped, that they didn't. The boy started scrolling through a flat, sandwich-sized computer he'd withdrawn from the pocket of his jeans.

'You're supposed to turn the stop-cock until it clicks, and the lever goes in,' the gasman went on. 'If it doesn't click, you can't be sure the gas isn't still coming through. And some of these old meters have been mucked about with so many times they're about as tight as a cheese-grater.'

The girl glared at the boy, who was still busy with his little organiser device.

'The meter's in that cupboard in the porch,' D.C. Orchard mused, 'so when the matches come through the letter-box…'

At that moment the boy looked up from his screen and said, 'I talked to Miss Adita Shah in the New Domestic Supply Team at 2.48pm on Wednesday.'

'Tampering with a gas supply for any reason is an offence…' began D.C. Orchard.

'So is sticking lighted matches through someone's letter box,' said Rex.

Bond cut in, addressing the two squatters. 'Detective Constable Orchard is right. Regardless of what you say happened at the front door, you shouldn't have fiddled with the gas main. Even if you had decided to go legit and pay for it. You should have left it to the experts.'

'We thought, if the gas company saw there had been an illegal supply, they would know this place was a squat and they wouldn't give to us it,' protested the girl, her English suffering as she became agitated.

Bond chuckled. 'I reckon the tin shutters and the Fuck the Pigs sign would have given them a clue or two, love.'

At length, the crowds departed: the firemen to the café down the road, the gas man to a call in Enfield, the police with their two sullen charges.

Terry had offered to hide the boy's bike safely in the back garden, and Rex went with him down an alleyway at the side of the house, which led onto a flat, muddy garden. He felt truly terrible now, the rush of energy having given way now to a full, body-and-soul type of hangover. His foot was grumbling too, and he needed codeine. He didn't have any, and the only way to get a decent dose would be to make an appointment with his G.P. Who wasn't talking to him.

'Why did you offer to stash it for him?' Rex asked irritably, as Terry pulled a muddy blue tarpaulin off a barbecue set and covered the seat-less bike with it.

Terry winked. 'So I could see if they had any weed growing out back.'

'In England? In the autumn?'

'My mate Terry grows it all year round in Consett.'

'You've got a mate called Terry?'

'I've got two,' Terry said, poking hopefully in a bush with an old chair leg. Rex gazed out over the landscape – a flat, unhappy plain of washing lines and huge satellite dishes. The air smelt of smoke and wet concrete.

'Doesn't your bird live out this way?' Terry said, peering distractedly into a tiny, green-painted garden shed on a dangerous lean.

'She's not my bird,' Rex said. 'But yes. She lives three doors down, actually.'

'The one that's on fire right now?'

Rex turned and followed the direction of Terry's finger to see thick palls of dark smoke swirling away and upwards from the back of Milda's house.

They ran towards it, across the gardens. Only the elderly couple had a fence; no one else's boundary was marked by anything beyond a bit of netting or a few blackened stumps in the earth. In the yard of the junkie squat next to Milda's, there was, inexplicably, a large, plywood Wendy-house. Rex and Terry took cover behind it from the flames and the fumes.

When the wind changed direction, it rapidly became apparent

that Milda's house was not on fire. Instead, someone had lit a huge bonfire in the back yard. Rex and Terry stood, momentarily transfixed by the primal drama of a roaring blaze. A man came out from the house with more fuel in his arms.

It was Vadim, and he was burning Milda's belongings in the back yard. Rex watched in horror as he threw a pale-blue, William Morris print file on the flames. It was followed by a pile of sketches, and a scarf Milda had sometimes worn around her head.

As the smoke blew back towards them, Rex motioned for Terry to take some pictures. The photographer obliged, eyes narrowed, mouth set in a grim, contented line, as if he'd finally been drafted to the war-zone of his dreams. More of Milda's clothes went onto the pyre and the smoke thickened. Vadim appeared in profile, vanished then appeared again, a spectral figure in combat trousers and a short pea-coat.

The scene didn't ignite Rex's worst fears. It gave him fears he'd never had before. He reported on crimes every day – rapes and stabbings and robberies – but he always arrived in the aftermath. This was different. A crime – he was sure it must be a crime – was actually happening before his eyes, involving people he knew, people he'd loved and slept with. It felt as if a character on the television had suddenly turned to the camera and spoken his name, the removed become impossibly near in an instant.

Why was Vadim in the garden, early in the morning, burning Milda's belongings? Why had nobody seen her for so long? He remembered Vadim's taxi to the airport when they'd first met. Isn't that just what a killer might do? First bolt for home? Then calm down, go back, and cover his tracks?

And intimidate the only person who might get close to the truth.

* * *

Two hours later, Rex was at the Police Station on St. Ann's Road. They would be moving soon, Detective Sergeant Mike Bond told him, from this ornate red-brick and sandstone HQ to something steely and modern on the Seven Sisters' Road.

'This was my first nick,' Bond said, glancing up from his cluttered desk to the corniced ceiling and the panelled walls. It was an oddly elegant place, with a glass-tiled hallway, and it always smelt of felt and wax polish, like a museum. 'My two best mates at Bramshill got West End Central and I thought I'd got the shit sandwich coming here.'

The shit sandwich. Rex suddenly remembered his trepidation as he'd opened that envelope in the office yesterday. After everything else, it had crossed his mind that there might be shit inside the jiffy bag. He'd have been almost relieved to have found a turd. A turd was a simple insult. Journalists were always getting turds. At the *Telegraph*, he recalled, they'd had special bags and gloves for them. But there were no special procedures for the stuff coming his way now. But could it really be Vadim behind it all? And why rubber handcuffs?

'Mike. I've seen something,' said Rex, waving aside the mint Bond was offering him.

He told the policeman about Milda, who was still missing, and clearly hadn't gone home. Then about Vadim and the bonfire. Bond took it all in, in a grave yet inscrutable way.

'You need to file a Missing Person's Report,' Bond said, reaching into his drawer for some forms. 'But I have to tell you. We've got a Latvian woman who works here. She speaks all those languages: Lithuanian, Estonian. And even before these attacks started, she's been in here twice a week, talking to some mum or dad back in the old country, who thinks their son or daughter's disappeared. Nine times out of ten, they're in a new squat. Or they've just gone to Leeds. Or Paris. Or their phone's run out of credit. They're just... kids. It rarely comes to anything.'

'But her boyfriend was burning her stuff on a bonfire. I've got photos.'

'I can't act on that, Rex. Unless Milda filed a complaint about her missing stuff. Or one of the neighbours didn't like the smoke.' Bond took another sweet. 'So, you want to do this report?'

Rex shook his head. Bond was right: what it looked like to him was not what it looked like to the police. They needed more. But he had nothing else to give them. Yet.

'People are pessimists,' Bond said, crunching his mint. 'They've got reason to be, sure, but this place isn't half as bad as people think. I'm not saying it hasn't been. Back in the Eighties. Broadwater Farm and all that…' He proffered the bag again.

Bond was a calming presence, Rex thought, as he unwrapped a mint and put it in his mouth. Yet in the whole time he'd known the man, only two things had ever given him cause for concern, and they'd both occurred in the last few days. There was his strange, crass comment about Eastern European girls looking for trouble. And then that book on Brenda's desk. Living With A Violent Man. Mike Bond wasn't a violent man, surely. Then again, he'd been a copper in Tottenham for a long time. Who wouldn't be a little on the violent side?

'What made it so bad back then? Unemployment?'

Bond chuckled wheezily. 'People have never worked round these parts. Not the tax-paying kind, anyway.' He stretched back in his chair, displaying a billowing striped paunch. He'd put on a lot of weight. And had he always looked quite so tired? 'The racial thing was really bad. Pakistanis. Blacks. National Front. Police.' As he mentioned each group, Bond slapped a hand on his belly, like a series of incoming blows. 'Compared to back then, we've been living in a multicultural paradise.'

A police civilian staffer, a young, skinny, white boy with huge, tribal holes bored through his earlobes, put some forms on

Bond's desk, occasion for the old detective to roll his eyebrows at Rex.

'Keith Powell doesn't seem to think it's the Garden of Eden,' Rex said, seizing the opportunity.

'Well…' Bond unwrapped another mint and sucked thoughtfully. 'Brenda and I saw this nature thing the other night. You know, the coral reef. It's got eight thousand different life-forms all swimming around there. Your crab eats the sand-worms, and the sand-worms need this special plant to lay their eggs in, but…'

'Global warming.' Rex caught the odd nature documentary, too.

'Exactly. The sea heats up, the worms die, and the crab dies, and then the… whatever it is that feeds on crabs goes kaput too. It's a finely-tuned engine. And this place has been a bit like that, the past twenty years. Turks here. Kurds there. Caribbeans doing this, Africans doing that. It's worked. But then, suddenly, umpteen thousand new people fly in from Stansted, and on top of that, you've got a recession, inflation, all these cuts…'

Rex frowned. 'So Powell's mob have a point?'

Bond shrugged. 'I'm not saying we should do this or that. I'm just saying, it's going to change things. It's like I said. This manor's been okay since the bad old days. But I worry it might not be for long.'

'So you've gone from saying I shouldn't be worried about my ex-girlfriend because this is a lovely place… to saying I should be, because it's all changing, and we've got too many immigrants arriving in the middle of a recession?'

Bond sighed crossly. 'I'm not delivering a lecture to the Police Federation, Rex, I'm just talking to you. I think both, okay?' He'd gone red in the face, Rex saw. 'I think your Russian girl is probably tucked up in her kip safe and well in Moscow or

Brighton. But sometimes I do get the impression it's getting a bit tense out there again. That's all.' He wiped his forehead.

'So have there been more incidents of one kind or another since all the Eastern Europeans arrived?'

Bond rubbed the loose skin of his neck, calming down. 'I can't give you any statistics. I just know what it feels like as a copper. And sometimes, it feels like we're back in the bad old days. It feels edgy out there. Like everyone's watching each other, in a not very friendly kind of way.'

'Might be something to do with an ex-offender setting up a right wing anti-immigration group.'

Bond gave him a strange look. 'Funny thing that, Rex. I checked Powell out when I got back. And there's nothing on him at all.' He started leafing through a buff-coloured file to the left of the pile the boy had just brought. He held up a finger, meaning Rex should wait a minute. 'Yeah,' he repeated, after a while, putting the folder down. 'Powell hasn't got a criminal record at all. Not even a late library book.'

'But he's on probation,' Rex said. 'And he's definitely got at least one overdue library book. *Mein Kampf,* by Adolf Hitler.'

'Yes, well the library book thing was a joke, Rex,' Bond said, a little sharply. 'The Police National Computer doesn't keep records of that. It does mention if someone's on probation, though. And Kieron isn't.'

'Kieron?'

'Keith,' Bond corrected himself. 'Powell.'

'Could it have been missed off?'

'No chance.' Bond sat up, moving the file into his desk drawer.

'So...' Rex struggled with his confusion. 'All right. Regardless of his disappearing criminal record, are you going to ask him what his British Workers' Action lot were up to last night? Three men, Mike. That's what the girl said. I saw Powell acting extremely dodgy in the loos at the Salisbury last night – with two of his mates.'

Bond shrugged. 'Investigations into the cause of the explosion are ongoing, and if and when we deem it right to update the media, we will issue a statement.'

Correction. Three things had happened to give him doubts about Mike Bond. And this was Number Three. 'Mike?' Rex waved a hand in front of the Detective's face. 'Have you suddenly been taken over by an alien robot?'

'Look – I do a lot of favours for you guys,' Bond said, lowering his voice and glancing around the office. 'But sometimes you push your luck. We investigate the crimes. You write about them.'

'And sometimes, I thought, we help each other out.'

Bond's face was reddening again. 'And you've given me – what? A criminal record that doesn't exist. And a report of three men in a pub loo. Thanks.'

Rex shook his head. He looked down at his notebook.

'So can I write that you're investigating the British Workers' Action Party in connection with the explosion at the squat?'

'If you want to report something that hasn't been said, or written, or confirmed, or denied by us, go ahead.'

'But it would be a reasonable line of enquiry for the C.I.D., wouldn't it? I mean – you've got three Eastern European girls being attacked, in the same way, in the same place. You've got a squat, in an area almost exclusively squatted by Eastern Europeans, being blown up by someone who shouts 'Piss off back to Russia', and you've got a group putting up posters saying that everyone from Eastern Europe needs to go home. You'd naturally want to talk to the members of that group, wouldn't you?'

Bond opened the fingers of his left hand, and then closed them again – a hand-shrug. Rex didn't know whether to feel hurt, or insulted, or laugh out loud. The truth was that Mike Bond, dependable, straight, Rock of Ages, Mike Bond, was being downright shifty with him.

D.C. Orchard, with his wide, shiny Edam-face, came downstairs at this point, pulling on a leather coat. It was a bad leather coat, Rex noted, the kind you'd buy if you wanted to look like a detective, but actually worked as a ticket inspector. 'Scrap at the Eski Dostlar, skip. Turk with stab wounds and a chair through a Merc's windscreen.'

Bond stood up. 'These Turkish social clubs,' he quipped to Rex. 'Ought to call them anti-social clubs. C'mon – you want a ride in a panda car?'

Rex declined the offer, knowing there'd be no point going to the Eski Dostlar Club on the heels of the police. Everyone would have clammed up tight. There'd be one, angry Turk sweeping up glass and blood, and an air of Byzantine indifference in all the surrounding premises. In any case, these incidents came and went, connected, mostly, to the business that went on at the back and above the bleak, strip-lit tea-houses. Years ago, back when he'd been on the dailies, he'd tried to research a piece about the secret life of these shuttered, anonymous little establishments and got nowhere. Got nowhere, and been given a careful shove as he left a shop doorway, gentle enough not to harm, firm enough not to be mistaken.

As Rex left, the ear-ringed boy was talking to a policewoman. Unnoticed, he stopped to listen.

'Another one?' the boy was saying. 'When?'

'One of the response teams just told me on the way in.'

'Same thing as before?'

A phone rang, and Rex strained to catch what the WPC was saying.

'Anna Semchuk she's called. Ukrainian. Ally Pally. Throttled and scalped. But this time he got his dick out, so Sapphire are taking over. '

Rex felt a shiver of distaste. He knew that Operation Sapphire was the specialist Sex Crimes Unit. So, the attacker wasn't just carrying on. He was upping his game.

Another phone rang, its sound obscuring the next few words. 'A rubber glove?' was the next clear thing Rex heard the boy say.

'Not like a Marigold,' the policewoman replied. 'I mean like the ones we use. On a bush nearby.'

Something caused them to notice him at this point.

'You need some help?' the boy asked. He had a gentle, pretty face and something about it reminded Rex of Milda. After this fourth attack up at the Palace, Milda's disappearance wasn't going to warrant much attention.

Rex shook his head and went out. It was mid-morning now, and the day was turning blustery but fine. He bought himself some stronger painkillers in a little Greek Cypriot-run pharmacy, then went into the Caribbean bakery next door. It smelt delectable in there, of Christmas cake and warm bread. His sweet tooth stirred into action, he ordered something called a coco pattie and a cup of tea and was then somewhat alarmed to receive a small, fiery beef pasty inside a sweet-tasting bap. It was good, though, and as he chomped through it, he started to feel better.

At the counter behind him, a pair of men greeted one another: one wore a bus driver's uniform, the other something civic with epaulettes.

'Seen about all these attacks in the paper?' the epaulette-man asked.

The bus driver sucked his teeth. 'Wennem fine out some white boy doing it,' – he glanced pointedly at Rex – 'me celebrate , 'ca me sick a de dirty look. First girl me pick up this morning. Five o'clock. Naabady else 'pon de bus – so she naa wanta get on it.

She tink a nasty big black bus driver gwan interfere with her!'
'Raas.'

The men exchanged oaths, bought buns and left. Rex kept his head down until they had done so, aware, not for the first time, that the multi-cultural bonhomie of the area frequently wore thin, especially when there was trouble.

At least the codeine was having an effect now. His mind felt calmer, clearer. Back at the cop shop, he'd started to suspect Mike Bond. He still suspected Mike Bond, but he also knew that he was hungover, sad and in pain. When any of these three states affected him, his mind slipped into a certain groove. He had to recognise that, and change gear. If he could. That was what they'd taught him.

The groove had begun to form after the accident. He could even pinpoint the day. Six days out of hospital. They were operating on Sybille again and he was in the back streets behind University College Hospital because he could no longer bear to be in that hot, sterile room with her parents and her sister and her sister's mute, sickly twins. A newsagent on Gower Street had seemed unfriendly, and for some reason, he was unable to get this out of his mind. It had felt as if the newsagent had been staring at him – seen something in his face, perhaps, or thought he recognised him from some other place, and not liked the associations. On the pavement outside, unwrapping the packet of mints he'd bought, he got in the way of a pretty girl in boots and a fawn coat, and she'd set her mouth and her icy blue eyes in a scowl, as if he was pestering her. He'd scanned the faces of the next people who went by, to see if they were going to have a problem with him, too, and was not that surprised when they – another pair of prepubescent twin boys – stared at him in a shocked, affronted manner.

He was just tired, he'd told himself. But in a very short space of time, he'd fallen into a nightmare. In this nightmare, life carried on as normal. He ate, went to the shops, attended appointments with doctors and physiotherapists, visited Sybille in hospital, met up with colleagues from the job, even went to a 40th birthday party. But everyone – almost everyone, except the blind and small babies – stared at him. Into him. Their stares shrivelled up his soul. Everyone hated him. He was a pariah. And it was only right, because of the mummified creature who had been his wife in the hospital bed. Part of him knew they couldn't know about all that, but still, on some unconscious, animal level, he clearly gave off a signal that he was wrong. Something that had to be killed off.

A few drinks could lift him out of the groove, as could painkillers that contained opiates. After the right amount of either, or both, he understood that it was all utter rubbish, delusions brought on by depression and guilt. But the next morning, the delusions would be back with a vengeance. And one morning, on the way into the office to have a chat about the future with his boss, he couldn't stand the silent persecution any more.

'What the fuck are you looking at?' he shouted, hoarse and high-pitched, at his fellow passengers on the Northern Line. Nobody replied. They all stared down, except for one old, grizzled Rasta, who'd found it quite funny. But somehow, the act had made him feel elated. He'd accepted their war. And he was fighting. And he went on shouting – what the fuck are all you fuckers fucking looking at me for and other variants on that theme – through Waterloo Station concourse, down the steps and along the South Bank to the newspaper's brand new riverside offices. He shouted it in there, too. And he never worked for a national newspaper again.

In the Mental Health Unit, and afterwards, at therapy sessions in a delightful old building on Highgate Hill, they'd taught him to see it as an addiction. That thinking that way, as if everything were joined up in some grand, arching, worldwide attack on him, was seductive. Painful. Helpful, perhaps. But also, in the end, deadly. A kind of psychic codeine.

When it happened, they said, he shouldn't just accept what his mind told him. He just needed to write everything down in his journal, and carry on. Carry on trying to change his thoughts, carry on resisting them. And, they said, he'd have to do that until he drew his last breath, because there was no cure, only a way of handling.

Rex ordered another patty – curried goat this time, but without the accompanying coconut bap – and jotted down in his notebook all the things he knew, or thought he knew, or just suspected. He saw that there were several facts, papering over a large number of uncertainties.

Milda was missing. Someone was still attacking girls. Vadim had been burning Milda's things. Bond had been strangely unhelpful. Powell had a probation officer, but didn't have a criminal record. And he conducted meetings in pub toilets.

And someone, somewhere, whether connected to the foregoing or not, was trying to put the frighteners on him. It couldn't be Vadim, because the first warning, the kid on the moped, had happened before he'd even met Vadim, and the second had occurred while Vadim was supposedly en route to Lithuania. Unless the kid on the moped was random. And Vadim had an accomplice. Or hadn't gone away at all.

He picked up his phone and selected Ellie's number. But he hesitated, remembering the morning meeting. It had been more of an inquest. The Estate Agents wanted to know why their half-page advert had been turned into a piss-take. So did Susan. Ellie had blamed Rex for not filing the correct copy before he'd gone out for the evening. Rex had blamed Ellie for rooting round in his files and pasting what he'd written into the mock-up without even reading it. The truth was that they were both to blame, but he more than her, on grounds of seniority. He'd said that, this morning. But possibly not with enough emphasis.

He rang her number, and he said it again. In the silence that followed, he told Ellie what he'd heard at the Police Station.

'So there's been another scalping up at the Palace. But you want me to go and cover a gang-fight at a Turkish social club?' Ellie spoke slowly, with evident disbelief.

'Chances are, Operation Sapphire are going to tell us nothing about this fourth girl. Not in the next 24 hours or so anyway. And we need to keep covering the other stuff. You're good with blokes, Ellie. You'll get more out of them than me.'

'Are you being straight with me?'

'Of course,' he lied. A more important reason was that the old men in the club would underestimate this slip of a girl with her big handbag and her notebook. They'd flirt with her and give her lumps of Turkish delight with glasses of cardamom tea. And tell her more than they ought to.

'Hundred-to-one it's the usual protection racket shit and you won't get much. But it'll be good experience.'

'And what will you be doing?'

He smiled wanly at his own reflection in the café window. 'Visiting some prominent local estate agents. And grovelling.'

* * *

The darkroom was cool and musty, and he had always loved it in there. Not just the privacy and the darkness, but the order. Here were the chemicals: developer and fixer and cleanser. Here was the paper. The trays and the drying line, and the clips. To the side was a separate workbench where he kept the enlarger, and mended the cameras. Something about opening up a camera gave him a light, trembling feeling in his stomach. Like he'd felt when he was a boy and saw things he shouldn't have.

He didn't need to win the newspaper competition, of course. His camera bag was a beautiful buckskin one, produced to publicise the launch of the Leica iii g in 1955. He'd snapped it up at a church jumble sale in Winchmore Hill. And in a Save the Children shop, right next door to the very same church, he'd found a Chinese copy of the Linhof tripod, identical to the original except for a slight snag in the foot shape. If you knew what to look for, you could get professional camera equipment for next to nothing. But he had had this idea, a silly idea; it made him blush when he thought about it. He thought that he might win the competition, and if he did, he would give the bag and the tripod to the girl.

She was pale and bird-like, with the softest, whitest skin. Like something that shouldn't have been allowed to exist, and only did so in constant peril. She reminded him of the girl he'd strangled in the hospital bed, all those years ago on a Christmas night. She reminded him, less clearly, less frequently, of something about himself.

She had been standing on a bus-stop bench when he first met her. A hot, June day. Over in the roaring bypass emptiness of Tottenham Hale, they were building, chewing further into the marshes, expanding the retail park to include a restaurant and a cinema and a big hotel, and for miles around, even down at London Fields and Victoria Park, you could see the three cranes they were using. The girl had a Lomo – an extremely rare tri-speed 35 mm model released by Zenit in 1991 – and she was standing on the bench, pointing her camera over the fence behind to photograph the cranes.

'They're like birds,' she said, blinking at him through thick, gawky spectacles. 'Big, river birds.'

'Cranes!' he joked. But she didn't understand that there were two kinds of cranes in English, and after a short while, he gave up trying to explain. Sometimes, he liked to use a cheap little digital just to give him some ideas about the composition – he wasn't a stick-in-the-mud – and while he waited for his bus, he flicked through the images he'd been taking.

Without invitation, like a curious sparrow, she came to his elbow and peered down at the screen. 'You are taking only just the drivers?' she queried, looking at him with a mixture of amusement and concern. It was close and muggy, and he could smell her sweat. Like fried onions.

He told her that he liked crane drivers. That he'd always wanted to be one himself. Because they sat there, so alone, so high up above the city, and they had so much power to see everything that was going on. They were like gods. She seemed to like that idea, laughing a rather deep, beautiful laugh and sending the smell of mints in his direction.

'Yes. Like gods. Maybe the crane drivers could see we were going to meet before we did!' she said. And then the bus came swinging round the huge roundabout, and she got on it with him, and he had an idea that she just did it because she was interested in him, although that hardly seemed possible.

The bus went north, alongside the Watermead Reservoir before heading west on the North Circular. They sat together at the front, upstairs, something he'd never done. He supposed it was a place you sat if you had children, or if you had ever been a child. And neither of those applied to him. It was a new way of seeing the city, he realized: the solitary training shoes on the top of bus-stop roofs, the fat, naked Indian in a second floor window over a betting shop. He saw more. He thought he would do it again, when he could.

The girl sat close to him. Close enough for him to smell her hair. It smelt of Chinese tea. And she told him about her camera, which had been her Dad's, but she'd never used it before. He didn't know what to say, but the girl just talked and talked, in English, but in such a low, quick way, with such a funny accent that he sometimes missed what she was saying. It was comfortable, though, rather than confusing.

As they went past the back of the North Middlesex Hospital, he said that her father must know a thing or two about cameras.

'He is dead,' she replied harshly. He gazed through a hospital window at that moment and caught a typical, clinical scene of screens and equipment. It made him shudder. 'This is just some communist rubbish,' the girl added, tapping it with a fingernail.

'It's not,' he replied hotly. 'You don't know because you you're too young. It's a beautiful model. And if you'd had the film on the right speed, you'd have taken some beautiful shots.'

She stared, and he felt his face going red. He never spoke to anyone like that. She took her spectacles off and wiped them on her dress, and he imagined droplets of steam from his face being rubbed off the lenses and onto the printed hem that rubbed against her bare, girl's knees.

'Can you teach me to make those beautiful shots, please?'

A breathy, wispy voice, like a little girl's. He knew he had to get off the bus. Luckily, the allotments were coming up, and he found himself jabbering about the patch of ground he had there, and how much work it took up. And all the time he was thinking of the crunch that came when he forced a spade into the thick, damp soil. He nearly fell down the stairs and his legs were trembling as he stood on the kerb watching the bus drive away. He had an idea that it had been stupid to tell her about the allotments, because they were real, and the girl could find him there, but by the time he reached the gates, he'd seen how unlikely that was. She was only a girl at a bus stop. People, strangers, spoke to each other all the time. He'd seen it happen.

Later, he'd made a simple salad for Caroline with the bits he'd gathered at the allotments. After the last operation, she'd moved to a bed in the front room, and the place was filled with the smells of illness. It was hot in there, too, because she was always shivering, so they still had a radiator on low; and they couldn't open the window at this time of year, because the smoke from the neighbours' barbecues and the traffic fumes from the main road settled on her chest.

The lettuce and the tomato had lain untouched on a tray next to a puzzle magazine and her reading glasses; he'd fancied he could see them wilting second by second. It would be another of the days when nothing passed her lips except morphine and lemon barley water.

'I didn't know you were going up the allotments,' she'd said, out of the side of her mouth. She was so used to speaking while in pain that she talked that way all the time, even in moments of relief. He felt caught out, as if he'd done something wrong. And he'd also known, in that instant, that it was his wife who stopped him from doing wrong. If she were to stop eating, she might not be strong enough to carry on that job.

'Eat some tomato,' he'd said, switching on the local news. 'Just half. It'll be good for you.'

It hadn't been good for Caroline, of course. Not good enough. Nothing he'd done had helped her. And now he was here, in the darkroom in the autumn, developing a film that had been in its can since June. He knew what he'd find when he developed it, but even so, he'd never got over that sense of wonder as the chemicals went to work on the paper, and in the midst of that stark, hospital smell, a vision formed.

In the tray an image appeared of the cranes. He'd only caught two, but that had been his intention, because both had their arms extended, in opposite directions, at almost the same angle, so they formed a letter 'Y'. The drivers, in their isolation, were close together, and they were the magnetic centre of the piece. But in the bottom right hand corner, he'd accidentally captured a fragment of the girl. Just a shoulder and a slice of arm. Bare arm, bright blue plastic watch, and the shoulder of that old-fashioned dress she often wore.

Did it spoil the picture, or add something to it? It might be just right for the title of the competition. The Changing Face Of Haringey. The hint of a girl in an old dress, but with a modern watch. Cranes behind her, chewing up the old marshes. And the two drivers, seeming to have a conversation in their separate cabs, so far above the scene. Maybe he'd keep her in.

She might be annoyed, he thought. But then again, if he won, she'd be delighted.

* * *

Dr Diana Berne knew enough about alcoholism, saw enough, every day, of its beacons and its wreckage, to know that wanting a drink was not, in itself, something to worry about. Nevertheless, every afternoon, just between the departure of the penultimate patient and the arrival of the very last, she wished she kept something in a drawer.

She wished it tonight. On Tuesday, after being stood up on the Monday night, another grim day in the Surgery and that awkward, unhappy pub-session with Rex, she'd come home to find her flat had been burgled. She'd tried not to take it personally. Almost everyone else on her road had been burgled. But this person had thrown her clothes and her underwear all over the flat and scratched over the Polaroid of Tigger, her first cat – and that, somehow, had troubled her much more than what had troubled the two young policemen who'd turned up.

That nothing had been taken.

Her first suspect was the taxi-driver. He'd known she wasn't going to be in, after all. But he was an old man. And he'd left all the IKEA stuff so neatly and carefully in the porch. It was still there, in fact, two days later, because she couldn't bear to bring any of it into the flat. It was all new, in its packaging. The intruder hadn't touched it. She still didn't want any of it now.

She glanced at her screen, and saw that Mrs Trail was due in next. Now she wanted that drink even more. With a chaser shot of morphine. Mrs Trail was a silly, fussy, sheep-faced woman in her late fifties, employed as a school cook, and constantly in pursuit of a large compensation package. She always insisted on the last appointment because then she could unburden herself in a slow, unhurried fashion, beginning with the unhelpfulness of the doctors' reception staff, moving on to the laziness of her largely African colleagues at work, followed by the physical and mental stresses of living in a house whose garden wasn't big enough and having a daughter with a weight problem.

Dr Shah routinely prescribed her antibiotics: given a fair wind, he said, Mrs Trail's immune system might be compromised and finally finished off when some deadly new superbug landed in Haringey from the Third World. Diana, on the other hand, tried to listen and give support. In return, while not listening to a word of her advice, Mrs Trail did a ghastly impression of bosomy, big sisterly concern for her.

Found a nice young man yet? Mrs Trail would no doubt ask. And then, before Diana had replied. *Shame. Still...*

Concern, fake or otherwise, was something Diana could take no more of. On Wednesday, reluctant to be alone in the flat, she'd gone up to Temple Fortune to see her cousin Avital. Or Abigail, as she'd been known before a muscular form of Zionism had seized hold of her in her first year at Manchester University. Now married to an Israeli mathematician, Avital wore a headscarf, and seemed to have children attached to every limb and garment. Amidst the smell and the clamour and the shiny trails of snot, she herself seemed to shine with fulfilment: a woman who loved sex, loved her husband, and simply loved having babies. The fact that God had given the thumbs-up to the enterprise was merely the icing on the cake. However much Diana shuddered at her cousin's lifestyle, she couldn't help but examine her own and find it wanting.

When the kids were in bed, Avital and Diana had sat in the conservatory, shared pizzas and some wine and giggled about men, just as they'd done when they were fourteen and living at the opposite ends of what Lawrence Berne, Avital's father, proudly called Finchley's longest street. Avital had reeled off a list of eligible suitors for her cousin, and was threatening to invite them all to her husband's forty-second birthday party in November. Diana had agreed solely to make her cousin shut up, and ever since that evening, Avital had been sending her links to various Facebook pages and Twitter profiles.

She'd looked at one of them. Already knowing, down to the last mole, what "@MarcusGreen333" was going to look like before the picture downloaded: handsome and dark, clean-cut but running slightly to fat. She saw the words 'Senior Partner' in his profile and harrumphed to herself, almost pleased to be disappointed. But then she saw the word 'Paris', too. She was even more pleasantly surprised to find a link to an architectural history group, of which the aforementioned Marcus Green was a founder-member. He couldn't be dismissed as just another successful Garden Suburb Jewish lawyer. Possibly none of the men Avital knew were the sort you could write off in a sentence.

And yet, she'd kept thinking, throughout today's parade of headaches and eczema flare-ups, none of them was Rex Tracey. This crumpled-looking reporter with the limp and the odd, quiet way of talking that seemed forever half-sad and half-amused. He'd come to her by way of a clerical error, when one practice in the area wound up, and the patients were divvied up among the others by alphabet. She had got surnames J through to R, and she'd been envisaging a magnificent six-foot transsexual hooker called Tracey Rex, when instead, one day at the end of July, this face, the sort of face that belonged in a French comedy film, just came in and said it wasn't sleeping too well. Without going over his records much, she'd asked all the usual questions about appetite and bowel movements and stresses at work, and at the end of it all, he'd said that, in his opinion, it boiled down to two factors.

'I've got new neighbours. Colombians, I think. They're having sex all night, with the windows open. And I can't get Okocim Mocne in any of the shops at the moment.'

'Can't get what?'

'Okocim Mocne. It's a Polish lager I drink. Quite a strong one.'

She'd laughed and told him lager never helped anyone to sleep. It turned out that, like a lot of her male patients, Rex Tracey was in a lot of pain, but expecting the Doctor to guess it, rather than to need to be told. The arthritis clinic at the Middlesex had washed their hands of him after too many missed appointments so she referred him to Chase Farm, aware that he'd probably do the same thing there, and that even if he didn't, the arthritis clinic wouldn't do much for him.

Two days later, she'd been in the Marks and Spencer on the High Street buying some underwear in her lunch-hour, when he'd appeared holding a basket of things from the sandwich chiller cabinet at the back. Startled, and blushing because of the intimate apparel in her hand, Diana had accepted his invitation to share a sandwich, and then done so, on Duckett's Common, amid the alcoholics and the gang-bangers on the basketball court and the listless clutches of Balkan men.

She'd known from that first meeting, that he was getting over some recent relationship. She hadn't minded that, because he was a patient. And then, over the course of a few drinks and Turkish dinners, he was a friend. She ignored the wisdom, tested and learnt long back in her life, that told her men and women could not be friends. She found herself looking out for the articles he wrote in the local paper, then looking up the things he said he'd written for the national press on the internet, and one day, not long ago, she'd actually touched the screen of her monitor as she printed up a repeat prescription for him. She knew then that Rex Tracey wasn't her friend any more. She felt something else for him.

That ought to have been a cause for celebration, but for the fact that he often showed up late for their meetings, or didn't come at all, and declared his phone to be out of juice with suspicious regularity. And if she ever sent him a jokey text, there'd always be a long, unnerving delay before he replied. She didn't expect him to wear her scarf wrapped round his wrist – they weren't kids. But everyone she'd discussed this with – not just Avital, but her two best friends – had drawn the same, blunt conclusion. The ex was still on the scene.

'Or she isn't, maybe,' Avital had said, mirroring her husband's irritable Israeli way of speaking. 'And there's something or somebody else. But either way. Come on. You haven't gone to bed with the guy after a whole summer? It's not happening. Look somewhere else.'

She was right. There was a wife with half her face missing. Some hideous accident that had left her in fairyland, him lame and doubled up with guilt. In his notes there was a single oblique reference from his old GP, from years back: *Traffic accident. Left foot injury. Post-traum. arth.?*

Diana rubbed her eyes as she looked at the clock on her computer. It was 5.50. Half an hour, if she was lucky, at the hands of Mrs Trail, half an hour on paperwork. She'd promised Ina, the receptionist, whose nephew worked at the police station, that she'd get a cab home, because there'd been rumours of a fourth attack, and if she stuck to that, she could be back in Upper Holloway by seven. Ten minutes in the Tesco Metro. Half seven and she'd be drinking wine in the bath. Except maybe she shouldn't lie in the bath drinking wine if Avital really was going to introduce her to a bazaar-load of bachelors in just under seven weeks' time. Maybe she'd be better off going to the gym. Was she still a member of the gym? What gym was it?

There was a polite knock at the door.

'Come in.' Diana was surprised. Mrs Trail must be learning some consideration for others. It was about time.

The door opened. 'You're not Mrs Trail,' Diana said.

'Well observed,' Rex said. 'I can see why you became a doctor.'

At around half-past eight – just an hour later than she'd predicted – Diana was in her bath drinking wine. And she wasn't the only one.

'Why are you smiling?' he said, as he soaped her left breast.

'Because tomorrow I'll have to move you to Dr Shah's list,' she said. 'And he'll want to know what treatments I've been prescribing.'

'Please don't,' Rex said, kissing her deeply. 'Sharing a bath with Dr Shah just won't be the same.'

She gave herself up to the steam and the heat and the taste of the wine and the feel of him. His hand slipped between her legs – it felt cool and dry even though they were in the bath. Her breaths became shallow. His phone rang.

'Ignore it,' he whispered. It wasn't difficult. She listened to the gentle splashing of his hand in the water, moving faster between her legs. She felt light-headed, heat in her stomach, a gentle, delectable ache. Then his phone rang again.

'Sorry, I'm going to just switch it …'

She breathed in deeply through her nose and opened her eyes slowly, trying hard not to lose the moment and the exquisite, promising sensations that came with it. But she lost it all the same, when she saw that he hadn't switched the phone off. He was pale, open-mouthed, listening to a message.

Just a foot away in one sense; a universe in another.

'They found a body in the park at Alexandra Palace,' he said quietly. 'It's Milda.'

Chapter Five

Rex had seen a film once, a dream sequence in some kooky American, made-for-tv affair, in which the character found himself in Heaven's waiting room. It was a no-frills reception area, with block-foam seating, a functional coffee table and a humming vending machine in the corner. The vending machine dispensed cans of Coke every time someone back in the land of the living said a prayer for the dead person's soul. Apart from that detail, the waiting room in the Hornsey Public Mortuary was exactly the same. Regardless of the fact that this low, Eighties-built compound housed the recently-dead of Haringey, its interior boasted pale carpets, pine-scented air freshener and copies of the council's free community magazine, entitled, ironically enough, *@Live! In Haringey*.

Eventually a wheezing, moist-looking Bond, wearing jeans with the dark grey jacket from his everyday suit, led him through a pale door at the back and down a sharply-sloping, brightly-lit corridor. No Coke machines here, just narrow doors off to left and right, two with slits for windows, two, more worryingly, without. Now the smells were of rubber and chemicals. One of the windowless doors was opened and there, with a certain sense of theatre, a rheumy-eyed, elderly man in surgical scrubs lifted a sheet which matched his outfit perfectly. Milda was under that sheet, on a slim trolley, her eyes closed.

He expected to feel overwhelmed. Perhaps he was. Perhaps that explained why he could only stare down at her, noting every detail, patiently and numbly. She looked less 'at peace' – or any of those other terms often used to describe the dead – more as if someone had made a model of her, a model that was all right, but not great. Her skin looked as if it was made of millions of tiny grains. A chunk of her hair was missing – smaller than what he gathered had been pulled from any of the other victims - and her scalp was still intact. He noticed the small, tea-coloured blemish on her left temple and remembered stroking it. Now the feelings came back. He nodded to Bond, who nodded to the man in the scrubs, who pulled the sheet back over. 'Sorry for your loss,' he commented, before he started to wheel the trolley away.

Rex turned to Bond. 'Mike – what happened to her? Did she just… die…?'

Bond put an arm on his. 'It all looks a bit iffy.'

The floor see-sawed beneath him. 'What do you mean iffy?'

'They haven't done the PM yet, but…' Bond seemed to be struggling with something. 'I'll see if he'll speak to you now.'

'If who will speak to me now?'

Bond didn't reply. More time in the waiting room followed. Rex bought a can from the vending machine, just because he found the money in his pocket, and flipped through the pages of @Live! In Haringey. It was like one half of a local newspaper. The touchy-feely, 'one big happy family' half, full of tales of Residents' Associations organising park clean-ups and African drumming workshops on various benighted estates. The other half, the headline half – Seven Sisters Man Stabbed In Eye – that wasn't in there. Nor was Beautiful Girl Found Dead In Park.

He had no socks on, and his feet felt wet in his shoes. As he'd rushed to get out, Diana had said all the right things, made the right gestures. But her eyes couldn't lie. And as he stepped away from the warmth of her flat into the sharp fresh night, they had asked one thing. Why? Why are you going? Because you ought to? Or because you need to?

He didn't know the answer. Milda was a lovely girl. She was

young and beautiful, with a bewitching voice and an enchanting, old-fashioned manner. But he'd understood some time before they parted that finding something lovely was not the same as loving. He had not been able to love her. The gulf between them, composed of age and language, background and so much more, had simply made it impossible and yet, however starkly he put that point to himself, he could not let go. He couldn't let go of Milda, just as he couldn't let go of Sybille. Perhaps, he sensed dimly, he couldn't let go of Milda because he couldn't let go of his wife. No wonder Diana had had enough.

Why did she have to be dead? Why had this man, this fragment of a person, cut the scalps of two girls, yanked the hair from the heads of two more and left all of them alive, but then taken the life of this one? Over the past few days he'd imagined terrible things happening to Milda. Usually, imagining something terrible happening meant it wouldn't happen. But now it had. Something worse than he'd imagined.

Bond returned and led him to an office where a tall Chinese-looking girl seemed to be packing the contents of her desk into a cardboard box. An odd occupation, Rex thought, at half ten in the evening. Behind the second desk, in a spotless, shapeless t-shirt, sat the elderly man who'd shown him Milda's body. He introduced himself as Dr Clore, the pathologist.

'We'll cut her open tomorrow,' he said, gruffly. 'But it's foul play.'

Bond seemed to stiffen in his chair next to Rex. The girl openly tutted, as she put a photo frame in her box. Dr Clore took an almost savage slug from his coffee mug.

'Bruising and redness around the neck,' he went on, fixing his gaze somewhere between his notepad and Rex's throat. 'Ocular petachiae. Involuntary evacuation, 1 and 2.' Now he looked, with bloodshot eyes, directly at Rex. 'Meaning she'd pissed and shat herself. Standard signs of death by strangulation.'

He broke off as the Chinese-looking girl pulled a white coat from the back of the door, added it to the pile in her box and started to leave. The box had once contained 48 disposable body suits.

'You're off, Bibigul?' The girl didn't reply. Rex wondered where the name came from. It didn't sound Chinese. Dr Clore made a stab at standing up, but sat down again. His chair creaked. 'Well, you know… wish you all the…'

The girl had slammed the door before he could finish. Clore shrugged and took another drink from his mug.

'We'll know more tomorrow. But you know – they found her half in and half out of a bush, didn't they, Mike? Someone must have stuck her in there.'

'The "kid" was called Milda Majauskas,' Rex said. 'She was an artist from Klaipeda.'

Dr Clore blinked slowly, like someone who was very tired, and rubbed his face. He had a stray lock of white hair, boyishly-long, and he shoved it back on the top of his head, before nodding, slowly, as if he'd got the point.

'There are no immediate signs of forced penetration,' he said, as if making a concession.

At that moment, the wide and shining head of DC Orchard appeared round the door. His eyes widened in surprise and disapproval when he saw that Rex was in there.

'Skip,' Orchard said, jerking his head back, to indicate the need for a private word.

'Girlfriend was she?' enquired Dr Clore, tugging at a desk drawer, when Bond had left.

'Sister,' Rex said. He didn't know why he said that. To get some reaction, he supposed. It didn't work. Clore continued to pull at the drawer. Bond returned.

'Better wrap it up there, gents,' he said, rubbing his hands.

Orchard came in behind him, fixing Rex with a cold glare.

'How long had she been there?' Rex asked the pathologist. 'Who found her? Can you at least tell me that?'

'Skip – this is seriously out of...'

'Are you saying this looks different to the other attacks?'

'Skip!'

Bond put up a hand to silence his younger colleague. 'I know. Come on, Rex.'

Rex found himself being gently, but forcefully propelled out of the room, first by one pair of hands, finally by two. He felt as if he was under arrest.

Had that been the case, of course, then officers Bond and Orchard would not have let Rex out of their sight. As it was, they couldn't wait to get rid of him.

'Should I try to get hold of her family or...'

'We'll do that,' Orchard replied, tersely, as he keyed something into his mobile.

'Best just go home,' Bond said, avoiding eye-contact.

'I'll get in touch with you tomorrow, shall I?' Rex asked, unable to disguise his frustration.

Orchard looked at him. 'We'll be getting in touch with you.'

Bond said nothing, but raised his eyebrows by way of faint apology for his colleague's manner. Rex left. He caught a bus by the old Pumping Station they were turning into flats. The Chinese-looking girl from the mortuary was on the bottom deck, arms clasped around her box and the white coat neatly folded up on top. She was in tears. Wrapped up in his own thoughts, Rex didn't speak to her.

* * *

As he walked up the stairs to the *Gazette's* office the next morning, he noticed he was less out of breath and that his limbs ached less than they had done in a long time. He'd gone home and straight to bed, sober, and as a result, physically, he now felt pretty well. The same could not be said for conditions inside his head.

When someone suffers a bereavement, the people around them behave in one of two, equally ineffectual ways. They either bombard the sufferer with sympathy, or they act as if nothing has happened. Within thirty seconds of appearing in the office, Rex had experienced both. Brenda, standing in a huge, mauve jumper at Terry's desk, shot him a look combining terror and concern, as if he were an apparition, but one nevertheless in need of a cup of tea. Terry, for his part, went on calmly handing Brenda black-and-white contact sheets as if nothing had happened. But that pretence became impossible to maintain once Susan appeared on the scene.

'Rex,' she said, in an urgent whisper, which had the effect of making the entire office fall silent. 'I want you to tell me…' Her mobile began to ring and, in an unprecedented gesture, she switched it off. 'I want you to tell us how we handle this.'

She was wearing a sort of ridged, off-white trouser-suit with a wide belt, giving her the look of a heroine in a Greek tragedy. Rex felt annoyed with her. Why did she have to make this into a scene? Why couldn't it just be what it was? Milda was dead.

'Body of Girl Found in Ally Pally Park,' he said, blandly. 'Police suspect foul play. I take it you want a murder enquiry to be a lead story?'

'It's definitely murder?'

'It's not *definitely* anything,' he said, suddenly angry. 'I only know what the pathologist thinks. They're doing the autopsy today, so in the meantime, we work on what we know and what the police will tell us, and we wait for the coroner's report to… Why am I telling you this, Susan? You know what we need to do.'

'And you intend to be the one doing it?'

'For god's sake, Susan. We went out for four months!' Rex exploded. 'I've been split up from Milda almost as long as we were together. Of course, I feel weird about it. Of course, I'm thinking this has got to be something to do with those other four girls. But I'm not going to take to my sick-bed over it. I'm going to get on with the story.'

Susan eyed him for a moment, then handed him a leaflet. It was another one from the BWAP. How Many More? – it asked.

> *How many more girls are going to end up dead in our parks? How many more attacks? How dangerous do our streets have to become before the government understands that uncapped emigration is turning parts of the city into 'No-Go' zones? If you feel like us, join us next Sunday at noon, at Duckett's Common. March to the Palace.*

Rex was simultaneously stuck by several thoughts. The BWAP had clearly abandoned the calm logic of Keith Powell's earlier pronouncements, in favour of tasteless, irrational scare-mongering. Who knew that Milda's death had anything to do with 'uncapped emigration', as the leaflet erroneously called it? Who could prove any such thing? Unless they knew something Rex and the police didn't.

But one thought dwarfed the rest in importance. The BWAP had had enough advance knowledge about Milda to churn out a leaflet about her death. *How had they known*?

'Are they actually allowed to put out shit like this?'

'If they are, it's a bloody cheek,' Terry cut in. 'Mate of mine got done just for having a gollywog on his van. Doing kiddies' parties, he said.

'I gather they are not allowed to put it out, no,' Susan said, gracing Terry with a brief, chilly look. 'They'll face prosecution. But they'll probably apologise and still benefit from the publicity. Anyway, do we starve them of oxygen or devote half the front page to calling them bottom-feeding scum? Discuss.'

She turned smartly on her heel and went back into her office, listening to the message on her mobile phone. Rex sat next to Ellie.

'Oxygen or bottom?' he asked. Ellie smiled, but looked troubled.

'The thing is. I mean – I've got absolutely nothing in common with those kinds of views at all. I mean, *at all* – I mean, my grand-dad's from India and... But in a weird way, it's like what they're saying... it's sort of happening... Or it could?'

'What makes you say that?'

'I went to Eski Dostlar like you asked me.' Ellie made a face. 'What makes men spend their time in places like that?'

'Their wives?'

'Yeah well, they didn't want to talk to me, but this one guy was in there making a delivery, and he said he'd have a coffee with me at the cake shop round the corner.'

'I bet he did.'

'He was totally old.' Ellie said, rolling her eyes. 'Like thirty-five or something. Anyway, he said it was all about cigarettes.'

'Cigarettes?'

'He said people buy cheap cigarettes round there, and they come in on the lorries from Turkey. But now, they've started coming in from Poland, and Lithuania.'

'So the fight at the social club was about the illegal cigarette trade?'

'He said that his uncle said it was about ten blokes – big blond boys from Poland or somewhere like that – came in and smashed everything up. And then this morning, I saw this, just over the road from my bus-stop.'

She showed him a picture on her mobile phone. It was a recently opened Polish supermarket, rather badly stocked on the lager front, if Rex remembered rightly. The door had been boarded up and a single Turkish word spray-painted across the right-hand window. *Sıçan*.

'Do we know when that appeared?'

'Overnight, the owner said.'

'Do we know what that word means?'

'Rats,' Ellie said, brushing a strand of hair behind her ear.

Someone else had used that word. The mini-gangster who'd attacked him outside Ausra's squat. He'd called the Eastern Europeans rats. Could someone have thought Milda was a rat, too? Something to be exterminated.

'That's not all,' Ellie said.

'Jesus. What time did you come in this morning?'

Ellie looked annoyed. Rex was making too many jokes. 'Sorry,' he added. 'I'm a bit – you know.'

'Why don't we go and get a decent coffee somewhere?'

Rex would end up waiting a long time for a decent coffee, because just at that moment D.C. Orchard swung in as if in the closing scenes of a low-rent police show. He'd cut his neck shaving, Rex noted.

'We'd like you to come down and answer a few questions,' he said, just loudly enough for everyone to hear.

'Is that the Royal 'we'?'

Orchard was so pleased with himself, he barely even frowned. 'Is it going to be a problem?' he asked.

'I doubt it's going to be a pleasure.'

* * *

'Autopsy found she was 15 weeks pregnant,' Orchard said,

sitting back and rubbing the back of his straw-blond head. From that relaxed position, he reached for his file and peered into it. 'Explaining the presence of an appointment card at the Chase Farm ante-natal unit in her handbag.'

'That's why you turfed me out of the mortuary last night was it? You found the card then and now the PM's settled it for you?'

'You told my colleague Detective Sergeant Bond that your relationship ended in the first week of July,' Orchard went on, ignoring Rex. 'In other words, a little over fourteen weeks ago.'

Rex took a deep breath, deeper than he ought to have done in the fuggy little interview room. It smelt of men and coffee.

Milda had been pregnant.

'Did you have intercourse in the final week of your relationship with Milda Majauskas?'

'Intercourse with Milda Majauskas, or intercourse in general?'

'Do you want this to get a whole lot more shit?'

'We'd... we sort of tailed off.' Rex could feel himself blushing. He stared into Orchard's close-set, blue eyes and longed to thump him. 'But we had a big row one night. And in the morning, we had, well, I guess I thought it was making-up stuff, but for her, it must have been a valedictory. That means goodbye,' he added. Orchard gazed at him with unchecked hate.

'So you had intercourse, and then you split up?'

'No. We had intercourse, and breakfast, then she went to her job, and I went to mine, and she met me in the park at lunchtime and we split up. Parks are full of people splitting up at lunchtime, have you noticed that?'

'And you never saw her again?'

'We met up twice. Once by accident. Once because we arranged to. Neither particularly successful. Then I saw her on the top of a bus one night. Start of September. I sent her a text. She didn't reply.'

'What did the text say?'

'It said: I just saw you on the 141 bus, hope you're okay.'

'Sorry?'

Rex sighed. Orchard had heard him perfectly well. It was a text-book ploy to get him riled or catch him out, or both. Journalists did it, too.

'I just saw you on the 141 bus, comma, hope you're okay,' he repeated.

'Why do you think she didn't reply?'

'Moved on, I guess.'

'You hadn't?'

'It took me a little longer.'

'Is that usual for you? You find it hard to deal with rejection?'

'I'd say that even though I invested less in the relationship than her, the age I'm at now made me feel it harder when it ended.'

'Did you know she was pregnant?'

'No.'

Orchard stared, disbelieving. Another interview trick. Rex remained silent.

'She'd never been pregnant before at any point?'

'Not while we were together. We used condoms.'

'So there's a chance she wasn't pregnant by you?'

'I suppose there is, but I'd be surprised. She wasn't like that. She was very... serious about relationships and that sort of thing. Anyway, I presume that pathologist has got some unpleasant way of telling whether it's mine. Whether it was mine,' he added.

Orchard appeared to nod. 'You say you split up in the park. But whose decision was it?'

'I did it, because she wanted me to.'

'Meaning?'

'If you don't know what I mean, Detective Constable Orchard, perhaps you need to get out and have intercourse yourself a bit more.'

Orchard didn't even blink. 'She told one of her friends she split up with you.'

'As she did. That's how some girls are, isn't it? They don't want to do it, so they make the bloke do it by behaving so badly that he has to split up with them. Which friend did you speak to? Aguta?'

'Behaviour including sleeping with someone else?' Orchard asked, ignoring his question.

'I doubt Milda was the kind who'd do that.'

'But some women might? To be honest, I think you're right. You can't trust them.' Orchard gave him what he clearly hoped was an encouraging, bloke-ish wink.

'Jesus. So you think I've been attacking all these girls, do you? Building up to the big one? How do you explain the smoke?'

'The what?'

'One of the girls said he smelled of smoke. I don't smoke.'

'Which wouldn't rule you out of killing Milda, and making it look like the work of someone else. Or being an occasional smoker as well as an occasional attacker of young women.'

'Is that what you think?'

'I'm not paid to think,' Orchard said, unaware of the irony. Rex was not in the best shape to appreciate it himself. 'For the moment, Rex, I'm just interested in your relationship with the deceased. Unless you've got something else you want to confess?'

'Something else? I've got nothing to fucking confess. My relationship with Milda had run its course. We kept bickering and falling out over silly things. All she needed to do was be a bit arsey over one last little thing and it would be the final straw.'

'What was it – the last little thing?'

'A sandwich,' Rex recalled, awkwardly, having forgotten that detail himself. 'I fetched us sandwiches, and the girl put black pepper on both, and Milda had a strop about it and said she'd have to go hungry, because she didn't want pepper.'

'A sandwich.' Orchard wrote it down. Rex suddenly remembered that a 'Cuban sandwich' had cropped up in his final, fateful argument with his wife. Was that meant to mean something? Or was it just another of life's senseless absurdities?

'Can I ask you something?' Orchard looked up. 'Did you find anything with her? I mean, like the glove that he left next to the third girl.'

Orchard glared at him. 'How do you know about that?'

'I overheard it in the cop shop,' Rex said. 'Don't worry. We won't print anything. I just want to know. Did he leave any more clues?'

Orchard shook his head.

'Anything useful on the glove?'

Orchard shook his head again. 'Can I fill you in on any other aspects of our work?' he added, sarcastically.

'Since you mention it – yes. How was she found?'

'Dog-walker.'

'May I know when?'

Orchard considered it. 'Early-to-mid evening.'

'So a body is found by a dog-walker early to mid evening. Long after all the press deadlines and local news bulletins. And yet the BWAP have got the resources to knock this out in time for the morning rush hour.'

He put the leaflet on the table. Orchard glanced at it, without touching it.

'A lot of people have complained about it. Do you wish to?'

'I'm not complaining. I'm asking you. How did they know?'

Orchard gazed at him. 'We imagine somebody tipped them off.'

'One of your officers?'

'However professionally you handle a crime scene like that, a large number of people is going to have access to certain details. The person who drives the ambulance to the mortuary. The person who finds the body. All sorts of individuals. We're looking into it.'

'We will be, too.'

'Given your connection to the victim, I'd be careful what you do and say, Mr Tracey, professionally and otherwise.'

'Are you threatening me?'

'You've had problems with paranoia, haven't you?'

'Piss off.'

'Tell me about your movements yesterday.'

It was the way Orchard said it. The school bully voice gone, replaced by a neutral gravity. Rex realised that this was a real enquiry. He was a suspect. He swallowed, and as he did so, he felt as if a finger of ice was passing from his throat down to the centre of his pelvis. He shivered, and told Detective Constable Orchard exactly what he needed to know.

'What about the day before?'

Rex did the same for Tuesday, concluding with the nuns and his wife and the parting from Diana at the bus-stop. Orchard, to his credit, made no comments on it, in voice or gesture. He asked Rex to provide a DNA sample.

While Orchard was sealing the sample of Rex's cheek cells in a plastic bag, a phone rang and rang unanswered. This made Rex remember what he'd been talking about when he was last in a police station. 'Have you asked Vadim where he was?'

'Vadim Kozyrev?' Orchard looked up. 'Gold-plated alibi. Repairing Oyster top-up machines at various locations on the Northern, Jubilee and District Lines.'

'So the fact that I've got photographs of him burning Milda's stuff at the back of her house... You're not interested in that?'

'It's not her house. Well – it's no one's house, is it? But the room she stayed in, in that squat, was Mr Kozyrev's. In the early part of the year, Miss Majauskas borrowed the room from him while he was working in Frankfurt. When he returned at the end of July, a relationship between them ensued.' Here, Orchard permitted himself a sardonic glance towards Rex. 'Subsequently, on Monday this week, in fact, Mr Kozyrev went back to Lithuania to sort out a family crisis, and his wife and son announced their intention to return with him, leaving Mr Kozyrev, as he put it, with no choice but to destroy the belongings of Miss Majauskas once he returned, for fear that his infidelity should be discovered.'

'Do you believe that?'

Orchard leaned back, ignoring his notebook to emphasise the power of his memory. 'A Captain Jonas Bendoraitis of the Lithuanian Police Foreign Liaison Office tells me that Mr Kozyrev's brother-in-law was recently shot in an argument over a stolen Honda Civic. In addition to which, a Mrs A. J. Kozyrevna and a Master P. P. Kozyrev were on Wednesday evening's flight RY3613 from Kaunas to Stansted along with Mr V. S. Kozyrev. So, yes, we do believe that, having little reason not to.'

* * *

It was a grey day now, proper London autumn, breezy with the threat of rain. He caught a bus back to the office, again sitting at the front on the top deck. In Milda's seat. There, so high up, so detached from the street below, he had a sudden, brief, powerful sense of being just one small soul on a teeming planet in an even vaster, empty universe. Below him, a young Chinese man was locking his bicycle to a lamp-post. Two headscarved girls went, laughing, into the newsagent's. All this could be going on, all these separate streams of experience, and just a few feet above, another one: a man whose former girlfriend had been found dead in the park. A man who already had one life on his conscience. A man suspected of murdering his former girlfriend and the child they had made, not to mention a string of other attacks on young women.

He felt numb, but as if he was thawing, too. As if there were strong feelings, and they might start to pour out, like the melting of the Alpine snows, and once they started, they would drag bridges and cars down. He got off, one stop before the bus joined up with Green Lanes. Green Lanes, once the route to the slaughter houses, he remembered. Milda and the life inside her had gone the way of the cattle.

Had it been at the hands of the man who'd attacked the other girls? If his behaviour was escalating, why progress from pulling out their hair to scalping them and then go back to the sort of half-hearted tug that must have removed part of Milda's fore-lock? Unless, perhaps, something else was taking over from the hair. Something that gave him more excitement – like squeezing their throats. Perhaps the bliss he got from that, from doing it until he extinguished life, cancelled out all his other techniques. The thought made Rex shiver.

In front of the bus a trim, neatly-dressed Hasidic man crossed the road. He was probably about Rex's age, encircled by small boys in skullcaps. There were little religious study-houses and schools tucked away all around South Tottenham, active only in the daytime, behind the dusty panes of neglected villas. And while some of the Hasidim in these parts looked otherworldly and wild, this man radiated confidence and dependability. He was a father to some of these boys in his charge, undoubtedly, probably also to some other children somewhere else, and it was a role he relished and took pride in. Rex had never looked upon fatherhood like that. Even with Sybille, it had been a future prospect he'd dreaded: bad news that was sure to come one day, like arthritis. Then, suddenly, he'd begun to see it differently. When it was too late.

It had been his baby inside Milda. He was certain of that. Certain, too, that Milda hadn't wanted him to know. How frightened must she have felt – here, in a squat, on a waitress' wage, with that life growing inside her? And how convinced must she have been that it was better not to tell the father of the child? It wasn't a child to him. Not at sixteen weeks. He could not mourn a number, a date. He could feel ashamed, though. And he did.

The junction of St Anne's Road and Green Lanes was directly opposite The Good Taste Café. As Rex drew near, he saw Keith Powell leaving with a newspaper under his arm. He was wearing a bright red fleece with the KP logo on it, and it made him look stockier than usual. Rex ran across the traffic and caught up with him just outside the *O' Pentadaktylos* Social Club. It was a relief to be able to turn some anger away from himself, if only for a moment.

'What was all that shit with the leaflets, Powell?'

An old West Indian lady with a shopping trolley backed into the doorway of the bank, as if sheltering from Rex's outburst. Powell looked startled and red-eyed. Had he been crying?

'I just – I just wanted to do something.'

'Like exploit a murder to whip up a bit of racial hatred?'

Powell zipped his red fleece as a breeze stirred polystyrene burger cartons and the cellophane ribbons from cigarette packets. 'I was fond of Milda, and I don't... our organisation doesn't want any more girls to get hurt.'

'Funny that your organisation was calling it a murder before anyone had even done a post-mortem. Funny you even knew about it, for that matter. You remind me of Neil Addison.'

Powell frowned, networks of fine lines appearing across his ruddy cheeks. 'Who's Neil Addison?'

'Neil Addison and I were trainees on the Lincoln Daily Dispatch together. He couldn't write for shite, but somehow, he got every story before me. Then one day, the editor noticed that ninety percent of his stories were about small fires and vandalism. Then he noticed that every time a skip got set alight or a phone box got smashed to bits, no one knew where Neil Addison was. You know what Neil Addison was doing?'

Powell pushed Rex out of his way. 'We're a local pressure group concerned about the effects of mass immigration. We had nothing to do with Milda's death, and the implication disgusts me.'

'Poor you,' Rex directed, at the back of Powell's head. But when he turned, he saw the owner of the Good Taste in the doorway, watching him, and shaking his head. When the old Greek went back inside his premises, Rex followed him.

'Don't blame Keith,' the owner said, over his shoulder, as he carefully repositioned a poster with a cheeseburger on it. 'He's okay.'

'Would you have thought he was okay in the Sixties, when you were trying to make a life over here?'

The man motioned to Rex to sit at a table in the window and joined him, sitting gingerly, as if in pain. 'There weren't so many people here then. Back then, if someone had a problem with foreigners, it was always because they didn't like foreigners. Now…' He waved a hand towards the streets, as two gowned Somali women floated by, their faces like burnished moons.

'Now it's just about how many people per cubic foot? Come on, I don't believe that.'

'Believe it,' said the man, picking something off a salt cellar. 'Keith, he is… he always talks nicely to the girls in here, he's got lots of Polish guys on his firm. He's not saying, you know, darkies go home and all that racialism stuff. He's just saying no more people. We're full now. Same as what I say when all the tables are taken.'

'So you're going to be marching with him?'

'I'll be here, cooking. We're doing a Marchers' Special, bacon roll and a coffee for two quid.'

'You were Milda's boss, and now you're doing the catering for the people who think she should never have been allowed in the country in the first place.'

The café owner stared at him through greasy spectacles. 'If she hadn't been here, she'd still be alive. He paused. 'And I wouldn't have the guilt.'

'What guilt?'

He took the glasses off and rubbed the bridge of his nose. 'I sacked her. I trusted that Czech girl's word. And you know what? When she saw that leaflet this morning, and she found out Milda was dead, she broke up. Told me the truth. She told Milda to take that box of stuff. Said it was okay. Did a lot of other things, too, and made it look like Milda's fault. I asked her – why? Why would you do that? She just goes like this.' He mimicked a moody, Slavonic shrug. 'I didn't like her. That's all she said. I didn't like her.' He shook his head and swore in Greek. 'I'm hiring boys in this place. Greek boys only, from now.' Two tears suddenly fell from underneath his glasses like little silver coins. Rex was shocked.

'You only sacked her,' he said, ineffectually.

'She was a nice kid.' He blew his nose and blinked at Rex. 'Different. You know. Interesting. Hard to get to know, kind of, but…'

'I know.'

He was right. She had been hard to know. Suddenly he understood something else. From the time of Milda's disappearance, Rex had been the subject of a range of anonymous threats and warnings.

And from the time of her death, these had abruptly stopped.

* * *

He knew he was going to have to give up the allotment soon. It wasn't just the amount of time Caroline needed him with her, nor the physical toll of travelling between Southgate and Palmers Green, nor even the fact that he seemed to forget such a lot. He was fit – he never smoked, never drank, walked or cycled whenever he could. If he ever ached, he took a hot bath with mustard powder. His foster-mother had taught him that.

No, he thought, as a woman's laugh rang out across the sheds and the seed beds, breaking through the dull roar from the North Circular. It wasn't because of that. The allotment was changing. He had sensed it starting to happen, round about the time they sold their house in Palmer's Green and moved to a smaller place in Southgate. Every time he journeyed the two miles back to tend his vegetables, one of the old, familiar faces was gone and another in its place. He hadn't had much to do with the old breed of gardeners, of course, only a nod in passing, a word or two about the weather, but he sensed they belonged to the same species.

The new ones were different. To start with, they were all so large. Even the women. Like some alien race, with loud, strong voices and bright clothes and broods of large, vigorous children with names that sounded made-up. They grew flowers and they drank wine and they came up to the allotments, all the way from places like Crouch End and Hornsey, in camper vans and on folding bicycles. They had barbecues, and they played music, and mostly they were English, like him, but they spoke in ways he could barely understand. Sometimes, in the summer evenings, the men played guitars and passed around pungent, home-made cigarettes. They kept their plots immaculate, they immersed themselves in all the necessary committee business and were never anything but polite. Even so, they were slowly, steadily pushing him off the land. It was just nature. He saw that. The strong pushed the weak to the edges, onto the poor soil where they withered and died. It was a process that had happened to him all his life. With one notable exception, when he had fought back.

He had been weeding today, bent to the clay-filled earth, throwing the green leaves into a Tesco carrier bag, when he smelt the smell of women's sweat. A pair of them strode by in immaculate wellingtons, hair in ponytails, bare arms glistening behind a creaking wheelbarrow. One spoke to the other one, in a low voice, and they both giggled. It wasn't about him. But he knew the tone of it. He knew the sort of thing they were talking about, and his face burned.

It was like a club, he thought, straightening for a moment and wiping his hands. Or two clubs. On one side was the club of everyone who could discuss it – discuss sex – like that woman with the wheelbarrow was doing. Of everyone who was able to have sex, was comfortable having sex, and announcing to the world at large that their sperm and their eggs were permitted to keep the human race going. On the other side, all those people whose broken, run-down genes had to be partitioned off, sent down cul-de-sacs to extinction and who, consequently, were neither having sex, nor comfortable having it, or seeing it, hearing it, all around them.

Because that was the other thing. The club of the people who were having sex wanted the club of the people who were not having sex to know. To know and to hurt with the knowledge. His foster-sisters had sent him on a fictitious errand. On a muggy, clammy afternoon, just like this one. The point of the errand had not been that he should fetch the shears, but that he should pass round the back of the rabbit-hutches and see June, the eldest of the sisters, with her navy blue knickers down around her ankles, panting as she held on tightly to the red-haired boy from the grocer's. An unfamiliar, foxy smell on the breeze that he found he liked and wanted more of. They had wanted him to see the thing that they all did, and that he never would. They had wanted him to hurt.

'You're a married man.' A doctor had said this to him in the hospital, shortly before Caroline's hysterectomy. Said it with a thin, mocking sort of smile, as if perhaps he knew that once, once only, in a shuddering, embarrassing squash of limbs and apologies, had this man and his wife managed what was, at that time, called 'relations'. He had felt nothing. She had cried out. But he'd been so horrified at the mess that he hadn't been able to ask her if she was hurt. They had lain there, in the lumpy bed at her sister's house in Rye, side by side, each pretending to be asleep, each knowing the other one wasn't.

That was their honeymoon. Not long after, Caroline said she was pregnant. He was unable to relate it to what they'd done in the bed at her sister's house. How could a baby result from that? It felt as if the post-war government, prone to capricious, mysterious announcements and restrictions, had merely issued another one: you will move to one of the new towns and you will have a baby.

So they had moved to Welwyn Garden City, to a new house on a new estate, but before they had even unpacked, Caroline went into the hospital. Some women's bodies rejected their babies. That's what they said. And he understood, of course, that any baby made half from his own flesh would have to undergo that fate. But before that, there were five months in hospital, five months of complete bed-rest, they said. By then he had started his own chiropody practice, and the hours were long. And at the hospital, they were very strict about visiting times, so the priest from the nearby Church started to go and see Caroline in his stead. He was a young, serious, good-looking man with red cheeks and thick hair. After the baby came still-born, the priest stopped visiting, and he even crossed the road a couple of times to avoid talking. And when Caroline came out, she said she didn't want to go to Church any more and she wanted to move away, back to London. Somewhere with more life in it, she said.

So they did. And Caroline's answers were so sharp whenever he mentioned Father Daniel – that was his name – that he assumed she must have had a falling-out with him. Perhaps the young Father had said that losing the baby was God's will, and she hadn't liked that, and turned her back on him and the religion, too. Years later, when there were strikes and power cuts, he'd been searching in a drawer for candlesticks and she'd shouted at him in the same sharp voice, that he was not to go in there, that there was nothing to see in there. So he hadn't. And when she was out at the shops, he looked again, but there were only cream-coloured napkins and wooden napkin rings and tablecloths. They never used them, any more than they ever discussed the things they wondered about.

'What you will do with those wades?'

He glanced up, alarmed. The strange girl was there, in her short, printed dress. She seemed so pale and fresh. She looked like she was naked, with a dress on top.

'Those...?' He followed her gaze to the carrier bag. 'The weeds! We call them weeds.'

She gave a laconic shrug. 'Strange language. You write one way. Say another.' She shrugged again, and put on a passable imitation of a posh, clipped English voice. 'What you will do with those wiiiiids?'

He found himself smiling, forgetting how much she scared him. 'I will give them to my rabbits.'

Her eyes widened. 'Why you do have rabbits? Do you eat them?'

'I don't eat them. I...' He could scarcely explain it to himself, let alone to this funny girl with the grey-blue eyes and the camera round her neck. He pointed at the camera as the skies darkened above. 'You're still taking photographs?' He was pleased that he remembered that. He'd had some worrying episodes lately – whole stretches of time lost. But he remembered the girl and her Russian camera.

She reached inside her handbag. It was canvas, with Indian writing. He couldn't understand why people did this kind of thing. On the bus, this morning, he'd sat next to a fat, ginger boy with Japanese letters all over his jacket. It didn't make sense.

'Do you want to see?' She was holding out a wad of photographs in a thin, semi-transparent envelope. Her smell – of shampoo and soap – cut through the soil and the exhaust fumes. She frightened him. But he wanted to see the photographs.

They sat on a bench and looked at them together. The woman who'd been pushing the wheelbarrow stared over from her plot. Other people walked past on their way out, and they looked as well. He found he did not care.

'SuperSnaps,' he said, glancing at the logo on the envelope.

'Close to my house,' she explained.

'They're everywhere,' he replied, sifting through the pile. 'And they're cheap. They're cheap because they're quick. But look – ' He pointed out a detail on one of the photographs, using a soil-rimmed fingernail. 'That's a pebble-dash wall, isn't it? A camera like yours could have captured every detail of the texture and the differences in the light. But it's flat. See?' She nodded, earnestly. 'It looks flat because they use the cheapest, least reactive paper. They don't care. Or this…' He moved to another photograph: a fresh, busy portrait of a dreadlocked girl standing in a children's playground.

'It's my friend, Birgita.'

'And you composed it beautifully,' he said. He watched as

she seemed to unfurl at the word. Had he ever said 'beautiful' to anyone before? 'The swing over here. The drunks on the bench on the other side. There's so much motion. And the way her hair seems to go through the ladder of the climbing frame. Very clever. But see.' He jabbed his nail at the top edge of the photograph. 'You go to all that trouble, and they chop off the end of her hair for you!'

She tutted as she took the photograph from him. Then she gazed at him, as if in wonder. 'How you do notice this things?'

He didn't know how to answer that. He didn't know why he noticed things. Sometimes, he wished he didn't. He was going to say that it was because he was invisible himself. But that wasn't right. At first, it was true, people tended not to notice him. But then they did. They noticed him, noticing them, and then they disliked him for it.

'If you want to take good photographs, you need to control the developing process yourself. That's why I've got a darkroom.'

Her eyes widened, as if he'd said he had a giraffe in his garage. And then she said, in a quiet, little voice, 'Could I use that darkroom please?'

He felt as if her words were tickling him. He liked that she just came out and said what she wanted, as well. He wished all people were like that.

'No, I'm sorry. My wife is sick and...' What else could he say? How could he be with her inside his darkroom? Stand behind this milky, fragile girl, with skin so thin he could almost hear the blood washing through her veins, and look at the hair, neatly plaited over the neck and the plastic zip against the soft white skin and smell the smell of her? He knew it could not be done. 'We're not set up for visitors at the moment.'

She looked so crestfallen that he nearly changed his mind. Then he had another idea. 'There's a Camera Club,' he said, reaching in his jacket pocket for a pencil stub and a scrap of paper. 'At Winchmore Hill library.' He wrote 'Camera Club, Winchmore Hill Library' on the piece of paper. 'They've got a darkroom for members.'

'You are a member?' she asked, taking the piece of paper.

He almost smiled at the idea of him joining a club. For him, the word 'club' meant only turned backs and whispers.

'It's supposed to be very good,' he replied. She gave a funny shrug, folded the piece of paper and put it carefully inside a compartment of her purse. There was a thoroughness about her that unnerved him. It was empty in the allotment now and the sky looked like a bruise. A breeze made his carrier bag of weeds crackle and he shivered slightly.

'Rain!' he said, pointing at the sky and gathering his things. He had an excuse to go now.

'It isn't raining,' she said, blankly.

And the rain didn't come. The skies got darker, and the air seemed to swell with foulness. Back in his yard, the rabbits sensed danger afoot, snatching the weeds from his hands, and retreating with each mouthful to the safety of the dark, urine-soaked corners of their hutch. He didn't know if it was the weather upsetting them, or the screams from the house.

A locum GP had come just before tea-time, because the Fentanyl patches weren't working anymore. Or rather, according to the GP, who was young and meaty-faced and hearty, the patches were still dealing with the 'baseline' pain, but because of the severe weight loss, and the way the larger tumour was now pressing on the nerves, Caroline was also experiencing regular 'breakthroughs'. It was an odd word, he thought, as if there was something triumphant about this chorus of suffering that began, every half an hour or so, with a low, horror-struck gasp, before twisting her helpless body into a screaming arc and flinging it down again like an unnecessary flap of skin. The GP gave her a lollipop to suck. A painkilling lollipop. She was meant to keep it in her mouth, and the extra drugs would get more quickly into her bloodstream that way.

From tea-time – it was ridiculous calling it that, of course, since neither of them ate or drank anything – to mid-way through EastEnders, the lollipop seemed to have done its job. She dozed while he pared the callous on her left big toe and filed the toenails. His mind drifted to the girl's feet: how slender and long her toes were, how exquisite the U shape between her hallux and the second phalange. Caroline's had been like that, once. No pretty girl, no beautiful woman ever thought she was going to die like this. Bedsores, incontinence pads, the stale smells at the far end of life's hallway. Yet somehow, none of it shocked him at all.

Later, he went out to see to the rabbits. The house was stuffy, but the yard was no fresher. The rain would not come. So he busied himself, feeding them more weeds, then changing their straw, and repairing the wire in the run. He never forgot the rabbits. By the time he'd swept the pile of sodden bedding and dung into a rubble sack, his wife was screaming again.

He washed his hands, and went to the refrigerator, where the Doctor had told him to store the rest of the lollipops. They needed to be kept cool or the drugs inside them would deteriorate. 'Lime, orange, cherry,' the Doctor had said, handing them over. 'Full set of traffic lights!' He couldn't decide what flavour to choose. The noise in the adjacent room told him that his wife wouldn't care. Why would anyone who'd reached the point of needing these things care? And in that case, why had they bothered giving them flavours at all?

As the next spasm came to an end, he switched off the tv, gently shifted her into a sitting position and unwrapped a cherry-flavoured lollipop.

'Remember what he said. Don't crunch it. Just let it dissolve.'

She barely had the energy to keep it in her mouth at first. She lay on the pillow, head to one side, staring at the wall. But after a few minutes, the combination of the sugar and the drugs gave her a jolt of artificial vigour. She tried to speak. He told her to save her energy. But she tried again, the lollipop clacking against her teeth and the stick in her mouth seeming to beckon like a finger.

So he took it out of her mouth and leant close. Her breath smelt of cherries as she said, in a whisper, 'Kill me.'

Chapter Six

Of course, Dr Diana Berne had eaten many a lazy Sunday breakfast with a man before. Sitting together cosily in your pyjamas, with smoked salmon and bagels and a pot of strong black coffee was, for her, the very symbol of being in a relationship, and the thing she most missed when single. Weekends in Paris, dinners with ocean views: she liked those things, but she knew she could live without them. Sunday mornings were what counted, just another part of life when you were experiencing them, an aching hole when you weren't.

This particular Sunday breakfast wasn't exactly filling the hole. Rex had gone to some effort, she could tell that: warm Turkish *pide* bread with black olives, salty *beyaz peynir* cheese and floral Cyprus honey. A classic Levantine breakfast, eaten on divan cushions in the narrow, low-ceilinged living room of his little house, with the French windows open onto the front yard. But instead of the Sunday papers, they were reading the autopsy report for Rex's murdered ex-girlfriend.

In a way she had asked for this. On Friday lunchtime, she'd seen the copy of the coroner's file on Dr Shah's desk – Milda had been one of his patients – and later that night, she'd rung and asked Rex if there was anything he wanted explaining. He'd accepted. Eagerly? Out of politeness? She couldn't tell. There'd been loud Middle Eastern pop in the background, but she'd suspected he was alone, at home, drinking. And she wasn't sure why she'd offered, except that she didn't want there to be a bad atmosphere between them. But what did she want?

Rex was angry today. He kept tearing his bread into little

shreds and rolling into pellets between his fingers. The cause of his anger was the autopsy report.

'Milda would never have taken heroin,' he said, for the fourth time since she'd arrived. 'I knew her. It's rubbish.'

The autopsy report said there were traces of injected heroin in Milda's bloodstream. Diana had been surprised to read that. But then, she hadn't known the girl. Not like Rex did. Or thought he did.

'She used to come here and complain about the lads at the squat smoking skunk. She thought drugs were stupid. And that guy… the pathologist… I swear there was something weird going on there.'

'You said yourself: Milda changed. You didn't see her for months. You don't know what might have happened.'

Rex shook his head. 'Never. She used to have a go at me for taking codeine. If she'd been some sort of smack-head, she'd have nicked them off me. They've mixed up the bodies. Seriously. That's what I think. '

'That can't happen,' Diana said, patiently. 'Unpleasant things come out when people die. I've seen it so many times. Abortions, missing kidneys. It's like opening someone's diary.'

Rex blinked, another piece of dismembered bread poised in between his fingers. Diana saw a slight trembling at the side of his mouth and worried she'd gone too far.

'I'm sorry,' she added, more softly. 'I know you still have feelings for her, and it must be hard, finding out drugs were involved.'

He shook his head again. 'I want to find out the truth. I don't have any feelings except that. And anyway, drugs weren't really involved, were they? Not as involved as some bloke covered in nitro-glycerine yanking out her hair and sticking his hands round her throat.'

'It was sodium nitrite.' She looked down at the report, and read aloud. 'Strangulation. Traces of sodium nitrite in and around the bruised area of the neck suggesting deposits left by the pollex and digits of a smaller-sized, male left hand. In other words, whoever strangled her had the stuff on his hand.'

'But what is it?'

'It's a chemical –'

'Yeah, I got that,' he said.

She sighed. His house, two streets east of the tube station, was clean and bright and sandalwood-smelling – nothing like the chaotic binge-site she'd envisaged. But its owner was hung-over, red-eyed, looking for someone to have a go at. She wondered if she should leave. 'It's a chemical used for all sorts of things.' She picked up the packet of beef salami from the table. 'It's in this, for a start. As a preservative. And it's in fertilisers.'

'So they're looking for a left-handed, salami-eating farmer with an interest in ladies' hair,' he said. His mouth smiled, after a fashion, but his eyes looked as unhappy as ever.

'I don't think you're being honest, Rex. I mean – she's been murdered, and she was pregnant with your child. You and her were together. There's no shame in admitting you feel something.'

'I felt something for her once. Maybe not enough. Certainly not enough to make a baby together. All right? I feel guilty about that, so… I feel I owe something to her. I owe her the truth. That's it.'

'Maybe you're never going to let yourself feel enough. For anyone. Because of your wife.' Diana felt her heart beating fast as she said it. But it was, she knew, exactly what she felt. And why she'd come here today. Because she hoped she might be wrong.

She thought he was going to be angry. But instead, he smiled, and bit into an olive. It was the first thing she'd seen pass his lips all morning. 'My problem,' he said, chewing slowly. 'Is that everyone I meet thinks that. They think it, but it isn't true.'

'Maybe you should ask yourself why they all think that.'

'I have.'

'And what did you decide?'

'They're all a bit stupid, basically.'

'Thanks.' She felt her eyes filling up. She was angry with herself for it. Even angrier than she was with Rex. The rude, self-pitying prick. She grabbed her handbag from the floor, concentrating internally, on the next few moves. Tissues. Lip gloss. Leave.

But before she could do that, there was a sharp rap at the front door, startling them both. Rex started to get to his feet. Diana nearly volunteered to go herself, but she quashed the impulse. Why did she always do that? Become the willing doormat?

She took advantage of his departure to blow her nose. She heard high, urgent, female voices at the door and wondered if it was a group of gypsies. In her part of town, troupes of ankle-skirted, fierce-looking girls knocked on doors on Sunday mornings, proffering stray copies of the Big Issue and dishcloths.

But it wasn't gypsies. Rex came back inside, with two women and a little girl. The little girl, who seemed familiar to Diana, was dressed as a pirate. The women smelt of cigarettes.

'This is Milda's friend Aguta,' Rex said. 'And Milda's sister, Niela.' Diana couldn't help looking with curiosity at the second woman, the sister of the girl Rex had loved. She was slight, dressed in a cheap red and grey tracksuit with bleached hair and big, hooped earrings. Her face looked hard, but her eyes were pretty. Milda had had those eyes, too: she'd seen them in the newspaper photos.

'Why's Doctor Berne here, Mum?' the pirate girl asked. The child must be one of her patients, although Diana couldn't remember her name, and Rex wasn't bothering to introduce her. 'Is he ill?'

'No he isn't,' her mother – who had plum-tinted hair and a blue leather biker jacket – replied. 'They're… friends.' She pursed her lips. The tracksuited woman glared.

'I was just going,' Diana said, with a tight smile.

'Were you?' Rex asked.

She didn't reply, just walked out through the French windows, crunching across the gravel. Rex caught up with her by the gate.

'Diana. I wasn't calling you stupid. I mean… I didn't mean to call you stupid. Sorry.'

She nodded. 'I've got to go anyway. Really. I want to get home before that march kicks off.'

Rex clutched the top of his head. 'Fuck! The march! I'm supposed to be covering it!'

His distress was so comical that she couldn't help smiling. This sweetened the mood between them, making the moment of parting harder to arrange. There was an awkward pause. She decided to kiss him on the cheek at the precise moment – so it seemed – that he decided that he wasn't going to kiss her on the cheek. She stumbled, there were a few, faltering words of good-bye and she walked back towards her bus-stop, cursing herself.

She reached the end of Rex's lane, where three roads met around an unkempt square of grassland. In the middle of the square, not drinking super-strength lager, not letting his bull mastiff do a shit, not kicking a ball or engaged in any of the other activities that traditionally went on there, there was a young man in a grey hooded top. She assumed it was a young man, anyway, from the height and build, but the face was obscured by the hood.

He was doing exactly what he'd been doing when Diana had walked past an hour or two before. Standing with his hands in his pockets. Staring at her.

She scanned the street ahead, reminding herself to stay calm.

Bad things had been going on up at Alexandra Palace. But this was a residential street, a full half mile away.

A very quiet residential street, though. Few people were up at this time on a Sunday. At the far end was a parade of shops: two grocers, an Afro barbers and a cab-rank. Normally there were people milling about, but now there was no one. She quickened her pace, feeling the man's gaze on her, and not daring to check if she was right. Surely the grocers would be open. She only had to get inside one of them to be safe.

She walked past a low, Art-Deco block of flats with abandoned mattresses and car parts scattered on its lawns. She crossed a road and turned around. The man had vanished.

She looked again. No. He hadn't vanished. He was following her. There was no one else around, and he was following her.

She sped up, feeling a numbness in her arms. She'd had enough. First the burglary. Now this. Being made to feel afraid, by some creep on a bright, cold Sunday morning. Why the hell should she?

She stopped and turned around, planting herself in the middle of the pavement, chin up, hands balled into fists. Fuck you, she thought, preparing to face off the shuffling, grey-clad figure coming towards her.

But there was no one coming towards her. She looked round in alarm. There was a skinny lad walking on the opposite side of the road. Grey top with the hood down, huge, grey tracksuit bottoms. Was that him?

She stared at him. Quite a handsome, fine-featured boy of nineteen or twenty. Golden curls and milky skin, with just a few remaining traces of acne on the cheekbones. The sort of boy girls fancy when they're twelve. Non-threatening. It couldn't have been him. But who else could it have been?

The boy seemed to redden under her gaze. He lowered his

eyes as he loped past her, as if she'd been the one spooking him. As, perhaps, she was.

Diana watched him until he'd crossed the bus station concourse and disappeared. She let out a long sigh, feeling the distant click of her heartbeat in her throat. She didn't have a clue what had just happened there – if it had been sheer paranoia, or an abandoned mugging, or worse. She knew something, though. She'd had enough. Even before this, and the burglary, she'd had enough of feeling scared and self-conscious all the time in the streets. Trying to ignore the posturing and the tooth-sucking. Pretending to herself that her puny armoury of anti-depressants and blood-thinners was making any difference to the misery of the place. Rex might bang on about the beauty of it all and the energy and the promise. He was welcome to it.

She had a plan, a plan half-ready for quite a few months now. It was time to put it into action.

* * *

After Diana left, Rex went back inside his house and offered coffee to his visitors. They examined the tin, saw it was Turkish coffee, and declined – exactly the sort of thing Milda would have done. Aguta picked up the autopsy report, and started talking, excitedly, to Milda's sister. Everything in Lithuanian sounded like an argument. When Milda had been round, talking on Skype to her Mum, he'd feel certain from the pitch of the voices and the sheer speed of the words that the pair were at the inception point of some 20-year-long blood feud. But they had just been swapping gossip. Something they would never do again.

'She agrees about the heroin,' Aguta reported. 'She says it's a joke.'

'I just said it to the doctor – she never touched drugs. She was totally against them.' Aguta and Niela exchanged a look. Rex noticed it. 'What?'

Aguta spoke a few sharp words of her native language to her daughter, who sighed as only a child can, and went into the garden. When she next spoke, it was in a low voice.

'Actually, Rex, sorry. You know, when we were younger, we tried some things. All of us. But I mean – just things you smoke.'

Niela let loose another burst of verbal machine-gun fire. Aguta explained. 'Milda hated needles. At the school, when they gave us all the tuberculosis injection, she ran away.'

Niela added more, running the zip up and down her track-suit top as she talked. Aguta translated. 'Forty kilometres she ran away. To the granny's village. It's because when she was a little kid, she had to go a lot of times to hospital. Lots of tests and er –' She mimed sticking a needle into Rex's arm.

'Jabs?'

'Yes, jabs.'

'Why did she have to go to hospital?'

Aguta shrugged, her electric blue biker jacket creaking. 'Due to some problem with the head.'

He frowned. Hadn't someone else mentioned her being ill? 'What problem? Like headaches?'

There was another short exchange between the two women.

'She doesn't remember. She was too young. But she's sure about the needles.'

Rex sat down on the corner of a chair. He couldn't remember who had mentioned Milda feeling ill before. Across the little hall, in the kitchen, the coffee pot bubbled away, untended. What Diana had said was right. You could think you knew someone, and later find out you'd been very wrong. But someone who ran away from needles didn't sound like someone who willingly injected drugs.

'We need to tell the police. It doesn't add up. And it doesn't sound like any of the other attacks that have been happening either.'

Niela reeled off a great long speech, in which Rex recognised the word 'Klaipeda', and something that sounded like 'carpe'. Carpe diem? They all had cause to think of that one.

Aguta glanced outside at her daughter, then interpreted in a voice so low Rex had to strain to make out the words. 'She is worried, if she makes a fuss, they won't let her take the body back home. That's why she didn't mention about moving house. It's not going to bring her back, is it?'

'What do you mean – moving house?'

'Milda sent her an email. A few weeks ago.' She checked a detail with Niela. 'On the 13th of September. She said she was going to move in for a while with a little friend.'

'A little friend?'

'That's the words she used. Move in for a while, with a little friend carpe.'

'Wait a minute. Carpe? That's the name of the little friend?'

Niela nodded. Aguta shrugged. 'It's not carpe, Mama.' Dovila said defiantly from the doorway. 'She's saying the letters like Lithuanian letters. It's Kay. Pee.'

K.P. Keith Powell. Two weeks before she was found dead, Milda had moved in with Keith Powell. Did that explain the strange array of herbal teas and the feminine touches in the bathroom? Had she been living there at the time when Rex visited to interview Powell? He felt his heart fluttering. 'Did she keep the email?' He didn't wait for Aguta to translate, he just grabbed Niela by the hands and spoke directly to her. 'We need to tell the police. It could be very important. Please.'

He looked into Niela's grey blue eyes. For a moment or two, they were Milda's. A colour like the Baltic Sea. She pulled her hands away.

'We want –' she spoke falteringly, in a surprisingly deep voice. 'To bring her to home.'

'So why did you come here today?'

Niela spoke again to Aguta, looking directly at him. Aguta translated. 'Because Milda said she loved you. Niela wanted to see him. The last man her sister loved.'

'But –' She'd never told him she loved him. It hurt him to hear it. He swallowed. 'Don't you care that the person who hurt Milda might never be caught? You want him to live free when she's dead?'

Niela looked unsure. Rex turned to Aguta. 'I know who K.P. is. It has to be Keith Powell. The man who's organised the march today. He knew Milda. He told me they were friends.'

'And that means he killed her? Rex, you heard her. She just wants to bring Milda home.'

'It means there's a detail they haven't looked into. And they need to. Please.'

Aguta relayed this to Niela, who was silent for a long time, chewing her lip. Finally, she said she would go with him to the police station. Tomorrow. Aguta would bring her to the newspaper office, then she would go with him.

'Maybe you could come along too,' Rex said, to Aguta. 'For moral support.'

She didn't answer, merely frowned slightly. Rex supposed it wasn't so easy for her to get time off work. In any case, he guessed, when it came to taking statements, Bond and Orchard would be able to rustle up an interpreter.

He walked them to the bus station – they were taking Dovila to a birthday party in the café in Finsbury Park. All down the road, across the over-grown green in the middle, and along the low parade of afro-barbers and takeaways, he kept up a playful interrogation of ten-year-old Dovila, who had wanted to dress up as a soldier, but lacked the necessary items of costume. It was easier to talk children's parties than to think about what Niela had told him.

The streets were swelling with people. All around the bus station, and coming in twos and threes up the steps from the tube station were men. They were dressed as if they were on their way to a football match: in clean, pressed, casual clothes, amongst which, on baseball caps and shirts, the cross of St George seemed to be a prominent theme. Some carried cans of lager. But unlike a football crowd, they were quiet. They streamed, in orderly, serious fashion, down to the crossroads, and over Green Lanes to Duckett's Common, which was ringed with orange-coated stewards and policemen. Inside the cordon, in the little park, were gathered more men like them. The local population – the Kurds at the cab-stand, the Bangladeshi lads who sold fruit from trestle-tables in front of the station, the Polish girls who ran the florists – had either disappeared, or else were watching the proceedings from behind closed doors. It was an eerie scene, full of movement, yet silent. Rex fancied public executions might have been a little like this.

Rex and his little party crossed onto the concourse of the bus-station just as a 253 was disgorging a further load of marchers. They had the collars of their shirts pulled up. A couple wore scarves around the lower part of their faces, as if deliberately hiding their identity. Rex suddenly saw that they were surrounded on all sides by strong, stony-faced, staring men. No one did or said anything: the men just filed past, the mood tense and hostile. One of them banged into Niela with his shoulder and carried on walking, not even turning around.

Shaken, they made their way to the bus, and Rex said good-bye. He wished Dovila a good time at the party. To Niela, he said one of the twenty-odd words of Lithuanian he could remember. *Rytoj*. Tomorrow. But she just sat on her seat, next to Dovila, staring ahead, seemingly lost in fresh grief over her sister. He hoped she wouldn't be too full of sorrow to talk to the police tomorrow. They needed to hear what she'd said, directly from her.

He considered nipping across the street to the Mini-Mart and buying a cold Okocim. Just one, enough to take the edge off his hangover. He caught sight of himself in the window of a parked taxi. As ever, he was dressed in a crumpled suit. If he took the jacket off, rolled up his sleeves, clutched a can of lager, he could look like one of the marchers, and that would be less conspicuous, easier to get the inside track. But he couldn't bear the idea of it.

He looked at his watch. There were twenty minutes before the march was due to leave the common, and make its way up Turnpike Lane, under the railway, past the old Pumping Station and the Saxon church tower to the Palace where Milda had been murdered. He bought his can and took it home to change.

Less than ten minutes later, he was back again, half a litre of Poland's strongest lager sloshing around his empty stomach. He felt better and worse in equal measure: stronger, healthier, but less in control. Perhaps it was not a good way to be going into that paddock of testosterone. He thought about buying another can. What stopped him was the singing.

The silence of the crowd had given way to something halfway between a melody and a chant. The tune, incongruously, was that old Junior School favourite, 'Sing Hosanna'. But the words came from a place that had nothing to do with hosannas, or Junior Schools.

'*No surrender, no surrender, no surrender to the Ta-li-ban.*

No surrender, no surrender, no surrender TO. THE. WOGS.'

The singers, a knot of about a dozen men, were some distance away from the main gathering on the common, but there was a steady stream away from the main body of the marchers to join them. They were young and drunk. They didn't seem to notice the stern-looking Bangladeshi elder who walked past them and up the High Street with a shopping trolley. Nor did he seem to notice them. Rex wished Terry were there to take a photograph: of the two groups, the bald and the bearded, sharing the pavement and so indifferent to one another.

Now that he thought of it, Terry probably was somewhere in the vicinity. Hadn't they arranged to meet?

'I'm stuck in a queue between the third and the fourth floor of the Morrison's car park,' Terry informed him, tersely, when Rex finally reached him on the mobile. 'I had to do the shopping.' He said the word with distaste, making Rex wonder if domestic life in the gated mews was beginning to lose its charm. 'You go and stand round the back, I'll chuck me cameras down and you can do the photos.'

Rex hung up and crossed the road to get a closer look at the choral society. He was held up, mid-way across by one of the cruising Romeos who used the High Street to show off their sound-systems. This seemed to be an exclusively Turkish pastime, indulged in mainly by young men with good jobs who dressed up as gangsters at the weekend. All the real gangsters were up in Hertfordshire, of course, sitting in their hot-tubs, counting their money. Down on the mean streets, meanwhile, off-duty insurance executives and estate agents played booming Turkish pop from their open-top cars, crawled up and down in the weekend traffic between the Mothercare and the Morrison's, and, occasionally, got a girl to look in their direction.

Marooned at the traffic lights, this particular Romeo increased the volume on his stereo to drown out the singers. When this attracted no attention, he tried turning it repeatedly down and up again. And when that failed, he revved the engine angrily. It cut out, ignominiously, just as the lights changed, prompting the delivery van behind to beep its horn in derision. A classic

Tottenham moment. Attention-seeking, mockery and aggro – those words could have been on the little civic crest over the library.

By the time Rex made it across to the singers, they had been joined by a number of BWAP stewards in bright orange tabards, who were trying to silence them.

'If you want to sing that, go home. It's not what we're about.' The speaker was none other than Keith Powell, kitted out with a flashy earphone and mouthpiece set. Beneath the orange vest he was wearing a dark suit, giving him the look of an architect visiting a construction site. And that was what Powell was. An architect of destruction. A builder of walls.

'So what exactly are you about, Keith?' Heads turned in Rex's direction. Rex was, himself, a little shocked that he'd spoken.

'Rex – can we have this out some other time?' A frown creased Powell's chubby, good-natured face.

'Why? You keep saying you want an open debate. Tell me: what's the difference between this lot here, and that lot over the road? Oh, I get it. This lot hate Muslims. And that lot hate Eastern Europeans..'

He was in the crush now, jabbing his finger at Powell. Smells of beer and aftershave and sweat were all around. Rex felt a familiar buzzing at the top of his skull.

'It's a peaceful march and we're not here to antagonise…'

'You fucking hypocrite!'

As he hurled himself at Powell, Rex felt as if he was in a dream, launching himself off a cliff. For a moment it felt strangely liberating, until his arms were jerked back, an expertly-placed knee jabbed his own legs to the ground and he found himself kissing the pavement.

'You want to be arrested?'

D.C. Orchard was on top of him, speaking, almost lovingly,

into his ear. Rex bucked and kicked, but he was pinned by an expert, someone who had studied the practice of causing maximum discomfort with minimum effort. Rex swore into the paving stones.

'Let him up!'

Rex felt the pressure ease for a moment, then he was hauled to his feet. Mike Bond was there, now, grey-faced and wet-lipped.

'Move on, Rex.'

'Ask him,' Rex shouted. 'Ask that bastard about Milda. Ask him why she was living in his house. Go on!'

Bond looked at Powell.

'I don't know what he's on about. He smells of booze.'

'KP!' Rex spat. 'My little friend KP!'

'Rex, you need to go home now, or I'm going to arrest you.' Bond was out of breath, but he spoke calmly and firmly, as if to an excitable dog. There were people all around, uniformed and otherwise, videoing everything.

'You're in it, too, aren't you?' Rex said quietly, looking Bond in the eye. 'All that stuff you told me in the police station – immigration upsetting the delicate ecosystem. Very clever. Whatever's going on here, you're part of it. Aren't you?'

Bond turned and walked away without answering. One of Powell's minions put a hand on Rex. He responded by giving the man a huge shove. The steward toppled back into one of the masked 'No Surrender' crew, and within seconds the two factions were trading punches. Those who weren't fighting struck up a chorus of 'The Long and the Short and the Tall'. Powell gazed at the scene in horror.

'Stop all this fucking about!' he shouted. 'This is about the future!'

'None of you've got any future,' Rex said, trying to swipe away a video camera that was being pointed right in his face.

There were several blasts on a whistle, and those of the stewards not actively involved in the punch-up began to gesture up the street. People began moving. Incredibly, the march was still going ahead.

'Quite a party atmosphere,' said Terry, who appeared at his elbow with cameras slung across his football shirt like Christmas tree baubles. The crowd was moving west. The fighters dusted themselves off, and the singing was replaced by whistles and klaxons.

'Why does the devil have to have all the best tunes?' Rex muttered. 'That's why the Nazis did so well.'

He and Terry joined the march, filing slowly past a mysterious, barely-used Somali internet café and a shop specialising in parts for hookah pipes. Suddenly D.C. Orchard emerged from the doorway of the Gujarati Sweet Centre, swooping down on them like a vengeful prefect.

'You were informed that you would be arrested if you didn't leave the area,' he hissed, flecking Rex's ear with spittle.

Before Rex could answer, an explosion ripped through the air. It was less like a bang, more a sudden blow. People began to run back the way they'd come, terror in their eyes. Wisps of cordite rose amongst the panicking stewards and the police. Rex's ears were humming from the initial blast, but he felt certain he heard more bangs, a succession of them, one after another after another, like firecrackers.

They had taken cover in the doorway of a sweet shop. The owner, a tall thin businesswoman in a sunset-coloured sari, rushed back and forth with a horror-struck face, trying to keep people out of her premises. Everyone seemed to be talking at, about and over him, in a multitude of tongues. Everything was confusion: the running of the feet outside, the howl of sirens and the ringing in his ears. More people piled in, ignoring the hoarse cries of the owner, shuffling in alongside sweets the colour of rainbows in gold and silver cases, bringing in smells of burning plastic that mingled with the coconut and the rosewater. Everyone was talking, and in their panicked chatter there was just one word he recognized: *Esou che bomb. Bomb hatou. Bomb nathe. Bomb.*

He turned to Terry. 'It was a bomb!' But the person next to him wasn't Terry. It was one of the marchers – a crew-cut boy in a pink polo shirt, breathing heavily. Where the hell was Terry?

* * *

Rex's hearing still felt strange as he left the house for work the next morning. There was a quietness in the street, as if everything had been wrapped in a thin shroud, and the people he passed seemed to be moving more slowly than usual, dazed and hesitant. Outside LesDrive! Driving School, all the identical black instruction vehicles were parked up on the kerb. Get In Mini Mart had, for the first time in living memory, closed its doors. There was an air of collective disbelief at what had happened. This was a hard place. Drug gangs took pot shots at each other. Kids sliced each other up, for straying over postcode boundaries. At a more basic level, people often got themselves thumped or shoved to the floor for looking at someone the wrong way or dithering too long at the cash-point. But a bomb was different.

Not here. Come on. Not here.

He'd been at the newspaper until three in the morning, on the phone to contacts in the emergency services, friendly charge nurses at the hospitals. He went back and forth between the office and the site of the blast – a side road of rented houses, with a single empty shop on the junction with Turnpike Lane. Without access to Mike Bond, Rex's news-gathering abilities were severely tested. He could say that a large blast had occurred at the empty shop, and that seven people were in hospital with minor injuries. Beyond that, not a lot. No one would confirm that it had been a bomb.

That hadn't stopped him from writing all night. At about midnight, a woman's voice, tipsy and perhaps a little unhinged, had floated up from the street below. She kept saying the same thing over and over again to her companion, her tone shocked and disbelieving. *Not here. Come on. Not here.*

It had summed up how Rex felt, and spurred him on. He wrote down everything. About the disappearance of Milda. The fire at the nearby squat. The fear of needles and the 'little friend'. Powell and the vanishing police record. The only things he omitted were the threats to himself. Not because he doubted them: every time he thought about them, he became more convinced of some concerted campaign to unsettle him. And more troubled by the idea that Milda herself might have been behind them. Why, he didn't know. But people were odd. Sometimes they became vengeful at the end of relationships. They went on the attack when they were afraid. And she must have been afraid.

When he was finished, he emailed the document to Susan, placed a hard copy on her desk and went home to sleep.

Now Brenda was at her desk again, in a sparkly leopard-print top, eating a slice of sponge cake. There were further slices of the cake in a round Tupperware on top of the reception counter, but she did not offer one to him. Instead she nodded stonily in his direction, as she did to the window-cleaner she suspected of stealing and the plumber who gave her the creeps. No doubt Mike Bond had gone home and told his wife everything. At various points during the night, Rex had remembered his words to the old policeman and his hurt, disgusted expression, and suspected he'd gone too far. But only suspected.

'There's someone waiting for you upstairs,' said Brenda.

'Who?'

At that moment, Lawrence Berne, Laureate of the Ladders, came in, and Brenda turned the full force of her charm on him. 'Where have you been, you naughty man? Come and have a slice of my sponge!' She was upping the pleasantry, Rex knew, to underline the point that he was out in the wilderness. He went morosely up the stairs, trying and failing to think of a visitor he would actually like to see in his office right now.

'Wanted to ask a few questions about what you saw yesterday,' Orchard said. He sat in Rex's chair, with his legs indecently wide. He wore a tight, pale brown suit, and long, thin Chelsea boots; the effect was to make his head seem even wider, like a round Dutch cheese balanced upon a garden cane.

'You mean the explosion? I saw what you saw. A big bang. Smoke. People running. It smelt a bit like fireworks at first. I thought that. Some of the other people I spoke to said that too.'

'It was fireworks,' Orchard said, sitting upright. 'A double chest freezer, inside the empty shop, filled with Chinese rockets.'

'Frozen fireworks?'

'The chest freezer wasn't working.'

'What set them off?'

Orchard lowered his voice. 'Did you see anyone taking out a mobile phone in the moments before the blast? Anyone doing anything with a laptop or an organiser?'

'You think they were detonated?'

Orchard tried to look inscrutable.

'So you're ruling out accidental causes?'

Another constipated look. Rex couldn't hold back a smile. 'You must be in trouble if you're asking me.'

'We're asking everyone who was there. And we want your editor to put a plea for information in this week's paper.'

'You're making a lot of effort over seven people with cuts and burns and a derelict shop.'

'Meaning?' Orchard scratched his knee.

'Meaning it's more effort than you've made over Milda Majauskas.'

Orchard stood up and adjusted his jacket collar. He pointed to Susan's door. 'Shall I talk to the boss myself?'

'She had a phobia about needles,' Rex shouted at Orchard's back. 'And three weeks ago, she wrote an email to her sister, saying she was moving in with someone else. Someone called K.P.'

Orchard turned around. 'How do you know this?'

'The sister told me. We were planning to come in later this morning to make a statement.'

Orchard raised his eyebrows. 'I drove Niela to Stansted this morning and she didn't mention a word of it.' He looked at his watch. 'As we speak, she's on a flight back home with the body.'

Rex tried to take this in. Why? Why leave, when she had such important information about the killer, information she'd only yesterday wanted him to know? What had made her change her mind? Or who? As he looked at Orchard, standing there like an Edam advert, he thought he knew.

'Are you sure she didn't mention it?'

Orchard glared at him. 'Positive. But now you have, we'll look into it. Along with all the other ongoing aspects of the case.'

He turned away and after a brief knock on Susan's door, entered her office.

'Rex. Look man. Look!' It was Terry. With trembling hands, the photographer pulled some blow-ups out of the envelope and laid them on the desk. The top one was very nearly a work of art. A blast, emerging like a crown of fire from the roof of the shop, a plume of black smoke curling out alongside it and twisting along the pavement and in the midst, seeming to leap through the very centre of the carnage like a gazelle in flight, a very fat skinhead in a lime-green Fred Perry top.

'So that's where you disappeared to,' Rex said, leafing through the photos, which were all of similar quality. Terry had found his war-zone at last. 'You could flog that one to the *Independent*,' he added.

'I have, man!' Terry beamed. 'And the *New York Times*, and the *Sydney Morning Star* and the *Frankfurter Allgemeine*. I sent the top three off to an agency and it's gone global. Half an hour's work and I've practically paid off me mortgage!'

Terry pulled a photo from the bottom of the pile.

'You're looking like a very ugly action hero in this one,' he quipped. He'd snapped one of Rex, moments after the blast, running for cover. 'Well, maybe a very ugly action hero's even uglier stunt double...'

Rex didn't acknowledge the joke. He stared at the photograph.

Just behind and to the left of Rex was a tall, thin figure in a grey hooded top. It was thrusting an object towards Rex. A slim, metallic object. A knife.

'Can you enlarge that?' Rex asked.

'It's a blur. All ye'll get is a bigger blur.' He peered at the photo and chuckled. 'Looks like he's trying to shank you.' His grin vanished. 'You think he *was* trying to shank you?'

Rex didn't have a chance to reply. The editor's door swung open, and Detective Constable Orchard left Susan's office, treating the room to a cold, mackerel-eyed glare before stepping out onto the landing. Susan called Rex in.

'I'm spiking it, Rex.'

'Did Orchard tell you to do that?'

Susan shut her eyes and rubbed a finger around her hairline. It was her way of composing herself. 'What you've just said confirms the worry I had as I read your piece. I think you're imagining things.'

'Thanks.'

'I don't mean it as an insult. You're a friend, and a colleague, and an employee. But my responsibility to you in the latter category compels me to step in. This piece…'

She pulled the hard copy into view from a pile of papers and mock-ups, tapping it with a long, red fingernail.

'This piece illustrates perfectly what a doctor once told me about psychosis. He said: the reasoning's all sane and logical. It's just built on a proposition that's completely barking mad. That's exactly what this is, Rex. It's well written. Coherent. It's a little flabby in the middle, but for the most part, it's as punchy as everything you write is. But it all rests on an idea that's round the twist. This isn't Chile in the 1980's.'

'Not here. Come on. Not here.' Rex repeated. 'A woman kept saying that outside the window last night. Because she'd seen a bomb go off in the middle of a fascist rally. Here. That happened. Why is it such a leap to imagine that Milda's death, and all these girls being attacked, are all part of it, and so is Keith Powell, and so are the police, and so are a bunch of things that just don't add up?'

'People can imagine whatever they like. We're in the business of printing facts.'

In answer, Rex put Terry's photo on the desk. 'Here's one for you.'

She frowned. 'What am I supposed to be looking at?'

'The kid in the hoody. What's he doing?'

'Running?'

'What's in his hand?'

She peered again. 'His phone.'

'It's a fucking knife! Last week, someone not a little similar to this twat,' Rex tapped the photograph, 'tried to run me over. Then they left a wheelchair outside my house. And sent me a pair of handcuffs. Now it seems they're trying to stab me.'

'Did you get a look at his face?'

'I didn't even know he was there until Terry showed me this photo!'

She blinked in surprise. 'So you don't actually know it was a knife?'

Rex hesitated. 'I know it looks like one. And I can see it's the same person who tried to run me over. For a while, I thought Milda might be behind it all, because it all seemed to stop after they found her dead. But this happened yesterday.'

'Rex. Every third kid on the High Street's got one of these tops. *I've* got one. Rex...' She rubbed the bridge of her nose. 'I'm worried about you...'

'Don't give me the speech, Susan. I'll resign.'

'I'll refuse your resignation. You're exhausted. You're traumatised by what happened to Milda. And you're not thinking clearly. I want you to go home and rest and come back this afternoon. Ellie can take over, and fill you in on what we decide at conference.'

'No,' he said, standing up. 'I resign.'

'Then you're sacked.'

'How can you sack someone who's already resigned?'

'You didn't give me a letter. It says that in everyone's contract. So you're sacked.'

Rex grabbed a pencil from the elegant Japanese tray, a letter from the top of her In-pile and scribbled 'I resign,' on it. 'I resign', he shouted, for good measure, slamming the door behind him.

On the stairs on the way down, he met Brenda, making her stately progress up for the Monday meeting with a pile of letters. 'You can stop looking at me like that,' he said. 'I've resigned.' The big woman stopped stock-still. Rex didn't look back, but he sensed her, watching him, all the way down the stairs and out of the building.

He didn't often see the street at this time on a Monday. This was normally the hour when he was in meetings, fighting with his boss and his colleagues about details that no longer seemed to matter. Green Lanes had the air of some vital, exotic port: Istanbul or Aleppo. Veiled widows were stuffing their shopping trollies with greenery, a haughty-looking waiter crossed the street, between motorbikes and buses, without spilling a drop from his tray of tea-glasses, and in the window of the Famous Manti Shop, a chorus-line of head-scarved girls was rolling out dough for the dumplings.

This was a hard place. Sad, if you chose to look at the gaunt old men raking through the reduced tins outside the Lidl. Maddening, when you saw bright young kids given a police escort from the school gates to the bus-stops to prevent them from being stabbed, or stabbing each other. But for all that, Rex had a sense of something new being born here, being hewn in the teahouses, forged in the internet cafes and the cab ranks, grafted and sculpted by each fresh set of incomers. No one knew what was going to emerge from the shower of sparks, any more than they'd known in New York in the 19th century, or Rome in the 1st. He loved it.

Was Susan right? Was he losing his mind? He only knew that many things did not add up. That the future of this place was under threat, as well as himself. Both needed to be fought for. And if that fight had to be conducted outside the newspaper, instead of inside, then so be it. He would survive.

It was 9.15. The Salisbury opened its doors at 9 and, according to a recent feature in the paper on local eating spots, served a handsome breakfast. Susan was right about one thing. He was exhausted. And he hadn't eaten properly since Saturday evening.

He had just enough time to read the menu, and to become very hungry at the prospect of herb sausages with black pudding and mushrooms, fried eggs and grilled tomatoes, before the pub's one barmaid came over and told him there was no food today. 'Cook sick,' she pronounced, with a certain gloomy satisfaction.

The problem was, he was in there now. With the smells of wood and beer in his nose. The weak autumn sunlight streaming through the coloured glass windows, giving the place the air of a sanctuary. He asked for a glass of Czech beer – Litovel. The girl served him with an air of disdain, but then she did the same to everyone, whether it was nine in the morning or just before chucking-out time. Another customer walked in, and she went off to bully him. Rex left for his corner table.

He was a few gulps in, already feeling the effects of it, and wondering if the barmaid would take his drink away if he nipped out and bought a paper. He noticed with irritation that the other drinker was heading in his direction, holding a coffee cup. Why did they have to sit so near him when the whole barn-like pub was empty?

'Beer for breakfast. Takes me back to varsity days, that does.'

'What are you doing here, Lawrence?' he asked, not a little gracelessly, as the Laureate of the Ladders sat next to him.

'I'm doing a little feature-ette... best coffee joints on Green Lanes,' Lawrence said, placing a pair of half-moon glasses on his tanned nose. 'And this place serves the best espresso this side of Milan. Or should I say, Danuta serves it.' He nodded his mass of dyed curls towards the barmaid who, to Rex's astonishment, broke into a dimpled grin. 'Seven miles of wonders, this road is,' Lawrence went on, before sipping his coffee and smacking his lips. 'But you know that, don't you?'

'I fear our love affair might have just come to an end.'

Lawrence shook his head. 'You fall in and out of love with places. And jobs. In and out and in again. Just like a marriage.' He tittered, making a sound like a magpie. 'Don't tell Diana that her uncle took you to the pub to discuss marriage.'

'I don't think Diana would mind either way,' Rex said, after a long swig from his glass.

'Not what I heard.'

'You talk to her much?'

'Well, she was sat at my table last night, between my wife and my son-in-law, eating our famous baked trout dinner. We had six guests.' He peered at Rex pointedly over the top of his glasses. 'At one point, earlier on in the week, we were informed that there might be a number seven.'

Rex didn't know what to say. The news cheered him up a little, then depressed him. He took a deep swig from his beer. He felt Lawrence staring at him and put the glass down.

'What? You're going to tell me to go easy? It's only going to make matters worse?'

'I'm guessing it's making things feel a little better,' Lawrence replied. 'In the short-term, anyway. You know, Jews don't really drink. So when we do, we use it like medicine. My Uncle Sonny used to drink one bottle of vodka a year. He'd pick a weekend, draw a circle around it in the calendar, and lock himself in the warehouse. He said it was like topping up his batteries.' He tapped Rex's glass with a manicured finger nail. 'Want another?'

Rex watched his strange companion at the bar, chatting easily with the normally frosty barmaid. Lawrence Berne, as no one was allowed to forget, was a committee member of North Finchley Golf Club, and he dressed, at all times, for that part. Today, he sported pleated front charcoal trousers with a black and white houndstooth jacket. There was a chunky gold bracelet on his right wrist, matching the thick gold watch and the decorative gold clasps on the front of his slip-on shoes. He wrote one of the most annoying newspaper columns in the history of the printed word. And yet, right now, he was a comforting presence. Benign and understanding, a rabbi-therapist in golfing slacks. Rex hoped he wouldn't go away.

'What I'm saying is… you should get very drunk.' Lawrence was back, with another pint for Rex and a Perrier for himself. 'Crawling-to-the-toilet-to-be-sick drunk. Then tomorrow morning, you crawl back to the office. Say sorry. Take your beating. It's not going to matter, is it? Nothing could make you feel any worse than you've already made yourself feel. That's the beauty of a hangover. You say sorry, and you go back to work.'

Rex found himself smiling. He also found himself thinking of Diana. Not just because of the faint family resemblance, but because of the style of the advice. Philosophical, yet also slightly cracked. It was exactly the sort of theory she would come out with. He wished to God he could have been the seventh guest last night. He wanted to belong to that world. Girlfriends and their uncles and their famous baked trout family dinners. Not death threats and mortuaries.

But then he remembered what he had been doing last night, and his smile faded away. He remembered Susan in the office, as good as calling him insane. How could he go back? Write neat little local interest pieces for a paper that blithely ignored the chasm opening up in their midst? He'd be part of it. Part of what had killed Milda and the life inside her.

'If you don't want to sit here and get rat-arsed, you could come with me. I'm going to have a look at an old synagogue on Quicksilver Place.'

Rex knew the road: a gauntlet of small factory units and warehouses between Wood Green and Alexandra Palace. He could not think of a less likely location for a place of worship. He said so, aware that this was just the feeder-line Lawrence Berne had been waiting for. He stretched his legs out, revealing socks with golf clubs on them, and began.

'I found a funny little article, years ago. Written in 1881. It said there was a firm of German hat-makers at Wood Green, and they had their own Temple next door. That's what they used to call synagogues, you know, so I went looking for it. And then I worked it out. Quicksilver. That's mercury. Used in hat-making for the curing of beaver pelts.'

'I know. I didn't know about the synagogue, though.'

'No one does. It's just this little clutch of industrial units, now. But right at the back, there's this building that's more or less bricked up, and there's a design in the brickwork at the top – a *magen dovid*. That's Hebrew. It means star of David.'

Rex smiled tightly. Lawrence always did this, in his column and in his speech – over-explained. Still, he'd rather hear about an old synagogue than think about the present.

'So can you get inside?'

'Well that's the weird thing. The first time I went, I got up to this little sort of light-shaft thing. It was dark inside, but I met this caretaker who said I could ring his boss and maybe he'd let me come and see inside. So I rang and rang the number he'd given me, but no one ever answered. So then I just went back on my own a week ago.' He paused for effect. This, too, was typical of discourse with Lawrence Berne.

'And?' Rex said, playing his part.

'And it was full of people in overalls. Packing sandwiches. There were great big piles of ham and sausage.'

'In a synagogue?'

Lawrence shrugged. 'Ever been to Ayia Sofia? That's a Church they made into a Mosque. Anyhoo –' He sipped his water, while Rex wondered if anyone else incorporated the word 'anyhoo' into daily conversation. 'I knocked on the door, but no one answered. And then I went back. And it was completely empty again. So I'm going to give it one last go. Fancy it?'

'What about the featurette? Best coffee on Green Lanes?'

'Hmm? Oh, that's pretty much done now. Shall we?' He dangled the keys to his Merc. Rex downed the rest of his beer and stood up. Why not, he thought.

By the time they'd reached Wood Green, Lawrence – with his funny little quirks of speech and patronising side-lectures on every subject, from the meaning of the word 'Hale' to the origins of asphalt – had begun to annoy Rex again. He wasn't sure how much that had to do with Lawrence, and how much it had to do with the fact that his initial drunkenness was now turning into a banging hangover, and his bladder was full to bursting.

Now the late autumn sun was beating down with unseasonal strength on Rex's throbbing head as they walked through a silent gulch of respray workshops and storage units. A dog barked somewhere. Somewhere else, there was the sound of grinding metal. They turned a corner, passed a barred and shuttered cabin entitled 'GREEK CYPRIOT BAKED GOODS', and a blank space, where weeds pushed up through the concrete. A train clattered by.

'Moorgate to Welwyn Garden City,' Lawrence observed unnecessarily. 'Here we are.'

They had reached a long, narrow, brick warehouse, clearly older than most of the surrounding buildings – the sort of thing you might have expected to see at the docks. At the top, just under the roof, were a couple of tiny, soot-covered windows, and round the side, by the railway line, a line of glass bricks set into the wall about nine feet off the ground. Rex could not imagine anyone worshipping in such a place but there, high above the glass, was a star of David picked out in lighter-coloured brick.

With surprising nimbleness for a man in his sixties, Lawrence clambered on to an industrial waste-bin and peered through the glass.

'It's full again!' he hissed. He held out a hand to Rex. Rex took it, and hauled himself with difficulty onto the bin.

The sight that greeted him was an eerie one. Lamps hung on chains from the rafters, casting a harsh light onto the balletic scene below. Pale-faced, solemn workers stood in rows as if in a church, assembling and packing sandwiches at long trestle tables. No sounds could be heard from where Rex and Lawrence peered in at them, nor did it seem as if any of them were speaking. A squat, neckless man in a suede jacket moved amongst them, inspecting, correcting. The workers moved as if they were part of a machine: here an arm applied mayonnaise, there a pair of rubber-sheathed fingers pressed down triangles of bread. One man was stamping bread-sized squares out of a mighty great industrial roll of pressed pink meat.

'Imagine doing that all day long.'

'At least they're all wearing gloves,' Lawrence said. 'Health and Safety will be delighted about that, if nothing else.'

'You reckon this is illegal?'

'Story of the area, isn't it?' Lawrence said, with a wry smile. 'I doubt the German hatters had a subsidised canteen and a crèche.'

A sudden rustling sound below made them both look down. Two large brown rats slithered over the assorted rubbish and vanished into a vent in the side of the building.

'And they make food in this place…' Rex whispered.

'At least it's only those nasty sandwiches they flog in newsagents,' Lawrence said.

'I eat nasty sandwiches from newsagents all the time,' Rex replied.

After a few more minutes of silent spectating, the pair separated. Remembering Lawrence's advice, Rex went to the nearest pub: a grim pub, named The Hope where there clearly was none, but at least the staff and the customers left him alone.

He left it just as the schools were chucking out. Befuddled and feeling unwell, he found himself at a bus-stop on Pretoria Road, with three, tiny Somali children clutching reading books. Bigger kids swept up and down the street in shrieking tidal fronts. The bus, when it came, would be full of them, so he decided to walk. But where was he going? What exactly did he want to do? He thought of Diana. She was a long way away, the far end of Tottenham. But he wanted her.

Even in the 21st century, parts of Tottenham still had the air of some flimsy Saxon settlement, clinging to the edge of the unfriendly marsh. Confident little rows of double-glazed terraces trickled away into light industry, car lots, then nothing. The names in this quarter – Durban Street, Pretoria Road, Johannesburg Place – all dated back to the Boer War, but the area had always been referred to as Little Russia on account of the poor immigrants who'd filled it up at the start of the 20th century. After the Second World War, much of the old housing had been knocked down; the little that remained was occupied first by West Indians, then Ugandan Asians, and more recently, people from the Horn of Africa. A rust-coloured Vauxhall Astra and a moped duelled over some issue of road etiquette as they went by, and Rex heard a burst of Slavic swearing from the car window. Perhaps the Russians were coming back?

He walked on. He had a long way to go. He heard a door slam – a car door, a house – then felt a polite tap on his shoulder and turned round.

Something hit him between the eyes. He lurched back, colliding with something that might have been a lamp-post, or another person. He felt punches and kicks to his ribs and his legs. A glimpse of a grey hood. Metallic blood and boot-leather. Someone, he was almost certain, said something about Milda, before something bright smashed into his face for a second time, splitting his vision and all his other senses into separate compartments of agony.

Then came the sound of someone shouting in English. Running footsteps. And hands. Gentle, firm hands lifting him up. He saw his blood dripping from some part of his own head onto a fleece. But the fleece seemed to be red already, and he thought he knew it from somewhere else.

Chapter Seven

He sat at the Formica table in the darkening kitchen, his fingers picking distractedly at the corded wicker spiral of a table mat. They hadn't eaten in here for a long time. There was a corkboard on the wall next to the refrigerator. They pinned bills on it, appointment letters, every claim from the outside world upon their inner one. He saw he had a dental appointment next Tuesday and the thought of it almost made him smile.

This was another of those side-by-side moments. Where God revealed the power and the mystery of Himself. In this room: the smell of lemon washing-up liquid and flowers from the allotment. Dental check-ups next week. A little fridge magnet in the shape of Anne Hathaway's cottage. Life continuing. In the next room, just across the hall: life brought to an end. Murder.

Was it murder? Whatever it was called, he couldn't do it. She'd asked him, louder and hoarser, until there could have been no mistaking what it was she wanted. And he'd just murmured something about changing the pillow-cases: anything so that he could get out of that airless, sweet-smelling room. He had even gone up to the airing cupboard on the landing and taken a fresh, lilac-coloured pillowcase from the pile. But it was sitting on the kitchen table in front of him now, an hour later. He couldn't go back in with it.

The storm still hadn't come. He drank a glass of water. It was warm and brackish, like the air. His foster mother had always said that tap water was bad on Sundays. What day was it today? Something else he couldn't remember. He remembered, though, that after he'd killed June's rabbit, he'd lain in bed, many a night, patiently going over all the details of what it had felt like to take a life by choking the breath out of it. Storing them, studying them, as if they were part of a book. The springy resistance of the neck. The silky feel of skin being rolled against tendons. The tidy juxtaposition of a moment where nothing was as important as another breath, and a subsequent moment where breath was irrelevant. He had shuddered at the memory of that power, felt something akin to a tickle passing down his diaphragm, through his belly to the twitching tip of his penis, and felt his cheeks on fire. Some nights, he'd fall asleep then, and wake in the dark to find a cold, stinking glue inside his pyjamas. He couldn't remember if that had happened when he killed the girl in the camp. He'd had the feeling. But the cold stuff – he knew what it was now, of course – had that been there, too?

He rose abruptly, the chair scraping on the linoleum. The lino had a pattern of bricks on it. And everything around him, the corkboard, the humming fridge, the warped door to the utility room, suddenly looked so solid and familiar, so normal that he found it impossible to believe there'd been any other kind of existence before it. How could he have taken any life, he who kept Morrison's carrier bags in a bundle behind the door? How could there be killing, here, in this house, where pegs were stored in a little cotton sack with a picture of a gypsy girl on it?

He went back into the front room. She was on her side, facing away from him towards the window, her angular shoulder moving with a rhythm that suggested she was asleep. He thanked God that she was. He folded the pillow case, placed it on the chair and picked up the water-jug to take it out and refill it. He'd tip-toed back to the door when her voice startled him.

'I never asked anything of you.'

He froze. Watched her turn over, slowly, like a stone rolling from the mouth of a cave.

'I knew you… weren't right pretty soon after we were wed. And that was just…' She licked her lips. Her mouth was dry. He moved forward to give her water but realised he didn't have any. He stayed where he was, transfixed, by the vision of her, now sitting up in the bed, suddenly filled with horrible strength. 'That was just how it was. I made my choice. Father Daniel made me understand that.'

'Why are you talking about him?' His voice sounded like water passing down a blocked drain.

'Because he…' She swallowed painfully, a blue veined hand to her throat.

'Do you need the patch replacing?'

'Shut up!' she hissed, fiercely, knotting the bed sheet in her fist. 'I don't want more medicine. I don't want to live. I want to die! And you're the only one I can ask.'

'You can't ask me,' he said, limply. 'I'm your husband.' Outside, the first drops of rain landed on the laburnum bush.

'We never had a marriage!'

'It's the drugs,' he said. 'The doctor said they might take you like this. It's the drugs.'

'Pull out the drawer,' she commanded him. 'Underneath the bed.'

He did as he was told, kneeling close to her. He smelt the artificial sweat given off by people who are being kept artificially alive. The drawer was stiff. In there, she'd kept newspaper cuttings – he'd never known why. Royal weddings. Mountbatten being blown up on his boat. A pull-out special on the dredging of the Mary Rose. She'd always had some sort of attraction to history, he realised. There was a tear-shaped locket in there, too, on a fine chain, its silver so dirty it was almost blue.

'Open it,' she rasped, finally resting back on the pillows. Her face was slack, exhausted. The rain came down a little stronger.

For a second, he even wondered if she'd fallen asleep, but then her eyeballs swivelled back round to him. He looked away and squeezed the little tear-drop open. Inside was a picture of a broad-faced, handsome young man with sideburns.

'Father Daniel?'

'I loved him. Do you understand? I fell in love with him, and I stayed in love with him. All this time. So you owe me nothing. There is no reason why you shouldn't help me to die.'

He opened his mouth and closed it again, ineffectually.

'What did you expect? You'd obviously had feelings for some-one before you met me. And you never wanted me, did you?'

'What do you mean…? Feelings for someone?' His head span.

'That lock of hair you keep in a tin. I've seen you. It was a girl, wasn't it?'

He shook his head. But she went on. 'It's all right. You wanted someone else. I wanted someone else. It hasn't been a very good life. I don't care now. I just don't want any more pain.'

'I can't do it.' The rain grew louder and he had to raise his voice. 'It's… wrong.'

'Wrong? Wrong is me lying here like this. What for? What are they keeping me alive for?'

He couldn't answer.

She raised herself again and spoke through gritted teeth. 'Do one, decent, brave thing in your life. I'm begging you. Do it. All you have to do is hold a pillow over my face. They won't get you for it. Just do it. It's just a pillow.'

He had to suppress an urge to laugh. No one knew how brave he was. Brave enough to take life. Brave enough not to. The rain seemed to drum down in time to her chant. He remembered how the girl in the bed had bucked and bowed, how the springs had creaked, the horsehair in the pillow crackled, her bare knees knocked against his back. His cock straining against the rough fabric of his orderly's uniform, and a muscle deep within him shifting and pulsing, like the pulse of the whole world. He swallowed.

A sharp, angry bang startled them both. His heart knocked painfully against his chest. He thought at first it was thunder. But it was the doorknocker – an ugly, heavy lion's headed thing that had been there when they bought the house. No one ever used it. No one ever knocked on their door. But the knocking went on, shaking the house. She lay back on the pillows, staring at the ceiling, still uttering her chant but without a voice, the fire in her eyes having ebbed to despair. Suddenly angry, he rushed to the door.

'What do you want?' he shouted. The girl was there, on the doorstep, soaked through.

'Ai! Such a doorknocker,' she said, as she wiped her glasses on the hem of her dress. 'Is it very old?'

'What are you doing? How did you find my house?'

She frowned. 'Address was on back of the envelope. You're angry with me?'

'No. I mean. It's… it's not a good time for visitors. I'm sorry.'

She said nothing, inclined her head a little to the scene behind her, which was a solid wall of thundering downpour, so thick the parked cars seemed to be shadows. She raised her eyebrows. From inside the house, he heard his wife cry out in pain.

'All right, all right.' He motioned her in. Smelt her wet hair and her wet skin as she shut the front door. 'Wait.'

He rushed back in to his wife. But she did not need him. She had died.

* * *

In the sixth form there had been a girl called Helen. He had found her neither attractive nor especially interesting, although, looking back, he allowed that she might well have been both.

Helen's skill had been that she was everywhere. At all the College Newspaper meetings. In the only pub that would serve them. At the only parties he was invited to. Always beside him, with a faintly aggrieved air, as if he were being ridiculous for not understanding that their destinies were entwined. Whatever Helen had wanted, it had never happened.

Helen had something in common with the North Middlesex Hospital. Its sheer ubiquity in his life made him loathe the place. He dreaded it. But he was always ending up there, in one capacity or another. This was just the first night they'd spent together.

Apart from curtains with a design of Tower Bridge and taxis, the only decorative feature of the Danny Blanchflower Ward at the North Middlesex was a long, mauve stripe that passed across the middle of each wall and finally pointed upwards, as if heaven were the destination of anyone lying there long enough to follow the entire route. Rex had already done so several times since being awoken with a strong cup of tea at around 4.30 am. He had not arrived in heaven yet.

But later, in spite of the sharp pain in his jaw, the dull throbbing at his temples and a myriad of further bodily complaints, he had polished off a surprisingly good plate of scrambled eggs. His neighbour, having ticked the box that said 'Afro-Caribbean' on one of the dozens of forms thrust daily at the patients, had been mightily disgruntled to receive a plate of rice and peas for his own breakfast, and had gladly passed it in Rex's direction when he saw him gazing curiously at it.

Wiping the last few beans away with a scrap of roti, Rex was thinking of revising his views on the North Middlesex when a visitor arrived.

'Curry for breakfast. You must be feeling good.'

'You got the blood out of your fleece then,' Rex said. Keith Powell looked down at his bright, logo-emblazoned garment.

'I didn't,' he said. 'This is a new one.'

'I should say thank you.'

'You should,' Powell said. He motioned towards a grey plastic chair. 'May I?'

Rex nodded. 'Thank you. I've been beaten up lots of times,' he said, wincing. 'But never quite so thoroughly.'

'They were shouting something about Milda,' Powell said, as he sat down.

'You're certain it was a "they"?'

'Three of them.'

'Hoodies?'

Powell frowned. 'One of them had a sort of silver cagoule on. He didn't have the hood up, though. And the other two were in those padded builders' shirts.'

'There was no moped?'

'Not that I was aware of. Why? Do you remember one?'

Rex didn't answer. He was still wondering if Powell and his cronies had something to do with all the recent attempts to frighten him. That he had saved him from the attack didn't quite fit this theory, of course. Unless it was a clever bluff.

'I guess it was someone who thinks I killed Milda,' Rex said, carefully. 'They wouldn't be the only ones.'

Powell took his media-glasses off and rubbed his nose. 'Well, you can strike Her Majesty's Constabulary off your list, at least. They've charged someone.'

Rex sat up, ignoring the pain. 'Who?'

'An Albanian. He's coughed to it. To murdering Milda, and all the other attacks. They nicked him completely by accident.'

'How?'

'Haringey Council got a tip-off about poor hygiene at a sandwich factory in Wood Green, so two inspectors went down with police back-up. One of the workers bolted when he saw the panda car. Legged it right across the railway line in front of the 13.02 from Letchworth. And when they caught up with him, he just coughed to the lot.'

Rex lay back on the hard pillow, feeling a wave of wonder and relief. The tip-off – that could only have been Lawrence Berne, surely? And the stuff around Milda's neck – the sodium nitrite – it must have come from the sandwich factory. 'But what about the heroin?'

'Says he shared it with her first,' said Powell. 'They used to live in the same squat, apparently.'

Rex remembered the bills piled up in Milda's porch. Powell confirmed his thoughts. 'Adem Dushku. Little bloke. Honestly, you wouldn't think he had it in him.'

Something still didn't quite fit. Milda had never mentioned an Albanian in the house. And could she have changed so much, that she'd have willingly sat down in a park, and injected heroin with some weird drifter? Rex felt a wave of nausea, and the rice and peas came back into his throat.

'You all right? Do you want me to get someone?'

Rex squinted at Powell as the sickness ebbed away. 'One thing I don't get, Powell. And that's how you know all this. Have you got an insider in the Tottenham nick?'

There was a pause. 'It's more like the other way round.'

'Tottenham nick's got an insider in you? You mean you're…'

Powell held up a silencing finger. 'SO21. Hate Crimes Division,' he said softly.

At the other end of the ward, a tall, olive-skinned young doctor was beginning his rounds.

'So the Hate Crimes Division is going round the place, actively setting up local fascist groups in order to… What? See who comes out of the woodwork? Isn't that entrapment?'

By way of an answer, Powell whipped out a phone similar

to Rex's, and connected it to YouTube. Rex found himself staring at some wobbly footage of the corner of Turnpike Lane and Green Lanes. Wind crackled in the microphone. Orange jackets and union jacks came into view. Then Rex himself. He watched, slightly appalled, as a street-brawl unfolded, with him at the centre of it.

'I think my old headmaster would be very disappointed.'

Powell showed him another clip: crowds of marchers running down Turnpike Lane in blind panic, away from the explosion. Smoke and sirens and shattered glass.

'These images are being downloaded thousands of times a day. Not to mention all the times they've been on the news, here and abroad.'

'So what?'

'So if you'd set out to show people that there's no such thing as a reasonable anti-immigration group, if you'd wanted to prove that every time someone starts talking about sending people home, you get this' – Powell tapped the screen – 'you couldn't have asked for much better, could you? You don't need to outlaw people like this. You just need to let them exist, and make such a fucking pig's ear of it all that anyone who might just be tempted to listen to them decides not to bother.'

'And if they don't exist, then you invent them?'

Powell shook his head. 'We didn't invent the BWAP. We infiltrated it.'

'So who did set it up?'

Powell glanced towards the doctor, who was approaching with a chorus of nurses and students. 'Look, we haven't got time for that. We're at a crossroads. I got involved yesterday and one of the lads who was putting the boot into you sort of... recognised me from another context.'

'What context?'

'I nicked him, four months ago, spray painting the back of Hendon bus station, but he got away. He recognised me.'

'So who was he?'

Powell frowned. 'I don't know. A graffiti artist. The point is…'

'Your cover's blown?'

'Now it's a question of damage limitation. This thing goes a lot further and deeper than I can tell you, but…'

'In other words there are coppers involved,' Rex interrupted.

Powell looked as if he'd had a sudden twinge of toothache. It was enough for Rex to know he'd hit a nerve. So there were coppers involved.

'Coppers around here?' he said.

'If you care about the things you claim to care about,' Powell said, ignoring Rex and the waiting medical staff, 'you will let us get on with what we need to do without compromising it for the sake of tomorrow's chip-wrappers.'

Rex absorbed this request. It would mean binning the biggest story he'd ever brought the *Gazette*. Ever brought to any paper, for that matter. 'Two things,' he said finally.

'What?'

'First, they don't wrap chips in newspapers any more. Health and Safety.'

'And second?'

'Did Milda move in with you?'

'No. She never even came to my house. Anything else?'

'You know that headmaster I mentioned? He once played Hitler in a pantomime.'

'And?'

'I always thought he was the least convincing Nazi I'd ever seen. Until I met you.'

* * *

In a quiet, northerly part of Muswell Hill there was a church, so incongruous amongst the wide suburban villas and the parked cars that it looked as if it had been dumped there. It was, in fact, two churches, shared by the United Reformed and the Russian Orthodox communities. A week out of hospital, and still sore in many places, Rex sat gingerly on a hard maple pew and wondered how the ecclesiastical sharing arrangements worked out. Did the Russians pack the icons away, so as not to offend their room-mates? What did the Protestants make of the wafers and wine that were said to have been transformed, magically, into Christ's own essence by a man?

There could be no doubting which of the two traditions was being served up today. The air was heavy with incense and the fatty smoke of candles. A ruck of bearded men in vivid robes moved back and forth, without any discernible order, swinging thuribles, inclining crosses on long brass poles and bowing before panels of gold-painted icons. A choir sang in deep voices, bringing Cossacks and onion domes to mind, and Milda's friends, a motley collection of squatters, anarchists and self-styled 'art terrorists', knelt and crossed themselves in memory of her soul. Birgita, her hair now cropped boyishly short, did not kneel, possibly because of the small bump now visible around her midriff, but kept her eyes closed in fervent prayer. Aguta and her daughter wept openly. DC Orchard had been in, performed some vague devotional gestures towards the front, and left, his mobile ringing. Others had also come and gone, all young, some known to Rex, others not at all.

Adem Dushku was in the high secure mental unit at Crews Hill. The group calling itself the British Workers Action Party had disappeared, and people who rang a firm called Keith Powell – Kill Pests were referred to a page on Haringey Council's environmental health website. Meanwhile, Rex gathered from a very well-crafted front-page piece by Ellie Mehta, gangs of Polish and Turkish boys from the local comp were regularly meeting in Morrison's car park for organised scraps. An enterprising local businessman – a certain Greek Cypriot cafe proprietor – was trying to get them all into football instead, sponsoring a team and a strip, with the support of a much-loved local newspaper.

Slowly, Rex found he could accept the police version of events. Milda had either taken heroin because she was no longer the person she had been before, or because she was in pain, or, perhaps, because she was under some duress from the person with the syringe. The latter was not a pleasant thought, but Dushku would be spending the rest of his days in a very bad place, and that was about as much comfort as anyone could hope for.

Was he 'KP'? It seemed unlikely. Milda's email had said she was going to stay with him, and Dushku had been living in some sort of hostel. But in the light of Dushku's confession and the evidence, the identity of her mysterious 'little friend' was probably an extraneous detail. Case closed.

So why did he keep running over it? Was that just how a sudden death left people: asking questions, refusing to accept the obvious? Was it also because he was out of work now, rattling around his house all day with nothing but a dwindling bank account for company? Or was there some tiny beacon signalling from his subconscious, tapping out in faint, but persistent morse the message that something still didn't make sense?

That morning another jiffy-bag had come through the post. It had felt thick and squishy. Inside, very carefully sealed within two zip-lock freezer bags, was a piece of raw liver. Calf's, he suspected. But he wasn't about to cook it and find out.

The persecution seemed almost artistic. Or elements of it did, whilst others, like the moped driven straight at him, were simply violent. He thought about the graffiti artist Powell had almost nicked. This almost-nicked graffiti artist had been one of the people beating him bloody on the pavements of Tottenham. Were they behind all these packages and messages, too? It was tempting to think so, but it didn't add up. A liver in a jiffy bag was a threat. A kick in the ribs wasn't a threat. Unless it was meant to be a threat of something worse.

His thoughts were broken by the arrival of two further mourners. A pair of milky-white men in identical, charcoal-grey suits, with the sort of shoes you'd feel very grown-up in – if you'd just started school. The Whittaker twins. Mark – or possibly Robert – glanced at him, pulled a block of yellow Post-it notes from his jacket pocket and scribbled something, handing the result past his identical twin to Rex.

We've come on behalf of all the staff at the paper.

A second Post-it note came his way.

How are you?

'I think it's okay to talk,' said Rex. 'These places are pretty noisy.'

The twins stared ahead, suddenly awkward. They'd clearly planned to communicate by Post-its alone.

'How's Susan?' Rex asked.

Without moving his head, the nearest twin turned a pair of cold, grey eyes towards him, and spoke out of the side of his mouth.

'She made us put a half-page advert in. To advertise for your replacement. But then she pulled it.'

Rex took this in. 'Maybe she's got someone in mind.'

'She hasn't,' the twins said together, loudly. Assorted heads and beards and kamelaukions swung round.

Later, there were vodka and pickled cucumbers back at the old restaurant where Birgita lived with the man she called Mark. He wasn't around, Rex noted – at least, he hadn't been in the Church and he couldn't be seen back home. He wondered if Birgita changed lovers every time she changed her look.

It was Parisian New Wave schtick now: gamin hairdo, black roll-neck sweater and matching pedal-pusher trousers. She drank peach juice, and very slowly, smoked her way through a single, thin roll-up, continually putting it out in a huge turquoise ashtray and re-lighting it. There was a boy with a ukulele, and an old, grey man, like a, convict, who played the accordion; together they bashed out *Ochi Cherniye* and something that sounded like *Bublitschki* but wasn't.

'So.' Birgita filled his glass and clinked her mug of juice against it. 'I told you I had a bad feeling for Milda.'

'You did.' Rex sipped the spirit. It was an odd, dirty yellow colour, and strong: more like an anaesthetic than a drink.

Birgita sighed. 'I knew she was pregnant, Rex.'

'She told you?'

'She came to visit to me here, and I told her about my baby,' she said, instinctively patting her abdomen. 'And she cried. And then it came out. You know, she said she saw you. On a bus. I mean, she was on a bus. And she saw you. And she had just done the test. It was inside her bag, and she went past you on the bus. And you... did you send to her a text?'

'Yes. She didn't reply.'

'She didn't know what to do. I'm sorry. I thought you should know, but... it was for her to tell you, not mine.'

He remembered something Birgita had said – something he'd been struggling to remember when he met Milda's sister, Niela. 'So that stuff about feeling dizzy and sick... that was just being pregnant?'

Birgita shook her head. 'She said no. She had it before.'

Rex pondered this for a moment. Birgita must have mistaken his expression for one of sorrow, because she patted him, surprisingly heavily, on the shoulder. 'I think she didn't feel ready for a baby,' she said, pouring more of the dark vodka into his glass.

'Does anyone?' Rex asked.

She smiled. 'I was ready when I was fourteen.'

'Lucky you. When is it due?'

'January. Yes, lucky me,' she added gnomically.

He was going to ask her about Mark, who was presumably the father of the baby, but she went to the toilet. Rex went through the kitchen to the back yard for some fresh air, and promptly found Mark, in fact, tinkering with a bicycle. He jumped as Rex appeared, and in his skinny black jeans and sleeveless t-shirt, he reminded Rex of a startled crow.

'Not joining in the fun?' Rex asked. He took in the man's appearance. Though he couldn't have been much younger than Rex, he had spots, and his eyes were the size of eggs. Mark held up his cigarette in response

'Biggsy doesn't like the smoke,' he said, in broad Salford dialect. 'Anyhow, I was just off to get some more booze. Don't suppose you'd er…'

Rex got the hint and handed over a fiver. Mark took it between long, yellow fingers, and vanished like smoke. The smell he left behind was one Rex remembered from his student days. Rolling tobacco and deodorant sprayed onto stale clothes. Was Birgita really having a baby with this bloke? But then, had Rex been a better prospect for Milda? Evidently not.

A collective roar of disapproval emanated from inside the house, as if perhaps the accordionist had started to play Barry Manilow. But there was no music. Instead, a voice droned from a television set. Rex went back to find everyone watching Newsroom South East on BBC 1. Newsroom So What? – as they used to call it, in the paper trade.

A young reporter with a long Tamil name stood outside the Muswell Hill Church, discussing the death of Milda, and the doubts that could now be put to rest. The only mourner on screen was DC Orchard, who had evidently shown up for his fifteen seconds of fame. He now delivered to the camera a thoroughly rehearsed statement.

'Milda Majauskas was a pretty girl, who'd done well at art school in Vilnius, and came here looking for work and adventure. We hope that some of the people considering a similar journey, and their parents, might take heed of what happened to Milda. She did not, as her family thought, share a flat with friends. She had a room in a dangerous, damp, squatted house. She left her job after accusations of petty crime and drifted into a life on the margins, accompanied by Adem Dushku, a drug addict who lived in her house.'

Across the room came a salvo of Slavic curses. *Kurva! Bletstva! Pashyal' ti!* Little Dovila giggled and looked up at her mother. But Aguta was silent, a tear rolling down each, perfectly made-up cheek.

'He encouraged her to try heroin, and she ended up murdered in a park. As safe as we try to make this city, some people will come here, and they will find danger. So to those young people at home, in Lithuania, and other countries, who are thinking about coming to London for money and fun, we say, think about the other possibilities, too…'

Orchard's face gave way to an item about a man keeping a donkey on the balcony of a high-rise flat in Wembley. The tv was switched off, and there was general silence. Rex couldn't believe what he'd just heard. It was like a manifesto for the now-disappeared BWAP. And no wonder they had disappeared. There was no need for them, with policemen reading out their mission statements on the lunchtime news.

Was that what Powell had meant at the hospital? 'This thing goes a lot further and deeper than I can tell you.' Orchard was one of them. And now that Powell's undercover investigation had stalled, people like Orchard could carry on unimpeded.

'Do policemen talk like that in your country?' he asked the person next to him, a thin, pretty boy with a knitted skullcap on. To Rex's surprise the boy frowned and walked away. Had he offended him somehow?

In the meantime, it became apparent that Aguta was in no fit state either to stay where she was, or to get home without help. Her daughter, Dovila, ten and bossy, helped her into her jacket, forced her to drink water, and painstakingly led her to the door. Then she turned an apple-cheeked face to Rex and asked, 'What train do we get to our house, please?'

He walked three doors down the road, past an off-licence and a tandoori, to the mini-cab office. He asked for and obtained a cab, established the identity of its driver and its probable cost – all without anyone addressing a single word to him in response. Was it rudeness? Indifference? Or just a kind of efficiency, in a city of so many tongues.

When he got back, Birgita asked if he'd bought any cigarette papers, which he hadn't. Why, he wondered, had Mark said she didn't like him smoking, when she smoked herself? For that matter, where had Mark disappeared to with that fiver? The off-licence was only next door. But Rex had other things on his mind. Like getting the inebriated Aguta and her daughter into a taxi.

The driver had his radio tuned to a jazz station, and as they drove slowly through the roadworks and drizzle, Rex felt as if they were in an advert or some painfully stylish movie. They'd only gone a short way along Green Lanes when the driver turned right.

'This isn't the way,' Aguta slurred.

The driver, a bird-like Sudanese in a heavy tweed coat, explained that most of Green Lanes was unpassable today. 'Dig dig dig,' were his exact words.

Listening to Billie Holiday, they headed east into Stoke New-ington, a land where council tenants, Hasidic scholars and tv producers dwelt uneasily side-by-side. There was a street where every shop sold cupcakes, or vintage clothing, or expensive retro toys. But the main high road – joining up with the old Roman route of Ermine Street as it headed to Tottenham – was markedly less chichi. There were bookies, several examples of what Milda had called 'Irish Man pubs', and a large, brightly-lit hall, where Yiddish-speaking women in wigs and flat shoes rummaged through bins of dried goods.

A sign announced a burst water main ahead. The driver clicked his teeth and swung right again, taking them into the Hackney borders.

Aguta wound the window down, and hiccupped. Rex gave her an Extra Strong Mint. Then he felt duty-bound to offer them to Dovila and the cabbie, leaving none for himself.

'I got to sober up,' Aguta said, shivering. 'I promised to ring Niela.'

'You're in touch?' Rex asked. Aguta responded with a shrug.

'One thing I don't understand,' Rex went on. 'What made her go home so suddenly? One moment she was going to come with me to tell the police about the email, the next she was flying home with the body.'

Aguta shrugged. 'Police rang and said they were releasing the body, so she just wanted to go.'

'But that email might have been important. At the time, we thought it was.'

'Important to us. Not to police.'

'You don't know that.'

'If you come from our country, you try to have as little to do with police as possible.'

He was about to say that British police weren't like that. Then he thought about Powell and Orchard and the BWAP, and suddenly wasn't so sure.

'But Niela was staying with you, Aguta. Didn't you try and persuade her to stay?'

Dovila started to say something, but caught a warning look from her mother.

'She was upset. I was upset. I don't remember all the things that were said. It's just... it's finished now.'

Aguta shrugged again and turned to stare out of the window, dead-eyed. Rex knew he would get no further. Besides, did it matter that Niela had had second thoughts about some stray email, now that the killer had been found?

It seemed inconceivable that there could be a third obstacle on such a straightforward trip, but they'd only gone a short distance when they again ground to a halt. There were cars in front, behind, and some sort of drama with flashing lights up ahead. They were in a smart, tree-lined enclave of tall villas, whose inhabitants gazed nervously from their windows onto the grey council blocks beyond. Used to trouble, many of them were out in the road now, talking to their neighbours, pointing, commiserating.

'Stop haunting me now. Can't shake you nohow,' Billie commented from the radio speakers. 'Good morning heartache, here we go again.'

Rex offered to walk ahead to see what was going on. His limbs ached and he wanted the air, even larded with exhaust fumes as it was. The flashing lights came from a police car, parked across the road. Next to it was a private ambulance. There was a light metal trolley in the driveway of a grand house, whose brick-built garage contained a car with all its doors open. In the driver's seat, Rex saw a white haired man slumped at the wheel, then a young, pointy-featured policeman blocked his view.

'I'm from the *Wood Green Gazette*,' Rex said, before he remembered that was no longer true. 'What's happened?'

'Car in garage. Dead bloke. Can't you work it out?' replied the policeman, in a not-unfriendly fashion.

'That's a Lincolnshire accent,' Rex commented.

The policeman's face creased with pleasure. 'Sleaford. You?'

Rex knew how he felt. No one else ever understood. 'Louth.'

He glanced over the man's shoulder. He thought of suicide as a teenage strategy, borne of an inability to see that things change. 'What makes someone that age top themselves?' he wondered out loud.

'Maybe it's the job,' said the policeman. 'I know I couldn't stand it. All those bodies.'

'What was he? An undertaker?'

'A Forensic Pathologist. Name was Dr Clore.'

* * *

Noise bothered him. It always had. As a child, he'd once stuffed cotton wool deep into his ears to block out the sound of his foster mother's coughing. A piece had got lost in there and given him an infection. But his hearing had turned out none the worse for it. It was extra sharp, in fact – another of the ways in which he noticed everything around him. Even now, when whole mornings and afternoons of his life vanish from his memory, he still saw and heard and smelt everything.

At first he thought the singing was the woman next door. The tenant of a West African housing association, she was a sturdily built woman with a baby but no husband. They hardly heard a peep from her, except once a fortnight or so, when she cooked in her kitchen, and sang along to gospel songs on the radio. The singing annoyed him. When it came, he would pace up and down the stairs, opening and closing doors, flushing the toilet, hoping to drown it out with sounds that were under his own control, hoping too that the woman would hear and be quiet.

When it started, this hadn't sounded like the woman's songs, but he couldn't imagine what else it could be, so he went into the hall and pressed his ear against the wall. The house next door was silent. He could even hear her clock ticking on the other side of the wall. But he could also hear singing. It seemed to be coming from higher up in his own house. He went up the stairs. It was coming from the bathroom at the back, looking out over the yard. He went in there and saw that the window was open. She had taken the gauze curtain down and must have washed it, because she was down there in the yard, in a pink blouse and a grey skirt, pegging the curtain out on the washing line. She was singing to herself as she worked. Nobody had ever sung in this house. Or any other of the houses he had lived in.

He had no memory of her asking to move in, or of any conversation on the subject, but that didn't mean it hadn't taken place. Nowadays, when he tried to consider things too deeply, it felt like a drill skidding on a surface it couldn't penetrate, giddy and dangerous. He just knew that the girl was here now. She washed and cleaned and cooked. He taught her to use the darkroom. Her photography was coming along. And if she hadn't arrived when she did, he might have killed his wife. She had saved him, as Caroline once had.

He had been very frightened of using the darkroom with her. One afternoon, not long after the funeral, he'd sat fingering the little lock of hair he kept in a Strepsils tin in a kitchen drawer, and thinking about his journey to this point, and he'd heard her upstairs, using the toilet, and been afraid. She was so soft, so pale and delicate – like the girl in the hospital bed, like the silver, dew-frosted spider's webs he used to find on hedges when he was a boy. So perfect he needed to take a stick and thrust it through them. He felt afraid that he might do that to the girl, one day, in the close, tight dark of the dark-room, pick up something heavy and smash it down on her, just because she was so perfectly made.

As he stood here now, looking down on her, he couldn't believe he had ever worried. She knelt daintily at the washing basket, her long neck bent as if in prayer, then straightened with her underwear in her hands, and strung it out, piece by piece, on the line taking pegs from her mouth, singing and humming all the while. The scene was so beautiful, he wanted to take a photograph of it. He turned to go to the dark-room and fetch a camera, in his urgency knocking a slim bottle of shampoo from the ledge. Something – the noise, his movement – must have startled her because she glanced up and stopped singing. He withdrew into the shadows. The moment was gone, but he would always have it in his head. Whatever else went, he would always have the pictures inside his head.

* * *

'It's been there for years. How can you never have seen it? It's about half a minute away from your office. And it's in between an off-licence and a pub.'

'Not my office any more,' Rex said, ignoring the alcoholism taunt.

'Anyway, it's called Sri Krishna Vegetarian Restaurant…'

'It's vegetarian?'

'I'm giving up meat.'

'Why?'

'I'll tell you when I see you. You are going to show up, aren't you? You can hardly use work as an excuse.'

'Nothing ever stood between me and a bowl of mushy cumin-flavoured vegetables. I'll see you at 12.15.'

Dr Diana Berne hung up. Rex felt encouraged. Given where

they'd left things, even an early vegetarian lunch was an augur of promise.

But in the meantime he had somewhere to go: the Famous Manti Shop on Green Lanes. He'd discovered after some judicious – if fraudulent – calls that this was where Bibigul, the late Dr Clore's one-time assistant was now working.

Rex stood outside and looked in the shop's window. She was in the window, at a low table, with a woman either side, rolling out dough and turning it into little parcels. Manti were everywhere: mandu in Korea, momo in Nepal. Portable snacks carried by the Mongol horsemen across the plains from Ulan Bator to the heart of Haringey.

Bibigul, fittingly enough, was from Kazakhstan. A highly qualified forensic pathologist who'd worked in Moscow and Hamburg, she was, understandably, bitter about her current role. She sat twitchily in her cap and apron at a little table at the back of the shop, aware, as Rex was, of her boss hovering nearby.

'We had a case come in,' she said, in quiet, clipped phrases that reminded him of horses' hooves. 'A baby. A cot-death. A mistake at the mortuary meant the parents couldn't give the baby a proper burial. Dr Clore and the Director told them it was because there was a power failure in the morgue, so the body… uh… deteriorated over the Bank Holiday. Do you remember – that very hot one, at the end of May?'

Rex nodded uneasily. It was hot in the shop, too – the charcoal ovens blasting smells of wood and lamb fat around. Not exactly the aroma you wanted when you were discussing cadavers.

'But it was Clore. He was drunk and couldn't operate the regulator. When I left on Friday for the weekend, I asked him if he wanted me to do it, but he shouted at me. He did things like that all the time. I wrote a letter to the parents. I thought they should know.'

'And you were the one who got the sack.'

'They didn't sack me,' Bibigul said, sharply, before the boss strode past for the fifth time. 'They invited me to hand in my notice, and I did.'

'Why do that? Why not report him? Take it to a tribunal?'

She laughed faintly and shook her head. 'You see this job? It's not what I trained to do. But the boss here... He's been here for thirty years, he's got a house in Cyprus, because he makes good manti. If he stops making good manti, he stops making money. It's not like that in pathology. Not for men like Dr Clore. He was old, and he was a man, and he knew everybody, all the professors and the judges, so it didn't matter that he wasn't good at his job anymore. He was at the top. And people like me can't report or make tribunals because we are at bottom.'

This final omission of the word 'the' had been Bibigul's only mistake, as far as Rex could tell. That, and, possibly, leaving Kazakhstan.

'He made a lot of mistakes? Not just with the baby?'

'The last case before I finished –' She shook her head. 'I can't say anything else.'

'But who was the last case? Can you remember? Can you tell me that?'

'It was the girl. That girl they had the service for. I remember, because they showed a picture of her on the news at lunchtime. And then at tea-time, the news said that Dr Clore had killed himself. I didn't know he had a... what do you call it... a conscience, but perhaps...'

'Why would he have had a guilty conscience about Milda?'

She shook her head again, and stood up as the boss walked back their way. 'Buy some manti. Please.'

He went, with a box of minced-lamb dumplings and a leaflet offering 20% off his next purchase, and he sat in the library at Wood Green searching forensics sites on the internet. The browsing history had not been deleted, and he saw that the last user before him had posed the eternal question: 'Where I can find free picture of naked lady?' Some other goodly citizen of the borough of Haringey had, on the day previous, typed into Google, 'if u hit sumbdy with a hamer on the head wil they die or do they jus like get a bruse?' He was tempted to click on it, and see what advice Google had offered.

As to his own forensic questions, little information was forthcoming. He didn't have the autopsy report with him, and he was now no longer sure what to look for. Since Dushku's arrest, he'd almost come to accept the idea that Milda had taken drugs with the Albanian Drifter, just as he'd come to terms with the idea that he had yanked out her hair and strangled her, for his own twisted little reasons. Clore's suicide changed things, though.

And there was no doubt: someone was trying to tell him something. Not just a simple 'fuck off and die'; it was easy to get that message across if you wanted to. Whoever was behind all these symbols – organs, handcuffs, wheelchairs – wanted him to know something important, something that could not be said outright. It had to have something to do with Milda. But what?

Then again, driving a moped at him, or beating him up: these actions were hardly subtle or encrypted... Were they even related to the other stuff? Or the work of someone else, who also hated him?

For the first time, sitting in the underheated, stale-smelling library, he admitted to himself how afraid he felt. How powerless. It was a physical, giddying feeling, like the one he'd had all those years back, when they told him Sybille would never recover. He'd been sick on that occasion, over some buff-coloured folders on the consultant's messy desk. He felt sick now.

He hurried out for some air, and when a couple of

bored-looking PCSOs began eyeing him with interest, moved on for a wander through the labyrinthine weirdness of Shopping City. It distracted him and took his heart rate down, eventually.

Built in the early Nineties around a disused railway station, Shopping City was six stories of glass, steel and discount, threaded together by steep, bare sided escalators from which you felt permanently on the verge of toppling. If Green Lanes was the old world, Shopping City was the new. A few, bewildered Turkish pensioners sat on the benches in the atrium in their caps and their multi-pocketed fishing vests, but everyone else in there – customers, staff, security – was very young, with a complicated hairdo and a diamante stud in at least one ear. The whole place glittered and shone – all of it, from the door handles on the shops to the quasi-military get-up of the security guards. But when you looked more closely, it had as much substance as a pub darts trophy. Everything was cheap. Much was counterfeit: a burger bar called Mad Donald's, The Barbadian Muffin Kompany. The only shops that lasted were Boots and Primark: all the others – the one selling fussy baby clothes for Africans, the specialist in religious statues for the South Americans, the leather 'n' studs outfit where Rex suspected Aguta had obtained many of her sartorial ensembles – these came and went. It was an illusion of Western abundance, frequented and staffed by people who were beginning to suspect they might have been duped. A year ago there had been riots throughout the borough. Shopping City had been attacked, windows smashed, fires started in the delivery area at the back. But nobody had stolen a thing. It was as if it wasn't worth the effort.

How had Milda felt about all this? Well-educated, full of promise, she'd come over here with her degree from art college, her luggage and her optimism like the rest of them, to find that the only skills required of her were cutting sandwiches and serving tea. Accused of theft. Left in the lurch, pregnant, by an alcoholic, arthritic local journalist. Living in a squat on the North Circular, threatened by Levantine gang-bangers and a local Nazi group secretly led and funded by a unit of the Metropolitan police? He could see now that she must have felt desperate. Who could blame her for accepting a little wisp of brown powder that might take that feeling away?

And perhaps someone else, someone close to her, might blame him for that.

At 12pm exactly, he was inside Sri Krishna, being reminded that the premises were not licensed. At 12.07 pm, he was back in there, with two large bottles of Svyturys – a Lithuanian beer – courtesy of the shop next door. At 12.09 pm, he remembered that he owed the owner of Sri Krishna money, having ordered 20 vegetable samosas to keep the *Gazette* staff going during a particularly tedious late shift, and lacked sufficient funds to pay for them. At 12.11 pm, he established to his relief that the place was now owned by someone else.

Diana came at 12.33. She accepted a glass of beer, which Rex took as another good sign. They shared a tali: a palette of assorted soup-like curries, with warm bread and pappadoms. Rex told her about the two searches he'd found on the library Web browser, and she laughed and told him about a cousin, who had once actually written 'Porn Mag' on a shopping list. She had had a haircut and was wearing a deep green blouse which perfectly complemented her eyes. He told her so.

Then things began to go downhill.

'I've got some news,' she said. 'Actually.'

'Ah. What's his name?'

'Kanta Bopha.'

'Senegalese? Bhutanese?' He was trying to sound playful, and failing.

She smiled. 'It's a hospital. Next to Angkor Wat. In Cambodia.'

'You've fallen in love with a building, three thousand miles away. You need help.' He kept the jokes coming, because he sensed what was on the verge of being said.

'I'm taking some time off from being a G.P.' she said. 'And I've always wanted to go out there. Well, you know… we talked about it. You lent me that book. So I've taken a job at the hospital. Three hundred dollars a month and all the rice I can eat.'

He nodded. It sounded like a great opportunity. He said so, and he meant it. 'When are you going?'

'Well… quite soon…' She took a breath. 'Tomorrow, actually. I'd been thinking about it for ages, and I had a month's worth of leave owing to me, and Dr Shah didn't mind, because…' She spiralled a hand in the air, short-hand for the various reasons. 'It's not to do with you,' she added. 'I want you to know that.'

'I'm not that self-centred,' he lied, offering her another glass of beer. She declined.

'Yes you are,' she said. 'We all are. That's part of the reason I'm going out there. To see if I can become a bit less.'

'If it works, let me know,' Rex said. 'I might come and join you.'

She squeezed his hand. Absurdly, he felt his eyes watering. He looked away. Waved at the waiter. 'Could I have another bottle of beer?'

The waiter – who looked himself not unlike a temple god of Angkor Wat – frowned. 'I told you, no license, sir.'

'I knew that,' Rex said, as a tear rolled down his cheek.

* * *

His front gate was wide open, swinging out into the narrow road. Rex slammed it shut on his way in, expecting to find a dozen pizza delivery leaflets stuffed through his letterbox. He would complain – it must have been the leaflet-deliverer who left the gate like that. But then he considered that he was an almost-40-year-old bachelor, about to get on the phone and complain about the leaflet delivery man leaving his gate open. It couldn't happen. He would not stoop that low.

There weren't any leaflets. Nor had the postman been. But someone had. Someone who had left the front door open. And who, judging by the sound of the tv in the front room, was still in there. Waiting for him.

He lingered in his hallway. Alert, on edge, but not as blind with terror as he'd imagined he would be. This was it, surely. The end of the message. The point to which all those augurs had been leading, from the encounter in the car-park to the wheelchair and the packages.

'Journalist!'

Vadim Kozyrev, Milda's some-time lover, was sitting on Rex's sofa, an unopened bottle of vodka on the coffee table, next to a felt-tip pen and a scrap of paper. The freckled Russian raised a hand in sardonic greeting.

'How the fuck did you get into my house?' Rex said, suddenly angry. Vadim mimed some kind of lock-picking procedure.

'I worked for time as lock-smith,' he said. 'In city of Turku, Finland. Sorry. I wanted to leave you a note, but I didn't have any pens. I thought, now a journalist must have a pens inside his house. So…'

The lock-picking motion again. There was, to be fair, a half-written note on the coffee table. Rex sat down at the other end of the sofa. A medical soap opera was showing on the tv. It made him think of the wheelchair.

'Have you been trying to frighten me, Vadim?'

Vadim frowned. 'I wasn't trying to frighten you. I came to give you something.'

'What?'

'That,' Vadim said, waving a hand towards the bottle on the table. It had a gold foil top, and silver Cyrillic writing around the label. 'Arkangelskaya. Seventy-two percent proof. Impossible to get it anywhere. Especially Arkangel,' he added, with a smile.

'Why?'

Vadim sat back. 'Because boys who beated you are sorry. They thought you did it. To Milda, I mean. They know they were wrong now. So they ask me...'

'So they changed their minds after Dushku was arrested?'

Vadim snorted. 'Dushku? Shit! Dushku was living in the house maybe five, six, seven years ago? When he was living there, Milda was in Klaipeda learning A, B, C! She didn't know Dushku and he didn't kill her. Are you really a journalist, to believe that? Come on, man.'

'So what made "the boys" change their minds about me?'

Vadim tapped his bony chest. 'I make change their minds about you. When I found out that they beated you, I made them. I explain them. This man is not police who just arrests some mad fuck Albanian and doesn't care. *On zhurnalist*. He is a journalist, a good man. And if you want a justice for your friend, you get him on your side, boys, because he is the only person maybe who find out what really happen.'

Rex took this in. 'So they were friends of Milda's then? The Boys?'

Vadim bit his fingernail and nodded. 'From art school.' He was silent. Then he chuckled. After a second or two, Rex began to laugh too.

'So you're saying I had the shit kicked out of me by a bunch of artists?'

'Yes. Painters. Illustrators.' He snorted. 'One of them does keramics!'

Rex remembered the funeral party – the thin boy who had been awkward, hadn't wanted to talk. He also remembered Powell, and his story about the graffiti artist. Now he understood. Or thought he did. He stopped laughing.

'And the boys… did they do anything else to me? Before you changed their minds.'

Vadim stopped smiling now. 'Do something to you? What would they do?'

'Try to frighten me. Leave things outside my house. Send me things.'

Vadim shrugged. 'Rex. You think everyone from Eastern Europe is gangster who leaves horse's head in the bed?'

Rex sighed. It looked like Vadim was telling the truth. Or the truth as far as he knew it. 'No. No, I don't think that.' He reached for the bottle and examined it. 'Please tell the boys thank you for the drink.'

Vadim nodded, thoughtfully. 'Somebody is trying to frighten you?'

'I think so. I can't work out why.'

'When did it start?'

'The same day I discovered Milda was missing. They leave things outside my house. They send me things in the post.'

Vadim nodded again. 'Maybe she is the answer.'

'Maybe so.'

The Russian reached into his jacket and pulled out a carrier bag.

'This was last remaining few things from Milda. A few things… from the bottom drawer. We thought to send to family, but then, maybe, they might… say something to you.'

Rex took the bag. The trace of her perfume made him sad. Inside the bag was a London Transport Oystercard, some sort of student identity paper and a well-thumbed copy of the Thomas

Cook International Rail Timetable. Rex looked at the Oystercard.

'You can get information off these, can't you?' he asked. 'If you know the login. Find out about journeys?'

Vadim patted him on the knee. 'My friend, you can get a data without login also. All you need is one Tube Station, and one computer engineer. Come!'

As they were coming out of the gate, the postman handed Rex a sheaf of letters. He stuffed them in his hunting bag and walked with Vadim the short distance to the Tube Station. The freckled Russian nodded approvingly as they descended the stairs into the modernist cathedral space of the ticket hall. One of the reason so many Slavic people lived around here, Rex often speculated, was the uncannily Soviet atmosphere of Haringey and its environs. The tube stations, most of them designed in the Thirties, recalled the democratizing grandeur of the Moscow Metro. Alexandra Palace – where Milda had met her end – was always full of people from the old communist nations, who found it a comfortable reminder of the Workers' Palaces of Culture. They even played Prokofiev over the loudspeakers at the bus terminus, though that was more to drive away the gang-bangers than to enlighten the masses.

With supreme confidence, Vadim produced his London Transport IT Team ID card on a piece of ribbon, which he hung around his neck, and approached a guard. 'Allo maite,' he said, in a distinctive mixture of Slav and London that some wags had started to call Pockney, 'Chast fitting apgrade, boss, awroight?' The guard nodded indifferently, and Vadim went straight to one of the large ticket machines by the side of the main stairs. He passed Milda's card over the yellow sensor plate and waited. Nothing happened. He licked the card and tried again. Strings of figures appeared on the screen. Vadim winked and motioned to Rex to have a look.

Rex peered in at the tiny digital screen. Line upon line of data was being scrolled through, detailing journeys by bus and tube, the times and dates and costs. Vadim held up a finger, tapped various keys and swiped a different, blank card across the sensor. The machine set about printing ten receipt tickets, with the whole of Milda's journey history printed on them in close, fine type.

'You are impressed, I can tell,' Vadim said. 'Don't worry. English people are not able to say these things, but I know.'

'He picks locks, he hacks computers, he fits kitchens. What else?' Rex responded dutifully.

'I told you,' Vadim said as the last of the cards dropped down into the hatch. 'Soviet system. Everybody must become resourceful, because no fucking resources. You want us to plumb, we plumb. You want us to make bomb, with a freezer and some Chinese fireworks, we do it.'

Rex stared at him. 'That was you?'

'What was me?' Vadim said, feigning puzzlement.

'Vadim. Shit. People got hurt by that thing.'

'Only fascists,' Vadim replied brightly. 'Come!'

In the little sandwich bar upstairs, they spread the tickets out on a table and tried to make sense of them. It proved pretty straightforward. For months, Milda's only regular journey was from a bus-stop on Bowes Road, outside the squat, down Green Lanes to a stop near the Good Taste Café. Between, there were occasional tube rides to the sort of places Milda had liked to go as a treat – Leicester Square for the National Gallery, St Paul's for the Tate Modern, Hampstead for walks and drinks. Rex remembered a few of these journeys himself: a glorious mid-May evening at The Holly Bush, a lost afternoon down Brick Lane, both in the salad-days of their affair. Even more sadly, he picked out the night she'd been on the top of the 141 bus and he'd spotted her: a Wednesday at the end of August.

Suddenly, in early September, when Milda had lost her job, the pattern changed. She began to visit Tottenham Hale, just for short spells, an hour or two at a time, then return to the vicinity of the squat. A week later, there was a trip to Newington Green on the 141 route – tallying with what Birgita had told him about Milda's last visit. Soon after that, for a fortnight, there was nothing except a couple of very short hops on the small back-street 'C' routes around Southgate. And then, on Thursday 6th October, the day Milda died, a final mammoth procession of public transport. Tube from Southgate to Wood Green. 29 bus from Wood Green to Turnpike Lane. 144 bus from Turnpike Lane to Priory Road. At Priory Road, she must have got off the bus, walked up the hill and through the woods to Alexandra Palace. Where she'd met her killer.

'She could have caught one tube and one bus to get to Ally Pally. Probably even done it all on one bus,' Rex said. 'Instead she did it in these short hops. Tube, bus, bus. It took her hours.'

'Being followed by somebody?' Vadim suggested.

'Or just unable to make up her mind.' Rex gathered up the cards. 'It looks like she went to stay in Southgate for a fortnight. You can see it all here. She lost her job, she argued with you, she spent a night with Birgita, and then she moved to Southgate. Who did she know there?'

Vadim shrugged. 'I fitted kitchen there the other week. It's all old people. Lot of Greeks. Jews people. Actually quite lot of English,' he added. 'Nobody… how I can say it… our sort.'

'Do you know anybody with the initials, K.P.?'

Vadim pondered. 'Only peanuts.'

He left soon after that, something to do with a friend's cousin's boiler in East Ham. 'You know why East Ham is becoming new capital of Lithuania?' he asked Rex in parting. 'Because even Rumanians don't want to live there!' He departed, chuckling at his joke, which perhaps had deeper layers of meaning to someone who knew East Ham, or Lithuania, or Rumania. And Vadim doubtless knew them all.

Rex, who had been given a cup of coffee hotter than the surface of the sun, tarried awhile, and made the mistake of deciding to look at the letters in his bag. There was a water bill. A credit card bill. Meanwhile, someone calling himself Ian Daley – Electrical had written to him in very fine old copperplate to say that unless Rex paid the outstanding £200 for the re-wiring done in March, Rex would find himself in court.

If he wanted to find out what had happened to Milda, who was behind the messages and the threats, he was in the wrong place. He looked down at his knees, where the fabric of his favourite suit was wearing a little thin. He thought he had better go home, and change into something with sturdier knees. This afternoon, he was going to be down on them, in Susan's office. Begging for his job back.

* * *

Apart from his short-term memory, his other senses were intact. His hearing, in fact, seemed to become sharper and more sensitive every day. In bed one night recently he'd heard the faintest of pattering sounds, so he'd got up to look out of the window. It was a squirrel running over the roof of the shed two gardens down.

He was losing weight, but it wasn't a surprise. He had started to find sounds and sights more nourishing than any food. He had spent a full hour in the Iceland, letting the contents of a bag of frozen peas roll and trickle and crunch past his ears, luxuriating in the sounds until a Security Guard had asked him if he was unwell. And now, in his own home, leaving traces in every room, was a creature so visually delectable, so much like silk and cream to his optic nerves, that he'd hardly had to take any photographs. Her towel on a radiator, the damp imprint of her bare body upon it. Her plate, with the dainty remains of a snack upon it.

Then, one day, he had seen too much. He was crossing the landing from the darkroom, and heard her in the bathroom. The wood of the door was thin, and years of steam and fluctuating temperatures had opened a long, narrow split in one of the panels. If he positioned himself just to the side, he would be able to see a strip of her. He had seen her like that the other day, drying herself, and fled down the stairs. But today, the light pulled him in.

He heard a zip. A soft fabric rustle, then the snap of elastic. The sounds caressed and coaxed the confusing shadows and flickers from the slit into a full, technicolour vision he could touch and smell. A vision of her undressing to stand there, pale as milk, with the golden light streaming between her legs. He groaned in awe.

There was a silence, then a rattle, a sound like a string of beads being cut. Little round, red pills cascaded out from under the door. She opened it, fully clothed, an odd look on her face.

'You are okay?'

'Yes,' he said, 'But –' He had picked up a few of the pills. 'These are my wife's…'

He shoved her aside and saw the bathroom cabinet was open. She had taken out and unzipped the plastic washbag where Caroline's drugs had been stored. There was a bottle on the floor. Another, unopened, on the sink.

She had humiliated him. Another one of them had humiliated him, after seeming to be different, seeming to hold out some promise to him. Anger streamed through him.

And then turned to joy. What a glorious, sharp, dizzying release it gave him to grab the soft, mocking flesh, to feel the fibrous chords and tendons underneath and then to hear the moan from her as a pink flush spread along her jaw and outwards.

He waited for the crack – like the shifting links of some huge fathoms-deep chain – but when the sound came, it was different. More like a distant crash. He felt only relief, though. She was gone. He was alone.

Chapter Eight

Susan Auerglass, Rex's friend and champion, his long-time colleague and his boss, was angry with him. She was angry because she needed him, because no one else like him would come and work on a weekly newspaper in the bleakest part of northeast London. She knew she had little choice but to re-employ him when he asked her to do so.

Susan's way of making all this known to Rex was to appear at her most charming. Even as she heard his confession, and granted him forgiveness, she was online, ordering him a special new ergonomic chair from the office suppliers. She also offered him her old laptop, a device upon which one could upload streaming video from Antarctica, should one wish to do so. She behaved, in short, as if he had been struck by some rare, embarrassing tragedy: something that should not be mentioned, but at the same time should be vigorously compensated for.

She informed him, too, that Ellie Mehta would be the lead reporter for the foreseeable future, and that he was to take charge of whatever shorter stories said lead reporter should delegate to him, as well as the judging and reporting of the photography competition. Rex got the message. He had to keep his head down, accept Susan's gifts with humility, and never walk out again. So be it.

He sat at his desk, and looked for the folder containing the entries for the competition. It wasn't there. He went over to ask Terry, who pointed to a grey canvas sack containing around ten kilos' worth of photographs and letters.

Unfathomably, the prospect of a free tripod had whipped the

population of Haringey into an image-capturing frenzy. Among the first few entries Rex opened were some tiny squares from passport booths; A3-sized black-and-white blow-ups; earnest, arty shots of abandoned textile workshops and cheesy Polaroid birthday ensembles. Rex glanced towards Susan's office, and could have sworn she looked away with just the faintest of smiles on her face.

Terry was not so discreet. Tapping his teeth with a viewfinder, he said that he would rather have gum surgery than go through that mailbag, and wished Rex luck with it.

'Is your entry in there too, Terry?' Rex sniped, as he hauled the bag back over to his desk. 'Or did your agent advise you against entering?'

'I haven't got a bloody agent,' Terry replied, gloomily. 'And it's actually a bit of a sore point, Rex, actually, so I'd rather you didn't joke about it.'

'What happened to the global overnight success story?'

'Thirty-five percent plus VAT!' he spat. 'That's what the cheapest of the bastards wanted in commission. Plus printing fees, postage fees, two-and-a-half per cent for internet reproduction, plus...'

'You decided against it,' Rex said.

'Aye.' Terry tapped his fingers against his skull. 'I thought, sod 'em. I'll be my own agent. So I stayed up half the night, rang up the *Sydney Morning Star*. Says – do you want this picture, like? And the bloke goes, we only buy from recognised agencies, sorry. Same for the lot of them. Bastards.'

Through the middle of Terry's lament, Lawrence Berne now strode, in a silver-grey suit. He'd had his roots done since Rex last saw him, and his tan reddened further. In his shining wake, were Aguta and her daughter, Dovila.

As usual, Lawrence was talking. 'So I said to the policeman, a man has just run out of this building and over the railway line, and I'm not doing railway lines in these shoes!'

At length, Aguta extricated herself from Lawrence and his self-glorifying tales. She approached Rex, followed by Dovila.

'We went to your house, but that Japan lady next door said you went back to work.' Aguta's sharp, elfin features looked aggrieved, as if Rex ought not have gone anywhere without telling her.

'She's Colombian.'

Aguta rolled her eyes. 'We got a message.' She swung Dovila round and unzipped her pink back-pack, rummaging through assorted bits of PE kit and packed lunch until she found a star-spangled notebook. 'Niela found other message from Milda. On the Skype voicemail. From Wednesday 5th October.'

'Milda's sister found another message from Milda? The day before she died? When did you find out about this?'

Dovila opened her mouth to speak, but Aguta cut in. 'Yesterday, Niela rang to us. She checked her Skype account at the internet café. She said it was first time for long time because factory is always late paying her wages…'

She ushered Rex out of the way and typed the Skype address on his computer. Some debate followed between mother and daughter about the precise details of the username and password noted down in the book, and whether a certain glyph was a 3, a B, an 8, or some jam. Their conversation was in Lithuanian, but conducted with such vigour that Rex, and everyone else in the office, was able to follow the gist. Finally, Aguta logged into Niela's Skype account and clicked on the voicemail.

And there, suddenly, was Milda's voice, issuing eerily from some far-flung ante-room of cyberspace. Rex didn't understand the words, but she sounded breathy and excited. It was just a day before she died.

Rex suddenly realised he had re-written the narrative of Milda's last days in his mind. He had turned her into a poor wretch, suffering ever-mounting torments until the final blow. But the truth was more disturbing. She sounded happy. Excited. She sounded like someone enjoying their life, and confident that it would continue. But what had she said?

'She said, I moved in with a KP now, into his house,' Aguta said. 'I am looking after him for now. But I've got a surprise for you. I am coming home. In a few days. I will see you soon.'

'She was going home. For good, do you think, or a visit?'

Aguta gave one of her classic shrugs. 'Maybe, from the verb she uses, for good. It's more like, I am returning to the home.'

'Who the hell is this KP?' Rex said.

'Could that be Keith...?' said Ellie.

Rex was about to answer when, suddenly, from the depths of a story-book, Dovila said, 'Kishkis Pishkis.'

'What did you say, Dovila?'

Dovila turned her book round. It was a Lithuanian book of folk tales, and the picture facing them was of an officious-looking rabbit.

'Kishkis Piskis, He's a very busy, bossy rabbit.'

'It's like a... a folks tale character,' Aguta said, shrugging. 'Bugs the Bunny kind of thing.'

'A rabbit? Someone like a rabbit?' Rex mused.

'Or someone who liked rabbits?' Ellie added.

'But was she – was she somebody who used nicknames?' Rex asked.

Dovila and her mother looked at one another and laughed. Aguta held a palm up. 'Er...durr?'

Dovila repeated the gesture.

'I'm guessing the answer is yes.'

'My nickname, since a juniors, is *skuja*. It's a needle,' Aguta

235

told him. 'Because of my nose. And Milda was *vezlys*. A tortoise, because –'

'She did everything so slowly,' Rex said. Suddenly he felt abominably, unbearably sad, not just at the memory of that lovely girl, who had always needed an hour and a half to eat a tiny bowl of muesli, but because he'd never known about the nicknames. They had never got that far. Having heard her voice, he now felt an overwhelming urge to see her again. Even just once.

'Dovila,' he said, clearing his throat. 'Do you still have that picture of Milda on your phone?'

Dovila frowned. 'It's gone.'

'You deleted it, you mean?'

She shook her head. 'I mean, one day I had it, and the next day, it wasn't there.'

Rex opened his mouth to ask another question, but Aguta cut in. 'She's just a child, Rex.'

She'd spoken so sharply that Rex held up his hands in surrender, as if to say he hadn't been accusing Dovila of anything. He'd just wanted to see Milda. That was all.

He stared at the picture book. Did this get them anywhere? That Milda might have moved in with someone who might have been like a rabbit, or like the particular rabbit-character in the Lithuanian children's stories, or just liked rabbits. Or KP might mean something else entirely.

Of one thing there was no doubt. She had sounded happy. She hadn't sounded desperate, or like someone who would put their own life at risk. She had plans. And from somewhere, from someone, she must have had some money.

Brenda, wheezing, came upstairs with the post. There was a hand-written envelope for Rex. N6 postmark. Just up the road.

He opened it. Inside was a sheet of A4 paper, with cut-out newspaper letters glued onto it: the classic blackmailers' and kidnappers' calling card. Everyone came over to examine it.

skewer iNTo mY

'It's an anagram of *New York Times*,' Lawrence said.'

'And it's OET,' said Susan. 'Old English Text – the typeface the *Times* uses for its masthead.

'Still think I'm imagining things?' Rex asked her. 'I've been getting lots of these. I think it's something to do with Milda.'

'Does the message mean anything to you?' Susan asked.

Rex shook his head. *Skewer into my* meant nothing.

New York did, though.

* * *

'Yes, but why,' Rex asked, through a mouthful of stuffed eggplant, 'why did the imam faint?'

'Because… it tasted so frigging good,' replied Terry.

The Turks, it was said, knew 256 different ways to prepare an aubergine. And you could sample a good sixty of them at the Pamukkale. Authentically cheerless, with a décor of white tiles, metal furniture and strip lighting, it served no meat before 8 pm, no alcohol ever, and was permanently, justifiably, rammed to the rafters.

This had been Terry's price for helping Rex out with the photography competition entries. Lunch at the Pamukkale. With double portions of *Imam Bayıldı*, the famous stuffed aubergine dish whose name, enigmatically, translated as 'The Imam Fainted'. Rex had readily agreed. He needed a treat.

'Yes, but' – Rex reached for a spoonful of the garlic-laden, sumac-dusted yoghurt before the last of it disappeared into Terry's mouth – 'Some people say the imam fainted for the opposite reason. Because his wife cooked him this beautiful dish for twelve days in a row, and then on the thirteenth, she didn't.'

'Aye well,' Terry commented, his face momentarily clouding over. 'That's birds for you.'

'Are things between you and your…'

'Shall we crack on?' Terry interrupted brusquely. Rex got the message, so he cleared a space amid the little saucers of seared artichoke and the courgette fritters, and began to lay out the thirty photographs he'd narrowed it down to over the course of the morning.

'Easy… daft… boring… FAKE… obvious… trying too hard, man… bollocks… not bad,' Terry reeled off a staccato list of verdicts as he went through the pile. He paused at a picture of Hasidic boys dressed up in superhero garb for the Purim festival. '*I* fucking took this one when I worked on the Highbury and Islington. Cheeky twat. Hmm…' He paused again at a startling image of two cranes, chewing up the earth near the Tottenham Hale roundabout.

They looked like dinosaurs, or giant yellow vultures, and the lurid red signage of the Tube Station behind accentuated the idea that some sort of slaughter was going on. Or if not exactly slaughter, then consumption. A feeding frenzy on the marshes. An old world being swallowed up by the new, the futility of the process underlined by the 'Y' formed by the cranes. A giant Why?

Meanwhile, Terry had moved on and was gazing appreciatively at a nice reportage of some Turkish girls primping for a Sunday wedding in one of the nearby hair salons. He squinted from various angles. 'A little too much light, but…'

'I think it's this one.' Rex placed the crane picture back on the table. He was glad to have been given this task. Every minute spent on photographs and aubergines was a minute away from Milda and the chilling message he'd been sent this morning. *Skewer into my.* Into whose what?

Terry glanced between the two contenders once, twice, a third time. He took a sip of cherry juice. And finally inclined his long Viking head.

'I think you're right. Who's the lucky boy?'

Rex looked on the back of the photo. 'He calls himself Arthur Chapman, and he lives at Number 44 Trentino Gardens, N14. Where is N14?'

'Southgate.'

Where Milda had seemingly moved. Every day would be like this, for who knew how long: full of tiny, barbed reminders, one loss, made into a million.

'He hasn't put a phone number.' Rex called Directory Enquiries, but there was no listing for that address. Arthur Chapman wasn't on the phone. Was that truly possible?

'This one's got a number,' Terry pointed out, flipping over the hair salon picture. 'Landline, mobile and email address...'

'But we decided this is the winner. And anyway, Terry, what has a bunch of girls in a hair salon got to do with the changing face of the area?'

'That one's having her make-up done, man. How much more of a changing face do you want?'

'Come off it, Terry. It's this one. Mr N14.'

'Well, if you want it to go in tomorrow's paper, you'll have to get up there with one of my cameras this afternoon, and get some snaps of him looking delighted with his new tripod.'

Rex was about to cajole Terry into giving him a lift over there, when Ellie came into the restaurant, all rosy-cheeked, excited and smelling of the outside. In her short, belted raincoat, she made Rex think of girls on the Paris Metro. She slapped a printed document on the table.

'My little friend at the council owes me a favour,' Ellie said, tapping her nose – a comic gesture, given the volume at which she was speaking. 'That's everyone in Haringey, Enfield and Edmonton with the initials KP.'

'Wow,' Rex replied. 'What made you go and get this?'

Ellie sat down. 'Adem Dushku's pleading Not Guilty.'

'Yeah, I know, on grounds of being a fruit loop.'

'No, on grounds of not having done it. Boy I know at the CPS just texted me. Dushku admits the four attacks, but he says he was co-erced into admitting the murder, and he's changed his plea.'

'Wow,' said Rex, for a second time.

'Is that all you're going to say?'

Rex stood up, slapped a pair of twenties on the table, and folded Ellie's papers into his jacket pocket. He turned to Ellie. 'Come on.'

'Where?'

Rex's phone rang.

'Hello.'

Silence. Then a quiet roaring in the background, just like before.

'Who is this?'

Over the roaring, a muffled voice said what sounded like, 'It's me, Rex,' and then hung up. Rex didn't know whether it was a woman or a man. He didn't recognise the voice. He wasn't even certain they'd said what he thought they said.

'Wrong number,' Rex said, ignoring the look Ellie and Terry exchanged. 'Come on. We're going to see Bernadette Devlin.'

* * *

If a single window-sign could sum up the ethnological history of the whole area, it was the one that announced, in gold, bold letters, the offices of Ozturk, Devlin, Berg and Mganga, Solicitors. The entrance was via a thin, frosted glass door between a Greek printers and a shop selling nothing but nuts. The office was upstairs in a long loft of a room, where each of the partners had a desk overlooking the Lanes. As in any truly multi-cultural enterprise, there was an ongoing feud between the various bosses and employees regarding the ambient temperature, and, depending on where you sat, you would be singed by hot-air heaters, or deafened by desk-fans, whatever the time of year.

As the daughter of immigrants from Guyana, Mrs Bernadette Devlin, LLM, LLB, MLS, was obliged to champion the hot side of the debate, but she did so in a half-hearted fashion, accompanying her own desk with a single-bar electric fire, which was in fact far too dangerous to use. She preferred to regulate her body temperature by alternating Polo mints with an obscure, fiery brand of Caribbean cough-drop.

'Have a sweet, darlin',' said Bernadette Devlin, holding out the pack to Ellie. Her voice always surprised people who didn't know her. With her long earrings and close-cropped silver hair, she looked as if she should speak some rich, lilting Creole. In fact, she sounded exactly as she was: Tottenham, to the bone. She winked at Rex as Ellie leaned forward and accepted a dark lozenge. Then they waited for the inevitable paroxysm.

'My husband says they're called cough drops,' Bernadette said, as Ellie staggered wheezing in the direction of the washroom, 'because they make you drop everything.'

'You never tire of it, do you?'

Bernadette beamed at him. 'I'm a black lawyer with the name of an IRA terrorist. I've got to have some compensation.'

As a man whose name attracted its own fair share of tiresome comments, Rex could sympathise. And he knew better than to correct Bernadette Devlin on the matter of the other, more famous Bernadette Devlin's occupation. No one ever interrupted, corrected, or questioned Bernadette Devlin, which was why half of Tottenham wanted her to represent them when they'd been arrested.

'How can I help you, Mr Tracey?' For all her larks with cough drops, she was a very formal lady – the deaconess of a hypermarket-sized Tabernacle Church in Seven Sisters. 'Have I won that photo competition? Mine was the one with all the cakes.'

'Adem Dushku. I take it he's one of yours?'

'Naturally.'

'Care to comment on his change of plea?'

'Care to spend a night inside Crews Hill?'

'Eh?' Mrs Devlin's utterances were often somewhat Delphic.

'Adem Dushku made the mistake of believing what he was told about secure mental hospitals being nice, gleaming white hotels with Playstations and En Suites.'

'In other words,' said Ellie, back from the washroom, 'the Feds told him to cop to the murder as well as the other stuff and he'd end up in a nice comfy hospital instead of a prison, so he did, even though he didn't do it, and now he's realised what a fucking awful place he's in, he'd rather go on the nonce-wing in prison than stay there.'

There was a long silence while Bernadette eyed Ellie. Rex half-expected her to leap across the desk and eat her head first.

'I don't like swearing,' she said at last. 'And it's only stupid kids who call the police the Feds. But that's basically it, yes.' She folded her hands together. 'He clearly has a problem with girls. He knows he has a problem. In the past eight weeks, he's been thrown out of two GP surgeries and an A & E unit, trying to get help.'

Rex and Ellie looked at one another, thinking the same thing. Dushku had gone to the Surgery Diana worked at. Tried to get help there. If that piece had been published, maybe he'd have got it.

'But what about the forensics?' Rex said. 'Sodium nitrite, used in exactly the sort of environment Dushku worked in, round Milda's neck. Are you saying the police made that up?'

'Sodium nitrite is used in all sorts of environments,' replied Mrs Devlin. 'No one is saying they made it up, but some people might say it isn't quite the evidence they have made it out to be.'

'And what do you say?'

'My job is to find all the holes in their side of things, and make sure the ones in ours are as small as they can reasonably be.'

'Why was he doing it? Attacking the girls, I mean. Has he given you any idea?'

'Mr Tracey, I have no idea, and I don't want one. I do know he had a job in a hairdressers once. I wondered if that might have something to do with it.'

'But you must have a view on whether he murdered Milda or not?' Ellie said.

Mrs Devlin gave her a broad, menacing smile. 'Another cough drop, dear?'

* * *

Around 3 pm, Rex found himself on a 329 bus, crawling up the Lanes to Southgate. The residence of Arthur Chapman, the winner of a brand-new tripod courtesy of Khan's Electrical and Photographic, was his official destination. Less officially, he had the addresses of three individuals who lived within a ten-minute walk of Arthur Chapman's house, within the N14 postcode and with the initials KP. There were forty-six people with the initials KP living in the N14 area, but these three would be a start.

Spilt lager and schoolkids: the classic odour of an afternoon bus was in Rex's nostrils as he cast his eyes over the list. He wondered what sort of a person Kyle Pinkerton might be. He marvelled at a civilisation that could confer on someone the public identity of Klianthis Panayiotopoulos. And he discovered, to his surprise, that the landlord of O'Mahoney's Shebeen was one Krishna Prabhu. At length, he arrived at Southgate.

With its chunky mansion blocks over rows of shops, it was less of a suburb, more like a Hertfordshire town that had been captured by the city. No flatbreads here, no shops selling amulets, just estate agents and chemists. Once Rex passed the commercial hub at the crossroads, he was immediately in a quiet zone of modest, between-the-wars semis. Trentino Gardens was remarkable only because it bore the name of an Italian province, whereas all the roads around it were named after shrubs. Arthur Chapman lived exactly half-way along, behind a front door with coloured glass panes. One red pane had a crack in it.

He was a slight, elderly man with small eyes that were perpetually staring. Rex was shown into a clean, worn-out little house unchanged since the seventies. It smelt of old people: sweet and slightly stale, like cake. He was about to go into the front room, but Chapman suddenly blocked his entry with what seemed almost like panic, ushering him down the wallpapered hallway into the kitchen.

'So, first of all – congratulations, Mr Chapman,' Rex said, after a long pause in which he'd expected in vain to be offered a cup of tea. Mr Chapman, whose hair was so white and fine it was more like a faint halo, nodded solemnly, without any sign of pleasure. Nor had he shown any interest in the tripod Rex had presented him with: it remained uninvestigated in the Khan's carrier bag on a kitchen chair.

'We'd like a photograph of you with your prize, and we also need two negatives so that we can print a copy of your prize entry in the paper.'

'Can't you scan it in?' Chapman asked quietly, for the first time showing interest in the proceedings.

Rex hesitated. The man was quite right. The truth was that, for legal reasons which only interested Susan, sending two negatives had been part of the competition rules. The further truth was that Arthur Chapman had included the statutory two negatives along with his competition entry, but that somewhere between Terry, Rex and the Pamukkale restaurant, they had been mislaid. The highest truth of all was that Rex didn't give a flying one about the negatives. They were an excuse to leave the office, and snoop around N14, so he could try to find out what had happened to Milda, and whether it had anything to do with the spooky messages and sinister parcels.

'I think we do need them for copyright reasons,' he said. 'Sorry to put you out. I mean, I'm sure the ones you sent will turn up, but…'

'They're upstairs,' Chapman murmured, staring at Rex as if he expected him to change into a butterfly. 'In my darkroom.'

There was another long, unnerving pause, during which the ticking of a clock in the hallway could be heard clearly. Rex looked out through the kitchen window into the yard beyond. What were those long wooden boxes? Rabbit hutches?

'Could I have a look at your dark-room?' he asked. 'Perhaps we could take your photo in there?'

Chapman nodded and headed out of the doorway. He moved silently. Rex followed him up a narrow staircase with an orange and gold swirly carpet. It was fixed in place with big ornamental clips, as his own grandmother's had been.

On the landing there was a mawkish painting of a little girl in a bonnet, and three doors, their once-white gloss paint turning yellow. Chapman opened the middle of these, and pulled a cord to switch a light on. Rex followed him in. Floorboards creaked beneath linoleum. At one point this must have been the box-room, or a child's bedroom, but now, with the aid of a wooden screen, a blind, and some insulating material around the door-jamb, it had been converted into a darkroom.

It was tidy, like Arthur Chapman himself. Obsessively so, with equipment on little racks, photo albums arranged in alphabetical order, no single item not in some symmetrical relationship to another. The room smelt of chemicals and dust, its bland, utilitarian look matching Chapman's beige shirt and grey trousers. The old man, with neat, precise movements that for some reason Rex found unnerving, moved a buff folder out of the way in order to retrieve a little card index filled with negatives, which he then began to look through, slowly.

Rex looked at the shelf of developing chemicals in front of him: white bottles with stark black writing, arranged so that each label faced the same way. Fixative. Emulsion. Stop-bath. Boric Acid. Silver dioxide. Sodium Nitrite. Rex read and re-read those five syllables. Milda had worn Guerlain on her neck. But she died with a different fragrance there.

Used in all sorts of environments, Bernadette Devlin had said. *Like photography.*

The light was dim, and his eyes began to hurt, peering at these little labels, so he glanced down to the bench, where some photographs from the displaced folder had spilled out. They were all versions of the image that had won the prize, some slightly broader or longer, with more detail in the frame. He moved the top photograph to look at the one beneath. Then, at the outer edge of the image, he saw a sliver of something that turned his heart into a jackhammer.

Chapman coughed. Rex dragged his eyes away from the photograph.

'Sorry.'

Chapman held out a little strip of dark brown plastic – the negatives. 'I'll get you a sleeve.'

He turned to a low metal filing cabinet. As he pulled out the drawer, Rex stuffed the photograph clumsily inside his jacket. It wouldn't fit in the pocket, so he was forced to trap it next to his body and hope that it didn't fall out.

Chapman placed the negatives carefully inside the plastic sleeve, then attached a label and wrote his name and address on it in maddeningly neat capitals, before handing it to Rex.

'Do you want to take your photograph now?' he asked. 'Where's your camera?'

Luckily, Rex had left it downstairs with the tripod, so he headed downstairs, the photograph nestling in his armpit. Trembling and sweating, trying not to look at the rabbit hutches outside, he took two very bad snaps of Arthur Chapman standing in his kitchen, and left, promising the pictures would be in tomorrow's paper.

He'd got a few yards down the road, when he noticed he no longer had the photograph.

Somewhere between the dark-room, the kitchen and the hallway, it must have fallen out. Chapman would find it. And he would know that Rex knew. That Rex knew he was KP. The rabbit man.

* * *

'Can I see Detective Sergeant Mike Bond, please?'

'I'm afraid he's gone,' said the heavily-pierced boy on Reception.

He was wearing eye-liner today, and an off-the-shoulder jumper with more holes than wool. The changing face of Tottenham nick.

'What do you mean, gone?'

'He had a heart-attack,' the boy said, scratching one shoulder to reveal a shower of tattooed stars. 'Do you want to talk to somebody else?'

Rex stood for a moment and collected his thoughts. 'When you say he's gone, do you mean he's dead?'

'Erm... no,' said the boy-receptionist. 'He's like, gone to the hospital in an ambulance? About an hour ago?' He raised his voice, as if Rex were elderly and confused. 'Do. You. Want. To. Speak. To. Anyone. Else?'

Rex asked to speak to a member of C.I.D, as long as it wasn't Detective Constable Orchard.

'Ah, that's cool, he's gone as well,' said the receptionist, smiling.

'Another heart-attack?' Rex asked.

'Nah, he's just, like, I dunno. Yeah. Gone.'

At last he was ushered past the barriers to speak to a thin, benevolent-looking Welshman named DC Brenard. He was not much more forthcoming on the matter of DC Orchard's unavailability, but he did sit down and take out a pen.

Rex told him about the photograph he'd seen in Chapman's dark room.

'The photograph you don't have any more,' said Brenard, twirling a wedding ring on a long, twiggy finger.

'I know. But it's there. Somewhere. In his house. And I know that arm.' Rex banged the desk as if the photograph was still in front of him and he could see the narrow band of his former lover's flesh along the edge of the image. 'And that watch-strap. It's Milda. She must have ended up staying with Chapman.'

'You're referring to the edge of a watch-strap,' Brenard said, after what seemed like much thought. 'A watch you bought from a fairground stall at Clacton…'

'I know. I know what you're going to say. Lots of arms. Lots of watches. But then there's the sodium nitrite. Around her neck. It's used in developing photographs – Chapman had some in his darkroom. And Kishkis Pishkis. In the answerphone message. It means a rabbit.'

Brenard held up a hand. 'What answerphone message?'

With a supreme effort of will, Rex marshalled his thoughts. He explained everything, while DS Brenard listened and took notes.

'We will have to look into this,' he said finally.

'Who will? When?'

'Trained detectives will, as soon as possible,' replied Brenard. His tone was serious, but infuriatingly calm.

'But he's out there. She's dead, and he's free! What if he does it to someone else while you're looking into it?'

'Someone has already confessed to killing Milda Majauskas.'

'And he's now withdrawn that confession.'

'In the meantime, since that person has been in custody, no one has been attacked. Which doesn't mean we won't be looking into this.' Brenard gazed back at him. 'Swiftly.'

Rex felt his stomach clench. There was nothing he could do. It would take time. Some things in life just did. Justice was notoriously slow. Slow for good reasons, perhaps. And waiting was often the right thing to do.

The trouble was that none of those good reasons mattered to Rex right now.

* * *

Early the next morning Rex, Susan, Ellie and Terry sat in the offices of the *Gazette*. Susan, as ever, was lily-fresh, but the rest of the team were pale and red-eyed with exhaustion. They had been up all night. Now Ellie was going through the plan one last time.

'Taxi's booked to pick up Chapman at 9.15 am. He's been told to dress smart, and bring the tripod. Sabjit Khan is coming here for 9.45 in expectation of being photographed handing over said tripod to the competition winner Chapman. Terry will find himself unavoidably delayed by twenty minutes, and then once he's here will come up with some suitable technical hitch to string the photo-session along a little more.'

For all the fatigue in the room, there was an unmistakeable air of excitement. Rex had been amazed he'd convinced Susan to go along with his scheme. In the end, two things had swung it. The fact that this was for Milda. And the fact that it involved some intrigue. Susan had a light in her eyes, a light that hadn't burned quite so fiercely since she'd manned the *Times*' foreign desk during the fall of the Berlin Wall.

That light was why Susan had driven to Chapman's house in Southgate in person – or rather, as a ditzier, softer, weaker version of her normal person – to apologise that Rex's photographs hadn't come out, and invite him to a special presentation at the offices. To everyone's surprise, Chapman had swallowed it, which could only mean that he hadn't found the photograph. That, in turn, meant that once Chapman was out of his house, Rex could break in and retrieve the vital evidence.

'Rex, have you spoken to your helper?' Susan asked.

'He's meeting me at the end of Chapman's road.'

'Even if you can't find the photo, take pictures. Pictures of everything.'

* * *

At 9.18 am, assured by means of text that Chapman had been picked up from his house, Rex turned the corner into Trentino Gardens. The day was grey and damp, cold as a morgue-slab.

His man wasn't there. Rex leaned against a bus-stop, lifting his bad foot a couple of centimetres off the cold ground. Was he really about to break into Chapman's house? He felt oddly calm about the prospect. His fear was that he wouldn't find anything.

Vadim appeared, crowbarred into a dark brown suit.

'Are you in court?' Rex asked. It was what people said, in his Lincolnshire hometown, if they saw you in a suit. He wasn't surprised to find Vadim understood the joke.

'Disguise. Nobody notices a smart man at nine 'o' clock in the morning,' Vadim replied, with a crooked grin.

They went to Chapman's house and into the porch. Vadim

rubbed his hands together and started work on the front door with its one cracked pane, whistling a little tune through his teeth. A postman had started making his way slowly down the road from the other end.

'Have you done it yet?' Rex asked, nervously, scanning the street.

'When I'm in,' Vadim hissed. 'You'll know it.'

'That postman's getting nearer.'

Vadim stood up and stared down the street to where a chubby man in a tracksuit stood, peering at the front of a package. 'He's a casual. Look. No uniform. Doesn't know who lives where. We'll be fine.'

He went back to work on the lock, armed with something that looked like an antique pair of forceps. These gave way to a knitting needle and finally, a paperclip, before the door gave a satisfying click – an event occurring just microseconds before the postman pushed the gate open. He stared at them, processing what he'd seen.

Rex froze. They had been caught.

'Okay, sweet-cheeks, I'm off to office, have lovely day.' Vadim cried suddenly, kissing him on the lips. 'Cook for me something nice!'

With a cheery wave to the postman, he waltzed back down the path and out of the gate. The postman handed Rex some letters and scurried away, embarrassed. Rex went inside, closed the door, and leaned back against it, breathing heavily.

Another text from Ellie: 'Eagle landed yet?'

Rex felt suddenly annoyed at how much his colleagues semed to be enjoying themselves, as if this were some kind of team-bonding Murder Weekend. But the corpse wasn't going to get up at the end. The corpse was a girl he had loved. Just not, perhaps, loved enough.

He wasn't enjoying himself. Every new thing he had to do made him nervous. More than that, it took him deeper, further from the fun and games of his colleagues, down a tunnel of dark feelings and sights no one should have to see, and which he'd already seen once before. He wanted justice for Milda, a bright young woman who had come here with hope and been dumped in some bushes. He wanted to know who was threatening him, and why. But most of all he just wanted it over. He was tired.

First he went into the front room, the room Chapman had seemed to be pushing him away from the day before. He was surprised to find a bed, no sheets or pillows, just a plastic mattress cover. Next to it was a pair of high-backed chairs – the kind only ever found in rest homes – and an old Strepsils tin on top of a coffee table. In the tin was a little swatch of hair. Rex stared at it with revulsion. It was the same colour as Milda's hair. He forced himself to take a picture of it.

There was nothing else in that stuffy room, around which hung the sweetish aroma of a medicine chest. He went directly upstairs to the darkroom and switched the light on. Scanning the work-top, he could see that Chapman had been up there and cleared the buff folder away. The photograph wasn't on the shelf of albums. It might have been in one of the drawers of the filing cabinet, or the sturdy cupboard – but these were all locked. Perhaps it was lying around somewhere, not noticed by Chapman. But how much chance was there of that, with this man who lined up all his pencils to face the same way?

He checked in the other rooms, half-heartedly taking pictures with his phone. Downstairs again, he scanned the kitchen cupboards and even the bin. Nothing. He sat on a kitchen chair, looking out onto the yard. What had Milda made of this place? Was it, with its faded, humble air, the big red torch on the shelf, the knives and forks draining in the little pot on the sink, a reminder of home? He doubted Milda's home had been like that.

The torch gave him an idea. Back in the darkroom, he went onto his knees, onto the cracked, chemical-spattered lino, shining the torch into the corners, behind and underneath the work-bench. He heard his phone ringing down in the kitchen, and it occurred to him that he should go and answer it. But there, between the bench and the wall, the pale edge of Milda's arm suddenly appeared in the beam of light, as if reaching out for help. The photograph had never left the room, it must have slipped out of his jacket almost immediately and fallen down.

He pulled at it and heard it tear. It seemed to be stuck. He tried to pull the work-bench out, but it was either too sturdy, or Chapman had secured it to the wall. The phone continued to ring downstairs. He supposed someone had left him a message, that it would keep ringing until he went down and listened to it. He wasn't about to do that now.

He found that by lying flat on the floor, stretching his right arm to its fullest extent, pushing with his knuckles against the back of the work-top and simultaneously squeezing the photograph along and out with his thumb, he was able to extricate it. As the crumpled, dusty item came towards him, he understood how so many of his own treasured possessions had vanished over the years. Strange quirks of gravity and dynamics had fetched them up in places like this: they were not gone, but to all intents and purposes they were unreachable. Some people were the same.

He knelt, staring at the picture, at what felt like the last living piece of Milda Majauskas. His phone had stopped ringing. He wondered if the battery was dead. He stood up with difficulty, and took a soft cloth from a box labelled CLOTHS on the worktop, wiping the photograph down tenderly. He had it. He had the key.

As he opened the dark-room door, he knew immediately that something had changed. The air was cooler; a top-note of damp leaves mingled with the cake-tin smell. On the hallway carpet lay the council's free magazine; he wondered if it had been there when he came in. Maybe the lifting of the letter-flap had let some air into this clammy little place.

He returned to the kitchen to get his phone, and found Arthur Chapman, dressed like a nine-year-old for a prize-giving ceremony – tie, tank-top, side-parting. He was holding the phone in his neat hands. Why the hell was he back already?

'What are you doing in my house?' he asked.

His eyes and his nose wrinkled as he asked the question, and Rex saw why Milda had named him after a rabbit. Pale and blinking, somehow fussy without even moving. With a pocket watch he could have come straight out of 'Alice in Wonderland'.

Quelling his urge to run, Rex put the photograph on the table. 'Milda was here, wasn't she?' he said. His heart was thudding.

Chapman peered at the photograph, then back at Rex. 'I don't understand people. I never have. They don't make sense to me. The things they do and say. The things they smile about. Why do they like dogs? Why do they watch football? Do you know?' He didn't wait for a reply. 'Just a few times in my life, I've met somebody, and I've let myself believe that I understand them. And every time, I've been wrong.'

'It seems Milda was wrong about you.'

'That depends what she wanted me for.'

'Wanted you?'

'She just wanted to take. I know that now. That's why she sought me out. Moved in. She was in the bathroom, filling her pockets with my wife's drugs.'

'Where is your wife?'

Chapman briefly raised his eyebrows. It was the closest thing he'd made to a gesture. The man didn't seem to create expressions, or do things with his hands. He was just a looking, reporting device. A Camera-Man. 'In St Pancras cemetery. She died. And that… girl moved in to help herself to the painkillers. I caught her with them.'

'So you killed her?'

Chapman's eyes widened slightly. He backed up against the sink. 'Killed her? I didn't kill her. Who thinks that? Is she… where is she?'

'In a cemetery in Lithuania, I imagine. They found her, dead in the park.'

'What park?'

Rex was confused. Chapman seemed genuinely surprised. 'Alexandra Park. Don't you follow the news? You obviously read the *Gazette*.'

Chapman shook his head. 'If you mean because of the competition, someone cut the piece out of your paper and put it on the Camera Club noticeboard in the library. I didn't…' He swallowed. 'I pushed her. I mean I had my… I had my hand. There.' He put his tiny left hand to his adam's apple. 'Just for a moment. I was angry. But she ran away. I swear she just ran away. Out of the bathroom, down the stairs and slammed the door. She broke the glass. I haven't seen her since.'

Chapman stood still, saying again and again that he hadn't killed Milda. His story made sense. It explained the traces of the developer fluid around her neck. In any case, how could this tiny, unworldly man have transported the body of a healthy young woman a mile and a half to Alexandra Park? He wasn't the right person. He was creepy. Unsettling. But not the killer…

Rex suddenly registered that Chapman had just said something new. Something very strange. He looked at him, and between the two men there passed a kind of recognition. Rex had grasped the significance of what Chapman had just said. And Chapman knew it.

The little man held out his arms in a strange, Christ-like gesture. That was the last truly clear image Rex had. Then there was a flash of pain as one of the man's tiny hands crushed his throat like a vice. Rex choked, his blood seeming to force his eyeballs out of his head, and as his vision began to dim, he struck out at the calm, smooth face staring up at him.

It made Chapman relax his grip for an instant, just enough time for Rex to move backwards. But as he struggled to find his breath, there was a flash of steel in the corner of his vision, a clatter of cutlery from the draining board.

The next thing Rex was aware of was a sharp, wet pain just above his cheek. His vision suddenly turned brown, as if his eyes were covered with onion-skin. He felt the same point of cold agony, this time in his chest. He staggered forward and heard a little cry as he hit the floor. It didn't sound like his voice.

Chapter Nine

Helen Fitch. That was her name – the girl who had followed him around in sixth form. Rex wanted to laugh out loud and clap. Now Helen Fitch was a nurse. One of his nurses, in the hospital. It was odd that she didn't seem to have aged. She looked better, though. Perhaps it was the uniform. At college there hadn't been a uniform, and given the clothes, hair and shoes fashionable in the Eighties, this had meant that everyone looked like shit. She did not look like shit now. When Helen Fitch changed his dressings, with her cool fingers and her soap smell, Rex thought he loved her. Was it too late to tell her?

The curtains around his bed opened, and he expected Helen Fitch to come in, in her crisp, starched dress. Instead he saw a tall, thin figure in a grey hooded top. His heart fluttered. The Reaper had come. It pulled the hood down. Rex saw his wife's blank, scarred, half-face.

He shot up in bed, sweating.

The painkillers were nice. Provided he stayed awake. If he slept, he had nightmares: sweat-bathed newsreels from the basement studios of the psyche. The nurse came across to him.

'Okay? Bad dream?'

He nodded.

'It's good news about your eye, isn't it?' she said. He looked around at the ward, divining from what was going on that they were in the long tundra of time between waking up and the arrival of the first doctor. For some reason, Helen Fitch now had an Irish accent. Perhaps she had been living over there. Rex would ask her later.

When the doctor came, he was angry that it wasn't Doctor Diana Berne, but a young, puzzled-looking Greek boy. He wanted Diana. Helen Fitch eased him back onto the pillows, and brushed his hair out of his eyes, speaking to him as if to a child.

'It's the medication,' she said. And she drew the curtains around his bed. He lay with his head to one side and looked through the fog at the printed images of Routemaster buses and Tower Bridge. He had been here before.

As the fog receded, pain took its place: a burning cord passing from the middle of his chest down the inside of both arms to the tip of his middle fingers. And a dull pulse behind his left eye, like the throb of a distant engine. They ebbed and flowed in intensity, sometimes together, sometimes separately. He tried to get out of bed, thinking he could run away from them, but he vomited.

He felt as if he were being passed through a sieve. But on the other side, miraculously, instead of being a mush, he seemed to reassemble into something like the person he had been before. Hour by hour – or maybe day-by-day, he had no idea which – more and more made sense.

He was in hospital. The North Middlesex hospital. Again.

Chapman had attacked him with something sharp. There was a patch over his eye. A dressing over the middle of his chest. And the girl from the sixth form... Yes, she might have been called Helen Fitch: his subconscious might have scored on that one. But she wasn't the Irish nurse whose soft cool hands gave him a hard-on. She wasn't even called Helen. Her name was written on her badge. He found he could not read it. But it certainly didn't say Helen.

'He's been doing fine off the ventilator,' he heard the nurse saying outside the curtains. 'The doctor's given him an excellent prognosis – provided he does as he's told.'

The other person outside the curtains – a woman – murmured something.

'He might seem a bit weird,' the nurse said. 'It's all the different drugs.'

'He's always been a bit weird,' Ellie said, as the curtains opened. She was wearing a green corduroy suit and she had her hair down. Rex sat up, but as she pulled out a chair at the side of his bed, he shifted away. He felt ashamed to be here, in this bed, in a thin gown, smelling of sweat and iodine and dried blood, next to a strikingly pretty young woman.

When he'd been a little boy, one of his teachers had come to see him at home when he'd been off sick with chicken pox. And he'd felt the same then, even though he was only six or seven: that she shouldn't see him, in his bedroom, in his pyjamas.

He tried to smile, but it made his eye feel like it was going to explode in a shower of sparks. He thanked her for the grapes. She said that the nurses all clearly fancied him, and they went on like that for a few minutes, strangely coy with each other.

'What's happened to him? Chapman?' Rex said.

Ellie seemed to relax a little in her seat, relieved to drop the small talk. 'He's in hospital. Don't worry. Not this one. He's in Chase Farm, with a policeman outside the door.'

'Why?'

'Because he's been charged with attempting to murder you with a vegetable knife.'

'Ellie. I mean, why's he in hospital?'

'You landed on him. That's what he says, anyway. He stabbed you, then you landed on him and you broke his femur. He had to call an ambulance on your phone.'

'Chapman called an ambulance?'

'Yep. Funny thing is, he saved your life. Because if he hadn't, you'd have died from your' – she pointed at his chest – 'punctured lung thing.'

'What I don't get is how come he was back at his house. I thought he was in a taxi.'

'So did we. Then the taxi driver rang, and said he'd just got out at some traffic lights. Didn't say anything. Just got out. We tried warn you, but you didn't pick up.'

Rex remembered his phone ringing downstairs as he searched in the dark-room. 'He didn't kill Milda.'

'That's what he says.'

'I think he's telling the truth.'

'Why did he attack you then?'

Rex lay back on the pillow. Why? Dimly, he remembered something at the end of his encounter with Arthur Chapman. The little man had said something odd. He had a feeling the strangling and the stabbing were related to that. But how? And if the man was telling the truth, then who had killed Milda? It made his eye ache to think about it. He gave up. For now.

'I'm here on a mission,' Ellie said. 'First of all, to give you this. It arrived this morning.'

He felt his bowels weaken as she unzipped her handbag. He wasn't sure he could take another spooky little token from his tormentor.

It was a postcard of Angkor Wat.

It was from Diana. He wanted to read it straight away, but he was too tired, and he knew Ellie would study his reaction, and relay it to everyone at the office. Who, of course, would also have read it.

'And secondly, to show you this… You're an internet superstar!'

She pulled out her phone and clicked on YouTube.

'If it's me acting like a thug at the riot. I've seen it,' he said. But Ellie shook her head.

'It's a mash-up of it.'

Someone, for reasons best understood by the under-25s, had

set the whole Turnpike Lane scrap scene to music, modifying people's voices through some clever mixing software so that they seemed to be singing along. The song, a nicely ironic choice for a racist rally, was 'Message To You, Rudie' by The Specials.

'Stop your fucking about…' sang Keith Powell. 'This is about your future…'

'None of you got any future…' came the riposte from Rex, before the scene exploded into speeded-up fighting and ska trombones.

'It's gone viral,' Ellie said. 'Isn't it brilliant? I mean – how stupid must that BWAP lot feel now?'

It occurred to Rex that some of the BWAP's senior leadership would be delighted with this thing called a viral mash-up. In fact, they'd probably put it onto the internet themselves. But he didn't say anything, just lay back and feigned an interest as she rummaged in her handbag for something else.

'Thirdly, as representative of the *Wood Green Gazette*, I am instructed to give you this…'

She handed him a large, green envelope. It contained a birthday card, reminding him that he had turned 40 while he'd been in hospital. The *Gazette* staff had all signed it, with comments ranging from the formal 'Best wishes, M. Whittaker' to the jovial 'You Old Coffin-Dodging Bastard, Terry'. Inside the card was another envelope. Rex opened it. He was booked on a return flight to Phnom Penh, at the end of next week. 'You can change all the dates for fifty quid,' Ellie said. 'I don't know if you'll be up to flying by then …'

She carried on talking, but he was too tired to listen. He lay back and closed his eyes. Would he be using that ticket? He doubted it. He had too much work to do.

* * *

The next morning he discharged himself. He was made to sign a disclaimer form, and a small group of nurses watched him struggling to put on the stiff, bloodied clothes he'd worn a week ago, without helping. They wanted him to see how hard it was, so that he'd change his mind. They didn't know how stubborn he was.

Help came from a strange quarter. He was in a chair, bent over, feeling as if molten lead had been poured into the front of his face as he tried to tie up a shoelace when a visitor sat on the bed. He looked up in surprise. It was Mike Bond, paler, scruffier, in a knitted jumper and grey tracksuit bottoms. He looked like one of the broken men of Wood Green, who sat in the library all day, staring at the newspapers.

'Going somewhere?' asked the old policeman.

'Home,' Rex replied. 'These places make you ill.'

Mike chuckled, the empty skin of his neck folding into hills and valleys, with a cover of silver furze. 'I felt the same. Brenda wouldn't let me discharge myself, though.'

'So are you still in here?'

'Christ no. If you have a heart attack these days, you're in and out in 48 hours. Quicker than a wisdom tooth… I had to come in for a check-up,' Bond explained, 'so I thought I'd look in on you. Hang on….'

He spotted Rex's feeble attempts to put his other shoe on.

'Mike, no…' Rex protested, but it was too late. The copper knelt and put his shoe on for him. Rex glanced from the bald top of Bond's head to the Nurses' Station and saw the looks. Bond got back up, flushed and a little breathless.

'I take it you're not back at work then,' Rex asked.

'Bren wants me to take early retirement,' Bond said gloomily, as he sat back on the edge of the bed. 'I might not have any choice. There'll be a review board in a couple of weeks.'

There was a silence, broken by the clatter of a surgical dish and a burst of polite African cursing.

'I'm sorry,' Rex said. 'And I'm sorry about what I said at the march, too.'

Bond nodded. 'Well, you had a point,' he said, scraping his index finger with his thumb.

'You *are* part of a racist conspiracy?'

'I did enquire about Keith Powell but I was told to stay away. I couldn't tell you that, because he was undercover.'

'I know.' Bond raised two white, curling eyebrows. 'I worked it out,' Rex said. He didn't want to land Powell in trouble.

'If you're going, you might as well go,' said the Irish nurse. 'We need the bed.'

As he picked his way painfully through the hospital's corridors, Rex thought this was what it must feel like to be old. Everything aching and weak. Vision blurred. The one-way system – devised to prevent the local gang-bangers from killing each other on the hospital's watch – had changed, adding to his sense of disorientation. He felt lucky to have an invalid policeman at his side.

'Your mate's gone,' Rex noted, as they left the medicated heat of the Reception area and went outside. The cold air stung his chest. He wondered if that was because of the wound. Perhaps he shouldn't have been so hasty about leaving.

'Orchard wasn't my mate,' Bond said. 'He was a... I don't know... Anyway, he wasn't my mate.'

'What did you have against him?'

A mini-cab tooted its horn. Rex nodded towards its driver, acknowledging the invitation.

'I don't know Rex... It's just that... Coppers... they're not political, you know. If they are, they keep it to themselves. You know, there are just unspoken rules. You don't talk about what books you've read down the staff canteen, and you don't talk about politics, either. But Orchard was... everything was politics with him. Politics, immigration, multiculturalism. It was like he was trying to get you into a conversation about it, all the time.'

Rex smiled. 'He'll have limited options for that when he's doing nights for Securicor.'

Bond frowned. 'What are you on about?'

'He's been Shanghai'd out, hasn't he?'

'He passed his Sergeant's exams six months back, and a vacancy came up for a D.S. in Brixton. That's where he's gone, Rex.' Bond chuckled. 'You could say it was down, but definitely not out.'

Rex took this in as the taxi – a battered Volvo, front window festooned with amulets and flags – drew alongside. Had Orchard been artlessly trying to find fellow-sympathisers, or almost as artlessly trying to entrap his fellow policemen? He suspected the latter. Something about D.C. Orchard – Detective *Sergeant* Orchard, as he now was – had always reminded him of the prefects at school, content to be hated, proud of the traitor-status. And now he'd been promoted. It was just like newspapers. If they couldn't sack you, they moved you up a rung.

'I read somewhere the other day... Know the average time a copper lives for after he retires?' Bond said, suddenly, as Rex got in the back seat. 'Twelve years.'

He looked almost tearful. Rex had never seen him this way before.

'Come on. Brenda will keep you busy for longer than twelve years. Do you want a lift?'

Bond shook his head. 'I've got to walk everywhere. For the exercise. Anyway, Bren's got a supervision going on in the front room.'

'A what?'

'She's training to be a – what do you call it – counsellor. God knows why.' He coughed. 'See you around, Rex.'

Rex watched the big man shuffle away, stooped and saggy. He felt sorry for ever having doubts about him. Living With A Violent Man. Now he knew why Brenda had been reading that book. She had a life outside her job, future plans. He worried that Bond did not.

The taxi driver was playing a kind of Nigerian pop called Highlife. A copy of the *Gazette* lay on the dashboard. There was a front page scoop for Ellie, all about the stabbing, the arrest of Chapman, and his connection to Milda. GAZETTE MAN IN SOUTHGATE STAB ATTACK SHOCK, read the headline, itself evidence enough that Ellie had been allowed to write it. But the piece was good. He sighed. Ellie would be on her way soon, to some lowly but coveted role on a national. Everything was changing. He felt an urge to act now, while there was still time.

'Can you drop me on the Lanes instead?' Rex asked the driver.

Wordlessly the driver changed direction. Rex steeled himself. The next task would be hard.

He got out of the taxi by the pub, just as a long line of school-children was being shepherded over the road by a group of harassed-looking adults. They were primary-age kids, divided by gender, but not – yet – by race. There was something heartening about the sight of them, the Polish girls primly tutting at the antics of the black boys, the Somalis, arm-in-arm, like sisters, with the Turks.

In the midst of the chattering line, huddled together, con-spiratorially, over the screen of a mobile phone, were the bent heads of Dovila and a classmate in a headscarf. Rex asked them where they were headed.

'We've got to go to Finsbury Park to count earthworms,' said Dovila without enthusiasm. At that moment, a teacher, a young, bald-headed man, edged across, frowning. 'It's okay, sir, he's my mum's friend,' the little girl said. Rex gave the man what he hoped was a reassuring nod. It seemed to work.

'At least you've got some entertainment,' he said, pointing at the phone, as he kept step with the line. It was a bright blue thing with a big screen – not the device he'd given to her mother. 'Is that yours?'

sIt's Mum's. We swap sometimes because this has got Sims Pet Vacation 3 on it, but she doesn't like me having it because she thinks I won't remember to tell her any messages but I always do.'

Rex suddenly had an idea. 'Did you have the phone when Niela rang? From Lithuania?'

'I answered it,' Dovila said proudly. 'I was coming home from swimming. And Niela told me the message and I told Mum. And I said to Mum we'd better go and tell you.'

Before Rex could ask another question, one of the multitude of teachers and assistants deemed necessary to take twenty kids worm-counting at the local park blew on a whistle. Dovila and her pals instantly pared down to single file against the window of a sofa shop and halted, awaiting further orders.

I said to Mum, we'd better go and tell you. So it was Dovila who had taken the call, Dovila who'd pushed her mother to come and see him. Rex remembered the taxi ride back from the funeral, when Aguta was drunk. How she'd been strangely evasive. But why?

* * *

The sign on the Famous Manti Shop said 'Famous Manti Shop – Restaurant', but it had no waiting staff. Anyone rash enough to dine there was sent downstairs, to be tended to, erratically, by one of the dumpling-rolling women from the window.

Armed with his 20% discount voucher, Rex strode up to the proprietor and asked for a table. The proprietor – a thin, melancholy figure who looked like he subsisted on a diet of coins – barked some words at the pair of headscarfed women in the window. Rex's gamble worked: Bibigul rose from her workstation and led him downstairs.

'What are you doing?' she asked, in a low voice.

'I need to talk to you,' he said. 'Bring me a bottle of Buzbag.'

She looked annoyed, but went to fetch the wine. Rex waited in the chilly, damp basement, glared at by an assortment of blue glass eyes on the walls and startled, every few moments, by a rush of water from the adjacent lavatories.

'I read about you,' Bibigul said, as she returned with a glass and a bottle. 'How is your eye?'

'They said it's going to be all right,' Rex said. 'When I was here last, you said some things, about the girl who was murdered at the Park. About the autopsy on her.'

'What about it?' she said, twisting the corkscrew in. 'I thought you'd caught the guy.'

'He says he didn't do it. But he is the reason she got the sodium stuff on her neck. She shared a dark room with him.'

'Clore didn't bother to see if there was any sodium nitrite anywhere else,' Bibigul said, as she poured him a drink. 'He just found it on the neck, and because the spread of it was like a man's hand, and he found petechial haemorrhages – that's little burst blood vessels – in the eyes he stopped there. If he'd looked on her hands, he might have found the sodium nitrite there, and then we'd have had a good indication about the… dark room.'

'So he jumped to the wrong conclusion?'

'He always jumped to conclusions,' she said bitterly. 'That was what he did. He found one or two things on a body to comment on, and he left it there.'

She looked at him, with her shining, steppe-land eyes. 'Maybe you think he just did a poor job on that girl because she was from Lithuania and no one cared. But the truth was, he was at the end of his career, he drank too much, and he did a poor job on everybody.'

'Can you remember anything else about the girl's body?'

There were footsteps on the stairs. The boss was hovering.

'I'll have six lamb, and six beef,' Rex said. 'Yoghurt sauce. No chilli.'

He didn't have to wait long. Soon he heard the ding of a microwave timer over the noisy plumbing.

'I remember she had mud on the back of her shoes, and on the heel of her tights,' Bibigul said, returning with a platter of manti, a fork and a napkin. 'There were indentations in the soil around her feet – like she had been drumming her heels against the ground.'

'Don't you do that if someone strangles you?' He remembered Chapman strangling him. The terrifying power of his grip.

'No, your energy's all focussed on stopping them. In any case, if someone strangles you hard enough for the blood vessels in your eyes to bleed, then you get bleeding in the throat as well. And there was no bleeding in the throat.'

Rex had speared a couple of yoghourt-covered dumplings with his fork. He couldn't bring them to his mouth, though.

'So... someone drumming their heels is what? More like someone having a fit? Could she have had a fit because of the heroin?'

'It doesn't cause convulsions. It doesn't cause anything, the amount she took.'

Rex frowned. 'I thought it was injected.'

'It was. But only a very, very small amount went into the skin, and an even smaller amount passed into her bloodstream. We almost didn't detect it. Some addicts do it that way if they can't find a vein, they call it skin-popping, but her veins were perfect.'

'So why would she have done that?'

'I don't know. Because she changed her mind? Because she wanted to try a little bit? Because it was an accident?'

'An accidental injection?'

'I'm not a detective. I know she didn't look like a heroin addict, though. She didn't have any of the signs.'

'They don't all inject, do they? Some junkies just smoke it, right?'

'Yes, but people who have this habit are emaciated. You know – you must have seen it – their eyes kind of look too big in their heads?'

Rex knew that look. He'd seen it recently, though he couldn't remember where.

'They have bad complexions and they don't take care of their appearance. This girl was clean, and she was healthy. Well. She was healthy apart from the fit.'

'You're sure she had one?'

'She had a violent fit. I think that's what caused the burst blood vessels in her eyes. And I think that had more to do with why she died than anyone strangling her. I said all this to Dr Clore when we did the Preliminary Exam, but he wasn't interested. And I…' She looked embarrassed.

'You were leaving anyway,' Rex concluded. 'So you think it was the fit that killed her?'

'Not the fit. But unless she had epilepsy, a convulsion is usually a sign of something serious. Tumours. Meningitis. Lots of things.'

Rex remembered all the talk of headaches, of Milda feeling dizzy and sick, visits to the hospital as a child.

'Is there anything that… I don't know how to put it… anything that she could have had for a long time that could have caused this? I mean, something she could have had since she was a kid?'

Bibigul frowned, trying to unpick his meaning. Then she nodded, with a faint smile. 'Could be. You can have something like AVM for years. A whole lifetime, unless it's triggered by a shock or a sudden stress.'

'What's AVM?'

He needed to know more, but the shop bell rang, and Bibigul had to go.

As he drank his way through the warm wine, ignoring the pile of tepid dumplings, Rex got his phone out. He connected to a site he'd spent a lot of time on in the aftermath of his wife's accident. Headmatters.org was a mine of information on the human brain, and the many things that could go wrong with it. It had helped him understand what happened to Sybille. The site's symptom checker was the sort of thing you should avoid, if you had a hangover or a tendency to hypochondria.

The connection was slow, unsurprisingly given that he was in a basement at the lower end of a built-up valley. Even so, by the time half the bottle of Buzbag was gone, Rex had worked out what had killed Milda. He also knew someone was responsible, and as he went back and forth over his conversation with Bibigul, he was almost certain he knew who.

* * *

The girl did not look out of place on a Saturday lunchtime in Newington Green. It was a sunny day, sharp and cold. The area had a hung-over feeling to it: people with bed-hair buying Cokes and *Guardians* in the newsagent; bleary boys eating fry-ups in the café; the odd, desperate soul staving off the doom with an early pint in The Alma. Shivering in a bomber jacket, with thin black tights and a denim mini-skirt, she got the odd stare, but it was more passing lust than disgust.

There were two old women waiting for the 73 bus. They didn't know one another, were of different races, but had already established a kinship based on it being cold, and the bus being late. They exchanged identical looks as the girl went past, although their thoughts were in fact quite different. Irene, 73, wondered why she didn't have a proper coat. Joyce, 71, thought that type of girl deserved all the trouble she got.

She could almost have been a trainee solicitor or a newly-qualified teacher: someone who had had a few drinks too many, passed out on a sofa a long way from her shared flat in Clapham or Ealing, and was now keen to get back there for a long bath before friends came round for dinner. It was a not-uncommon Saturday scenario. But if you went close to the girl you might have found a different story, detected something more disturbing in the unwashed, tied-back hair, the greasy circles around her eyes, the streaming nose.

One man saw it all instantly. It was a visual language, common to all who followed this particular path to destruction. She caught his eye as he came out of the chemist's with his dose. He caught hers. He didn't need any trouble right now. But trouble, somehow, always found him.

'Anyone got any brown around here?' she asked hoarsely. He looked her up and down. Too pretty for a policewoman.

'I might know someone,' he said, addressing his trainers. 'They're in Clapton, though. Might be hard for you to find.'

She wiped her nose on the sleeve of her jacket. He tried not to look disgusted. 'If you go with me, I'll give you a tenner's,' she wheedled. 'Please.'

'It's a long bus ride,' he said.

'Please. I'll give you two bags,' she said. 'I've got a car.'

He should have listened to the thin, reedy note of warning that sounded when she said she had a car. But he was thinking of the two bags. Two little twists of a carrier bag, plump and tied-off like sausages, stuffed with the pinky-brown powder that clung to the bag like pearls of sap on a plant. It melted on the foil with a seductive hiss, smelt like cocoa. So much better than the methadone.

He followed her across the Green. A few, grumpy young Dads were pushing small children on swings. He tried not to look at them. They crossed the road at the zebra crossing – funny that a bag-head should be so careful, he thought. She was approaching a gold-coloured Vauxhall Chevette. An odd car for a skinny young bag-head bird to drive.

Then one of those wiry, bone-headed blokes got out – the kind who never had an ounce of fat on them, lived on speed and Wotsits, and could still out-run a bus in their fifties. He felt a little disappointed, but not too much. He wasn't that into the girl anyway. He just wanted the bags. Was he still going to get them, though, with this knucklehead in tow?

The man gave him one of those hard, upward nods, enough to communicate that he wasn't going to rip his head off right now, then opened the passenger door for him. Surprised, he got in, and found himself in a clean, lovingly tended leather interior. The bloke got in next to him.

'What the –'

The other passenger door opened, and another man got in on his right side. This one was bulkier, in a crumpled suit, and wore an eye-patch. The girl slipped into the driver's seat. Were they Old Bill?

'Hello Mark,' Rex said, turning to the captive sandwiched between himself and Terry. 'Shall we go for a little ride?'

* * *

The Server Room didn't have any servers in it. Susan was always saying that the *Gazette* was going to go online, and was always having meetings with bright, sharp IT consultants in equally bright, sharp suits. So far, though, the only concrete step in that direction had been earmarking an oversized stationery cupboard on the floor below the main office for the purpose.

Earlier that Saturday afternoon, Rex Tracey and two accomplices – fellow employees of the *Gazette* – had found another purpose for the Server room: that of imprisoning a twenty-nine year old heroin addict named Mark Crosby, along with a mattress, a sleeping bag, six bottles of water, three buckets and a radio. The moment he saw the amenities that had been laid on for him, Mark had begun to hammer on the door.

On the other side of the door, flushed and frightened, Ellie unzipped the bomber jacket she'd borrowed from her flatmate's sister.

'What's with all the shit in the Server Room, Rex? I thought you just wanted to talk to him.'

'I do. But I anticipate it taking some time.'

Ellie's eyes widened. 'Hang on. Then technically you've just kidnapped him.'

'Indeed,' Rex said, rubbing his shirt over the spot where the bandage was. 'You have, too, since you willingly impersonated a heroin addict to lure him into Terry's car.'

'You said… I just thought that was to get him to talk to us! Jesus.' She glanced in panic at the door. 'What if Susan drops in?' Ellie demanded.

'If anyone tries to drop in, they'll have problems,' Rex said, 'because I've changed the entry code.'

'What if someone hears him?'

'On the High Street? On a Saturday?'

'What if he's still doing it on Sunday?'

'Trust me, by Sunday, he'll be so desperate for his scag that he'll be singing like Domingo.'

'Who? I don't care, actually.' Ellie's voice became louder. 'Rex – you're a bastard. If this gets out, and I'm an accessory, my whole career's over! You lied to me about what you were going to do!'

'It isn't going to get out,' Rex said. 'And if it does, we'll just say we persuaded some obliging young sex-worker from the Brownswood to act as bait.'

'Aye,' Terry chipped in. 'Ratty looking Indian tart she was. Fat arse and flat tits. Never asked her name.'

Rex sensed a softening in Ellie's mood. 'And if your career is over, you could always go back to the acting. You were brilliant, you know. First-class.'

'Now go off and buy your vintage frock and stop worrying about it,' Terry said. She was going to a party in Dalston that evening.

'How about a lift?' Ellie asked. Terry looked at Rex.

'It's fine, Terry. I'd rather handle him on my own. Go.'

After they'd gone, Rex sat in the office, vaguely clicking on one website after another. A distant sound of hammering and shouting came from below. After an hour or so, there was silence. He went down to check on the prisoner, knocking on the door.

'F-f-fucking let me out, you t-twat!'

The shivers had set in. Rex knew there would be shivers, then sweats, then stomach cramps. After twelve hours, just after midnight, Mark would be at the lowest point of withdrawal, with aching limbs, a streaming nose and a hectic, whirring mind. But maybe they wouldn't need to go that far.

'You were with her, weren't you? You were with Milda when she died.'

'I d-don't know what you're on about!'

Rex had expected this answer, but he was sure he was right. Mark was a junkie. His path and Milda's had crossed. And his behaviour at the funeral suggested he had something to hide. He was something to do with her death. Rex went back upstairs.

He returned every half hour after that. The voice behind the door became more strained, less sure of itself, but no more co-operative. Rex decided to lay his cards on the table.

'I'll give you some scag, Mark, if you tell me what happened.'

'Nothing happened. Fuck off,' Mark panted. From what he could discern, Mark was pacing up and down the room at high speed.

He had stopped doing that by seven pm. He said he wanted to talk.

'Go ahead,' Rex said. 'I'm not into torturing you. I just want the truth.'

'I agreed to meet her,' Mark began, in a slurred, quiet mono-tone, so that Rex had to push his ear hard against the door to catch the words. 'At Ally Pally.'

'Why?'

'She wanted an Interrail ticket. To get back home.'

'And what are you? The Newington Green branch of Thomas Cook?'

'I know these guys. At a printer's in Clapton. They're doing snide Oysters and railcards and that.' He sniffed loudly.

'You know all the leading citizens in the Clapton area, don't you? What was your fee for the ticket?'

'Eh?'

'What did you charge her?'

'A ton. But when I got there with it, she said it was too much. We had a row. I went. Look, Rex, man, I really, really need…'

'Not yet. So you had a row. And you went.'

'Yeah. I swear. I just went.'

'So Milda went to an isolated spot to meet a known smack-head scumbag, namely, you. You left. And Milda, with no ap-parent history of drug use or abuse, ended up with heroin in her bloodstream.'

He listened. There was silence.

'How, Mark? Osmosis? Telekinesis? Through the fucking air?'

There was another long pause. Mark sighed. 'I don't know,' he said, finally, in a tiny voice. 'Please will you just give me my –'

'You're lying. I'm going.'

Mark's voice went loud again. 'I'm not! Please. Don't go, man.' He thumped the door, three times, with what sounded like his head.

'Mark. You lied about the money, because I know she didn't have any money, and I know she tried to steal some painkillers from the bloke she was living with, and I imagine that was to pay you.' He waited. Mark said nothing. 'So I don't believe you.'

He went back upstairs and closed the double doors to block out the sound of Mark going wild. It wouldn't be long now.

His chest was aching – in fact, the centre of the wound, where the stitches were, felt as if it was on fire. He took some painkillers, which made him care less about the pain without exactly reducing it, and finally tore off the eye-patch, savouring the delicious damp touch of his palm against his eyelid.

He went to look at himself in the toilet mirror. His eye belonged in a horror film. He could still see through it, but the vision was grainy and blurred. He put the patch back on.

An hour later, after the end of X-Factor – which Rex had tried to enjoy on Susan's wall-mounted flat-screen – and Mark still wouldn't answer.

Another hour, and Mark was answering, after a fashion, his responses amplified by the bucket. He was being sick.

Rex began to wonder if this was going to work.

In his imagination, the junkie would first get a bit antsy, then desperate, then tell him everything. But he was getting really sick now. It gave Rex no pleasure to be torturing someone. Indeed, he felt a lot of sympathy for anyone who depended on some powdered poison to feel all right. At least he knew what was in a can of Okocim. He wondered whether he should give Mark the methadone he'd been carrying when they picked him up, but he also knew that would scupper the whole thing. The pain would be gone. He'd go to sleep, and Rex would get nothing. It was time to move things on.

He took a package from his desk drawer and decanted some of its contents into a clear plastic coin bag from the petty-cash box. Then he went downstairs. There was no noise from Mark.

Rex knocked on the door softly. 'Mark?'

Silence. Rex tapped the door. Again, there was nothing.

He began to feel worried. What if Mark had choked on his own vomit?

'Mark!' Rex tried again, banging the door hard.

'*Wafukizit?*'

Rex's legs nearly buckled with relief. 'I'm going to open the door, and I want you to stay on the floor, on the opposite side of the room. Do you understand? If you're anywhere else, doing anything else, when I come in, I'm closing the door again and the deal's off.'

There was a long wait before Mark's weak reply came. 'I couldn't stand up if I fucking wanted to.'

Rex opened the door. Mark was on the mattress. He'd taken his shirt off and was bathed in a greyish, granular sweat. His hair was plastered to his forehead and the room smelt of vomit.

'You can have this scag,' Rex said, holding up a bag of brown powder, 'when you tell me what really happened at Ally Pally. If you make any sudden moves, it goes. If you say anything that's a lie, it goes. Do you understand? I want the whole story.'

Mark nodded, and took a draught of water. He began to speak, with his head against the wall and turned to one side. It was more like he was letting the truth fall out of his mouth than speaking.

'I didn't know her that well. Just seen her round. She come up to see Biggsy a few times like, and I thought she were alright. Then one day, I seen her, up at Choices.'

'What's Choices?' Rex sat on the end of the mattress, a move which, for some reason, made his stitches sting.

'It's a drug counselling place.'

'You're having counselling?'

'No one goes there for the fucking counselling!' Mark spat. 'It's where all the dealers hang out.'

'So what was Milda doing there?'

'I never said she was there,' Mark objected. 'I said I seen her. I mean – she was just round there. I was on my way there, and I saw her.'

'Where is it?'

'Southgate. She said she was trying to get home. Back to Russia, I mean.'

Rex wondered how Mark could be living with a woman from Lithuania, by all accounts have made a woman from Lithuania pregnant, and still think she was Russian. 'Go on.'

'I think Birgita must have told her about my mate at the printers or something because she knew about it. And I told her it'd be two hundred for an Interrail. She said she only had one-twenty, but then, this guy came up to us in the middle of it. I sort of know him, from around, like. And he asked us if I had any syrup.'

'You mean methadone?'

'I told him to fuck off. I didn't want Milda catching on and it getting back to Biggsy – Birgita, you know – but Milda twigged. I thought she was just going to walk off, but she didn't. She said she could get me lots of pills. Diamorphine and that. So I agreed to meet her, a week later, with the ticket.'

'So what went wrong?'

'Nothing went wrong my end. I brought the ticket, up to Ally Pally. But when she turned up, she was all upset. I dunno why. And all she'd brought is fifty quid and one poxy bottle of codeine pills.'

'So you were angry. Is that why you attacked her?'

'I was angry because I'd told my mate he was going to get double his money back when I sold all the pills.' He suddenly lifted up his head. 'I never hurt her, though, man. I swear.'

'What was she doing when you left her?'

'I just walked away. I was fucked off, that I'd got this stupid ticket, and no pills, and now she knew, and she might tell Biggsy, so I just walked off. But she... she grabbed on to me... onto my shirt.'

'And you pushed her away.'

'No. Seriously, I never. I pulled my shirt back, but she grabbed onto my legs. She pulled me down. Like a rugby tackle.'

It was an odd, athletic simile for a heroin addict. It reminded Rex that somewhere, underneath the layers of grease and lies, there was a very ordinary person. Someone who had watched rugby, perhaps even played it.

'I fell over. And she was on me, saying all this Russian stuff.'

'It's Lithuanian. Milda and the woman you're having a baby with – they're Lithuanian.'

'It's all part of Russia, isn't it?' Rex didn't reply. 'Look, I don't know what she was saying, but she was trying to get the ticket off me. And I got away from her, but my works come out of my pocket.'

'Your works?'

'Syringe. We was rolling round, and it got stuck in her arm. And then she just stood there, staring at it, and staring at me. It's like she was frozen. I said – I dunno why I said this, but it's what I'd think if I got someone's sharp in my arm – I said, I'm clean. I've been tested. It's true. But she didn't hear me. She was just staring at it, in her arm. Shaking.'

'Why didn't you take it out?'

'I tried to. But it was proper stuck in, and when I grabbed it, she grabbed my hand. I told her to get off. I could see there was a little bit in there. In the works, I mean. And she was pushing and puling my hand, and I was worried some of it was going to go in her. But then someone came along.'

'Really? The police called for witnesses. Nobody came forward.'

'It was a woman.'

'What did she look like?'

'I didn't see. They called out, but they were just on the other side of the hill, you know, so I couldn't see them. I thought it might be someone she knew, so I just legged it.'

'Why do you think it was someone she knew?'

'When they called out, Milda span round. Like there was something about it she recognised. The voice. Or what they said.'

'But they didn't call out her name?'

'I don't think so. It was something different. Look – are you gonna tell Birgita about this? I just –' His voice cracked. 'She's the only good thing I've got going on. I can't fuck it up. Do you know what I mean? Please.' He started crying. 'I can't lose her, man. I know I'm a fucking waste of space. But I can't lose her. Please.'

This hadn't gone the way Rex had expected. He held up the bag he'd been carrying and looked back at Mark, who slowly took hold of his shuddering emotions., peering at him through snot-webbed fingers.

'You know what's in the bag, Mark? Cumin. I was going to give you a bag of cumin, so you knew you'd confessed for nothing. I was angry. I thought you'd caused Milda's death and hidden it all this time. I was wrong.'

Mark took his hands away from his face. 'She was all right when I left her, I swear. I mean, she wasn't all right, but…'

'I can't imagine Milda having anything to do with drugs,' Rex said, mainly to himself. 'It's the opposite of the person I knew.'

'You know what Karl Jung said, don't you?' Mark brushed a greasy strand of hair out of his eyes. 'Everyone has three selves. How they see themselves. How other people see them. And how they really are.'

Rex looked at him in surprise.

'See?' Mark said. 'That's the bit you see. Thick junkie scum. There's two-thirds more, of me, that you'll never see. Biggsy sees it. She's the only one. I reckon there were two-thirds more of Milda, too.'

Perhaps he was right. 'We kept your methadone,' Rex said. 'I'll go and get it.'

'No!' Mark almost shouted.

'You don't want it?' Rex asked.

'I've come this far,' Mark said, biting on one of his knuckles. 'I might as well make something out of it. You never know. I might even stay off it this time.'

Rex nodded. He let Mark clean himself up in the washrooms, gave him a vast mauve fleece that he found under Brenda's desk, and let him out into the wild of a Wood Green evening.

'Who do you think it was?' Mark asked, turning to Rex in the doorway. 'The person who came along?'

Rex shrugged. 'Maybe we'll never find out.'

He watched Mark's unsteady progress across the car-park, strangely concerned for the person he'd loathed a few hours before. He hadn't told Mark the truth, of course. There was nothing to find out, because he knew already. He knew how.

And he knew who. But he didn't know how to handle it. He didn't know if he could.

Chapter Ten

It was one of the remarkable things about the city that in a place containing so much variety, so many forms of life, someone would always be doing exactly what you were doing, at the same time. No one was original. Like ants, everyone scurried on set paths in a vast, ordered nest. This notion had first struck Rex on his honeymoon. He and Sybille had flown to the South Pacific, to New Caledonia, a journey originating humbly in a ride on the Number 27 bus from Camden to Paddington railway station. There was a solid, red-cheeked and sandy-haired man, farmer-like, waiting at the bus-stop on Camden Parkway. He caught the train to Heathrow with them. Later, they were marginally surprised to see him at the bar at Charles de Gaulle airport, as they changed flights in Paris. But not as surprised as when he turned up at a waterfront Pizzeria in Noumea. For his part, the sandy-haired man remained indifferent to their presence as he had been at the first bus-stop: he recognised them, but it meant nothing to him. People were just everywhere, always, doing the same things.

So Rex wasn't surprised to find people having their nails done at a beauty parlour at the back of Shopping City at 8.30 on a wintry Sunday morning. There were African ladies, in dazzling dresses, on their way to church; Kurdish girls sporting plain black chadors over diamante-studded jeans. Most of the staff were Chinese – nails seemed to be a Chinese business, right across the capital. Only one person who worked there was not: she specialised in make-up, skin-care and head massage, for which there seemed to be no call this morning. This person sat reading a tv supplement, occasionally glancing out of the shop.

In Shopping City the rents became cheaper, the further away from the High Street you went. The atmosphere near the beauty parlour was more like a covered market. A Bangladeshi clan sold cheap cookware. Some tough-looking Essex lads had a unit purveying belt buckles, Confederate flags and cannabis-related paraphernalia. And a pair of twin sisters, London-Jamaicans, ran a little café selling fiery pasties and sorrel punch, as well as regular teas and coffees, to the other market-traders. It was to this place – named The Jerk Shack – that Aguta took Rex. A reggae cover version of 'Amapola' played on the radio, as steam rushed into the milk jug.

'Have you listened to this station?' Rex asked. 'In the mornings, it's old reggae. In the afternoons, it's a Nigerian pastor casting out devils over the phone.'

Aguta didn't smile. She lit a cigarette: in this part of the precinct, nobody objected.

'Eye is looking okay now,' she said, gesturing towards him with the cigarette. He'd taken the patch off. She said it as if she had seen his eye at its worst. But she hadn't. She hadn't come to visit him in the hospital. Now he understood why.

'How did you know?' she asked, sending a jet of blue smoke to the ceiling.

'Niela. Milda's sister.'

Aguta frowned. 'You have spoken with her?'

Rex shook his head. 'I spoke to Dovila.'

'I don't know what you mean, Rex.'

'Do you remember, in the taxi, coming back from the funeral service. I asked you – what would make Niela suddenly go home? What would make someone so concerned about finding out the truth one day, then go home the next? And you couldn't answer me.'

Aguta said nothing, merely looked at her cigarette.

'I might have forgotten about it, but then you came to see me about that message. It didn't add up. Someone who just wanted to bury her sister and grieve, gets back in touch. With another clue, another bit of evidence. That's not someone who went home because they weren't bothered about finding out the truth. That's someone who only went home because they thought that someone here was going to keep on the case for them. And who could that have been?'

Aguta swallowed, and he knew he was right.

'Then I saw Dovila. She had your phone.eAnd I realised – you swap them sometimes, don't you? So she was the one who got the message from Niela. And she was the one who made you come and see me. If the message had just gone to you, you'd have ignored it, wouldn't you? Strung Niela along, and let it lie. Because you were the one who wanted to let it lie. Not Niela. You were the one who called out to Milda, weren't you, in the park? Just before she died. Some words she recognised, but not her name. That's what the witness told me. A nickname.'

He paused as one of the café-owners brought over two mugs of coffee. When she'd returned to her counter, Aguta blew on the coffee, then pushed it away, tears in her eyes..'I couldn't understand why you got so cross, when I asked Dovila for that photograph on her phone. I couldn't understand how come it could have been there one day, and gone the next, unless someone had deleted it. And then I realised. It was you who'd deleted it. Because you didn't want to look at her. You couldn't face being reminded. What I don't understand is why,' Rex went on more gently. 'I was hoping you could tell me.'

Aguta sighed. 'Today, Dovila is at a friend's house. Every weekend, I try to find a different friend for her to stay, so I can work, and I don't have to pay a babysitter.'

'That must be hard,' Rex said, not understanding where the conversation was heading.

'Few weeks back, I saw an advertisement. In your paper, actually. A day-time care assistant. Weekdays. 8.00 to 4.00. I've done this kind of work in Lithuania, sometimes, you know, so I called up them, and they invited me for an interview. You know where it was?' She frowned, half-amused. 'Such a strange. It's a nuns-house, in the woods, at the bottom of Alexander Palace. They look after people there.'

'The Sisters of Saint Veronica of Jumièges,' Rex said, as the circle closed.

'You know place,' she said, with a shrug. 'I didn't. So I went for an interview. On a Thursday 6th. In the afternoon.'

'You didn't get the job?'

Her face suddenly looked bitter. 'Most places, you know, Rex, if they don't want you, they don't telephone and tell you. They just say nothing. And maybe after two, three weeks, you stop hoping and you get the message. I thought maybe some nuns would behave a bit better than that, but...' She ground her cigarette out on the floor, and blew on the coffee again. 'I don't know. Job was cooking, cleaning, helping with laundry. I could do it, but... That nun who was interviewing me, she had a very strong... erm... accent. Was a bit difficult for me to understand what she was saying and sometimes, I think, she didn't understand me, either.'

Rex could easily imagine Sister Florence frowning and squinting, and Aguta doing the same back to her.

Aguta let out a long sigh, and lit another cigarette. 'So it wasn't success. It would have been so good, Rex, that job. So much better for Dovila. But...' She gestured expansively with her hands, and a bit of the smoke from her cigarette followed their path, as if that had been her dreams, passing beyond reach, finally vanishing. 'So I decide to walk over the park, back to here, to work. To clear my... brains. And you know the place where the water-fountain is? The path goes down, and up again. I saw her. I saw Milda there, with a skinny boy.'

'Mark. His name is Mark.'

'For how many weeks she was missing? Two? All that time, I was so worried. Visits to you. Calls to Klaipeda. And there she is, in the park. So I called out to her. Actually, I called her by the nickname. *Vezlys*. Tortoise. And I ran to her. I thought perhaps maybe she was a ghost, because she didn't turn around. The boy was gone. And she just stood there, like she was in a dream, with that... with disgusting bladdy needle in her arm, staring at it. You know, I felt I was like her mum. I was crying, saying to her, where have you been, we've been so worried of you. But she doesn't say anything.'

Rex took a sip of the coffee. It was still too hot to drink. The little bit he'd swallowed scorched his insides. He pictured it, briefly, melting the stitches in his chest.

'I don't know, Rex.' Aguta's eyes filled with tears. 'I just got so mad with her. We are same age. You know. Same class in the junior school. We shared desk. And she always does what she wants Goes to art school. Lives in squat, has parties, boyfriends... ' She rubbed her temples. 'I work, all day, every day and I can't even buy Dovila a new uniform. She's in the last year's uniform at the school. And Milda can just play with her life. She quits job, goes missing, makes a big drama, that's what I thought, and now she's in the park with a needle. Taking drugs.'

'The needle was an accident.'

'I know, I know. I understood that after. I remembered what she is like about those needles. But at the time, I just saw, I don't know. I only saw how angry I was. Fuck you. A silly, selfish little girl.' Her face became angry as she remembered. 'I pulled that needle from her arm and then I pulled her hair. I pulled it hard as I could.'

Rex shuddered as he imagined how hard she must have pulled. 'And she fell, or… what?'

'No. She just looked straight at me. And then…' Aguta held a hand to her mouth and swallowed, as if recalling it made her sick. 'She said my name. My nickname. *Skuja*. Or…' She frowned. 'Or maybe she was talking about that needle…' She shook her head. 'And then she said a lot of other things, but it didn't make any sense, like backwards. And I said, 'What? What?' And then her eyes. Her eyes went up. I mean, they rolled up inside her head. Like zombie film. And then she fell. And she shook. A lot. And then she went.'

Tears were rolling down her cheeks. The café lady looked across, vaguely curious, through the steam of the dishwasher. Rex handed Aguta a serviette, and she took it.

'I took that needle, and I ran,' she went on, in a hushed, horror-struck voice. 'I'm sorry. I killed her. And I didn't know what to do. If I went to police, maybe they would take Dovila some place. Or send her to my mum. My mum is alcoholic, Rex. She lives on the 18th floor in Kaunas. No lift. Junkies on the staircase…' She stopped, taking several deep breaths. 'I killed her. And I thought to go and hide away. But then I thought, you were looking for her now. And if I stopped looking for her, then you would know. So I kept on, pretending to be worried. I am sorry. She was my friend. I loved her. But I killed her.'

'You didn't.'

She lit another cigarette, trembling so much Rex thought she would set light to herself. 'I did,' she said. 'I killed her Rex. I killed her.' She was in tears now, almost hysterical.

'Aguta, you didn't kill her. Listen to me. It was an AVM. An arteriovenous malformation. Milda had had one since she was a child. Remember the headaches? The hospital visits?' Aguta nodded hesitantly. 'It's like a little knot in the blood vessels of the brain. A tiny thing. But it's a time-bomb. It can burst, at any time.'

'So I pulled her hair, and the bomb went off.'

Rex shook his head. 'No. Or maybe. You pulling her hair could have caused it, but equally, maybe rolling round on the ground with Mark caused it. Or Chapman strangling her. Maybe none of those things caused it, Aguta, and it would have happened at exactly that time if she'd been lying in bed on her own, or playing the flute. Nobody can know.'

'*I* know.'

'It's up to you what you think. But nobody's going to do anything to you, Aguta. I'm not going to tell anyone. Even if I did – the police, the courts, they wouldn't do anything. It's up to you to decide how you are going to live your life. Are you going to accept that something bad happened? That you were angry, and you lost control, but that you couldn't help it, and move on? Or are you going to live your life all eaten up with it? Carrying it around with you like a...'

He stopped The word he'd been on the verge of saying was 'limp'. And he realised, in that moment, that he had been talking as much to himself as to her. About Sybille as well as Milda.

'...like some piece of luggage,' he finished. 'It's up to you.'

Aguta stared down at the table, tracing with one fingernail a swirl-pattern in the split coffee. It was almost as though she were making a list, trying to work it out. Decide, in coffee and sugar whether redemption was to be found. 'Don't Worry, Be Happy' played on the radio. She looked up at him with a brief, weak smile. For once, Rex thought, there could be no other pair of people, in London, or anywhere, experiencing this moment.

'I'm not the other one, though.'

Rex frowned. 'What?'

'You said if you found who killed Milda you would find the

person who was sending you those... messages. But that wasn't me.'

'I know. But...'

Rex trailed off. He hadn't given his persecutor much thought over the last couple of days. Nor they him, it seemed. Perhaps they had given up. Either that, or they were gathering their strength.

* * *

Arthur Chapman had a sunny room to himself at Chase Farm, overlooking a garden in which gowned people with drips in their arms sat smoking on plastic chairs. He was not, as Rex had been told, under police guard – the police having deduced, correctly, that whatever Chapman had done, he wasn't going anywhere now.

He looked smaller in bed, with the jacket of his cream pyjamas ballooning out around his wizened frame. There was a canula in his left arm, just above the wrist, inexpertly tied on with a patchwork of tape, like a poorly-wrapped present. A tuft of his thin, colourless hair stuck up. He did not seem surprised to see Rex. He looked as if nothing would surprise him now. As sun streamed in, he moved his lips wordlessly. Rex had no need to hear any words, because he knew what Chapman was asking.

'Because I remembered,' Rex said.

He had remembered it only this morning. As he walked Aguta back to the beauty parlour, he'd told her he knew the nuns she had approached for a job, and offered to have a word on her behalf. If Aguta wanted to make atonement, he said, then couldn't be a much better way than working there.

'What it does mean – atonement?' she had asked.

'Trying to make up for something you've done. Trying to make sure you never do it again.'

She had shaken her head. 'Do it again? You think I might kill again?'

290

Outside, on the still deserted High Street, he remembered someone else saying something similar. Just before Chapman stabbed him, he had said, 'I never killed again'.

'So you killed once?' Rex said, now standing at the end of Chapman's hospital bed in Enfield. 'You did kill someone?'

Chapman nodded, and looked out of the window. Then he glanced back and, with difficulty, sat up in the bed. With a wavering arm, he reached out for the plastic water-jug on the bedside table. Rex intervened and poured him a glass of warm, slightly cloudy water. Chapman took a sip, and then seemed about to let the glass fall from his grasp. Rex took it and put it back on the side.

'I killed a girl,' he said, in a weak, ratchety voice. Rex had to lean close to hear him, catching the decay on his breath. 'A very long time ago.' He swallowed painfully.

'What do you mean – in the war, or…?'

Chapman shut his eyes, by way of saying no. Then something approaching a smile passed across the old man's face.

'It was in a refugee camp. After the war. I enjoyed it.' He stared straight into Rex's eyes, and Rex shuddered. It wasn't evil he saw there, but the complete absence of anything. People did bad things, he knew, in wars and in their aftermath. But were they best left unexamined? In Chapman's case, he sensed, there was little choice.

'For years, I told myself that I hadn't. Even that I hadn't done it. But then I came back to my house, and you were there, in my kitchen.'

'That's what I don't understand. What made you get out of the taxi and come back?'

'I kept something. A memory. In a little tin. I always put it away after I'd looked at it. But that day, I don't know why, I didn't. I left it out. I keep forgetting things now. And when I remembered, I had to come back. But then you were there. And by mistake I told you. And I looked at you, and I saw that you knew. And your neck was just... there.'

Rex nodded, remembering the little metal tin with the lock of hair in it. He'd thought it was Milda's. 'And you thought I'd tell someone.'

Chapman laughed, a dry, wheezy sound, like some ancient wind instrument. 'What would that matter? I tried to kill you because I felt an overwhelming urge to do it. Just one more time, before it was too late.'

'Too late for what?'

Chapman touched his forehead. 'It's Alzheimer's. I forget things, and I see things that aren't there. That's the start of it, apparently.' He licked his lips. 'I'm going to be eaten away, piece by piece until there's nothing left.'

'What do you think it will be like?' the journalist in him couldn't help asking.

'Like nothing,' Chapman said, closing his eyes. He looked as if he had already died.

* * *

As dusk drew near, a thick, damp fog settled on Muswell Hill. As Rex took the little path to the convent through the woods, he had a sense of walking through clouds. It felt serene, other-worldly, dream-like. He wasn't paying attention as he came to the stone steps at the end of his journey, and was startled by a tall, thin hooded figure coming the opposite way. He might have thought it was a ghost, but for the fact that it banged into him and trudged past, without a backward glance.

Rex was about to utter some minor admonishment when he saw that the figure had dropped a postcard. He picked it up from the damp stones. It wasn't the sort of card you'd send someone from your holidays. It dated from the war, and depicted a row of European bodies being inspected by a clutch of officials.

He turned it over and saw that the card was addressed to him.

He shouted after the figure, which was just about to be swallowed by the fog. It didn't stop. He ran after it, back uphill, almost slipping on the wet pathway. It seemed to slow down a little, without turning round, almost inviting him to catch up. Out of breath, angry as much as afraid, Rex grabbed the arm of a grey hooded top and span it round.

'Who the fuck are you?' he shouted. 'Why were you sending me this?'

'Oradour sur Glane,' said a voice from the depths of the hood. '1944. 642 villagers killed by the German SS.'

Rex pulled the hood off to reveal a thin young male face with blond hair and large eyes.

'If you go to school in France,' continued the young man, in an accent suggesting he had done so himself, 'everyone learns about it.'

The penny dropped. 'And you had a very good education. Didn't you, Olivier?'

The young man frowned, and coughed. 'Olivier is in prison. I'm Sylvain.'

'You were just a pair of twelve-year-olds when I last saw you. Well… that's not quite right, is it? Because I've seen you since, haven't I? Seen you and heard from you quite a bit.'

Sylvain. His wife's nephew. One half of the unit always referred to as 'the twins'. Now almost a man, and entirely fucking messed-up. Sylvain swallowed, and then spoke.

'It's to show you what you did to my family,' he said, pointing at the card. 'You, Rex.'

Rex sighed. The wheelchair: Sybille. She wasn't in one, but she might as well be: she never went anywhere. Why hadn't he made that connection? Some part of him had always known the payback was coming, and another part refused to admit it.

'Why is your brother Olivier in prison?' he asked.

'Dealing cocaine,' the pale boy said, leaning against the wall and rubbing his throat, anxiously. 'He chooses that. Our mother chooses vodka. So you see...'

'Handcuffs for Olivier. Liver for your mother.' Rex nodded. 'Yes, I do see. And the anagram... If it hadn't been for me going to New York, the accident wouldn't have happened, and your life wouldn't have been ruined.'

He could understand how it would have seemed that way to a child, in search of something, or someone, to blame. For your parents' divorce. For your mother hitting the bottle. For your twin brother going to the bad. It hadn't strictly been like that, of course. Sybille's sister's marriage had been on the rocks for a long time before the accident – not least because of her fondness for clear, grain alcohol. And even from an early age Olivier had always been the one who climbed too high up the tree, waded too far out in the river, forever seeking some kind of self-obliteration. Rex couldn't say all that to this pale, edgy boy, though. Something else seemed more important.

'One thing I don't understand, Sylvain. Sybille and I did argue about me going to New York, the night of the accident. But I never told anyone. So how do you know?'

The boy swallowed. 'Aunt Sybille told me.' He swallowed again.

'But Sybille can't tell anyone anything.'

Sylvain gave a laugh, which turned into a cough. 'Is that right?'

Rex didn't know what to say. 'Why didn't you stab me when you had the chance, at the march?'

'Because that bald guy was taking a photograph,' Sylvain replied. 'Anyway. I changed my mind. I wasn't finished.'

From his long-lashed eyes, he flashed Rex a look of hate so strong it was like a stench from a bottle. Rex looked away.

'I started coming here in September, when my course began. The nuns don't know who I am. They just think I'm a nice Catholic boy who comes to visit the poor fucked-up people. I don't say anything to them. But I listen to them. Every time since I first come in here, saying what a good man you are. To stay so close. The great journalist, who works in the shit little newspaper, so he can be still with his wife… You're not good.'

'I don't pretend to be, Sylvain.'

The kid said nothing. He pulled an asthma inhaler out of his jeans pocket. Rex remembered the sickly child of five years ago, with a back-pack of medications. And headphones permanently in his ears.

'So you thought I deserved to be taught a lesson. Because of what some nuns said about me? You didn't think, maybe, you could just come to the newspaper and talk to me? Maybe find something out about the life I've been living all these years since it happened.'

Sylvain shrugged. 'I wanted to hurt you, not be your friend.'

A pigeon fluttered in the trees. Both men fell silent for a moment.

'So the nuns think you're a language student with a fondness for the sick and infirm. What about Sybille?'

Sylvain looked straight at Rex. 'She knows everything.'

Something about the way he said it made Rex shiver. Then he remembered how angry he was.

'Shall I keep this card then?' he asked. 'Save you buying a stamp? Tell you what – why don't we meet up here every week and you can give me a bucket of shit?'

Sylvain murmured something into his collar.

'What?'

'I said I'm not going to do anything else,' he said sullenly.

'Why? Why stop? It's not like I can turn back the clock, Sylvain, so why should you?'

'You're not what I thought you were. I made you into a monster, but you're not a monster. With your bad foot, and your eye-patch and your cans of lager… Actually, I feel sorry for you.'

The boy pulled up his hood, thrust his hands into the pockets of his top and strode away into the mist. Rex tore up the postcard and threw the bits into a hornbeam bush. Then he felt guilty, so he gathered the bits back up and put them in a bin. It was probably the sort of thing that made him look pathetic to Sylvain, but he didn't care.

* * *

Sister Florence took a long time to answer the convent door. When she saw Rex, she said nothing about his injuries. She just clapped her hands and exclaimed, 'Everything is illuminated!'

'Is it?' Rex asked, wondering what brand of religious fever had seized the household.

'It's wonderful film, Rex. Have you seen it? We watched it today. But now we are watching *policiers* again.' She sighed and bustled off down the scrubbed, shabby hallway. Rex assumed he was meant to follow her, and did.

In the tv room, with Ironside tracking down jewel thieves in the background, Sister Florence made Rex the sort of cup of tea one might expect a Belgian nun to make and Rex, politely, took a few sips as he heard all about the film. It was about a young Jewish American who went in search of his roots in Ukraine. Since Sybille was in one of her non-communicative moods, Rex took advantage of the topic to mention Aguta. Sister Florence flushed.

'*Cette fille pauvre*! I wanted to telephone to her, but Rex…' She lowered her voice and leant closer. He smelt lavender talc

– a very holy sort of smell. 'I believe that Sister Columba moved my book in the office when she tidied it up. I cannot find it.' She looked heavenwards. 'I feel terrible. I think we will have to make again an advertisement, and pray that this girl comes back.'

'You were going to give Aguta the job?'

'Of course. Not Catholic, of course. Orthodox. But – good hands and heart, as my father used to say!'

Rex was writing down Aguta's number on a slip of paper when Sybille decided to speak. Had she been angry that he had not visited for a few days? Had she noticed? No one knew.

'He's got it wrong,' she said.

Sister Florence and Rex looked at her.

'It's wrong.'

'What is, Sybille?' Rex asked, taking her cold hand in his. She had her tweed skirt on. He had been with her when she bought it. On Regent Street, in one of those strange, shabby, expensive knitwear shops. They had laughed about the Americans in there, coming to the centre of London to buy Harris tweed and clan tartan. 'What's wrong?'

She squeezed his hand, something she did every now and then, and it always felt as if she was squeezing his heart, with this trace of the affection there had once been between them, without anything else around it.

'Ironside,' she said. 'He gets one person at the end of every mystery. But it's never one person.'

'What do you mean, Sybille?' asked Sister Florence.

'Everyone is guilty,' Sybille said. 'We are all born in sin, and we're all redeemed through the love of Christ.'

Sister Florence looked at Rex and said in a low voice, 'That new priest was here today,' as if that hadn't been an entirely good thing. Then she stood up and rubbed her hands briskly.

'So many visitors for you today, Sybille! Like the Grand Central Station.'

She bustled out and Rex was left wondering if Sister Florence had ever seen Grand Central Station. In tv shows, he guessed.

'Did anyone else come today, Syb?' He wanted to hear it from her.

'The priest.'

'I mean anyone apart from him. Anyone apart from me and the priest?'

She didn't answer. Later, at the door, Sister Florence pressed her lips together and said, 'I wish I knew if there was some sense to the things she says sometimes. Ironside!' And she gave a high, musical laugh that reminded Rex of Julie Andrews. He wasn't sure what holiness was, but if it existed at all, then it existed in Sister Florence: in her kindness, her battiness, in the way she made him not want to leave her at the door and go on with his journey.

He walked down Muswell Hill, descending through the fog onto the wide, flat plain of Tottenham, which smelt of slow-burning leaves and Indian takeaways. He walked slowly, gingerly, as he always did, all the way down, as the light seeped from a sky etched with the vapour trails of peoples departing and arriving.

He felt a strong urge to be on one of those planes, heading somewhere hot and steamy and strange. After all, he had the ticket.

ABOUT THE AUTHOR

Born in Nottingham in 1971, M.H. Baylis is a novelist, journalist and scriptwriter. A former 'EastEnders' storyliner, his first novel, *Stranger Than Fulham* ('Fast, funny and funky' *The Times*; 'Original enough to get noticed and pickled in black humour' *Daily Mail*) was published by Chatto & Windus in 1999. His second novel, *The Last Ealing Comedy* ('A triumph' *Daily Express*; 'The excellent dialogue makes you snort at least once a page' *Kirkus UK*) was published by Chatto & Windus in 2003.

After adapting Catrin Collier's series of novels for BBC One, he went to work in Kenya and Cambodia, training local scriptwriters and creating TV dramas for the United Nations and BBC World Service Trust. After a spell living in a remote mountain village on the Pacific island of Tanna , he returned to Britain in 2005, to take up his present role as television critic for the *Daily Express*. He continues to write films and TV dramas for the Far East.